Vixa was trapped in a clear crystal globe surrounded by water. The water was filled with sea elves. They didn't speak, only stared and pointed with long, webbed blue fingers.

"Stop it!" she shouted at them. "I am Princess Vixa Ambrodel, daughter of the house of Kith-Kanan!"

They showed no sign of hearing her, but continued to stare with blank faces, their eyes glowing. Furious, Vixa struck the walls of her crystal prison with her fists. The blow stung her knuckles and caused cracks to appear in the glass. The fractures radiated outward from the point of impact, and water began to seep into the globe. Anger turned to horror as Vixa realized what she'd done.

The cracks raced around the glass, spreading faster and faster. The water rose up to her ankles. A blink of her eyes, and the water touched her knees. In seconds, she was neck-deep and had to tread water to keep her face above the icy flow.

Vixa flung out a hand and felt the roof over her head. Silver fissures met and crossed above her. Water closed over her head. She pounded at the domed ceiling.

"I—will—not—die!"

From the Creators of the DRAGONLANCE® Saga

THE LOST HISTORIES

DragonLance® Saga

**The Lost Histories
Volume 3**

The Dargonesti

Elves of the Sea

**Paul B. Thompson &
Tonya Cook**

DRAGONLANCE® SAGA
The Lost Histories
Volume Three

THE DARGONESTI
©1995 TSR, Inc.
All Rights Reserved.

First Printing: October 1995
Printed in the United States of America.
Library of Congress Catalog Card Number: 94-68153

9 8 7 6 5 4 3 2 1

ISBN: 0-7869-0182-9

TSR, Inc.   TSR Ltd.
201 Sheridan Springs Rd.   120 Church End, Cherry Hinton
Lake Geneva, WI 53147   Cambridge CB1 3LB
U.S.A.   United Kingdom

For my nephew
Matthew Craig Carter
enfant chéri
—T. C.

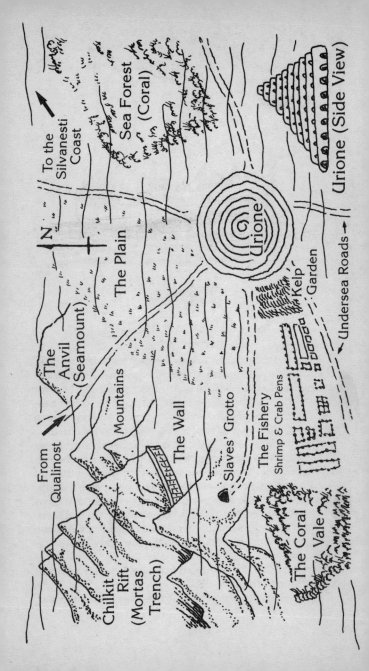

Chapter 1

A Rescue Mission

Tall columns of smoke, bent by the southern wind, rose above the thick forests at the mouth of the Greenthorn River. Even more telling than the smoke was the debris filling the river delta and the Gulf of Ergoth: wrecked wagons, burnt timbers, and the bodies of men and horses. The civil war in Ergoth was moving ever nearer this once-peaceful coast.

High up in the crow's nest of the Qualinesti ship *Evenstar*, Princess Vixa Ambrodel watched with concern the evidence of distant devastation. Her uncle, Speaker of the Sun Silveran, had dispatched her to this spot on Ergoth's southeastern shore to rescue certain important Qualinesti elves fleeing the strife in that country. For two days she and *Evenstar* had waited in the sunny waters of the gulf. Of Ambassador Quenavalen, his family, and his entourage, there was as yet no sign.

"How now, lady? What can you see?" called a white-haired, older elf from the deck.

"The fires are on both sides of the river," Vixa replied,

squinting her eyes against the sun's glare.

"General Solamnus is moving fast. No sign of Que-navalen's party I take it."

"There's nothing on the river but wreckage. Watch out, Colonel. I'm coming down."

Vixa swung her mailed legs over the rope rail of the crow's nest and climbed down the shroud lines. She jumped from the lines, dropping the final four feet to the deck. Climbing in armor was never easy, but in this heat and humidity it approached torture. Vixa was puffing with exertion.

Evenstar's mostly human crew lolled on deck, trying to keep cool. Not so the elves in Vixa's party, twenty hand-picked Qualinesti from the city garrison. They'd been girded for battle for two days, eating and sleeping in their armor since *Evenstar* had dropped anchor. They were restless, eager for action. The smoke of far-off battles drifting over the ship only heightened their anticipation.

A cluster of fishing smacks, canoes, and flat-bottomed river craft dotted the water around the Qualinesti ship. Most of these were laden with refugees fleeing the advance of the army of General Vinas Solamnus. The Imperial Army of Ergoth was in disarray, unable to offer Solamnus open resistance. Instead, they continued to retreat, harassing the enemy at every opportunity. The fires along the Greenthorn had been set by the retreating troops as they burned crops and storehouses to deny supplies to Solamnus's men.

Every hour brought to the river mouth more wretched refugees, desperate for passage away from the fighting. Most were simple farmers or foresters who had been caught up in events. They welcomed the overthrow of their mad emperor, but no one was prepared for the cost—in homes destroyed, crops burned, and family members killed or injured—of such an uprising.

Vixa relieved Colonel Armantaro of her polished silver helmet, but did not don it. The slight breeze felt good on her face, ruffling through her short blond hair. At six feet, the princess was two inches taller than her colonel. The two stood shoulder to shoulder, scanning the distant shore.

Their silent watch was interrupted by Harmanutis, corporal of the city guard, who came to Vixa and saluted.

"Lady, we would like to know, how long are we to stay here?" he asked, standing at stiff attention.

Armantaro frowned. "As long as it takes, Corporal."

"He has a right to know," Vixa conceded. "Corporal, if the ambassador is not here by midday, we'll have to act." Harmanutis saluted once more and departed to share this word with the others.

Alone with his princess, the old colonel allowed himself a slight smile. "Just what does *that* mean, lady?"

"I'll let you know when I do." A smile eased the lines of worry on her face.

To a human, Vixa would appear to be eighteen or twenty years old. But elves aged much more slowly than humans, and her actual age was sixty-five. She had served in the army of Qualinesti for six years, mainly under the tutelage of her warrior mother, Lady Verhanna Kanan, daughter of the great Kith-Kanan, first Speaker of the Sun. In spite of her proud lineage, Vixa had come up through the ranks on merit and hard work. Her mother had seen to that. This mission was her first independent command.

A commotion on shore brought everyone to the port rail. A mob of Ergothians was swarming down the banks to the water. Though burdened with rolls of clothing and valuables, they ran down the sandy slope and waded into the river. The slow and the weak fell, were trodden upon, but no one stopped to help them.

Soon the elves saw the cause of the panic. Emerging from the trees on the south bank of the river was a band of mounted humans. The men, who wore remnants of Ergothian uniforms and carried lances, swooped down on the unarmed refugees.

"Is that the army of Ergoth?" asked Vanthanoris, another of Vixa's soldiers.

"No," replied Armantaro. "They're deserters—brigands —I'll wager."

The elves watched in mounting anger as the lancers rode down the defenseless folk, trampling them in the shallows, spearing them on the riverbank. Several of the brigands dismounted and tore through the refugees' sad bundles. There was obviously precious little to steal.

"Scum," Armantaro was heard to mutter. Vixa put a hand on the old warrior's shoulder.

"You know, Colonel, those scavengers pose a grave threat to Ambassador Quenavalen's safety," she said slowly. "It would never do to let His Excellency or his family be inconvenienced by such as they, would it?"

Armantaro's blue eyes widened. "No indeed, lady. It would not do at all."

She nodded once. The colonel turned away from the rail and hailed *Evenstar*'s captain. "Break out your longboats, Captain Esquelamar! Soldiers, stand to arms! Leave your helms and bucklers behind. I want swords and bows only!"

Evenstar's deck boiled with activity. Vixa set down her helmet next to her embossed shield. She stepped into her stubby recurved bow and bent it against her thigh, stringing it. By the time she had shouldered her quiver, the Qualinesti contingent was mustered in the ship's waist. Elven sailors lowered two longboats, one on each side of the ship. Armantaro took command of one boat and ten warriors, Vixa the other.

The sea was glassy calm. Sailors bent to their oars, and the longboats soon reached the tiny island at the mouth of the Greenthorn. Some of the Ergothian refugees had sought the supposed safety of this sandy spit of land. When they beheld armed elves coming ashore, they screamed and started back into the river.

"Hold!" Vixa cried. "We've come to protect you!"

Warily the exhausted men and women trickled back. Armantaro asked one sturdy fellow, a blacksmith by the look of him, where he had come from.

"The village of Piney Brook, m'lord," said the man, eyeing the colonel's sparkling armor.

"Did you follow the river downstream?" asked Vixa.

"Aye, lady, for forty miles or more."

"Did you see any elves along the way? Well dressed perhaps, a group of some twenty-five?"

The smith nodded. "Oh, aye. I seen folk like yourselves four or five miles back on the north bank," he said.

"When did you see them?" Vixa pressed.

"Yesterday it was, lady."

Just then the brigands, who had finished looting the bodies of those they'd killed on the riverbank, formed up and shouted threats at the refugees across the way. The Qualinesti soldiers stepped out in front of the unarmed Ergothians, bows ready.

The sight of the small party of elves failed to intimidate the mounted deserters. They held up stolen trinkets, taunted the Qualinesti.

"Go home while you can, Long Ears!" screamed one bandit.

Vixa's brown eyes narrowed. "Amend their manners," she said calmly. The elves nocked arrows, and soon a hard rain was falling over the brigands. Half a dozen saddles were emptied when the arrows landed. The bandits ceased their shouting, wheeled their plunging horses, and fled into the woods.

"That was simple enough," Armantaro remarked.

"And I was hoping for a good fight," complained Harmanutis.

Vixa glanced at him. "You may yet get your wish, Corporal."

She ordered the sailors to take one longboat and ferry the Ergothians off the spit. They would have to be distributed among the various boats in the gulf. The other longboat, with all twenty warriors and Colonel Armantaro, Vixa took to the north shore.

It was nearly noon, and the heat bore down like the blast from a Thorbardin forge. The still air was darkened by smoke. Nosing through the smoldering wreckage that drifted downstream, Vixa's longboat made for the far shore. The oily river water seemed to cling to the oars, hampering their progress.

"Strange," Vixa mused. "The air feels heavy, but there's not a cloud in the sky."

One warrior, Paladithel by name, looked up from his

rowing. Sweat streamed down his face. "More's the pity," he muttered.

Vixa nodded absently. Where in the name of the Abyss were Quenavalen and his party? The priests and mages in the service of the Speaker of the Sun were certainly working all manner of spells in order to send word to the ambassador that rescue was coming.

The longboat's prow bumped sand. Vixa and several warriors leapt overboard and steadied the boat, and the rest of the soldiers clambered out, dragging the craft ashore.

"Follow the shoreline," Armantaro advised as the warriors readied their weapons. "Watch the trees. I don't want to walk into an ambush."

Strung out in single file, the elves moved along the shore. More signs of war floated down the Greenthorn: broken and smoking rafts, their occupants lying slain upon them, casks and boxes, smashed canoes. In the distance, faintly, came the sound of shouting voices. Far-off trumpets blared, and every elf paused, alert and worried. Trumpets almost certainly meant the advance guard of Vinas Solamnus's army.

A crashing in the trees caused Armantaro to bark quick orders. The warriors formed a hollow square on a wide stretch of sand. The colonel and Vixa took up positions inside the center of the square just as a group of horsemen galloped into the open.

"Bows ready!" Armantaro called. Twenty bows rose as one. "Steady, lads. No one is to loose until the command is given."

The riders approached on thundering hooves. They were Imperial cavalry all right, but once they cleared the trees, Vixa and her warriors could see that most of the horsemen were unarmed. Their faces were bloody, their cloaks torn; only a few retained armor.

More and more horsemen appeared. Those in the lead slowed and milled about in confusion, clearly unsure how to proceed now that they'd left Solamnus's army behind. They were still some thirty yards away and had not yet noticed the Qualinesti. Soon a hundred or more riders filled the clearing.

At last they saw the elves. A cry of "Infantry! Solamnic infantry!" went up. Horsemen tightened into a thick column and charged straight for the tiny band of elves.

"Target the leading riders!" hissed Armantaro. "Ready! Loose!"

Arrows peppered the horsemen. Those in front fell, tripping those behind. A ghastly pileup began, with elven arrows pouring death on the screaming mass. For a time, the elves held the cavalry back. Then the arrows ran out.

"Draw swords!" Vixa shouted. Twenty bows dropped to the sand. The remaining Ergothians rode wide of their fallen comrades and charged again. The horsemen weren't properly armed—most had no weapons save their horses— but the twenty-two Qualinesti were greatly outnumbered. The elven square broke into isolated pairs and trios. Swords flashed as they battled for their lives.

Vixa found herself paired with Vanthanoris, an elf of Kagonesti ancestry and the best sword fighter in Qualinost. He spun, lunged, dodged a stream of terrified horses. The Ergothians spurred their mounts. Vanthanoris emptied four saddles with graceful leaping thrusts, but the fifth trooper bowled him down in a flurry of iron-shod hooves. Vixa stood over her fallen comrade, trying to protect him.

Like a wild thunderstorm, the fight was over quickly. The Ergothian cavalry vanished downriver, leaving half its number dead or wounded. Vixa's small command was also cut in half, ten elves down with broken heads or limbs. Vanthanoris rose from the sand, bruised and winded.

"I am in your debt, lady," he said, pushing his silvery white hair from his eyes and bowing.

"Nonsense," she replied, grateful the battle was over.

The elves held a hasty conference at the river's edge. Most of the warriors were for pressing on to find the ambassador, but Vixa was none too sanguine about their chances.

"Another encounter like this, and my mother will have one less child to bully," she noted wryly.

. "Lady Vixa is right," agreed Armantaro. "We'd best return to *Evenstar*—for now."

Carrying their wounded, the elves made their way back to the longboat. *Evenstar* rose like a hawk amid the lesser river craft. The banner of Qualinost—green tree and golden sun—fluttered from the mainmast.

As her troopers launched the longboat, Vixa noticed an odd sight. A wall of pale clouds was rapidly approaching the cluster of ships assembled at the river's mouth. The cloud was white as snow and so thick as to appear solid. At a word from Vixa, the elves rowed harder.

"What can it be?" the princess wondered. "Smoke?"

Armantaro shaded his face against the sun, staring at the enormous cloud. "It's not natural, lady, that's for sure. See how the land breeze carries the smoke from Ergoth over our heads and out to the bay? Yet that cloud is coming up fast from the opposite direction!"

Then, half a mile from *Evenstar*, the cloud appeared to stop. Its edges swirled and billowed, but it did not advance farther. The delay allowed the longboat to reach the Qualinesti ship. Vixa was the last of her company to regain the deck.

"Raise anchor!" bawled Captain Esquelamar, as soon as she was aboard. "Stand by the mainsail, lads!"

The princess protested. "What are you doing, Captain? We are to wait here for Ambassador Quenavalen. Our orders come from the Speaker of the Sun himself!"

"Lady, there's magic afoot in that unnatural cloud, and I'll not risk my ship for an elf who may already be dead," Esquelamar replied bluntly.

Sailors on the capstan wound the anchor up from the gulf's muddy bottom. The sound of clanking chain echoed over the water. Other small boats and rafts that had been hovering near *Evenstar* slipped their anchors and raised sail. Some resorted to oars, for the light wind had ceased to blow.

"Here it comes!" shouted a sailor in the rigging. The cloud was moving once more, churning and billowing toward them.

"Starboard helm—unfurl the mainsail! Stand by the mizzen and the spritsail!"

With maddening slowness, *Evenstar* made a turn to the right. Vixa and Armantaro watched, transfixed, as the wall of white engulfed a pair of smacks and a white-hulled ketch. The smaller vessels vanished inside of it without a trace.

Every square inch of canvas *Evenstar* carried was spread, but to no avail. The sails hung uselessly from their yards. All the wind was gone.

The strange cloud continued moving rapidly toward *Evenstar*, though no breath of wind stirred the air. The oppressiveness that Vixa had felt earlier, as though a storm were brewing, was even more pronounced now. A sense of dread swept over her, and she heard Armantaro whisper, "May the gods have mercy."

Hull creaking, the Qualinesti ship met the oncoming cloud stern-first. The wall of white swallowed it.

Vixa flinched as the vapor flowed over her. It was cold, finger-numbing cold. One instant she was bathed in the glaring heat of the sun, the next, an icy chill dried the sweat on her face and penetrated her baking chain mail.

Everyone had braced for catastrophe, but the fog's main effect was to make teeth chatter. Sailors and warriors stood and compared reactions to the bizarre mist enveloping them. No one felt ill, or unusual in any way, only very cold.

"What do you make of this, Captain?" Armantaro asked Esquelamar.

The elven sailor waved a hand through the cloud. "Feels like a sea mist such as mariners find off the cape of Kharolis," he said. "But it moves and holds its shape like no natural mist. It's an enchantment, I'd say."

"I agree," Vixa said. "Perhaps it was called up by the emperor's sorcerers to screen his failing army from General Solamnus."

"Damned uncomfortable, if you ask me," grumbled Harmanutis, stepping out of the white cloud.

Shivering sailors and soldiers wrapped themselves in their cloaks. The captain called up to the crow's nest, asking the lookout if he could see anything.

"Nay, Captain. It's like trying to peer through milk."

"Come down then, before you freeze."

The captain, the princess, and Armantaro went to the rail. Esquelamar knelt in the scupper, thrust his head over the side. "Can't see a damn thing," he muttered. "Not even water, nothing!"

"It feels as if we're moving," Vixa offered.

She was right. Although the sails hung slack, the creak of the hull and a slight rolling of the deck caused them to sway on their feet.

"The emperor of Ergoth does not command such power," Armantaro stated.

Evenstar was mysteriously adrift, her crew and passengers unable to rescue their ambassador—unable, even, to rescue themselves.

Chapter 2

The Teeming Sea

It was impossible to measure the passage of time. Sailors collected in small groups and whispered fearfully to each other. They called out long and hard, but received no answering hails from any of the smaller craft that had dotted the waters of the gulf. Captain Esquelamar resolved to curb the growing terror. He assembled his mariners before the mainmast. On the quarterdeck, Vixa and her company stood listening.

"Now, lads, there's no reason to fear," the captain said firmly. "We've seen fogs before. And we've been in much worse situations than this. Why, remember that time off Sancrist Isle? We thought we were goners then, didn't we, lads? And yet, here we are. *Evenstar* is a strong ship, the finest of her size in Qualinost, and she'll come through this."

"But this is an evil spell," one sailor insisted.

"We don't know that, Pellanis," Esquelamar replied in a matter-of-fact tone. "Nothing so ill has befallen us yet, has it? In fact, this could be a good sign. Mayhap the gods called down this mist to protect us."

"Do you believe that, lady?" Armantaro whispered.

Vixa shrugged. "I never studied sorcery," she replied. "But Esquelamar is right about one thing: neither we nor the ship has been injured by the fog. I prefer to know where we're going, and I don't like being taken away from my proper duty."

Captain Esquelamar dismissed his crew. The sailors went to their posts looking less fearful, though some still fingered lucky talismans. The captain climbed the steps to the quarterdeck.

"A good speech, Captain. Do you believe it yourself?" asked Vixa.

"I have to, lady. Those lads look to me for their safety."

The crew and passengers of *Evenstar* settled into a state of uneasy watchfulness. Despite their initial dread, as time passed with no untoward occurrences, they gradually grew accustomed to the silent, impenetrable cloud that enveloped them. The captain kept his sailors busy with all the usual shipboard tasks: swabbing decks, mending sails, and polishing the brightwork. Vixa kept her contingent on the quarterdeck, where they would be out of the way. Time passed.

When their stomachs told them it was time to eat, the elves did so. Then Paladithel broke out his pipes. He wasn't much of a player, knowing only one song, "When We're Coming Home Again." He played this mournful tune eight times in a row and would've launched a ninth, but his comrades protested. Suddenly there was a shout from the bow.

"Ahoy, Captain!"

"What is it, lad?" called Esquelamar, emerging from his cabin. A napkin was tucked under his pointed chin.

"Dead ahead, sir! A break! A hole in the fog!"

A cheer went up from every throat. "Two points to starboard, Manneto!" the captain barked.

The helmsman tried to comply, but the whipstaff refused to budge an inch. With both hands and a shoulder braced against the tall lever, Manneto struggled to turn the ship. Esquelamar joined him, grunting and groaning as they hauled on the whipstaff.

The dark spot ahead was a welcome change from the monotony of cold, white cloud. It was featureless and black, like a doorway into night, and grew larger all the while. Either they were drawing nearer to it, or it was approaching them.

The two elves continued to struggle with the whipstaff. At last, Esquelamar and Manneto stepped back from the helm in defeat. The helmsman cursed eloquently in three languages, then remembered who was listening.

"Begging your pardon, lady," he said.

"I thought my mother could curse, but helmsman, you are a master."

In any event, they were heading straight for the opening in the cloud. The mist thinned to gently billowing streams. Warmer air washed over the ship, filling the sails and offering a respite from the biting cold. In spite of the head wind and the straining sails, *Evenstar* ploughed onward, against the wind. The hole grew taller and wider.

"Stars! I see stars!" cried the sailor in the bow.

Remnants of the fog peeled away from the ship like petals dropping from a flower. The dark spot was simply the night sky, clear and star-spangled. Once *Evenstar* was free of the last tendrils of mist, her sails rippled and caught a cross breeze. The ship heeled under a sudden gust as the sails bellied full. Without having to be ordered, sailors scaled the masts and trimmed the sails. Manneto saw the whipstaff lever flopping from side to side. He grabbed it and turned *Evenstar* against the wind. The ship came about smartly, turning a half circle in the open sea.

"It's gone!" Armantaro cried, pointing. The odd cloud had vanished behind them. As soon as the ship was free of it, the fog had disappeared without a trace.

Esquelamar called for his sextant. The princess and Armantaro stood at the captain's elbow as he aligned his instrument with the stars. Within minutes he had their position.

"Charts—fetch my charts!" he ordered. A nimble sailor scampered into the captain's cabin and returned with an armful of rolled maps. Esquelamar scrutinized the writing on the sleeve of each, handing back those he didn't want. The fifth chart he unrolled. Squinting in the flickering light of a lantern, he found their position according to Krynn's stars.

"By the Blue Phoenix!" he exclaimed.

"Where are we?" Vixa demanded. She peered over his shoulder, her mouth falling open in astonishment. Esquelamar's long finger rested on a spot at least a hundred leagues east of Cape Kharolis—some three hundred leagues east of their original position at the mouth of the Greenthorn River!

"It can't be," said Armantaro, dazed. As word filtered back to the soldiers and sailors, they echoed his sentiments.

"Hard about!" Esquelamar shouted. "Bring us to a new course: due west!"

Lanterns were lit, hung from the bow and stern. Corporal Harmanutis pointed out that as far as elven eyes could see, they were alone on the sea. Vixa ordered her warriors to serve as extra lookouts.

To Armantaro, she confided, "I fear for Ambassador Quenavalen. Our absence may cost him and his party their lives. How long do you think it will take us to get back to the Greenthorn?"

The colonel put this question to the captain, who replied, "With fair wind and no ill magic, we should enter the Gulf of Ergoth in eleven days."

"By Astra! That long?" Vixa exclaimed.

"Lady, three hundred leagues is nine hundred land miles," Esquelamar explained. "*Evenstar* cannot cover such a stretch overnight."

"And yet she just did," Armantaro observed dryly.

* * * * *

Solinari, the white moon, rose from the sea and shone brightly on the lonely ship. The brisk westward wind continued.

Vixa, Armantaro, and Captain Esquelamar were alone on the quarterdeck. The old colonel, his white hair shining in the moonlight, was swapping stories with the captain, nearest of all aboard to his own age. Vixa listened with interest for a time, but the gentle rocking of the ship and the rushing of water by the hull soon conspired to make her eyelids heavy. She sat down on deck, leaning against the starboard rail. Once the drawstrings at the throat of her mail shirt were untied, she luxuriated in the feel of the warm breeze washing over her. She slept, her sheathed sword lying across her knees.

Perhaps it was the sound of the rushing water or the motion of the ship, but in her dreams, Vixa found herself swimming in a black ocean. Silver shapes darted around her. They were fish. Enchanted, Vixa tried to reach out and touch them, but they managed to elude her and were swallowed by the darkness. Then she heard the faraway skirling of pipes. It was strange, remote music, tuneless yet lyrical. The black water coursed by her face, as if she were hurtling at great speed through the dark sea. A roar of crashing waves filled her ears.

"Your Highness! Lady Vixa!" Armantaro was calling. Vixa's eyes opened, and she sat up, blinking in confusion.

"What?" she said. "What is it, Colonel?"

"Look at the sea, lady!"

Unsteadily, she hoisted herself to her feet. The strong wind of the night before had diminished. Though the sun had not yet risen, the predawn light was sufficient to show a marvelous sight. The sea surrounding *Evenstar* was alive with fish. Fingerlings, cod, perch, mackerel, and hundreds Vixa could not name leapt and swam across the ocean's surface, heading away from the Qualinesti ship. They scrambled up from the depths and kept going, swimming over each other. Fish that normally would have feasted on each other ignored each other in their mad haste.

Now dolphins appeared, arcing in and out of the water. They raced ahead of the sailing ship, zigzagging across *Evenstar*'s bow. Vixa was amazed at their speed and grace. She ran forward along the railing, trying to keep the dolphins in sight. After them came pilot whales and blackfish—dark-skinned animals twice the size of the dolphins.

Then, most astonishing of all, several whales breached. Huge gray backs broke the surface, water and other fish cascading over the smooth hides. The whales were mottled with barnacles. Flukes as wide as the ship's waist waved in the air and plunged down again, sending surges of water against the hull. Vixa braced herself as *Evenstar* rolled in the whales' wake.

The tumult brought all the sailors up from their hammocks. Some of them seized the opportunity to drop nets over the side. Laughing, they hauled nets full of bluegill and sea trout aboard, spilling the flopping fish over the deck. The noise also roused the Qualinesti soldiers. Rubbing their eyes, the warriors joined the others on deck.

"Have you ever seen the like, Captain?" Vixa shouted over the splash of fish.

"No, lady, and I wish I weren't seeing it now!"

"How so? It's a splendid sight."

" 'Tis not natural. All those creatures do not commune together. Something has disturbed them—frightened them into flight."

"What can frighten a whale?" she wondered, watching a massive gray head break the surface.

Esquelamar's worried eyes scanned the teeming ocean. "I don't know, my lady," he replied, shaking his head. "I don't know."

The furious activity lessened. The dolphins wheeled about the ship like cavalry and departed. Whales submerged and did not return. Within half an hour of Vixa's awakening, all the commotion had ceased. On the main deck, sailors busied themselves with cleaning and salting their bounty.

Esquelamar leaned over the rail, staring at the empty waves. His high brow creased in a frown. "Bosun! Where's that laggard of a bosun?"

A lean, barefoot elf with carroty hair ran to the captain's side. "Aye, sir?" he said.

"There's mud in the water. It could've been stirred up by the fish, or we could be in uncharted shallows. Take the lead line forward and sound. Be quick!"

The lead line was a length of twine with a lead weight tied to one end. At certain points along the line knots were made, indicating various depths. The bosun took the lead line and climbed out on the ship's beak. He let the weight drop into the water, paying out line as it sank. When the weight hit bottom, his sharp eyes read the mark at the ocean's surface below.

"Three fathoms and a half!" he sang out.

"Twenty-one feet," Armantaro advised his princess.

"In the open sea? Sound again," ordered the captain.

The bosun hauled in his lead and dropped it overboard again. "Two fathoms, even!"

"What! There should be more than forty fathoms under us," Esquelamar insisted. "Reef in all sails!"

Sailors clambered aloft and gathered in the sails. The captain mounted the rigging. "Damn it," he mumbled. "There's mud everywhere. Sound again, bosun!"

In seconds the reply came back: "Ten fathoms and a quarter!"

"What?" roared the captain. He swung around to the elves at the capstan, who were preparing to heave the anchor overboard. "Belay the anchor, lads."

"Captain!" The young bosun's voice was full of astonishment. "Full forty fathoms!"

"This is madness," Esquelamar said, shaking his head.

"Not so, good Captain," Vixa called. She descended the steps from the quarterdeck and made her way to where the captain clung to the rigging.

"There are accounts of such upheavals happening all over Ansalon," she continued. "The sages taught me that the skin of the world is not unyielding. It flexes every day, rising in some places and falling in others. Such are the circumstances of earthquakes."

"I never heard this," he said gruffly.

"Her Highness is correct." Armantaro stated. "I myself have read of these earthquakes and volcanoes, where the gods shake the ground, great buildings topple, and people are swallowed by new fissures in the land."

"Have the gods cursed us?" cried a sailor overhearing

this exchange.

"Belay that! If the learned lady and the colonel say these things happen naturally, then we're not the object of the gods' disfavor," declared the captain loudly. The light of the rising sun showed his lean face shiny with sweat, but he managed a smile. "Raise sail, lads! Let us begone from these strange waters!"

Evenstar wallowed westward under renewed sail.

* * * * *

Vixa shed the last of her armor and dressed herself in a plain leather jerkin, baggy cavalry pants, and boots. Despite her highborn status, she had little use for fine clothes, expensive jewelry, and courtly manners. Her father, Lord Kemian Ambrodel, despaired of her ever becoming a refined princess. He had to content himself with the fact that at least his youngest daughter had inherited his love of learning. In her rooms in the palace, books and scrolls vied for space with swords, armor, maces, and bows. Vixa's mother, Lady Verhanna, commander of the armies of Qualinost, wholeheartedly endorsed Vixa's military bent. "There are thousands of delicate elfmaidens," she was fond of saying, "but shockingly few good warriors."

Verhanna had nicknamed her youngest child "the scholar." She believed bookishness to be a waste of time for a warrior. However, as it didn't diminish Vixa's fighting skills or detract from her duties as a royal princess, Verhanna kept her views to herself. Most of the time. After all, she reasoned, the child's father was also bookish and it hadn't kept him from proving to be a fine general.

Vixa made her way forward between decks to the galley to collect her breakfast. The only open fire allowed on the wooden ship was kept in the brick oven abaft the mainmast. *Evenstar*'s cook was also her healer, a Kagonesti named Barbalthin. He greeted the princess cheerfully and gave her a trencher laden with griddlecakes and a cup of mulled nectar. She bit into the crispy cake. Ah! There were no bakers in the royal household who could match Barbalthin's griddlecakes. Vixa raised the pewter cup of nectar to her lips—

—and suddenly the entire contents splashed in her face as the ship lurched sharply. The nectar stung her eyes as the deck canted beneath her feet. She and Barbalthin collided with the brick hearth, fell, and rolled to the starboard wall. Glowing coals spilled from the firebox onto the wooden deck. Barbalthin scrambled against the tilt, dousing the embers.

Evenstar held its starboard list. The stout hull groaned, and a distinct grinding sound filled the ship.

"Now what?" groaned Vixa.

A chorus of shouts and the sound of tramping feet resounded overhead. Vixa made for the ladder and climbed up. Sailors scrambled fore and aft, cursing every god in the heavens. Vixa slid down the deck on her hips and heels until she collided with a red-faced Captain Esquelamar.

"We're aground!" he said fiercely. "A hundred leagues from land, and we're aground!"

"Are we wrecked?" she wanted to know.

"Never fear, lady. *Evenstar* will not sink."

A sailor popped out of the same hatch Vixa had emerged from. "She's tight below, Captain! No water in the hold!"

"Thank the gods for that," Esquelamar breathed.

The world heaved again as the ship rolled back upright. Esquelamar bounced to his feet like an acrobat. Vixa got up more slowly and saw Armantaro trying to stand, hampered by his armor. Vixa found herself wondering if the old colonel slept in his armor, too.

"On your feet, Colonel," she said genially.

"Now I know why I never served in the Speaker's navy," Armantaro muttered. "At least land doesn't trip a soldier at every opportunity."

The ship appeared to be surrounded by yellow mud—land where nothing had been seconds before. To the southwest, the low peak of an island was just visible in the early morning light. Esquelamar ordered a sailor over the side to see if the bar they were on was shifting. As his fellows held his legs, the elf stabbed a boat hook into the swirling, muddy water. It was only ten inches deep.

"We're fast aground," Esquelamar reported, his expression grim. "This shoal is not on any of my charts!"

"Can we lower a boat?" asked Armantaro. "Kedge off the bar?"

"Nay, the water's too shallow, even for the longboat."

The sun rose higher, and the island to the southwest stood out more clearly. It was a large, flat expanse of sand, with a single high dune in the center.

Knowing elves have to eat even in the direst of situations, Barbalthin came on deck with some food. He brought griddlecakes for the landlubbers, kippers for the sailors. Armantaro picked up a flat cake and was about to bite into it when an idea struck him.

"What about a raft, Captain?"

"Eh?" said Esquelamar.

"Why not build a raft? We could pole it ashore," said the colonel.

"To what end, sir? There's nothing out there but a hill of sand."

Armantaro pointed. "It is the tallest spot around, is it not? From there we should be able to spot open water."

"Aye. I see your meaning. Perhaps we can lighten the ship and float free of this bar." Esquelamar cupped a hand to his lips. "Manneto! Heronimas! Collect all free hands and assemble on the foredeck. And break out the carpenter's tools. We're going to build a raft!"

Empty water casks were dragged up from the hold, sawn in half, and lashed together. A makeshift deck of planks was hammered in place across their cut sides. Oars and oarlocks from the ship's longboats were attached, and the crude raft was hoisted over the side.

Vixa looked down at the newly made raft. "Who else is coming?"

"Lady, you would be safer on the ship," Armantaro ventured to suggest.

Vixa frowned. The obvious concern in the old colonel's face caused her to swallow her sharp retort. Clapping him on the shoulder instead, she said lightly, "Fear not, old friend. I doubt if the mosquitoes on that island are very dangerous."

A party of eight was chosen to explore the island: Captain Esquelamar and three of his sailors, Vixa, Armantaro, Harmanutis, and Vanthanoris. Manneto was left in charge of the ship, and Paladithel put in command of the remaining warrior contingent.

Although Armantaro and the other two warriors in the landing party had donned full battle dress, Vixa demurred, saying, "I'm only going to climb a hill, not fight a battle. Why should I wear armor in this heat?" She did, however, take along her fine Qualinesti sword.

A section of the ship's rail was removed, and supplies for the landing party lowered by rope to the raft. Vanthanoris and two sailors went down first, holding the raft steady by its mooring lines. The others followed. Below the waterline the hull was studded with razor-sharp barnacles. Deprived of water, the creatures made eerie clicking sounds as they gasped in the air.

From the deck, Manneto called down, "How long will you be, Captain?"

Esquelamar shaded his eyes, checking the position of the sun. It was perhaps two hours after dawn. "We'll be back before sundown," he called back.

"Aye, aye, sir."

With the captain at the raft's plank rudder and the sailors and warriors on the oars, they set off for the unknown island that had risen from the bottom of the sea. And Vixa said a silent prayer to the Blue Phoenix, lord of the sea.

Chapter 3

Marooned

The glare off the still water was harsh, though the sun was hours yet from its highest position. Gulls and other seabirds wheeled overhead, screeching in the steamy air. To shield her head, Vixa made a sort of short burnoose with her kerchief and a length of thong.

The going was slow, as almost every dip of the oars struck bottom. Lurching from side to side, the raft made its way. Twenty paces from the shoreline, the raft ran aground. Captain Esquelamar pulled in the steering oar and called, "From here on, mates, we walk."

They piled out. The footing was firm. From their vantage point, they could see *Evenstar* high and dry, looking like a child's toy left on the bank of a pond. Esquelamar shaded his eyes and scanned the low line of dunes left and right.

"From the look of these ridges, I'd say the water drains off from a central point. There, I think," he said, indicating the highest point on the island.

They set off, Esquelamar and Vanthanoris leading. It was

not a pleasant walk. The hollows between the sand ridges were full of stagnant pools, seaweed, and other debris. A foul stench rose up from this soupy mess. There was no way around it, only through.

Vanthanoris drew farther and farther ahead of the rest of them. Suddenly, at the top of a ridge, he drew his sword and flung up his free hand.

"Hold!" Vixa ordered. She, the colonel, and Harmanutis each dropped to one knee. Confused, Esquelamar and the sailors stood and stared.

"Get down!" hissed Armantaro. They did so at last.

Vanthanoris disappeared over the hill, sunlight flashing off his naked blade. A few tense minutes passed, then he came jogging back to his worried companions.

"I saw movement," he whispered. "To the northeast, yonder. Whatever it was, it disappeared behind some dunes. I ran forward, but all I found were tracks."

"What kind of tracks?" Vixa demanded.

"Hard to tell. This ground doesn't hold them well. Maybe a four-legged animal of some kind. Big, too," Vanthanoris replied.

"How big were the tracks?" Esquelamar asked.

The elf warrior held his hands apart about sixteen inches.

"Show us the trail," Armantaro said, rising. In a flash, the agile Vanthanoris was loping up the hill. The others struggled through the sand after him.

On the lee side of the ridge, they saw a line of prints starting on the left, southeast, and moving in a curve, paralleling the contour of the ridge.

Harmanutis dropped on his stomach and sniffed the prints. "Saltwater," he reported. "Whatever it is, it came out of the sea."

"A sea turtle?" suggested one of the sailors in a hopeful tone.

"Nay," Esquelamar said, dismissing the suggestion with a wave of his hand. "A turtle's got flippers. This creature leaves a distinctive trail."

"Well, it went that way," Vanthanoris said and started off again. His long legs covered the ground rapidly. The rest of the party hurried along in his wake.

They headed right, following the gully's curve. Vanthanoris, his hunting blood up, forged ahead. Vixa and Harmanutis jogged after him, panting with exertion. The fetid
sea-stench grew stronger.

Suddenly, Harmanutis lost his footing and slid down the
slope. Vixa, one hand on her sheathed sword, went after
him. About the time she reached the bottom of the slope, a
shout split the air. It was Vanthanoris from above—calling
for help.

Vixa was still several steps away from Harmanutis.
Struggling to his feet in the stinking bog, Harmanutis called
to her, "Go, lady! I'm with you!"

The princess ran splashing along the bottom of the gully,
scanning the landscape for sight of Vanthanoris. She caught
a glimpse of movement at the top of the next ridge. Then
she froze in place. Harmanutis, coming up behind her, likewise halted. A tall, upright figure was silhouetted against
the bright sky. All she could make out was a dark figure. It
was not shaped like the stocky, muscular Vanthanoris, but it
seemed to be a person, definitely not a four-legged animal.

"You there!" she shouted. The dark figure turned away,
disappeared over the hill.

"Go help Van!" Vixa ordered Harmanutis. Out came her
sword. She charged up the slope.

By the time she reached the top of the hill, Vixa was puffing. Her labor went unrewarded. There was no sign of the
dark figure, only more undulating ridges of sand. She stood
for a moment, scanning left and right. Still nothing.

Vixa turned right, strode along the rim of this dune until
she saw the rest of her group collected in the bottom of the
gully. Esquelamar and the sailors had caught up at last. She
called down to them, "Hello! How's Van?"

Armantaro and Harmanutis moved apart, revealing the
young warrior. Vanthanoris waved to the princess. Vixa
skidded down the dune. When closer, she saw that Vanthanoris had a gash on his forehead.

"What happened, Van?" she asked.

"I was hard on the trail, lady. As I rounded the bend

there, I caught a glimpse of something green moving. I challenged it, and it split in two!"

"Split in two?"

"Yes, Highness! What we thought was one four-legged animal turned out to be two two-legged people, walking in step together."

Vixa looked back at the ridge top. "I saw one of them," she said. "Did you get a close look?"

"No, my lady. I couldn't see them well. But they were covered with this." He held out a hand. In it was a swatch of green material. "They were lying in wait for me as I rounded the bend. When they attacked, I managed to tear this off one of them."

Vixa took the green material from the warrior's outstretched hand. It was damp. "Looks like seaweed."

Esquelamar examined it. "The fisherfolk call it eelweed," he told them. "Comes from the deepest parts of the ocean. Most people see it only when it gets caught in a fishing net."

The stems of the weed were woven together, like cloth. There even appeared to be threadlike strands of green sewn through the seaweed, for all the world as though it were a square of cloth. This was no bit of camouflage picked up at random. Someone had taken time and trouble to fashion the fronds of seaweed into a leafy covering.

"Well, these two brigands were draped in it," Vanthanoris stated. "They saw me, jumped apart, and one of them thrust a short spear at me. I ducked, but it grazed me. That's when I gave the call. One ran over the hill, that way. The other one ran down the draw."

Armantaro was nodding. "This changes everything," he said. "If there are armed foes about, the ship may be in danger."

The sailors were all for turning back right away. Esquelamar glared at them until they subsided into silence. "There's no need to panic," he said calmly. "Some other boat has fetched up on this unforeseen land, that's all. Vanthanoris ran into another scouting party. He startled them, so they attacked and ran away. There were two of them—if they'd wanted to kill him, why didn't they?"

"But the seaweed—" objected Harmanutis.

"There's probably several hundredweight of eelweed lying around here. This sand heap rose up from the depths, did it not? It must have brought the eelweed with it," was the captain's reasonable response.

"I agree with the captain," Vixa said. She tucked the swatch of eelweed into her belt. Esquelamar was probably right in his reading of events, but the woven eelweed was certainly one more peculiar detail in an increasingly odd situation. "We should finish what we came here for."

A bandage was tied around Vanthanoris's head. With Harmanutis in the lead, the small band continued their march toward the center of the island. The hills got higher, and the ravines between them got deeper. Here and there were more tracks in the sand, pairs of deep indentations, but they saw no more figures, weed-draped or otherwise. They plodded up hill and down dale, sweat-drenched, until Harmanutis topped the final rise and cried out, "I see smoke!"

The rest of the party slogged up the ridge to join the corporal. "Smoke means people," Esquelamar said.

One of his sailors muttered, "What is there to burn on this sand pile?"

Standing alongside Harmanutis, they saw the white smoke soaring skyward from a distant point. The smoke did not rise in long plumes, but in distinct, rolling puffs.

"How odd," Vixa said. "Is someone signaling?"

"That's not smoke," said Armantaro. "See how it disperses so quickly? That's steam, by Astra! There must be a geyser behind that hill." The old colonel allowed himself a smile. "No wonder this island is not on the charts. It must have been created by a recent upheaval of the subterranean regions."

The elves hurried on. Vixa and the younger soldiers arrived first at the pinnacle. As they had hoped, the view was spectacular. Looking back the way they had come, they could see *Evenstar*, surrounded by muddy water. A considerable distance to the west, a strip of brilliant blue revealed open water. However, it was a long, long way from the stranded ship.

A fresh billow of steam erupted below them. As the wind whipped the steam away, the source of the eruptions was revealed. Two large openings marred the hillside below.

"This I must see," announced the captain. He started down the hill.

"Keep clear, Captain," Armantaro called. "The steam can scald you." The master of *Evenstar*, acknowledging the warning with a wave of his hand, kept going, followed by his crew.

The warriors lingered atop the sandy hill, discussing how best to move the ship to that tantalizing stretch of blue ocean. A flurry of action interrupted their debate. Just as Esquelamar and the three sailors reached the closest steam vent, three large, weed-draped figures burst out of the cave-like hole, brandishing short-handled spears.

"Out swords!" Vixa ordered. "Charge!"

The elves ran down the hill, shouting Qualinesti war cries. The attackers had seized Esquelamar. His sailors tried to free him, and one received a spear in the chest.

Vixa raised her blade in a high overhand swing and brought it down on the closest foe. Keen elven steel sliced through the eelweed cape, and a broad section fell away, revealing some type of shiny green armor.

The attacker let go of Esquelamar and turned to face Vixa. He towered over her by at least a foot, though she herself was six feet tall. He jabbed his short spear at her. She batted it away with her sword. The head of the spear was a reddish, glassy material, barbed like a fishing hook.

The other Qualinesti warriors poured into the fight. Vanthanoris ran up behind the enemy and grabbed one of them, spinning him around and slashing hard across his opponent's chest. Eelweed fell away, revealing a cuirass of bright green. The elf dodged a spear thrust, lunged, and felt his sword tip strike home. His moment of triumph was short-lived, though. His tall opponent grasped the blade and wrenched it from Vanthanoris's grip. He then brought up his own spear, willing to continue the battle with a sword in his side. The now weaponless Vanthanoris hastily withdrew from this display of fortitude.

The other two weed-robed figures were retreating. They had abandoned Esquelamar and dashed back into the steam vent, bowling over Harmanutis, who tried to block their way. The third antagonist staggered toward the other steam vent. After wrenching Vanthanoris's blade from his body, he plunged into the cave.

Vanthanoris and Harmanutis gave a shout and started after the fleeing foe. Armantaro called them back. The old colonel and Esquelamar were kneeling by the dead sailor.

"Sir! The enemy escapes!" Vanthanoris exclaimed. The bandage on his forehead had slipped, and blood trickled down his face.

"Stand your ground, soldier!" snapped Armantaro. "Will you charge blindly into a dark cave, like some wild kender? Retrieve your weapon and stand guard at the mouths of those caves, both of you."

Vixa went over to the spot where one of the strange creatures had been wounded by Vanthanoris. Drops of greenish liquid were soaking into the sand. She touched the colored spots and raised her fingers to her nose. It was blood—of a completely alien shade, but blood nonetheless. She showed the others the odd bloodstains, saying, "I know of no race on Krynn with green blood in their veins."

"Do we go after them?" the colonel asked her.

"Yes," was her grim reply. "I want them alive, to question."

She led them to the mouth of one of the caves, guarded by Vanthanoris, who was cleaning green stains from his sword with his kerchief. The opening had an arch to it and looked to be made of some smooth stone. Esquelamar scratched the rock. "Limestone," he reported.

"Two of our marauders went in here," Vixa said. "We'll go after them. Captain, you and your lads should stay and guard the entrance."

"Nay, lady," Esquelamar contradicted. "It's my comrade who lies dead. I want a hand in catching his killers." The captain ordered his two sailors to remain on guard, then the elves entered the cave. The sudden change from bright sunlight to damp darkness left them all temporarily blind. They paused inside, allowing their eyes to become accustomed to the gloom. The sound of their footfalls echoed in the tunnel.

The floor tilted downward. Harmanutis and Vanthanoris lost their footing, slid down the slippery slope, and fetched up in a heap at its bottom. They called warnings to their companions, but too late. Vixa, Armantaro, and Esquelamar joined the pile.

"Your pardon, lady," Armantaro said, untangling himself from Vixa's long legs.

"Think nothing of it." Vixa stifled a chuckle at his unfailing politeness, then grunted as something dug into her ribs. "Mind that elbow, Captain."

"Beg—*oof*—your pardon, lady," Esquelamar puffed. They managed to separate and get to their feet, all except Vanthanoris. He remained crouched on the floor, feeling with his long, sensitive fingers.

"What is it, Van?" asked the princess, straightening her clothing.

"The floor is ridged," he replied, curiosity in his voice. "The gap between the ridges is filled with something soft." Vanthanoris drew his dagger. "I'll nip out a piece, and we can examine it."

As soon as his dagger penetrated the soft layer in the floor, the island convulsed. The floor rose up under their feet, then dropped away, knocking them all down.

"Earthquake!" yelled Harmanutis.

It was no ordinary earthquake. A great inrush of air howled through the cave, tearing at their clothes and ripping the burnoose from Vixa's head. Sand, sucked in from outside, stung their skin. Then the rush of air reversed direction, bellowing out as hard as it had previously roared in. Thick steam came with the outward flow, soaking them to the skin.

"We must get out!" Esquelamar cried.

Vanthanoris and Harmanutis cupped their hands, and Esquelamar placed his feet in them. The soldiers boosted him to the top of the slope.

"Gods preserve us!" Esquelamar shouted over the screeching wind. *"The cave is closing!"*

He offered his hands to Harmanutis. After the two of them pulled the rest of the party up, they all ran in a body for the shrinking exit.

Indeed, the walls of the cave mouth were closing together. The faint light that penetrated the cave was fading fast. Creases appeared in the floor, and the whole tunnel seemed to be folding in on itself like a concertina. Air shrieked inward once more, blowing Vixa and Vanthanoris off their feet and back into the others. When they regained their footing, they saw that the opening was sealed tight. They were trapped.

Before they could take in what had happened, the floor dropped out from under them once more. A mighty rushing sound filled their ears, as though the entire ocean roared around them. Vixa shouted for her comrades. If they replied, she couldn't be sure, but a hand reached out from the darkness and clasped her own. She would know those knobby fingers anywhere. Armantaro.

The floor continued to rise and shake, throwing them about like pebbles tumbling in a gourd. In spite of the thundering sound of water, no torrent breached the cave.

The walls of the cave had begun to glow a dark red.

"Armantaro," Vixa gasped, "what is happening?"

"The fires of the deep underground," he replied, drawing her closer. "Don't look, Your Highness. Turn away."

She could not resist a glance. By the ruddy light, she saw the warriors and Esquelamar huddled on the floor. The walls and the ceiling of the cave seemed to be shifting. Was the cave collapsing?

With loud wheezes and gulps, they fought for breath. Sweat broke out on their faces. The temperature was rising.

They would be crushed, if the heat and pressure didn't kill them first. Clumsily, her chest heaving, Vixa drew her sword. It had been presented to her on her last birthday by her mother. Ten ingots of dwarven iron forged by the finest smith in Qualinost into a single blade. The hilt was finely wrought with leaves and twining branches, forming a lattice handguard set with a large topaz.

Vixa was determined that if this was her time to die, then Astra and E'li, the highest gods of her people, would find her with sword in hand when they came to collect her soul. She would face death as befitted the granddaughter of Kith-Kanan, as befitted the daughter of her mother.

The air, compressed by the closing walls, battered the companions into oblivion. Esquelamar and Harmanutis lost consciousness first, and Armantaro felt himself joining them. Vixa tried to reach out to the colonel, but before she could do more than contemplate the action, her sword dropped from her nerveless hand. Van had likewise drawn steel. But finally, even the stalwart Vanthanoris, skilled hunter and warrior, could fight for breath no longer. His sword fell from fingers suddenly gone numb, and he knew no more.

Chapter 4

The Deadly Depths

Vixa was very surprised to open her eyes and find herself alive.

Her head pounded as if all the smiths of Thorbardin were busy inside, and with a groan, she sat up. Captain Esquelamar and the warriors remained unconscious, scattered around the shrunken cavern. The walls still glowed a dull red. Vixa massaged her aching temples.

Armantaro stirred. He sat up slowly, clutching his head. A smear of blood stained his upper lip.

"Ahhh," he moaned. "My head feels as if I drank a barrel of nectar." He winced, and added, "Very bad nectar."

"Your nose bleeds, Colonel."

He dabbed at it, and they spoke in whispers because the throbbing in their heads wouldn't allow anything louder. This strained quiet was suddenly shattered by a skull-piercing roar. Captain Esquelamar had fought his way to consciousness with a great bellow.

"For mercy's sake, Captain!" Vixa hissed. "Be quiet!"

"Astra have mercy, I'm dying!" he roared, heedless of her

entreaties. He thumped his head with the heel of one hand. The captain cried, "I'd give my right arm for a beaker of nectar!"

Armantaro muttered, "I'd give mine if you'd lower your voice."

Esquelamar stood, reeled about, and blundered against the glowing wall. Vixa expected him to cry out, but he did not.

Armantaro asked softly, "Captain! Are you not burned?"

"Burned?" The captain lifted one eyelid and took in his surroundings. Frowning, he stepped back from the wall and said, "Nay, nay. 'Tis no warmer than a maiden's cheek."

Vixa regained her feet slowly, waited a moment while her knees trembled, then walked carefully to the wall. She placed one hand against it. Esquelamar was right. It was only mildly warm, but yielded to her touch, like living flesh.

Harmanutis and Vanthanoris awoke at nearly the same instant. The corporal croaked for water, but they had none to give him. The small store of food and water they'd brought with them had been swept away in the tumult of the earthquake.

To take her mind off her own thirst, Vixa studied their prison. She dropped to one knee and scraped away debris. Soon, she had exposed more of the odd ridges they'd seen deeper in the cave. Between the ridges was the softer material Vanthanoris had described. Like the walls, it was spongy and gave easily to her touch. Suddenly, the myriad thoughts chasing around her aching head coalesced into a single idea—an idea so startling, she gasped aloud.

"Your Highness?" Vanthanoris had come to see what she scrutinized so carefully on the floor. He dropped to one knee beside her.

"This is not a cave!" Vixa exclaimed.

Vanthanoris and the others regarded her blankly. "What, lady?" whispered Armantaro.

"This is not a cave," she repeated slowly and carefully. "I believe—I believe we are inside a living creature!"

All their faces registered puzzlement. The colonel frowned, trying to marshal his scattered wits. "What?" he demanded in a low voice.

Vixa looked at each of them in turn. "This island is no island," she stated, forcing her voice to remain calm. "It is some sort of creature."

"Your Highness has injured her head," Harmanutis blurted.

"Mind your tongue, Corporal," Armantaro said absently. "Lady Vixa, how do you know this?"

"Captain," she replied, "the other night, when we saw the fish fleeing on the surface—had you ever seen such behavior before, in all your years at sea?"

"No, lady. Never."

"And the soundings that changed, deep then shallow then deep again—ever experienced that before?"

"No."

"The sea was stained with mud for miles, right in our path, yes? And *Evenstar* fetched up on a shoal no one had ever charted." They still regarded her with skepticism. "Don't you see? This creature rose from the bottom of the sea. It frightened the fish, and they fled before it. It swam under the ship, and that's why the bosun got different soundings. When at last it arrived at the surface, we ran into it, thinking it was an island!"

During her recital, doubt had crept into the faces of the other elves. When she finished, worry appeared, as the logic of her words sank in.

"How can it be?" asked Vanthanoris, standing by Vixa. "The monster would be more than a mile wide. How can the gods permit such a creature to exist?"

Armantaro shook his head, dazed. "The gods do as they see fit."

"This cave," Vixa continued, "must be inside the creature. The walls are made of flesh. That's why they're so soft and warm."

Vanthanoris's head snapped around, and he stared at her in horror. "I roused it," he whispered. "When I dug into the floor with my dagger, I roused it from its slumber!"

Silence reigned for long minutes as each of them digested the implications. They contemplated their surroundings, trying to recognize this place as the inside of a living beast and not a natural rock formation. A cave that was no cave.

"What shall we do?" Harmanutis asked at last. "Will we ever see dry land and sunshine again?"

Vixa straightened her shoulders staunchly. "There must be hope. We don't seem to have been devoured. In fact, judging from the wind that tore through here just before the beast went under, I'd say we're in the creature's nose or spout-hole. The principle danger, as I see it, may occur when the beast next draws breath."

"We could get out then," Vanthanoris said, hope dawning in his hazel eyes.

"If it breathes only air, yes. But if it breathes water—" Vixa's voice trailed off.

Captain Esquelamar ran his hands through his long, sand-colored hair. "I forced the guards to stay on duty," he said softly. "I left them out there. When this monster submerged, they must have—" Armantaro put a hand on his arm. However, there was no comfort to give. When the sea creature had submerged, certainly the elves left outside on guard must have drowned.

"But the ship is probably all right, Captain," offered Vixa, as much for her own comfort as for his. After all, she'd left her own soldiers aboard the vessel.

Esquelamar forced a smile, saying, "Aye, lady, she's a good ship. The best I ever served on." The smile vanished. He swallowed hard.

"There's a legend I heard once," he murmured, "a long time ago, when I was a lad not yet gone to sea. It told of a creature called a kraken, a beast so huge it could drag down a ship entwined in its tentacles. Now and then a ship would be lost in fair weather, or on an easy run to Hylo or Balifor, and the old salts would say, 'They're food for the kraken now.' "

This vignette did little to lift their spirits. Armantaro finally stood and declared, "We'll never get out by sitting here. We should explore farther down the passage. Perhaps there is another way out."

"Don't forget, the ones who attacked the captain and killed Theleran must be in here with us," Vanthanoris reminded them.

"If we meet them, we must offer a truce," Vixa decided. "It would be folly to fight each other in a situation like this."

The younger warriors drew swords and made for the slippery slope. The others trailed, picking footholds with care. The air grew moister and warmer as they descended the passage. Out front, Harmanutis murmured, "I don't fancy this." His and Vanthanoris's faces seemed bloodied by the lambent red glow from the walls. "I feel like a worm in a bird's gullet."

Vixa followed close on their heels. She found herself growing curious about the kraken—for a kraken it must be—in spite of her fears. "How would you classify this creature, Captain?" she asked. "Among other sea beasts, I mean?"

"Hard to say, lady," replied Esquelamar, ducking his head under a flap of leathery flesh hanging from the ceiling. "It vented like a whale."

"That would be fortunate. Whales breathe air as we do. When next this one surfaces to breathe, we could escape."

"Even if that's so, we've no way of knowing how often it needs to breathe," Esquelamar said. "It could be hours or—considering this beast's size—even days."

The gently sloped passage leveled off and ended at what looked like a pair of doors, each half-round.

They scrutinized the barrier. Vixa poked one of the doors with her fingers. The surface was soft and rubbery. At her touch, the doors parted slightly, and a foul, fishy smell assaulted them.

"Phew! That must lead to the monster's gut!" Esquelamar gasped.

They certainly didn't want to investigate that chamber. As there was no other way to go, they turned and retraced their steps, stopping just inside the closed nostril.

"The only way out is the way we came in," Vixa stated, gesturing at the sealed entrance.

Vanthanoris ran a hand through his silvery hair. "I wonder what happened to those two spearmen? The ones who led us in here."

"Maybe they fell into the kraken's stomach," Harmanutis said flatly. "Good riddance, I say."

"It's all very odd," Armantaro mused. "They didn't appear to be shipwrecked mariners. Yet, if they were not, then how did they get on the island—er, on the kraken?"

The princess had her mind on more practical matters. "We've no way of knowing when this creature will next draw breath," she announced. "We cannot hope to survive for long without food or water, so we must devise a way to escape. Suggestions?"

The warriors were out of their element. With charging armies, they could cope. With a monstrous sea beast, they were at a loss. A long minute passed, and no one spoke.

"Captain?" Vixa said, turning to that elf. "Any notions?"

The mariner folded his hard, tawny arms and replied, "I can't tell if we're moving or not. We might be lolling back on the surface, or lying on the bottom forty fathoms deep. As you said, lady, we have no option but to try to escape. As to the how—" Esquelamar smiled. "Kraken or no, if an animal gets something up its nose, it usually sneezes it out."

Vixa's own smile brightened her grimy face. "It does indeed. A splendid idea, Captain."

They resolved to get as close as possible to the opening through which they'd entered, then jab the kraken with their swords. With luck and the gods' intercession, the monster would expel them on the surface, or at a depth from which they could swim to the surface.

Armantaro, Harmanutis, and Vanthanoris shed their mail and heavy boots. Esquelamar pulled off his own footwear—beautiful, hand-tooled boots that reached to his knees. Vixa stripped to her smallclothes, which caused the old colonel some embarrassment.

"My lady, this is—this isn't seemly," he said haltingly.

"I won't risk drowning for the sake of modesty, Colonel. My clothes will weigh me down if we must swim," she pointed out.

The younger soldiers followed her example, stripping to their breechcloths. Armantaro stubbornly refused to remove his shirt and trousers, and the captain retained his emerald green corduroys as well.

"They're new," he said simply.

The elves drew their weapons. On Vixa's signal, they began to jab the leathery walls of their prison. The kraken's hide was tough. None of their thrusts drew blood or seemed to discommode the creature in the least.

Frustrated, Vixa raised her silver blade and stabbed it into the ceiling. This proved more tender than the walls. A twitching shudder rippled through the tunnel.

"Everyone! Concentrate on the ceiling!" Armantaro ordered.

All four elven blades were driven deeply into the ceiling, over and over. A violent quaking knocked them down. Two swords fell out of the ceiling. The other two—belonging to Vixa and Vanthanoris—hung quivering, embedded in the soft flesh.

The arched opening parted slightly. Water spewed in. "We must be underwater!" Esquelamar cried.

The beast shook itself again, rattling them helplessly.

Vixa was determined to reclaim her treasured sword. With the floor lurching and the ceiling swaying, this was not a simple task. She made two fruitless attempts, her hand missing completely. She finally grabbed the hilt on her third try.

At that moment, the nostril opened fully, and a wall of water smashed in. They were blasted back down the passage.

Vixa struggled frantically for a handhold. She knew they could be washed to destruction in the kraken's gullet. Water dark as ink roared over her. She couldn't see a thing.

The torrent slammed them against a barrier that buckled under the impact. This must be the "door," to the monster's gullet. They squirmed against the membrane, but the rush of water held them pinned in place.

Suddenly, they were rocketing in the opposite direction, back up the passage. The mad torrent of seawater had reversed itself as the kraken exhaled. Vixa hurtled on, battered by the water, debris, and the bodies of her friends. A stunning blow landed across her back as she shot through the nostril opening, then all was darkness and cold, swirling water. She was spinning free, weightless.

Her lungs were burning. Frantically, she began to swim. Was she heading for the surface? She couldn't tell. The buffeting of the water had knocked nearly all the air out of her. She had to breathe! Vixa put out her hands, groping for her comrades. Nothing.

Something streaked past her, brushing her outstretched arm. The kraken? There was a face staring at her. A strange, un-elven face. Smiling.

It was a dolphin. She'd never seen a dolphin this close before, and now that she had, she was nearly dead. She simply had to breathe. Her lips parted. Before the water could fill her mouth, something hard was shoved against her lips.

Air! Not cold seawater, but air flowed into her starving lungs. The dolphin had pushed a hard, white object against her face. With both hands, she pressed it to her mouth. It looked like a big seashell, but it held air—sweet, delicious air!

The dolphin bumped her right arm with its dorsal fin. On its second pass, she grabbed the dark gray fin and held on tight. The dolphin's powerful flukes propelled her through the inky depths.

Water rushed over her face, and she gripped the precious airshell even more tightly. Casting a look behind, she saw other undulating forms that were probably more dolphins. Had her friends been rescued as well? She sent up a silent prayer to Astra to keep them safe.

They swam for many minutes; then Vixa noticed a faint yellowish glow ahead and below. The dolphin changed direction, swimming toward the yellow light. They entered a zone of warmer water. A cherry-red glimmer beneath them told Vixa there were volcanic vents here. Columns of water warmed by the vents streamed upward.

The dolphin took her between two spires of stone. One, she noticed, passing just a foot away, was carved with geometric shapes and strange glyphs. Between the bases of the spires ran a long, white ribbon. It looked astonishingly like a road. A road on the bottom of the sea!

The dolphin slowed, fell in with a school of other dolphins. To Vixa they all looked very much alike—nine feet long, gray backs and flanks, lighter bellies. The school swam above the surface of the white road.

The water was brighter than before, suffused with a warm yellow light. Once more she looked over her shoulder. Vixa could make out the shapes of her friends, likewise being towed by dolphins. They all had shells clasped to their mouths, as she did. The number was wrong though. Her three comrades from Qualinost were there, but of Captain Esquelamar she saw no sign. Still, the sight of her friends cheered her tremendously.

She faced ahead again just as her slowly swimming dolphin reached another pair of stone spires. These were carved to resemble giant squids. The road rose, then dipped. Beyond was a sight that almost caused Vixa to drop her breathing shell.

It was a city.

This was the source of the golden light that brightened the depths. A vast structure rose from the seafloor in a swirling curve. Light shone through arched doorways. Vixa could see white shapes that resembled towers and buildings. Dolphins passed in and out of the lower reaches of the framework. She could only guess at the height of the peak. It was far beyond the limit of her blurry sight. The Tower of the Sun in Qualinost was over six hundred feet tall, yet this structure seemed much taller.

Her dolphin dove down to the lowest levels. Vixa could see beings walking on two legs near one of the structure's openings. Were there *people* down there?

The dolphin slowed and sank until its belly rested on the white marble road. He shook himself violently, and Vixa let go of his fin. Her rescuer darted off, leaving her alone.

As she floated there, pondering her next move, Vixa became aware that the water was filled with the sound of odd clicks and whistles. The dolphins bearing her friends drew up beside her, depositing the rest of the party on the road. Armantaro grasped her arm. She nodded vigorously to assure him she was unharmed.

Harmanutis tugged at the colonel's arm and pointed. Silhouetted against the city light came six very tall figures. The elves closed together.

The six strangers were the tallest beings Vixa had ever seen, easily a head taller than herself. Their skin was deep blue. It appeared they wore green-enameled armor, helmets, and short kilts. The water blurred her sight too much for her to make out details. What they bore in their hands was easily recognizable: short-handled spears. These were the beings draped in eelweed cloaks whom the elves had followed into the nostril of the kraken.

The blue-skinned strangers surrounded them. Vixa felt a pang of regret as her sword and scabbard were taken from her. Regret turned to surprise as she got a close look at the hand that gripped her sword; the fingers were unnaturally long, with a thin webbing of skin connecting them to each other.

The strangers herded them toward the city. It was awkward for the elves, half-walking and half-swimming, but Vixa had to admire the grace of their guards' movements.

As she drew closer, Vixa saw that the delicate-seeming city structure was actually made of pink granite. The walls of the lowest course were extremely thick. The group passed into a tunnel twelve paces deep, hollowed out with many side passages. Light came from pumpkin-sized globes attached at intervals to the overhead stonework.

The road forked, and the guards guided the elves to the left. The road inclined upward. They swam up the ramp and emerged into a large, air-filled chamber, twenty paces long and ten wide. The ceiling was dappled with waves of light reflected off the water. Vixa removed the shell from her mouth. The air here smelled sweet enough, and it was pure bliss to be able to breathe freely once more.

At the top of the ramp was a stone pier in the style of a seaside quay. Assembled on this pier were more tall, blue-skinned strangers. These wore silky robes of pale green, sweeping cloaks of mauve, and elaborate headdresses of shells and gemstones. Their hair ranged from apple green to deepest jade and was cut to shoulder length. At the center of the group was the most striking water-dweller of all. His short green hair was fixed in ringlets around his face, and he wore no headdress. Numerous necklaces of shells and gems covered his smooth chest. As she drew closer, Vixa saw that his nose was long and straight, his cheekbones high. Large violet eyes dominated his face. She pushed her sodden hair from her eyes, and something else attracted her notice. Astonished, she halted in her tracks.

The water-dweller's ears were upswept like Vixa's own. He was an elf. All the blue-skinned water-dwellers were elves.

"Greetings," he said in excellent Elvish. "I am Coryphene. Welcome to the city of Urione."

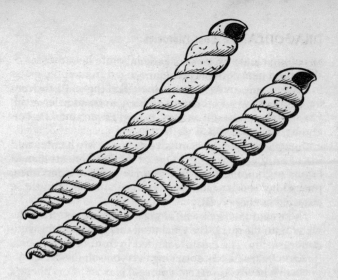

Chapter 5

Protector of Urione

No one spoke for several long seconds. The Qualinesti remained standing on the ramp, shivering in calf-deep water. None of the richly dressed strangers smiled or spoke. Clad as she was in only her sodden smallclothes, Vixa found their expressionless stares most unnerving.

"We had n-no idea you or your city existed," the princess finally stammered through chattering teeth. "It's lucky for us you found us."

At that, Coryphene smiled. "Has the landed race so soon forgotten their brothers, the Dargonesti?"

Dargonesti. Here was a race thought extinct for more than a thousand years. As Vixa, Armantaro, and the two warriors exchanged silent glances of wonder, one of the sea elf soldiers held out Vixa's confiscated sword to Coryphene. He examined it closely, testing the heft and workmanship. Turning to Armantaro, Coryphene asked, "Who are you?"

The colonel, evidently taken for the leader because of his age, introduced everyone. He carefully omitted Vixa's title.

No sense stirring up ideas of ransom.

"Your wife?" Coryphene inquired.

"My . . . niece." Armantaro smoothed the wet hair from his face and forced his shivering body to stand more erect. "There was another elf with us, named Esquelamar. Do you know if he was saved as well?"

Coryphene made a dismissive gesture. "My heralds told me of only your arrival." One of the Dargonesti leaned closer and spoke softly to Coryphene. He nodded once, then said, "It is possible your companion was brought in through another portal."

As he said this, a powerful gray dolphin burst from the water onto the quay. The Qualinesti flinched from this sudden intrusion. The creature landed in front of Coryphene. Its wide flukes flailed, splashing everyone on the dock.

"Is this how you present yourself, Naxos?" Coryphene's tone was as chilly as the water.

The dolphin uttered a shrill whistle. Its back arched, and a violent shudder ran through its muscular body. The Qualinesti stared in stunned amazement as two sinewy arms appeared from the animal's sides, arms as gray as the dolphin's flesh. With a sharp sucking sound, the tail split down its length, becoming a pair of long gray legs. The snout shrank to a rather prominent nose. In less than twenty heartbeats, the dolphin had transformed into a lean, hardmuscled elf with short, greenish blue hair. His gray coloring faded, first from his extremities, and the usual blue skin tone of the Dargonesti washed over him.

The transformed elf knelt before Coryphene, his body glistening with seawater. "Forgive me, Excellence," he murmured, though his expression was more amused than contrite.

"Is everything in order?"

"Ma'el is put to bed, Excellence." The elf called Naxos glanced at the Qualinesti shivering on the quay.

"Was another drylander found, Naxos?" Coryphene asked.

"A fifth was discovered, Excellence. He had drowned."

Vixa and Armantaro exchanged an unhappy look. Coryphene gestured at the two of them, saying, "You shall remain. Naxos, have the other two taken to the grotto."

More dolphins appeared in the pool, blowing and whistling. Armantaro had to shout to be heard. "Your Excellency! These are my retainers. I wish to keep them with me."

"You have no need of retainers here. Come."

The newly arrived dolphins began transforming just as Naxos had. Vixa watched in rapt wonder as, one by one, they became tall, yellow-eyed Dargonesti elves.

Armantaro, thinking it unwise to annoy their host, tugged at her elbow. He spoke briefly to Harmanutis and Vanthanoris, and the warriors reluctantly allowed themselves to be separated from their commander.

Vixa and Armantaro followed Coryphene. The entourage stood aside to let the Qualinesti pass. Up close, Vixa saw that these sea elves were more than mere officials or courtiers. Under their mauve cloaks they wore breastplates of green tortoise-shell. Short scabbards hung from their belts. Vixa thought longingly of her own treasured sword and took hold of Armantaro's arm.

"Why do I feel less rescued than captured?" she whispered.

He gave her an encouraging smile, but couldn't hide the worry in his own eyes.

Coryphene had donned a tall headdress made with dangling shells and gemstones. His guard closed in behind them. A wide stone staircase led upward through the pale pink ceiling of this level, emerging in a busy street. Hundreds of Dargonesti bustled about in what appeared to be a marketplace. Fish of a dozen varieties lay piled in gigantic seashells or baskets of woven seaweed. Vendors trundled two-wheeled barrows back and forth. The air was heavy with damp and the smell of the sea.

Everyone made way for Coryphene. The common folk, who wore gray leather vests over knee-length green or yellow kilts, bowed deeply as he passed. Striding through the respectful crowd, Coryphene looked neither left nor right. His escort was similarly sober. Once the Dargonesti lord had passed by, the sea elves turned their gazes upon Vixa and

Armantaro. The looks the two received were less friendly.

"No one seems happy to see us," Vixa remarked softly.

"No, they don't. We'd get a warmer greeting in Silvanost, I'll wager."

"Speaking of warm—" Vixa tugged at her skimpy clothing. Armantaro frowned. He lengthened his stride.

"Your Excellency," he said, catching up to the Dargonesti lord. "My niece is cold. Could we borrow a cloak for her?"

Coryphene glanced back at Vixa, shrugged, and gestured to a passerby. In moments, Vixa was wrapped in a blue cloak made of some surprisingly soft material. Warmer now, the Qualinesti princess looked about her with more interest.

Another vaulted ceiling topped this market, with many light globes strung about. In some places, on pillars or bare stretches of wall, stone spouts protruded. Formed to resemble sea horses or squid, these spouts poured forth streams of water into stone basins. They seemed too numerous to be drinking fountains. The mystery was solved when Vixa saw a Dargonesti set aside the basket of fish he carried and duck his head into one of the streams. It was then she realized that below each ear, on the sides of his neck, the sea elf had a semicircle of lacy gill. She commented on this to Armantaro.

"I see," he said, nodding. "They seem to breathe both water and air. Perhaps they must keep their gills wet when not in the water."

As they neared the far edge of the market, Coryphene stopped. An elaborate open sedan chair, borne by four helmeted elves, arrived. The bearers lowered the chair to the floor, and Coryphene stepped in.

Vixa looked around for another conveyance. None appeared. "Looks as if we walk," she said with a sigh. Her feet, bare and damp, felt like twin ice blocks. None of the Dargonesti were shod, so she'd probably have trouble securing new boots here.

At a shout, the bearers hoisted Coryphene's chair to their shoulders. The Dargonesti formed a line on each side. He clapped his hands, and the bearers were off at a trot. The

Qualinesti were obliged to jog just to keep up.

The Dargonesti guards drew swords and held them up as they ran. The lead soldier, ahead of Coryphene's chair, began to chant in a very deep voice. The guards echoed his words. To Vixa it sounded like nonsensical singsong.

"Look at their swords," Armantaro puffed.

Coryphene's escort was armed with an assortment of edged weapons—Ergothian sabers, dwarven short swords, sailors' cutlasses. It was clear that these were salvaged pieces, probably from shipwrecks. Why would this elite guard be armed with such a random mix of blades?

A lustrous marble path wound tightly around an enormous pink granite pillar, most likely the central support of the city's outer shell. The grade was rather steep, but the long-legged sea elves maintained their exhausting pace with no sign of discomfort.

As they trotted around the broad sweep of the ramp, Vixa looked up. The central shaft reached all the way to the city's apex. She swallowed hard and looked away from the sheer, dizzying height of it.

Round and round they went, passing every level in Urione. Some levels were air-filled and contained houses and shops. Others, walled off from the spiral ramp by panes of quartz, were open to the ocean. Dolphins coursed through the passages—or perhaps they were Dargonesti in dolphin form, for these animals wore necklaces of shells and gems. On other flooded levels were gardens of waving sea plants, schools of trout and tuna that surged from wall to wall with the restless energy of the wild sea, and pens teeming with crabs.

They passed a level with especially high ceilings. Roads, inlaid with alternating bands of black basalt and mother-of-pearl, radiated from the central ramp to a complex of wedge-shaped temples constructed in the finest style. Elaborate, brightly colored bas-reliefs on the buildings displayed a variety of sea life—octopi, starfish, sea horses, and fish of every shape and hue. An odd odor, similar to the sweet incense used in Qualinesti temples, yet strangely different, permeated this level of the city, leaving a sickening aftertaste. Then, as Coryphene's sedan chair swung around the ramp ahead of them, Vixa and Armantaro beheld a sight that froze the blood in their veins.

In a plaza between two brilliant temples stood an enormous statue, easily thirty feet wide and about half as high. It portrayed a creature shaped like an upside down bowl, with myriad tentacles hanging from its underside. A vast mouth opened on the side of the thing, and two onyx eyes were buried in the dull white flesh above the mouth. This was horrible enough, but scattered across the broad back of the monster were tiny carved models of ships. They listed this way and that, their sails slack and useless. Stranded ships, just like *Evenstar*.

"Ma'el is put to bed," the shapeshifter Naxos had said to Coryphene. And what had Captain Esquelamar told them when they were first trapped inside the sea monster? He'd spoken of the kraken, a creature so huge it could drag down a ship entwined in its tentacles.

Their pace faltered. Lines of Dargonesti warriors surged past.

In front of the grotesque statue was an altar of white coral. Several Dargonesti, clad in red and mauve robes that swept the floor, stood before the altar. In their hands they held seashell bowls. As each passed the statue, he poured liquid from his bowl onto the altar. The Qualinesti saw oil, sand, and a dark substance they feared was blood dribbled onto the flawless white coral.

Someone shoved them from behind. Vixa whirled, fists at the ready. Armantaro squared off as well.

"Move on!" barked one of the Dargonesti guards who had dropped back from the rest to ensure the Qualinesti kept up. "The Lord Protector awaits!"

Vixa frowned. "I am weary of being dragged around by these people," she stated. "I say we go at our own pace."

"An excellent suggestion, Niece."

The Dargonesti advanced, both aiming for Armantaro. They obviously regarded Vixa as no threat. Vixa lashed out with her foot at the soldier nearest her. Hooking her adversary's knee, she brought him down hard on his back. This distracted the other guard. Armantaro grasped his right fist with his left hand and drove his elbow into the Dargonesti's side. The blow propelled the sea elf into his fallen comrade, and both ended in a tangle on the floor. With a grim chuckle, Vixa shoved the flailing warriors. They rolled, like a pair of blue logs, down the steep ramp. The soldiers disappeared around the bend, and the sound of a loud crash reached Vixa's ears.

Dusting her hands, the Qualinesti princess asked, "Shall we continue?"

"After you, noble niece." The colonel was smiling.

They went up the ramp at a more leisurely pace. Around the curve, they came upon the rest of Coryphene's guards, waiting with swords drawn. Coryphene had left his sedan chair and stood tapping one foot impatiently.

"You must not leave my protection," he told them. "The people of Urione are not accustomed to strangers. You endanger your own lives."

"I don't feel all that safe with you," Vixa muttered.

Coryphene stood aside, gesturing for the Qualinesti to precede him. The bearers walked two paces behind.

The roof of the city was nearer now, the ramp narrowing to meet it. With no word of warning, the Dargonesti warriors suddenly halted in close ranks. When Vixa and Armantaro stopped as well, Coryphene ordered them to continue. It was then that the Qualinesti found themselves engulfed in a blazing white light.

Vixa threw up an arm to protect her eyes. Heat washed over her. In seconds she was dry and warm for the first time in what seemed like days. The sensation lasted perhaps five seconds; then the light disappeared. Vixa stood blinking in the dimness. When she could see once more, she realized that Coryphene was gone. She and Armantaro were alone.

"Colonel?" she said softly. "What happened?"

"I have no idea. At least I'm not so cold now." Armantaro rubbed his eyes and looked around, adding, "But where are we?"

Above their heads, the thick stone arches that made up the framework of the city beneath the sea had ended, revealing a transparent dome composed of millions of quartz crystals, fitted together with supreme skill. Beyond this clear barrier could be seen the deep blue of the ocean depths. Schools of fish swam overhead, the reflected light from the city flashing off their silver bodies.

Vixa and Armantaro stood in the center of a large disk of white marble situated in the center of a great round plaza. At the plaza's perimeter rose a colonnade, supporting a palatial building made of green stone. Though the building's facade was pierced by hundreds of unglazed windows, none of these openings showed any light. The only illumination was a subdued, shifting, greenish glow.

"Magnificent," Vixa sighed, turning round and round. "Really quite beautiful."

Armantaro was frowning. "Where is everyone? And where in the name of the Abyss is the entrance?" Try as he might, he could find no trace of the spiral ramp, only the smooth disk of white in the middle of the green-paved plaza. The old colonel slipped a hand under his battered shirt. Vixa saw the hard gleam of a dagger hilt.

"Put that away," she hissed. He made no reply but tucked the slim knife back inside his clothing.

The faint sound of footsteps reached their ears. Out of the shadows of the colonnade to their right came a tall figure carrying a glowing yellow globe. It was Coryphene. The light beneath his chin cast weird shadows across his sharp features.

"I know that landed folk require a great deal more light than we Dargonesti," said Coryphene, his voice echoing in the stillness. He stopped several paces away. Armantaro's fingers touched the dagger hilt through his shirt. There were no guards in sight. If he could take Coryphene hostage, they might be able to force the Dargonesti to release them.

Coryphene threw the glowing globe into the air. It rose to twice his height and vanished in a silent yellow burst. Instantly the plaza was filled with the tawny golden illumination of a summer evening in Qualinost.

"You're a sorcerer," Vixa stated.

"I have some skill in the art of magic. Another example."

He pointed a webbed blue finger at Armantaro. To the colonel's surprise, he felt the blade of his hidden dagger growing warm. He tried to ignore it, keeping his face impassive, but the blade grew hotter and hotter, until it burned like a branding iron. With a yelp, Armantaro snatched the dagger out and flung it away. He put his scorched fingers into his mouth.

Coryphene picked up the dagger. He tested its edge with his thumb and slapped the flat of the blade against his palm. With a nod, he slipped the knife into his own belt.

Vixa spoke up quickly. "Are you the ruler of this place? Are you Speaker of the sea elves?" she inquired.

Coryphene's violet eyes narrowed. "I am Protector of my people and First Servant of our divine queen." He clapped his hands twice, and a troop of servants appeared from the shadows of the colonnade. For Coryphene, they brought a chair carved from a single concretion of blood coral. Two large, flat-topped sponges were set in place to serve as stools for the Qualinesti. Two lackeys carried a hamper of woven seaweed. It was evidently quite heavy.

"Sit," Coryphene said, the word more a command than an invitation. "Refresh yourselves."

Supporting his chin with folded hands, he rested his elbows on the arms of his scarlet chair. Armantaro and Vixa sank gratefully to the stools, glad to rest their tired feet. Eagerly, the princess opened the hamper.

"Our food may seem strange to you, but I am certain you will find it superior to any you have ever eaten."

Vixa hesitated. Was it possible this odd elf wished to poison them? She glanced at Armantaro, who was likewise uncertain, then she looked at Coryphene.

A frown was gathering on the Protector's face. He was clearly ready to take offense if they refused his hospitality. Shrugging fatalistically, the Qualinesti helped themselves.

The food was indeed strange. There were planks of dried, spiced fish; greenish cakes made of seaweed; a smoky, strongly flavored meat paste; and cups of sweet relish that might have been animal or vegetable. Servants handed them goblets made of bell mussel shells and filled with a light, fermented beverage rather like the nectar of Qualinost.

Coryphene waited until the edge was off their hunger before asking, "What ship were you sailing on?"

"*Evenstar*, out of Qualinesti," Vixa answered, seeing no reason to lie.

"I have heard of that place. What was your destination?"

"The Gulf of Ergoth, specifically the Greenthorn River," replied Armantaro. "If it please you, my lord, may I ask how it is you know of our country, when we know nothing of yours?"

"Do none of the ancient race remember the Dargonesti?"

Vixa swallowed a mouthful of nectar. "I've heard legends that tell of sea-dwelling elves, but I always thought they were stories for children—tall tales passed around the fireside. I never honestly believed such a race existed."

For some reason, this answer pleased Coryphene. He smiled and ordered the servants to bring him a cup of nectar.

"For thirteen hundred years my kind has dwelt in the depths," he told them. "The Graystone transformed us, and we were able to escape the unfair rule of Silvanos by taking to the sea. Untouched by landed folk and their bloody wars, we perfected all the arts and sciences. The Quoowahb, or Dargonesti, are the most perfect of all the races created by the gods."

Vixa, trying to maintain an attitude of polite interest, nearly choked at this calm statement of superiority. Armantaro thumped her on the back. Unconcerned, the Protector of Urione went on.

"From time to time, the ships of the landed folk fall into our domain. I have seen many of the land races: humans, dwarves, kender. Thus have I learned of your cities and nations." He handed his empty cup to a hovering servant. "What rank are you and your niece?"

The swift change of subject caught Armantaro by surprise. "I am freeborn, Excellence, a subject of the Speaker of the Sun in Qualinost. My niece is an orphan, so I have adopted her as my own child."

"Qualinost is ruled by Silveran, son of the mighty Kith-Kanan, yes?"

"Why, yes. You know of Kith-Kanan?"

Coryphene stared off into space. "The birds of the air and the wind above the waves have spoken the name of Kith-Kanan," he murmured. His gaze returned to them, and he next inquired, "Are the nobles of your country required to bear arms?"

"Ah, no. No one is compelled to serve," Vixa replied warily.

"What is the size of Speaker Silveran's army?"

Armantaro placed a hand upon Vixa's wrist, but the warning wasn't necessary. The princess had no intention of giving this arrogant fellow such important information. She opened her mouth to deliver an evasive answer, and suddenly the air was split by a loud chorus of bleating notes. Coryphene leapt to his feet, knocking aside his cup of nectar. Vixa and Armantaro exchanged a baffled look as the plaza erupted into furious activity.

Servants came running and cleared away the food and chairs, practically dumping the Qualinesti from their seats. Four Dargonesti sped from the colonnade bearing a suit of exotic armor and arms. As Coryphene stood with feet apart and arms held out, the servants girded their master as though for battle.

"What is it?" Vixa demanded. "What's happening?"

"An attack," Coryphene said tersely.

The bleating grew louder, and Vixa spotted the source of the terrible racket. A trio of white-robed Dargonesti had appeared as if by magic on the disk of marble in the center of the plaza. The three sea elves stood blowing on large conch shells, their sonorous notes reverberating through the area.

Coryphene was now fully armed and armored. He turned a grim look on his captives and said, "Come. You may understand things better if you see the peril we face."

Vixa and Armantaro had little choice in the matter. A phalanx of at least one hundred soldiers formed around them and the lord of Urione. With the sound of conch shells bellowing all around them, they marched to the disk of white marble. A flash of light blazed. Vixa felt the heat once more through her borrowed cloak. When the light faded, they were heading down the great spiral ramp. Urionans lined the way ahead, shouting, waving, and blowing conch shells.

The din was bewildering to the Qualinesti. It appeared they were to be sent into battle—completely unarmed—to fight the-gods-knew-what type of enemy.

The sea elves were chanting. The cacophony of voices coalesced into a single word, repeated over and over.

"Chilkit!" cried the sea elves. "Chilkit! Chilkit!"

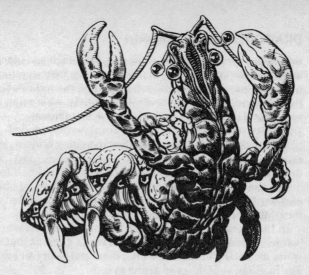

Chapter 6

Nissia Grotto

Harmanutis and Vanthanoris were taken by Dargonesti soldiers outside the city, given two whelk shells filled with air, and fitted with belts of sharkskin to which flat stone disks were attached. The weight of these belts helped them move better underwater, anchoring their feet more firmly.

The eight guards walked ahead, apparently unconcerned whether their charges kept up. It wasn't difficult to figure out why. The air in the shells was not infinite, and once it was gone the two Qualinesti would drown. They were imprisoned as surely as if bound with manacles and chains.

Underwater, the sea elves conversed in clicks and whistles, much like the noises the dolphins made. Gills bloomed from behind their ears as they moved through the dark water. Vanthanoris and Harmanutis trudged after them, watching everything, trying to figure out some way to escape this underwater city.

Once outside the city shell, they found themselves in an area of coral formations. The coral grew in branching, treelike shapes in a variety of sizes—some only knee-high and others towering twenty or thirty feet. There was the more common red coral, but also white and a faintly luminous yellow. The two Qualinesti could see several Dargonesti swimming in and around the coral, tending it as if it were a garden.

Twenty paces from the city, the coral gardens ended. A paved road, as wide as four soldiers marching abreast, led away into the shadowy depths. In several places, sand had drifted over the paving stones. Brightly striped fish followed the Qualinesti, darting through the streams of bubbles emitted by the whelk shells. Vanthanoris swatted at them, and the curious little fish swam away.

In the distance, a dark shape loomed. It took a while before Harmanutis realized that this was a gigantic underwater mountain, hundreds—if not thousands—of feet high. The road ran straight as an arrow to it.

Pillars appeared on each side of the road. These bore inscriptions in an angular script. As the Qualinesti drew nearer the mountain, they discovered that some of the pillars evinced a sinister purpose. Corpses in every state of deterioration were chained to them. Some of the bodies plainly showed signs of the predations of sharks; others were little more than skeletons. Harmanutis recognized most as human remains—the heavy bones and wide skulls made this plain. Now and then a smaller body could be seen, perhaps a dwarf or kender. In all, they counted forty-seven corpses lashed to pillars along the road. None elven.

Just then, Vanthanoris's air began to give out. He tried harder to inhale, but still there was nothing. He threw a startled look to Harmanutis and saw that the corporal was having the same difficulty. The guards walked on, oblivious to their captives' plight. The Qualinesti quickened their pace, catching up with the guards and making their distress plain. The guards merely prodded them to continue.

The road led to a cave entrance dressed with a pediment and columns. Vanthanoris hurried inside. Above him, ripples betokened a surface. There were stone steps ahead, and he fairly flew up them. On the ninth step, his head broke into open air. He tore the empty shell from his blue lips and gulped down huge draughts of chill, damp air.

Harmanutis surfaced beside him, likewise gasping. The Dargonesti soldiers rose with supreme indifference and herded the pair onto a rough stone landing. Vanthanoris staggered and fell. Harmanutis didn't bother trying to rise, merely crawled where he was bidden. While he lay inhaling and exhaling gratefully, he studied his surroundings.

Beyond the landing was a long, wide tunnel that ran straight back into the mountain. A few lighting globes were stuck high on the walls, but they were dim compared to those they'd seen in the city. Along both walls were piles of seaweed, scraps of leather, blankets, hanks of rope, and chests salvaged from sunken ships. An aisle passed down the center of the tunnel. Harmanutis realized he was looking at a prison for dryland captives.

One of the sea elves collected the exhausted whelk shells, and without a word, the eight Dargonesti submerged and departed.

Harmanutis helped Vanthanoris stand. "Is this our new home?" the latter asked hoarsely.

"Not for long, my friend. Trust our good lady and the colonel to find a way out for all of us," Harmanutis replied.

"We must be a mile or more from the city. Too far to swim without air. No wonder they don't need bars or locks to make this the perfect dungeon. Try to escape, and you would surely drown!"

"We'll escape, Van. I don't plan on dying a prisoner of these blue-skinned barbarians!"

Name boards of ships long sunk and forgotten were attached to the walls: *Sinar's Pride*, *Sea Dragon*, *Balifor Star*. Craft from all over Ansalon had ended their days here.

"I wonder if *Evenstar* survived," Harm said quietly.

"Poor Paladithel," murmured Van. "How he hated fish."

The cave stretched on and on. If every squalid pile of bedding denoted one prisoner, then there were hundreds of captives in Dargonesti hands. Why? Why did the sea elves hold so many land-dwellers?

A huge pile of debris blocked the end of the cave, leaving only a narrow space between it and one wall. It divided the inhabited section from the empty darkness beyond. In this moldering heap of debris were yards of rope, mounds of sailcloth, lengths of rusted and broken chain, clay pots, amphorae, and smashed wooden boxes—the detritus of centuries of shipwrecks, yet nothing that would help them get out of here.

Harmanutis kicked the nearest object, an empty flour barrel lying on its side.

"Oof!" said the barrel.

Harmanutis froze, his foot still in the air. "Did you hear that?" he hissed.

In reply, Vanthanoris kicked the barrel himself, saying sternly, "Come out. We know you're in there."

A pale, craggy face, framed by matted hair and a black beard, popped out of the barrel.

"A dwarf!" Vanthanoris exclaimed.

"You're not blueskins!" said the dwarf, crawling out of the barrel. Drawing himself up to his full height—just over four feet—he added, "You're Qualinesti, aren't you? Well, that's new. My name's Gundabyr."

Harmanutis introduced himself and Vanthanoris. "Are there any other elves down here?" he asked.

"Nope. No elves at all except the blue-skinned variety. I guess the Quoowahb don't care that you fellas are cousins, eh?"

"Quoowahb?

"The blueskins. That's what they call themselves." Gundabyr pulled up a battered sea chest and hauled himself up onto it. His feet dangled above the floor. A stick of some whitish stuff protruded from his vest pocket. He pulled it out and gnawed on it.

"Dried cod," he explained. "That's about all we get to eat around here." He looked them up and down, noted their abbreviated attire, and sighed. "It's a pity you fellas aren't carrying some ale on you."

"How did you get here, Gundabyr?" Harmanutis asked. "How long have you been a prisoner?"

"Nobody's a prisoner here. We're slaves." The dwarf shrugged in reply to their stunned expressions. "I was forgemaster for the Ironmongers Guild in Thorbardin. We hired a ship, *Sea Queen*, in Tarsis to carry a load of copper and iron ingots to Balifor. Me and my brother Garnath got stuck with the chore of tagging along with the ship to sell the ingots. Garnath said the ship's name would bring us luck, and it did—all bad. *Sea Queen* ran into fog off the Silvanesti coast, and when it cleared, we were a hundred leagues off course."

Vanthanoris smiled sardonically. "I know that fog," he said, then went on to describe *Evenstar*'s encounter with the mysterious wall of cloud.

"Sounds familiar," Gundabyr agreed. "Well, next thing we knew, *Sea Queen* was aground on the biggest sandbar Reorx ever created. Me and Garnath took a work party ashore to try to dig a trench under the ship to refloat it, but the whole filthy sandbar sank under us." A mighty frown creased his face. "Me and Garnath went down like anvils."

"The kraken." Harmanutis felt the heat of anger wash over him, despite the coolness of the cave. "It's no coincidence then. These Quoowahb use the monster to sink ships!"

"Yep, they do." Gundabyr finished his strip of cod. "Dolphins carried me and Garnath and a handful of other survivors down here. We've been in this hole for—" He looked up at the stone wall, on whose surface were drawn a number of white chalk lines. "—Um, forty-eight days."

Harmanutis related the story of their own arrival in Urione, including the fact that Princess Vixa and Colonel Armantaro were getting "special treatment" in the city, at least as far as they knew. Gundabyr rubbed his hairy cheek when he heard that.

"Hmm. Wonder what they want with your lady and the colonel?"

"Ransom?" Vanthanoris suggested.

Harmanutis shook his head. "Not unless Her Highness reveals her true status. I'll wager this Coryphene is questioning them about Qualinost, since we seem to be the first land elves they've captured."

Vanthanoris paced between the piles of wreckage. He turned suddenly to the seated dwarf. "Slaves? We're to be *slaves*, you say?" Gundabyr belched and nodded. "What sort of work are we supposed to do?"

"They're building a wall," explained the dwarf. "A very high wall across the Mortas Trench, from this mountain to the next."

"Why?" asked Harmanutis, curious.

"To keep the chilkit out."

Vanthanoris planted his fists on his hips. "And what, by Astra, are chilkit?"

"More like 'who' than 'what.' The chilkit are the mortal enemies of the Quoowahb. Now and then they come down the valley and attack the blueskins."

Harmanutis's blue eyes gleamed. "So the sea elves have enemies, do they? This may be our opening. Could we treat with these chilkit, Gundabyr? Would they help us get away from the blueskins?"

"Nope. The chilkit aren't people at all. They're monsters. Big, ugly crab-things. They eat any Quoowahb that they capture. We might be a different flavor, but they'd surely eat us too."

"Nonetheless," said the corporal, hanging on to hope, "our best chance may be to make our escape when the blueskins are distracted by their enemies. If we—"

The cave filled with the sound of churning water. "Work parties returning," Gundabyr said quickly. "I hafta hide from the guards!" In a flash he was back in the barrel.

"Wait! Gundabyr?"

"Go away! Don't let on I'm in here!"

Puzzled, the two Qualinesti left the dwarf and walked toward the pool. A troop of wet, semi-naked prisoners was rising from the water. Armed sea elves made a double line through which the captives passed. The last pair of Dargonesti held woven bags. As the prisoners went by, they deposited their used airshells in the bags.

The first slaves, emaciated humans with long beards, passed the Qualinesti without a second glance. There was more recognition from some dwarven captives—eye contact and slight nods. Then, to the elves' astonishment, Gundabyr came marching out of the cavern pool at the rear of the line.

"Eh?" Vanthanoris said, looking back toward the flour barrel. "What's this?"

Harmanutis jabbed him with an elbow. "His brother, remember? Must be his *twin* brother."

In a flash the Qualinesti warriors understood the dwarves' trick. Because they were twins, one of the brothers could hide from the Dargonesti guards, while the other went out to work. By alternating days off, the dwarves spared themselves half the work, along with half the jeopardy.

They followed Gundabyr's twin, Garnath, as he trudged to the rear of the cave and flopped heavily onto the hard stone floor. Water trickled off him, pooling in the low places in the rock. He became aware that someone was standing over him and opened his eyes.

"Whaddya want?" Garnath rumbled.

After performing introductions, Harmanutis dropped hints of their meeting with Gundabyr.

"*I'm* Gundabyr," said the sodden dwarf. "My brother, Garnath, succumbed to an ague weeks ago."

"Of course. My condolences," Harmanutis murmured.

"He was a fine dwarf," said Garnath mournfully.

"And a good forgemaster," put in a voice from inside the flour barrel.

"Salt of the earth," Garnath added.

"You can come out now," Harmanutis told the flour barrel.

Gundabyr worked his head and shoulders out of the barrel. Garnath sat up, and the dwarf twins shook hands.

"Your turn tomorrow, Brother," Garnath said with an exhausted sigh.

"Yup." Gundabyr brought out more strips of dried cod for his brother, and the two dwarves sat side by side, chewing noisily. Harmanutis asked again about the chilkit.

"Don't expect help from them," Garnath said, echoing his brother's earlier advice. "They have some intelligence, but not even the blueskins can talk to them. They come down the valley now and then and attack anything in their path. They're bigger than Quoowahb are, and pretty damn tough."

Next Harmanutis asked about the airshells.

"Nope, can't use them," Gundabyr stated, dashing yet another hope.

"Why not?" Vanthanoris demanded.

"The Quoowahb count every one they bring in and every one they take out. And even if you could get your hands on one, there's no knowing how much air's in it."

"And the sea brothers would get you anyway," put in Garnath.

Vanthanoris dropped his head into his hands, his brain reeling with all this unhappy news. "And who are the sea brothers?" he asked despondently.

"Shapeshifters. You must've seen them—the dolphins who rescued you."

Harmanutis remembered them well. "Can all the Quoowahb become dolphins?"

"Nope, just the sea brothers. They live outside the city. A fella called Naxos is their chief, but he takes his orders from Coryphene," Garnath explained.

"So Coryphene is Speaker of these elves?"

"Him?" Gundabyr spat. "He's a veritable butcher, but he's not the leader."

Vanthanoris swore, which caused the dwarves to smile. Harmanutis motioned for him to be still and asked, "Then who does rule in Urione?"

"Her Divine Majesty, Queen Uriona," said the dwarf twins in unison. Gundabyr added wryly, "Uriona the Mad, that is. They say she's been touched by the gods. 'Touched' is right."

A distinct *clack-clack* rang down the tunnel. Gundabyr vanished into the barrel again. Garnath jumped to his feet, crying, "The blueskins are coming back! Whatever the reason, it can't be good!"

The clacking noise had been made by one of the other dwarves. He'd seen a disturbance in the water and had signaled his fellow slaves by beating the floor with a rock. Seconds after his alarm sounded, a troop of Dargonesti warriors burst out of the pool, weapons in hand. One, with a golden sand dollar on the front of his helmet, boomed out, "All prisoners line up! Take a shell and proceed outside!"

Slowly the tired slaves rose. When they didn't move fast enough to suit their captors, a squad of sea elves came down the aisle, prodding the laggards with spear points. Harmanutis and Vanthanoris glared at the seven-foot-tall Dargonesti. Garnath straightened his soggy shirt and muttered, "Twice in one day! You owe me, Brother!" A muffled grunt from the barrel was the only reply.

The Qualinesti stood shoulder to shoulder, their proud bearing in marked contrast to the ragtag look of the rest of the slaves. When he reached the water's edge, Harmanutis addressed the Dargonesti who wore the decorated helmet, who he assumed was an officer.

"What's happening?" he asked. "Where are we going?"

"No talking!" snapped the Dargonesti.

With no other option, the two Qualinesti fit their airshell mouthpieces into place. They were still wearing their weighted belts as they walked down the steps and into the cold water. As soon as their ears were submerged, they heard a riot of strange noises. It almost sounded like . . . a battle?

The Dargonesti soldiers drove the mass of prisoners forward. They quickly left the road to the city and turned toward the great mountain. Dark gray shapes hurtled overhead. The chorus of clicks and bubbling beeps revealed that these were dolphins, all heading in the same direction.

Suddenly, the Qualinesti saw a wall looming over them. Made of great blocks of stone, the wall rose sixty feet from the seafloor. There was a gate in the center, and four unfinished stumps of towers at the top. Unused blocks of stone were piled here and there. Crowded among the waiting blocks were hundreds of armed sea elves, facing the wall.

Floating aimlessly in the water above the Dargonesti were the injured and the dead. Some were missing arms or legs. Some were missing heads. Dolphins circled around, tugging Dargonesti wounded away from the battle and fending off prowling sharks. Blood drifted like smoke, coloring the water ahead.

Atop the wall, between the centermost towers, Dargonesti were fighting. The inside gate on the wall was open, and the Quoowahb were herding the slave workers into the breach.

As the Qualinesti, who were at the rear of the line of prisoners, reached the blocks lying on the seafloor at the base of the wall, something dropped among them from above. The prisoners scattered. Mud swirled around the Qualinesti warriors, and Harmanutis was knocked backward and trampled on. Once he got clear of the stampede, he saw what had caused even the sea elves to flee so frantically.

A chilkit had landed in their midst.

The creature reared eight feet tall, fiery red armor on top of pale gray flesh. Four jointed legs stood out from its thick, barrel-shaped body. A torso encased in a crimson carapace was attached forward of the legs, and the torso had two pairs of arms. The lower pair ended in articulated fingers sporting sharp talons. The upper pair was even more fearsome. A massive set of scissorlike claws tipped each of these arms. The chilkit's head was hard to discern—its torso simply came to a blunt point. Whip antennae sprouted from this point, and four wide-set black eyes protruded on flexible stalks below the antennae. Lastly, a vertical mouth, surrounded by horny palps, opened and shut as the chilkit forced seawater through its gills.

Harmanutis backed away. He feared no normal enemy, but this was a monster indeed, and he had no weapon. The chilkit scuttled forward, attacking the nearest man. The human scrambled madly, grasping the sandy bottom with both hands. The monster strode over him, its hideous claws upraised. Harmanutis watched in horror as the chilkit seized the man in both claws. The terrible pincers closed, cutting the slave in half.

Vanthanoris, also scrambling away, found himself atop a massive block of cut stone. Other prisoners followed, until they were spilling off the sides. The chilkit advanced toward the block and swept a dozen slaves from the side with a backward swipe of its claw.

Vanthanoris heard the staccato call of the dolphins, and a school thirty strong rushed in. Like a fleet of battering rams, the dolphins bore into the chilkit. Van lifted his head in time to see that the animals were wearing special helmets studded with shards of rock crystal. The chilkit backed away, slashing and grasping at the dolphins. The racing creatures eluded it and drove their spiked helmets into the monster's armored hide. Now it was chilkit blood that darkened the water.

From behind, Harmanutis heard an especially loud, trilling whistle. He saw a powerful dolphin ram full-tilt into the chilkit's chest. Armored claws closed around the muscular gray flanks; then all was lost in a welter of churning sand and blood.

Something nudged Harmanutis. He turned and saw a dolphin hovering behind him. Why did they always look like they were smiling? It nudged him again with its snout, then sank to the sand by his feet. The Qualinesti warrior got the message. He widened his stance, and the dolphin glided between his knees. The animal gave a warning shake, so Harmanutis held on to its dorsal fin. The sleek creature shot away with a few strokes of its powerful flukes.

From above, the struggle with the chilkit was easier to see. The monster that had dropped among the prisoners lay on its back, dead. Sharks tugged at its lifeless limbs. Harmanutis's mount swam higher, and he saw a wedge-shaped formation of Dargonesti warriors pushing chilkit back to the wall. The blue-skinned sea elves made a startling contrast to the bold red chilkit. One by one the attackers were isolated and battered to death by Dargonesti wielding stone-headed maces.

One group of chilkit held fast, and they got behind a building block and used it to ram a phalanx of sea elves aside. Harmanutis's dolphin mount saw this and nosed sharply down. The corporal almost lost his seat, but held on to the dorsal fin with both hands. The dolphin twisted and bore in for a ramming attack on the back of the chilkit nearest them. That was enough for Harmanutis. He let go, and the weighted belt he wore caused him to drop slowly to the seafloor.

He was on his feet promptly as he touched bottom, for to his astonishment he had seen whom the chilkit was attacking. A small knot of sea elves stood between the monster and two smaller figures. These two had airshells in their mouths.

Princess Vixa and Colonel Armantaro!

Harmanutis tried to shout a war cry, but the only result was a gurgle of bubbles past the mouthpiece of his airshell. He lost his footing and pitched down on his face.

The chilkit grabbed the shaft of a sea elf's spear and hoisted up the unlucky fellow. The warrior held his grip for an instant too long and toppled forward, into the monster's claws. The chilkit tossed the lacerated foe aside to face the next soldier, who used his shield to fend off the monster's talons. Undaunted, the chilkit bored in, bowling the elf over by sheer bulk. Now, only one fighter stood between the towering chilkit and the two Qualinesti elves.

This sea elf carried no buckler, but wielded his short-handled spear in one hand, like a dueling sword. He jabbed at the chilkit's eyes, and the creature backed off warily. The Dargonesti advanced quickly, thrusting with both hands. His opponent tried to snag the spear with its claws, but the warrior shifted his aim only slightly, deftly avoiding the claws. The needle-sharp tip of his spear pierced the chilkit through a chink in its body armor. A strangely emotionless cry broke from the monster. It gave ground. The Dargonesti shoved his weapon farther in. Talons reached for him, but found only water. The sea elf twisted hard on his spear shaft until there was a distinct crack as the spear tore into the creature's vitals. Its arms dropped and it toppled over. The victorious fighter recovered his spear.

Harmanutis had at last fought his way through the mud and blood and reached his princess's side. Vixa clapped him on the shoulder. Her eyes and Armantaro's spoke eloquently. The corporal pointed to the milling mass of slaves and soldiers still fighting at the base of the wall, the last place he'd seen Vanthanoris.

The three Qualinesti started toward that spot, but before they'd taken more than two steps, Vixa's wrist was seized. She was yanked around, and found herself face-to-face with the Dargonesti who'd single-handedly defeated the chilkit. Harmanutis charged to her defense, but the Dargonesti leveled his spear point at the corporal's chest, bringing him up short. They could see the fierce face inside the helmet. It was none other than Coryphene.

Coryphene's throat worked, and a loud series of clicks rang through the ocean. Soldiers and dolphins not otherwise engaged gathered around him. He gave Vixa over to four warriors, then bade the rest accompany Harmanutis and Armantaro. The Qualinesti were tempted to resist this separation, but Coryphene placed a proprietary hand on Vixa's airshell. The two veteran warriors subsided immediately and were herded back to the other prisoners.

The battle was over. No living chilkit remained in the area. The three started back to the cave, but armed Dargonesti stopped them, sending them back toward the wall. It seemed they were to join in repairing the breach.

Though they were bursting with questions for each other, and anxious over their princess's fate, the Qualinesti had to content themselves with working in silence. The airshells in their mouths, and the vigilance of their guards, made any type of conversation impossible.

Armantaro joined the gang that was busy fitting a heavy net around a dislodged stone block. Bladders inflated with air were used to lift the massive block to the parapet of the wall. As the colonel watched, Dargonesti in civilian dress filled the bladders from airshells heaped in a litter borne by other sea elves and closely guarded by soldiers. He counted four large bladders filled from one whelk shell.

The problem, he mused to himself, is to get several of those shells secretly. Perhaps with enough air, the Qualinesti could walk to land.

The colonel paused in his work and stared with a worried frown toward the city, where his princess had been taken. Of course, even if they had airshells, they still faced the dangers of ocean predators and the Dargonesti themselves, not to mention . . .

Which way was land?

Chapter 7

Divine Queen

Coryphene conferred with his lieutenants in their odd, clicking language. In a studied display of nonchalance, Vixa waited, leaning against an ornate pillar by the road. The battle had frightened off all the sea life around the city, except the sharks. Packs of wary dolphins cruised above, chasing predators away from the wounded and the dying.

Coryphene rapped on the road with the butt of his spear. Vixa came out of her reverie and saw him motion for her to follow him back to the city. Bone-weary, she obliged.

Large crowds greeted the victorious warriors on their return. The quays were jammed with Dargonesti of every rank, cheering the repulse of the chilkit. When Vixa and Coryphene emerged from the water, a roar went up. The Protector of Urione removed his helmet but did not acknowledge the acclaim.

Over the enthusiastic cheering, Vixa said, "Your people appear to love you."

He pointedly took the airshell from her hands. "I am one

of them," he said simply. "And they will love me only so long as I win battles."

He climbed the ramp. Soldiers with mismatched iron swords appeared, parting the crowd. Coryphene's personal guard drew up for review as their commander passed by. One soldier, his armor dented from the fierce fighting, barred Vixa's path for a moment—just long enough to put some distance between her and Coryphene. It would not do for an outsider to intrude upon the Protector's moment of triumph. The Qualinesti princess, her borrowed cloak lost, stood shivering and dripping, while all around her the sea elves went wild.

An elderly sea elf, clad in a simple silver robe, stood at the end of the guard ranks, his bearing proud. Coryphene halted a few paces from this elderly fellow and raised one hand. Loudly, he intoned, "Greetings, Voice of Her Divine Majesty!"

The elf bowed his head slightly. Vixa was astonished at how quickly the cheering and screeching died down. One minute there were thunderous cries, the next, virtual silence.

The elderly sea elf replied in Old Elvish: "Greetings to thee, great Coryphene, terror of the enemies of Urione. Her Divine Grace desires thou to attend upon her instantly."

"I would like to make myself more presentable, noble Kytheron."

"As thou wishes, great Protector. Her Divine Grace desires thee to bring the maiden from the landed race as well."

Vixa was startled, but Coryphene merely nodded.

The Protector strode away, and Vixa was forced to jog after him.

"My uncle is leader of our party," she said. "You should send for him. I'm sure the queen would rather meet Armantaro than me."

Coryphene looked down at her disdainfully. "All must obey Her Divine Majesty. Refusal brings death. Remember that."

*   *   *   *   *

Vixa was shown to a room where the only furniture was a table upon which was a pitcher of fresh water, a fishbone comb, and a small pile of clothing. The Qualinesti princess washed her hands and face, relieved to remove at least a few layers of the grime and accumulated salt. Her hair—kept short because of her warrior status—she rinsed as best she could, then combed back from her face.

A pile of clean garments awaited her. There were several articles that were obviously undergarments and a flowing, ankle-length robe. Everything was made of a strange fabric. It didn't feel like cloth at all—more like tissue-thin leather, if there could be such a thing. Quickly, she peeled off her salt-stiffened smallclothes, doused herself with the remaining water, and donned the clean clothing. The robe was white and had a wide red stripe winding from hem to neck. It was astonishingly comfortable. Material such as this, soft as silk yet tough as leather, would fetch a handsome price in any market on Krynn. Around her waist she fastened an elaborate girdle of tiny white coral beads. She had to wrap its free ends twice about her, otherwise they would have dragged on the floor.

Coryphene entered unexpectedly. Vixa whirled, her hands still occupied with tying the belt. "Don't you believe in knocking?" she snapped.

"Her Majesty awaits. Come," was all he said.

He was resplendent in a long purple cape and jeweled torque. On his head was an elaborate headdress of shells and gemstones. Coral beads hung down in long streams across his bare chest. His fresh kilt was held up by a heavy, braided gold sash. Wide ankle bracelets completed his outfit.

They walked out of the barracks and down the narrow street to the ramp. An honor guard of twelve Dargonesti in silver robes met them. On the way, Coryphene advised Vixa on protocol.

"Do not speak unless you are spoken to," he told her. "Answer fully all questions put to you. Her Divinity has the gift of sight, and can see far more than ordinary mortals. Lastly, do not look Her Divinity in the face."

Vixa couldn't resist. "Why not?"

"To do so means death."

They ascended the spiral ramp and passed through the magical portal. After the flash of light and heat, Vixa was once more standing in the palace plaza. The honor guard had drawn off a short distance and donned silver hoods. Coryphene straightened his shoulders and walked firmly ahead.

He led Vixa to a pair of enormous doors, set just under the colonnade on the far side of the plaza. The doors were made of quartz crystals the size of logs, bolted together with rods of the same material. The shadows of servants could be seen on the other side, hauling the doors open. Once inside, Coryphene paused to remove his headdress. He tucked it under his arm before continuing.

The corridor was illuminated by greenish light from the domed ceiling. The odd color of the light came from the filtering effect of many fathoms of seawater. The sun's rays barely penetrated to this depth. Incense, its sweet-sour smell like that in the temple complex, filled the long passage. Vixa spied censers located between the pearl-inlaid columns lining the hall. Dargonesti women in scarlet robes tended these braziers, feeding them small pellets of some waxy substance.

The passage wound around the curve of the upper level of the city and ended at an antechamber. Tall, gaunt sea elves in priestly garb stood to each side of the chamber, conversing quietly among themselves. They fell silent when Coryphene entered, and bowed to him.

"I come in answer to Her Divinity's summons," the Protector announced.

"She awaits within," replied a shell-bedecked priest.

Coryphene nodded to the servants at the inner doors. One struck a hanging assembly of pink shells, which rang sweetly in a cascade of bell tones. The priests and the honor guard turned their backs to the door as it opened.

"Remember!" Coryphene hissed. "Avert your eyes!"

Vixa lowered her gaze to her bare feet. Fine treatment for a member of the royal house of Qualinost, she silently fumed. The blood of Kith-Kanan and Silvanos ran in her veins. Why could she not look on this petty undersea queen?

The audience chamber was lit by a shifting greenish light. The Protector dropped to one knee, signaling for Vixa to do likewise by tugging on her hand.

"Divine Queen, your servant Coryphene has come as you commanded," he said. Vixa resisted his pull. A princess of the Qualinesti kneels to none but the Speaker, after all. Coryphene gave a stronger yank, and she lost her balance, dropping unceremoniously to her knees.

A light voice, low in timbre, replied, "Is this the dryland maiden of whom I have heard?"

"Yes, Divinity."

"There were others with her, were there not?"

"Yes, Divinity. There were five in all. One drowned, and the other three are lodged in Nissia Grotto, to work on the wall."

A moment of silence. Vixa could hear the queen's light breathing. At last, the queen said, "You are small. Are you a child?"

Coryphene nudged her. "Answer," he whispered.

"I am not a child, Your Majesty," Vixa said. She felt silly staring at the floor while she spoke. "In my land I am counted as unusually tall."

"I see that we Dargonesti have surpassed the landed race in height and strength," observed the mild voice. "Just as we have in wisdom and divine favor."

That rankled. Vixa was about to offer her opinion of Dargonesti superiority when the queen commanded, "Approach."

Coryphene stood up, hauling her to her feet. They went forward six steps and knelt again. This time there was a large segment of polished basalt in the floor in front of Vixa. It displayed the queen's reflection faintly. Vixa squinted at it, trying to make out the woman's features.

"Who reigns in your country, girl?"

"Speaker of the Sun Silveran, Majesty."

"And who was his father?"

"The great Kith-Kanan. His mother was a Kagonesti named Anaya, who transformed into a tree while pregnant and delivered her son many, many years later."

There was a brief pause, then the low voice asked, "What is a tree?"

Vixa was so startled by the question she nearly raised her head to stare at the queen of Urione. She checked herself, explaining as briefly as she could what trees were.

"I see. Rather like our coral gardens. Tell me what you know of Silvanesti."

Again the abrupt change of subject disconcerted the Qualinesti princess. Coryphene nudged her, and she responded, "I've never been there, Majesty. The elves of Silvanost have little to do with those of Qualinost."

"Why?"

Vixa explained about the Kinslayer War and the schism between Kith-Kanan and his twin brother, Speaker of the Stars Sithas. It was slow going, because she hadn't studied history in some years, and it was by any reckoning a long and complicated narration. She stammered her way through the story, and her account seemed to satisfy the queen. Vixa gathered her nerve and asked a question of her own.

"Your Majesty, when may I and my companions return home?" she inquired.

Without warning, a stunning blow landed on the side of Vixa's head, making her ears ring and sending her sprawling. Her belt broke when she landed, and the tiny coral beads went flying.

"It is not your place to ask questions!" Coryphene growled. His fury was plain, though his voice remained low.

This was too much for Vixa. She had followed their ridiculous rules, crawling about on the floor like a commoner, and had only asked one simple, polite question. Immediately, she sprang at Coryphene, knocked him down, and aimed a kick at his ribs. It landed solidly; then many hands seized her and dragged her away from the Protector. She struggled against the grip of at least three Dargonesti, but they forced her to her knees and shoved her facedown on the cold, hard floor.

"Enough," said the queen, her voice still low and un-ruffled.

Coryphene tried to recover his wounded dignity, but this was a difficult proposition as he had to remain upon his knees, head bowed, before his monarch. The guards released Vixa at the queen's order, and the Qualinesti princess slowly sat up. She kept her gaze averted, though she was now filled with a burning desire to stare directly into the eyes of the queen.

"Though you are of the ancient race, it is apparent that our kindred have fallen into barbarism," observed the queen. "Your behavior demonstrates this. As the gods have told me, the time has come to unite our ancient peoples into one great nation."

Surprised, Vixa blurted, "What?"

"Know this, girl, I am Uriona, chosen of the gods and queen of this my city," the queen said. "Five hundred years ago the gods Abbaku and Kisla came to me in my dreams and bade me leave the deep lands of Watermere and found this city. Since then, I have dreamed many times of a shining tower, reaching far up into the dry air. The gods have given me this promise: when I am crowned in the Tower of the Stars, all those of elven blood will bow down and swear fealty to me."

Vixa was taken aback. The Silvanesti would never permit Uriona to set foot in the sacred Tower of the Stars in Silvanost, much less be crowned ruler of all elves. Did she think they would allow her to defile the purity of their city with her presence?

The queen was still speaking, saying that once she and her armies had marched to Silvanost she would be installed as the ruler of all the elven nations. She spoke as if accomplishing this would be the merest trifle. Vixa shifted position slightly and felt the cold tip of a spear digging into the thin material of her robe.

The princess's mind was racing. Not only did she desire freedom for herself and her friends, she had a duty to warn the Silvanesti about Uriona's crazed scheme. But how to escape? And how to warn the Silvanesti? She had about as much chance of getting into Silvanost as this crazy sea elf.

The chamber's odd, greenish lighting was constantly shifting. Momentarily it brightened, and Vixa caught her first clear glimpse of the image of Queen Uriona in the polished black surface of the floor tile before her.

The sea queen was seated on a bench whose wide, flat seat curved up slightly at each end. She was robed in some bright material—probably the same silver mesh her guards wore. The Dargonesti queen had a dark blue complexion and large eyes. Her hair, unlike that of her subjects, was shining white. It swept back slightly from her face but fell in a loose cascade over her shoulders and into her lap. Her age was impossible to determine from the fuzzy reflection, and her voice sounded neither old nor young.

A pinpoint of green gleamed in Uriona's reflected eyes. Vixa thought this was a trick of the shifting light, but it happened a second and then a third time.

"Impudent girl," murmured the queen.

A dazzling flash of green light erupted from the queen's eyes. The flare seemed to rebound from the floor and strike Vixa full in the face. She had no time to shield her eyes, and agony filled her head. She cried out, toppled to the floor. The glare was replaced by darkness as she dropped into oblivion.

*　*　*　*　*

Once the break in the top of the wall was repaired, the guards marched the slaves back to Nissia Grotto. The work had taken several hours. Harmanutis and Vanthanoris staggered to the rear of the cave, collapsing on piles of tattered sailcloth. Armantaro, more than twice their age, seemed to have held up better, but then he had the advantage of a decent meal, courtesy of Coryphene.

Garnath walked up to the flour barrel housing his twin and kicked it smartly. A snort erupted, but no dwarf appeared. Grimacing, Garnath pounded the staves with his thick fist.

"Wake up, Brother!" he bellowed. "Wake up!"

Gundabyr rolled out, dazed. "What? What is it?"

"I want the barrel," said Garnath. "You owe me two days' work now."

Gundabyr yawned. "By Reorx! Couldn't you have waited till morning to tell me that?"

"It *is* morning." Garnath shouldered his twin aside. "Good night!"

Gundabyr sighed and surveyed the long, dim tunnel. The unhappy slaves slept where they dropped. The grotto resembled a battlefield, with bodies strewn all about.

The only other person still awake in the entire cave was Armantaro. He tried to assemble a decent pallet from the assortment of junk littering the cave floor. Gundabyr yawned once more, stretched, and ambled over to the elf.

"Hail, friend. My name's Gundabyr."

Armantaro nodded and said, "Yes, so I heard. Your brother has an excellent set of lungs."

"Yup, he got that way shouting over the forge hammers in Thorbardin. I can't convince him not to shout here."

The old colonel reclined stiffly, pillowing his head on one arm. He told the dwarf his name and rank, and how he'd ended up in this wretched place after his visit to the city.

"I figured as much," said Gundabyr. He aimed a thumb at the inert forms of Harmanutis and Vanthanoris. "They told me you were down here. Ain't there a lady with you?"

"Yes, indeed, and I fear for her. Coryphene has kept her."

Gundabyr tugged at his black beard. "He's never done that before. The blueskins don't give a fig for any of us drylanders, you know."

"I'm certain he has designs on her. He may suspect she is something other than my niece. A princess of the house of Kith-Kanan would be quite a prize for an ambitious warlord." In spite of his worried tone, Armantaro's eyelids were drooping. His breathing slowed. As his eyelids finally closed, he added, "He'll get more than he bargained for with Lady Vixa, though. One unguarded moment, and she'll split him . . . wide open."

Armantaro was asleep. Shrugging, the dwarf got up and went back to a pile of wreckage behind the flour barrel. This seemingly worthless collection of rubbish was his tool kit. During his free days, and in the wee hours while Garnath slept, the restless Gundabyr spent his time exploring the recesses of Nissia Grotto. He'd fashioned some crude tools from bits of wood, bent nails, and loose rocks. Far back in the remote areas of the cave, he kept his collection of mineral samples. The grotto had not been formed by the slow process of erosion. Instead, it had been created by an ancient volcano. As a result, the interior was rich in minerals such as sulfur, niter, and bitumen, which oozed out of crevices in the lowest regions of the cave system.

Gundabyr slipped his tools into his ragged pockets and walked off into the darkness. His greatest wish, aside from freedom, was for a light he could take along on his explorations. The Dargonesti globes were fastened to the walls, and any attempt to remove them always ended badly. The dwarf carried out his research by touch and smell, often bringing back samples to the inhabited portion of the cave for final identification.

He'd gone only a few hundred paces into the deep cavern when he noticed a strange noise. Holding very still, Gundabyr heard it again. A sort of scratching, or maybe a scraping sound, coming from far away. The prisoners were all fast asleep, and there was no one else in the grotto. Gundabyr took his homemade pick, fashioned from a long ship's nail driven through a length of decking, and scraped the cave wall in front of him. He listened hard, but the noise had stopped. He did not hear it again.

Chapter 8

A Gift of Fire

Vixa was dreaming.

She was trapped in a clear crystal globe surrounded by water. The water was filled with sea elves, all staring at her and pointing long, blue, webbed fingers. They never spoke, but only stared and pointed. It became extremely annoying.

"Stop it!" she shouted at them. "I am Princess Vixa Ambrodel, daughter of the house of Kith-Kanan! Begone, I say!"

They showed no sign of hearing her, but continued to stare with blank faces. Their eyes glowed. Furious, Vixa struck the walls of her crystal prison with her fists. The blow stung her knuckles. It also caused cracks to appear in the glass. The fractures radiated outward from the point of impact, and water began to seep into the globe. Anger turned to horror as Vixa realized what she'd done. If the water got in, she would drown!

The cracks raced around the glass, spreading faster and faster. The water rose up to her ankles. A blink of her eyes, and the water had touched her knees. In seconds, she was neck-deep and had to tread water to keep her face above the icy flow. What was she to do?

Vixa flung out a hand and felt the roof over her head. Silver fissures met and crossed above her. Water closed over her head. She pounded at the domed ceiling.

"*I—will—not—die!*"

With a gasp, Vixa sat up. She was on a flat couch in a dimly lit room. From the green color of the walls and floor, she surmised that she was somewhere in the palace.

Her legs were tangled in her Dargonesti robe. She freed them and swung her feet to the floor. The room tilted slightly; she put a hand to her head. In a few seconds the dizziness passed. A small sound behind her brought her to her feet, whirling to face whatever threat might come. The room was divided by translucent curtains, and behind these she could see a seated figure.

"Who's there?" she demanded. "Show yourself!"

The figure rose and stepped forward, parting the curtains. It was Naxos, the shapeshifter, Coryphene's dolphin-herald.

"Forgive me," he said, though his tone was far from contrite. "I came to see if you were all right. Don't give me away, will you?"

"Give you away?"

"To Coryphene. I'm not supposed to be here."

He was dressed in a simple shark-leather kilt. His aquamarine hair was held away from his face by a headband carved from blood coral. His powerful physique, insolent manner, and daunting height made him an unsettling presence. Vixa, accustomed to looming over most people, found herself taking a step back, so as not to have to tilt her head to see him.

"What happened to me?" she asked.

"You've been unconscious a full day. I wanted to see if you survived your audience with Uriona."

"I guess I did—barely."

Naxos grinned. His smile was infectious, and Vixa found herself smiling back.

"You don't speak of your queen the way Coryphene does. Don't you consider her divine?"

"I've known Uriona since she was this high." He held a hand level with Vixa's forehead and grinned again, adding, "She's hardly ever divine."

"She seems . . . distracted," Vixa said carefully.

"She's mad," was his blunt rejoinder. Naxos sat on the couch, leaning back on one hand. "Since no one else will tell you the tale, I suppose I'll have to.

"Uriona is the fourth daughter of Kedurach Takalurion, Speaker of the Moon and ruler of Watermere. As such, she had few prospects in life other than marriage to some noble whose support the Speaker desired. She was not content with this fate and turned to the study of sorcery and high thaumaturgy. Whatever else it did for her, her magic frightened off half-hearted suitors. By the end of her first century, Uriona was one of the most powerful magic-users in Watermere."

Vixa, remembering the effect of the queen's glance, had no trouble believing him.

"The increase of her power affected her reason," Naxos continued. "She decided she was chosen by the god Abbaku to reunite all those of elven blood into one nation. This message had an appeal to other ambitious Quoowahb, who were tired of the boredom and constraint of life in Watermere."

"Others such as Coryphene?"

"Yes, and my humble self as well. When I was younger I craved adventure. I wanted to visit distant seas and walk upon dry land, where the sun scorches the air." His face twisted in self-mockery. "I pledged myself to Uriona's cause. Many hundreds of Quoowahb believed in her, and two centuries past, she led us out of Watermere to found a new kingdom."

Naxos gave Vixa a sidelong glance, as if to gauge her reaction to his next words. "She has visions, you know. One of them was of a great city protected by walls of fire. My sea brothers and I scouted for such a place, finding it in this valley between two volcanoes. And here we are, in the city of Urione."

Vixa sat down beside him. "You no longer believe in her," she said.

"Her dream has become evil," he explained. "It's Coryphene's doing. He hungers for conquest, for power of his own. He sees himself as the guarantor of Uriona's dream—and her dynasty."

Her brown eyes widened. "Does he love her?"

This time his smile was savage. "Desperately! But she listens only to her visions, not to his attempts to woo her." He leaned close, and Vixa felt herself tense. He had an aura that was palpable—an aura of what? Physical power? Magic? She couldn't define it.

Naxos lowered his voice to a whisper. "She foresaw your coming, little dryfoot. 'Elves from the ancient land will come to Urione,' she prophesied. And then you did."

"With the help of your kraken!" she exclaimed indignantly.

"Ma'el? Yes, Uriona's pet. Only she can control it. Our enemy the chilkit are creatures of the sea, but are less adept at swimming than even we Quoowahb. When Coryphene demanded workers to build the wall across the Mortas Trench to stop their predations, the queen sent Ma'el to drag down the ships of the land-dwellers."

"If you think she's so evil, why do you follow her?"

"I have sworn it."

Vixa folded her arms. "You don't strike me as an elf who would betray his conscience for the sake of an oath to a mad monarch!"

He shrugged and spread his webbed hands. "My brothers and I remain for the most part outside the air-filled city. Soon, we will swim away, and Urione will know us no more."

"Then help me!" she urged, taking hold of his arm. "You and your sea brothers can help us get away from here!"

He shook off her grip. "I can't do that—at least not yet. We're not strong enough to elude Coryphene's soldiers and defy Uriona's magic. The time will come when both are stretched to their limits. Then the sea brothers will depart. Only then."

"But I can help you! In Qualinost I have powerful friends,

friends who will shield you and your comrades." Vixa glanced around cautiously, though the room was quite empty. In a conspiratorial whisper, she said, "I am a princess of the house of Kith-Kanan. My uncle is the Speaker of the Sun!"

"I know."

She recoiled from his words and his aggravating grin. "What? How?"

"Uriona read it in your mind while you were unconscious. Coryphene is very angry, by the way, because you lied to him. He wanted to send you to the grotto, but the queen ordered you held here. She has some plan for you, I daresay."

Fear gripped Vixa's heart. Uriona had read her mind!

"Just how deeply did the queen intrude on my mind?" the princess asked, striving for a nonchalant tone.

His eyes still danced, but Naxos said quite seriously, "Don't worry, Princess. She only used the lightest and quickest of probes. Anything else would require greater effort—and its intensity might leave you quite useless to her."

Footsteps echoed beyond the thin curtains. Naxos was on his feet in a flash. "Be brave, Princess. Nothing is done until it is done."

With these singularly unhelpful words, he ducked through the curtains. Vixa lay down on the couch and closed her eyes. Her heart hammered, but she wasn't sure if it was because someone was coming, or because the infuriating Naxos had just left.

Coryphene swept the curtain aside. "Awaken, *Princess* Vixa!" He pronounced her title with venom. She feigned sleepiness and dawdled at rising.

"I didn't expect to wake again," she told him, yawning widely.

"No other drylander has dared look upon Her Divine Majesty and been allowed to live. It is only because our divine queen saw through your feeble deception that you still breathe. She would not kill the blood kin of Kith-Kanan," he declared.

"My feeble deception fooled you well enough."

Coryphene's fingers flexed around the pommel of the dagger in his belt. It was Armantaro's weapon, Vixa realized. "Take her out!" Coryphene snapped to the soldiers accompanying him. The towering warriors ringed Vixa.

The Qualinesti princess itched to launch into them, but she didn't feel like being beaten senseless. Coryphene would need very little provocation to thrash her. She was determined not to give him any. She rose coolly, straightened her robe. Coryphene stalked out, followed by Vixa and the guards.

Coryphene led her through a series of archways into the palace plaza. The whole of his private guard, some five hundred warriors, were drawn up in formation. Vixa entered the square of soldiers. At the center had been erected a table—a huge slice of mica supported by white coral legs. The hide of some large sea beast, tanned and whitened, was spread over the tabletop. Coryphene went to one side, while Vixa stood on the other.

On the hide was drawn a crude map. The seafloor around Urione was rendered in fine detail, but the farther regions were vague. Along one edge, Vixa saw a thin line drawn. It took her a moment to realize that this represented the southern coastline of Ansalon.

"Indicate on this map where Qualinost is," Coryphene said.

Vixa folded her arms across her chest and said nothing.

"We know Silvanost lies on the Thon-Thalas—how far inland is the city?" She only stared at him, lips pressed tightly together. "How deep is the Thon-Thalas?"

He might as well have asked a statue. The blue color of his face deepened to indigo. They stared at each other for a full minute, she with pale face set and impassive, he with ever darkening countenance.

"I can have you flayed alive!" he shouted at last.

"I will tell you nothing," Vixa said evenly.

He whipped out Armantaro's dagger and raised it high. For a heart-stopping moment, Vixa was certain he was going to plunge it into her. But the weapon's downswing

DRAGONLANCE Lost Histories

ended with the dagger embedded in the middle of the map.
Coryphene drove it in with such force that it stuck in the
mica tabletop. He released it, and it stood there, quivering.

The Protector's color returned to normal. In a much
calmer tone, he stated, "I know your kind, lady. Brute force
only reminds you of your duty. Very well. Let us see how
stiff your neck is after a few days in the Nissia Grotto." He
spat a command, and eight warriors ringed the Qualinesti
princess.

"To the grotto with her. Let her work alongside her servants. If the cold and damp don't soften her pride, perhaps
the close proximity of the chilkit will."

A hood was dropped over Vixa's head, and her hands
bound behind her back. Blinded, she stumbled along,
guided by the shoves of her guards. Having been up and
down the city's central ramp several times, she tried to
visualize her path. She recognized the incense of the temple
level and the noise and odors of the nearby fish market.
When at last the hood was dragged from her head, she saw
she was at a quayside pool identical to the one by which
she'd first entered the city. Dolphins coursed through the
water, and for an instant she thought Naxos had come to
rescue her.

But only for an instant. As the bonds were removed from
her wrists, she shook herself mentally. She couldn't depend
upon outside help to rescue her and her friends. They
would have to save themselves.

Coryphene's guards tied a weighted belt around her
waist, handed her an airshell, and shoved her down the
ramp. With one last glance at the dolphins swimming
around her, Vixa walked into the pool. The chilly water
closed over her head.

* * * * *

Sleep time in the grotto was always punctuated by the
coughing and moans of the prisoners. The cold and damp
constantly sapped their strength. Many were already sick
with ague and consumption. The others were only waiting

to get sick. The Dargonesti didn't know (or didn't care) that their land-dwelling captives needed warmth to survive.

Armantaro had slept curled up on his pile of bedding, teeth chattering all night. His first day as a slave had been more difficult than he would admit. The backbreaking labor on the wall combined with his constant anxiety over the welfare of Vixa Ambrodel gave him a very difficult time. His dreams this night were filled with visions of his tower room in Qualinost: book-lined, with a high ceiling and tall, narrow windows he left open on summer nights. His family always complained that the room was too drafty. In memory, it seemed like paradise.

The vision of home was interrupted by a tantalizing smell. A wonderful, mouth-watering aroma invaded his sleep and finally woke him. He opened his eyes, expecting the smell to vanish with his dreams; instead it grew stronger. It was the unmistakable odor of frying fish!

Flickering light cast grotesque shadows on the cave walls. Armantaro sat up, looking for Harmanutis and Vanthanoris. Their pallets were empty. He walked to the great heap of rubbish that divided the inhabited section of the grotto from the dark depths. On the other side were his companions. They were gathered around a campfire!

Vanthanoris was holding a plank to the flame. Pegged to the plank was a white fillet of fish. Harmanutis noticed the old colonel and greeted him.

"Where did the fire come from?" Armantaro demanded, hurrying to the welcoming light.

"Gundabyr did it," said Vanthanoris. "But it's not like any fire I ever saw."

Armantaro knelt and held his hands out to the heat. The dwarf had piled loose stones into a rough hearth. In the midst of the stones sat a seething cauldron of yellow liquid. It gave off only a little smoke, but a great deal of warmth. Armantaro noticed there was no wood or flame beneath the pot. The yellow liquid boiled on its own.

"What is that?"

"Gnomefire," replied Vanthanoris. "Gundabyr explained it to us, but all I got was the name."

Beyond the circle of light the dwarf appeared, his arms laden with old clay pots. Harmanutis helped him unload his burden. Gundabyr's clothes were dusted with ores of various colors. He looked as if he'd fallen in some lunatic flour mill.

Armantaro asked about the bubbling pot. Dusting off his hands, Gundabyr said, "Gnomefire is a compound often used by the folk of Sancrist Isle. There isn't much wood on the slopes of Mt. Nevermind, so some gnome invented this mixture, which burns without need for wood. I learned to make it in my younger days, when I traveled often to gnome country. Garnath used to say nothing useful ever came from a gnome's mind, but this stuff just might make the difference between living and dying down here."

"Gnomefire," Vanthanoris murmured. "Can you imagine the failures its inventor had before he hit on the right formula?" The gnomes of Sancrist Isle were known throughout Ansalon for their weird (and nearly always useless) experiments and inventions.

"It's wonderful. What's it made of?" Armantaro wanted to know.

"Sulfur and quicklime and bitumen and niter, plus a pinch of this and a scrap of that. I'd thought about making it before, but hadn't found enough bitumen until last night. By Reorx, there's tons of the stuff in the lower galleries!"

"How did you ignite it? None of us has a flint."

The dwarf's blue eyes gleamed. "That's the special secret. All it takes—"

Vanthanoris jumped to his feet. "We have company," he warned.

Scores of prisoners had awakened to the smell of cooking. Bearded, haggard faces stared with longing at the flickering bowl of light. The sight of the steaming fish caused mouths to drop open and tongues to move over cracked lips. So intent were they upon the fire and food, the prisoners overcame their habitual lethargy and crowded round the elves.

"Is there enough for all?" Armantaro asked Gundabyr.

"There's enough for the whole Daewar clan."

"Wait. Won't a lot of fires exhaust our air?" Harmanutis cautioned.

The dwarf shook his head. "Nope, I don't think so. There's over three hundred people in this cave, but unless I'm wrong, the blueskins are supplying us with fresh air somehow."

Even so, it was decided to limit the number of fires to five, just to be safe. Eager men clawed rocks from the floor and walls and built hasty firepits. Gundabyr went from one to the next, mixing powders into pots in just the right proportions, then stirring in thick bitumen to bind the ingredients together. Finally, he asked for water from the pool. As soon as the water was dribbled onto the black-and-yellow paste, a plume of smoke hissed upward. The mixture burst into flame with a soft *whuff!*

On first seeing this, one of the humans exclaimed, "You're a wizard!"

"I'm a forgemaster of Thorbardin, which is better," Gundabyr shot back.

Soon Nissia Grotto was warmer and lighter than it had ever been. Men crowded around the fires, warming stiff limbs and cooking their fish rations. They praised Gundabyr's brilliance. For the first time, Armantaro heard laughter.

Vanthanoris voiced a worry. "What will the Dargonesti say?" he wondered.

"I doubt they'll object too much," Armantaro replied. "After all, warmth and cooked food can only keep their slaves alive longer, right?"

The elves sat back to watch their fellow prisoners enjoy Gundabyr's gnomefire. They conversed softly about the battle of the day before.

"The chilkit bungled their attack yesterday," stated Harmanutis. "Had they scaled the wall in more than one place, the Dargonesti could not have stopped them."

"Let us be grateful you weren't leading them," Vanthanoris said dryly.

"Coryphene is no tactician, that's certain," put in Armantaro. "He simply met force with force. He didn't maneuver his warriors at all. His greatest advantage lies in his store of captured metal weapons." The old colonel frowned, etching deep lines in his thin face. "One of which is my own dagger."

"Have the blueskins no metal of their own?" asked Harmanutis.

"None but some gold and silver trinkets. Oh, and some copper buttons."

Gundabyr returned from his fire-starting and dropped heavily to the floor. "Phew! That's work! Any of that baked cod left, Van?"

"I saved you the best cut."

"Ah, many thanks, friend elf." The dwarf tore into the fish with gusto.

"Should we rouse your brother?"

"No indeed. Let him sleep. He groused so much about working a double shift, I don't want to hear him grumble about being disturbed again, even if it is for hot food."

While Gundabyr ate, Armantaro asked him why the Dargonesti set such store by the iron and steel blades they found.

"Because they've got no forges, that's why. You can't smelt iron underwater."

"But they do have gold and copper."

"Huh! You can work them with no more than a candle flame." More thoughtfully, he added, "Those volcanic vents would smelt soft metals, I bet. Maybe the blueskins use them."

Armantaro ran a hand over the hard black surface of the wall behind him. "Didn't you say this tunnel was part of an old volcano?" Gundabyr nodded, his mouth full of cod. "Well, that might be our way out!"

"How so, my lord?" Harmanutis inquired.

"Volcanoes by their nature tend to rise to the surface of the sea. If we can find a vent that goes all the way up—"

"Sorry, Colonel, but it ain't likely," interrupted the dwarf. "The blueskins wouldn't make it that easy. You can be sure they've checked this cave. It has only one opening, and *that's* it." He jabbed a thick thumb toward the pool.

The Qualinesti lapsed into discouraged silence. Gundabyr was about to finish his meal when the ringing of rock on rock signaled that the lookout had spotted activity in the pool. The men and elves hastily smothered their gnomefires with dirt, as Gundabyr had taught them.

Just as the cave was dim and quiet again, sea elf warriors emerged from the pool. Behind them came Princess Vixa. Armantaro jumped to his feet and ran to greet her. Harmanutis and Vanthanoris quickly followed.

"My dear niece!" Armantaro exclaimed. "Are you all right?"

A guard took Vixa's airshell. "There's no longer any need for that deception, Colonel," said Vixa. "They know who and what I am."

"Did they hurt you?"

"No. I did meet their queen, though. She used magic to see the truth in my mind."

Armantaro glanced at her guards, who were standing impassively to one side. "If they know you're a princess of Qualinost, why did they bring you here?"

"Queen Uriona imagines she can become ruler of all the elven nations. Coryphene tried to make me tell them about the armies of Qualinost and of the Silvanesti, but I refused. For that I was sent here." Her nose wrinkled as she sniffed the air. "You know, I could swear I smell baked fish."

"Ah, come this way, Your Highness," Vanthanoris said quickly. "We'll make a place for you."

Vixa lifted the hem of her Dargonesti robe to climb out of the pool. Only minutes after leaving the water the silver cloth would be dry. The sea elf in charge of her blocked Vixa's path.

"Prisoners will form for work parties immediately," he ordered.

"Now?" exclaimed Vixa. "I just got here."

The lanky Dargonesti ignored her. "On your feet! Prisoners will report for the day's work!"

The slaves were slower than usual in leaving their pallets. While his comrades rounded up the captives, the leader did something odd with Vixa's airshell. Around his neck, the Dargonesti wore a pendant made from a large aquamarine crystal. This by itself was not unusual. The sea elves loved to festoon themselves with all manner of shells and gems. However, he touched the pendant to the mouth-piece of the airshell he'd taken from Vixa. Wide-eyed, the princess saw the bright blue-green gem fade, becoming pale and lackluster. After several seconds, the Dargonesti let the pendant fall to his chest.

As Vixa stood pondering the significance of this new information, other Dargonesti appeared in the pool. They brought hampers of airshells. The weary captives each took a shell and trudged into the water. Vixa held back and drew Armantaro to her side.

"Did you see, Colonel?" she whispered, gesturing to the Dargonesti wearing the pendant.

"Yes, lady. If we could get a necklace like that—"

Gundabyr, impersonating his twin, finally joined the line. Harmanutis introduced him to the princess. As they made their way closer to the basket of shells, Vixa said, "If Cory-phene thinks he can break me by putting me to work, he's grossly mistaken. I don't know what Dargonesti princesses do with their days, but I'm no stranger to hardship."

One of the guards commanded her to be silent. She and Armantaro took their airshells. The line of slaves entered the pool. As they waited to submerge, the colonel touched his princess's arm and whispered, "It might be a good idea not to trumpet your resolve too loudly. After all, we're more likely to be kept alive and well if Coryphene thinks we'll be useful to him."

Vixa nodded thoughtfully and murmured, "You may be right, Colonel. But I wonder if the chilkit will stand by long enough for Uriona to put her mad dreams of conquest to the test."

Chapter 9
Hard Labor

Beneath the crystal roof of the city, Queen Uriona was surrounded by mirrors, light globes piled around her. The queen sat in the midst of a bright glare, her eyes covered by a sharkskin mask.

Outside the circle of mirrors, Coryphene waited. The queen's handmaids and her court of priestly advisors stood to one side, shielding their faces from the light seeping between the mirrored panels.

"You know I never question your actions, Divine One," Coryphene said carefully. "But how can I prepare for an invasion of the land when we are not yet free of the chilkit?"

"The creatures from the depths will be overcome. I have seen it. The elves of the sun will help bring this about." As she spoke, Uriona turned her masked face until she directly faced the gap in the mirrors behind which Coryphene stood. Her perception was unnerving.

"How will they do this, Divine Queen?"

"The method is unimportant. It will happen."

"Will it be soon? Should I muster the army?"

"You will do the right thing when the time comes, Lord Protector. The gods and I shall guide you."

Her conviction eased his doubts, save one nagging problem. "What if the Qualinesti woman won't talk? I must know the strength of the enemy."

"Patience, Lord Protector. She will provide what we need to know. In the meantime, send Naxos and the heralds to the coast of Silvanesti. They may learn something of importance by observation."

"Yes, Divine Queen. We will miss their reconnaissance against the chilkit, though."

"When the chilkit attack again, you shall destroy them utterly. This will be the first step toward our impending victory over the land-dwelling elves. Send Naxos away. Today."

He couldn't miss the agitation in her voice. Coryphene wondered if there was some hidden agenda associated with Naxos and his sea brothers. He'd long suspected the leader of the shapeshifters of disloyalty. Coryphene sometimes wished his queen-goddess would make her warnings a bit more plain.

"Open the mirrors. I am done for now."

Coryphene gave a command. The servants dashed forward to remove the encircling wall of mirrors. They did so with eyes tightly shut and faces averted—from the bright light and forbidden face of their queen. The standing panels were taken away, leaving only the queen and the piles of glowing globes in the center of the audience hall.

"Why do you do this to yourself?" Coryphene asked gently. He alone was permitted to gaze upon her countenance and, as always after one of these sessions, she was bathed in sweat and nearly fainting. "Why torment yourself with this light?"

"If I am someday to sit upon my throne in the Tower of the Stars, I must be able to bear the light of the sun." She removed her mask, her hand trembling.

He stepped closer. "I cannot bear to see you suffer."

"It is nothing."

Coryphene took the mask from her, allowing his hand to rest on her fingers. Her eyes fluttered at the unexpected contact, but she didn't draw her hand away. "Will Naxos betray us, Divine One?" he murmured. Uriona's languid gaze faltered. Her body went limp on the throne. Coryphene stepped in, kept her from collapsing onto the floor. The maidservants and priests closed around, looking anxiously at the Protector.

"Get back," he said scornfully. "Our divine lady endures much for our sakes. Go and prepare her bedchamber; I will bring her there."

The servants hurried to do his bidding. Coryphene lifted the unconscious queen in his long arms. The priests protested, scandalized by his familiarity, but the warrior lord carried his queen tenderly to the door of the audience hall.

"Chamberlain? Chamberlain!" he called.

"Yes, my lord?" Uriona's chamberlain, fresh from a dousing in seawater, appeared smoothly at Coryphene's elbow.

"Have Naxos of the sea brothers brought to me at once. This is the command of Her Divine Majesty." The chamberlain bowed, dripping seawater onto the mosaic floor.

"It shall be done, great Protector."

* * * * *

The line of prisoners trudged toward their day's work. The weighted belts they wore kept their feet on the path. The sea had lightened to a clear emerald green, and by Dargonesti standards it was a bright day. As the captives left the mouth of the grotto behind, Vixa could see a chain of peaks stretching away from the city. The mountain containing Nissia Grotto was the last in this long line. Some of the mountains were low and flat-topped. Others had sharp, jagged tips, thrusting toward the surface. Vixa wondered just how near the surface they reached.

They entered a wide ravine, whose mouth had been quarried for stone and cleared of coral, leaving it a flat, hard plain. All around, prisoners had taken up mauls and stone wedges and were pounding blocks of stone into rectangular shapes. When the blocks were finished, they were laid in nets spread out on the ground. At the four corners of each net were fish bladders sewn together and filled with air. These bladders floated the blocks up to the top of the wall, where other slaves wrestled them into place. No mortar was used, so the blocks had to fit together precisely.

Harmanutis and Vanthanoris were put to work dragging rough stones to the carvers for dressing. Armantaro was added to the gang that hauled blocks to the nets and attached the inflated fish bladders. Vixa was sent to the top of the wall to work with the stonelayers.

She started to remove her belt, so she could swim to the parapet. A guard stopped her, pointing to an opening in the base of the wall. She headed toward this opening. Before she went inside, a prisoner smeared her arms with a sticky paste that glowed greenish white. Vixa was surprised, but once she went inside she was glad of the glowing substance. The interior of the wall here was hollow and black as pitch.

Like ghosts, the phosphorescent shapes of other workers moved ahead of her. It was impossible to ask questions with the airshell in her mouth, so she just followed those in front of her. She stumbled against a stair step and started up. It was eerie, moving in the inky stairwell with only a faint glow of light. The steps reversed direction several times, and continued higher and higher. The wall had to be close to sixty feet tall.

She emerged in open water at the top. The area was thick with busy workers shoving stones into place. Someone grabbed her arm and tugged her to the edge. From there she could see the city of Urione shimmering in the distance.

A rush of water hit her, sweeping her off her feet. Vixa fell backward, slipping over the side of the wall. Automatically, she grabbed the parapet edge to stop her fall. No one came to her aid. As she hauled herself back up, she saw what had caused her fall: a block of stone had arrived, buoyed by its net and air-filled bladders, rocking the water with concussive force.

Workers pulled in the swaying net and levered the six-by-four-foot mass of rock onto the wall. Vixa tried to help, but her bare feet gave her little purchase on the smooth parapet. None down here were shod, but the other captives were more experienced underwater, and the Dargonesti's feet were obviously adapted for just this environment. Like their fingers, their toes were long and webbed.

The block thudded into place. The buoyant net rose a few feet over the workers' heads and hung there, tethered to the ocean floor by a long strand of woven seaweed.

The image of the net tugging at the line intrigued Vixa. She gazed up at the swaying net and thought again about the distance to the surface.

She wasn't the only one having such thoughts. A skinny human elbowed his way through the horde of workers, untied his weighted belt, and leapt from the parapet. He hit the seaweed net and clung to it. He had a sharp shard of stone in his hand and began to saw away furiously at the rope below him.

All at once soldiers were among them, battering prisoners with shields and spear shafts. The human managed to hack through the seaweed rope, and the net began to rise swiftly upward. The human clung to it desperately. Vixa wanted to scream encouragement, but she dared not remove her airshell.

A Dargonesti cast a spear at the escaping man. It missed. Another raised a conch shell to his lips and blew. Bubbles and a bleating call sounded in the sea.

Shrill whistles filled Vixa's ears. The ocean was immediately alive with dolphins, wheeling and diving. They raced after the escaping human. Fast as they were, they couldn't catch the rising net. The human rose upward with remarkable speed.

Sunshine filtered down from the world above. Against this backdrop, the man and the rising net were black shapes, shrinking rapidly. Suddenly, there was a violent explosion, and the man and the net dissolved in a mass of silver bubbles. In all, four separate eruptions were heard as each bladder exploded.

Slowly, the human came sinking down, enmeshed in the net. The dolphin sentinels circled the body, whining in mournful tones. The net passed Vixa, and she recoiled in shock at what she saw.

The thing that descended five feet in front of her no longer looked human. Blood oozed from his mouth and ears. His entire body was contorted as though in pain, arms and legs twisted and bent, head thrown back, mouth gaping wide. Vixa couldn't take her eyes from the dreadful sight until the Dargonesti guards cuffed the prisoners and shoved them back to work.

Vixa gripped a block, straining her muscles to help shift it. All the while her mind was working furiously. What had happened to the man? He was almost free. The dolphins were nowhere near him. Had someone used magic? She'd heard mutterings among the slaves about a death that could reach out and strike any air-breather who dared attempt to escape. Up to now, she hadn't given their talk any credence.

The day's work went on without pause. All the prisoners were racked by thirst, an ironic agony for people immersed in water. Their hands and feet swelled. Vixa found herself grateful for her Dargonesti robe. It didn't split or bind after hours underwater. She also discovered that her swollen feet gave her a better grip on the parapet stones.

A sea elf beat a crystal chime to signal the end of the day's work. Slack and drooping, the workers trooped down to the seabed to join their comrades. About the only thought Vixa's tired brain could manage was a mild amazement that her shell still had air, though she'd been using it for hours.

The dim grotto was a welcome sight as the Qualinesti walked out of the pool into the air. Armantaro waited for Vixa and offered her his arm, but she refused his aid. He seemed worse off than she.

Food was their first concern. Not only was the labor difficult, but the drag of the water seemed to double the effort necessary for even the simplest tasks. Their appetites were tremendous. The guards collected every airshell, dumped freshly caught fish on the floor, and departed. The elves collapsed on their bedding. Gundabyr set about preparing their fireplace with loose stones.

Garnath crawled out of his hiding place looking rested. "How did it go today?" he asked cheerfully. Gundabyr gave him a murderous look.

"This is no life for a warrior." Harmanutis sighed wearily. His hands were cracked and bleeding. "I don't think I could grip a sword even if I possessed one."

"This is no life for anyone," Gundabyr growled.

"I hate fish," Vanthanoris murmured. "Oh, for a roasted squab and a cup of steaming nectar, and maybe some thick, hot soup with plenty of . . ." His voice trailed off into soft snoring.

Armantaro just sat, silent and trembling. Vixa watched him and worried. He was too old for this mistreatment. His face was so pale, she feared he was ill.

Gundabyr was busy lighting fires around the grotto. His twin fell to cleaning the fish provided by their captors.

"Garnath," Vixa said, "why would a float explode going up to the surface when no one was near enough to prick it?" She described the escape attempt she'd witnessed and its gruesome result.

"Hmph," said the dwarf. "Sounds like the Law of Clouds to me." Vixa gave him a blank look, and he explained. "The Law of Clouds states that air expands as it rises. I'd say that a buoy filled with air at the sea bottom would certainly burst long before it reached the surface. And a man, likewise filled with air at the seafloor, would also—er—explode, unless he exhaled as he rose."

"But even if he exhaled properly, the bladders would still have burst," put in Armantaro quietly.

"Nope, nope. Had he opened small holes in the floats, the air might have leaked out quickly enough to avoid bursting yet slowly enough to allow him to reach the surface."

Vixa regarded him thoughtfully, rubbing her chin with one cracked hand. "But would he have enough breath to reach the surface?" she wondered. "Or would he exhale it all before getting there?"

Her musings were interrupted by an involuntary groan from Armantaro. Vixa dragged over a patch of sailcloth and used it to cover him, though he protested that he was perfectly fine. She pushed his shoulder gently until he lay down, his head resting on her leg.

"We must do something," the princess stated flatly, smoothing wet hair from the colonel's lined face. "Either by force or by guile, we've got to get out of this place."

"There is no way out." Gundabyr interrupted.

"No way at all," his twin agreed.

"Of course there is," she insisted. "We simply have to find it."

Garnath shook his head. "It's hopeless, lady. Me and Gundabyr've been working on the problem for weeks. I tell you, it's hopeless."

Angry, Vixa grabbed the nearest small object and threw it. It was a clay jar, which Gundabyr had filled with gnomefire paste. It smashed against the far wall, the sticky paste clinging to the black rock. Dew on the wall ignited the gnomefire.

"Hey!" Vanthanoris cried, scrambling to get out from under the dripping flames. A droplet of gnomefire fell on his pallet, which immediately caught fire. With much cursing and flinging of dirt, Vanthanoris and Harmanutis put out the small blaze.

"You must be careful, lady," Gundabyr chided. "Once ignited, that stuff is very hard to control!"

Vixa stared at the smoking pallet.

"Gundabyr, can you make more of this stuff?" she asked unexpectedly.

The dwarf blinked his heavy-lidded eyes. I've already made half a hundredweight. How much do you need?"

"We need all you can make, my friend. All you can make, and more!"

*　*　*　*　*

Coryphene was waiting at the quay for Naxos. It was half an hour beyond the appointed time, and there was still no sign of the shapeshifter. Furious at the insult to his dignity, Coryphene ordered his personal guard to search for the insolent wretch.

"Bind him, if you must, but bring him to the palace at once!" he shouted. His troopers dove headfirst into the water to carry out their master's order.

Coryphene stalked back to the palace, leaving the bearers of his sedan chair to puff along behind. He was oblivious to the praise called out to him by the common folk. Snarling a dismissal at his bearers, the Protector went through the magical barrier and swept into the palace plaza alone. There, lounging against one of the many green columns, was Naxos.

"You! You have earned my displeasure! How dare you keep me waiting!" stormed the warlord.

Naxos's face showed nothing. "I, sir? Kept *you* waiting? I have been waiting here for you for some time."

"What?"

"I was told to come to you, Excellence. Where else would I go but to the royal residence? I did not suppose you would come to the city quay to meet *me*."

This reasonable explanation cooled Coryphene's rage. He put a hand to his temple. His gills were dry, and his head had begun to ache. Seeing his leader's discomfort, Naxos went to the nearest pump and filled a shell with water. By the time Coryphene had splashed the water over his head and shoulders, his fury had abated. He savored the touch of the life-giving fluid on his gills. After several moments, he was able to speak in a calmer tone.

"Her Divine Majesty has a task for you and the sea brothers," he said.

"What's that, Excellence?"

"You are to go to the coast of Silvanesti and survey the area for us."

Naxos's green-blue eyebrows rose. "May I ask why?"

"It is enough that Her Divinity wishes it done. Go at once."

The shapeshifter bowed with a flourish that bordered on mockery. He whirled and took four long strides away, but stopped and turned back. "Does this perhaps concern the Qualinesti we captured, Excellence?" he inquired.

"You ask too many questions. Our Queen has ordered it. That is all you need to know."

"I obey her divine will," Naxos said smoothly. "I was just wondering—forgive me, Excellence—why the coast of Silvanesti interested Her Majesty, and not the waters off Qualinesti."

Coryphene smiled. "As we have visitors from Qualinesti, it is not surprising that we don't need *your* help in learning more about that land."

Naxos's smile was mirthless. "Ah, thank you for enlightening me. I am grateful for any scraps of wisdom Your Excellence deigns to bestow. I go, with all speed."

The shapeshifter departed. Coryphene found his hands clenched around his sword hilt and dagger pommel. He forced his fingers to relax. Damn Naxos anyway! His insolence was infuriating. Every time they met, there was a battle of words, and Coryphene always found himself somehow coming off the worse.

As he walked into the palace, the Protector consoled himself with the thought that it was only a matter of time before the arrogant shapeshifter's wit got him in deep trouble. That was something Coryphene would enjoy. Wholeheartedly.

Chapter 10
Fire and Flood

A strange thing happened on Vixa's fourth day in Nissia Grotto. Morning arrived, what morning there was two hundred fathoms down, and no Dargonesti came to lead the captives to work. Men awoke and wiped their bloodshot eyes, yet no taskmasters broke out of the pool with airshells and brusque commands.

Hours passed, and still no one came.

"I don't like it," Harmanutis said. "Something's amiss."

"Obviously," replied Armantaro. "But what?"

Gundabyr and Garnath returned from the depths of the cave, covered in all sorts of colored dust. Garnath announced they had the makings for a full hundredweight of gnomefire, but not enough pots and jars to hold it. Vixa had insisted the paste be divided into dozens and dozens of smaller containers, rather than concentrated in only a few larger ones. The dwarves and elves had scrounged up almost thirty pots. These lined the cave walls now, filled to their brims with sticky yellow goo.

Surveying the dusty twins, Armantaro asked, "Were you up all night? You must be exhausted."

"I couldn't sleep anyway. The quarrying kept me awake," Gundabyr said. He looked around at the grotto. "Where are our morning visitors? Haven't the Quoowahb come yet?"

"No, they haven't," Vanthanoris put in, yawning.

"You say the quarrying kept you awake—what quarrying?" Vixa wanted to know.

Garnath spoke. "The diggers working outside. I guess they found a new vein of limestone for the building blocks."

The elves exchanged looks of surprise. "No one's been working outside since yesterday," Harmanutis said.

"What exactly did you hear?" Vixa asked.

Gundabyr tugged at his black beard. "I dunno, but they are still at it, I think."

"Show us!"

They passed word to the other prisoners to cover for them should the Dargonesti appear. Then, pausing only to make a gnomefire lamp, the elves and the dwarf twins plunged into the deeper recesses of the cave. Twenty paces beyond the Qualinesti's sleeping area, the tunnel was dark and dank, the floor irregular. Crystals glittered in the black lava walls. Thirty paces in, the passage opened into a high chamber where dew dripped from the ceiling in an unending shower. This was their main source of fresh water. To keep the other prisoners from meddling in their explorations, the dwarf twins had made it their practice to tend the many buckets and seashell basins kept here to collect the dew.

Garnath raised the lamp over his head. "Listen," he hissed.

In the quiet, the elves heard a faint sound—*tink, tink, tink*—regular as a heartbeat. It sounded like sharp blows on rock, muffled by many feet of stone. Indeed, someone was digging on the mountain!

"The Dargonesti, do you think?" asked Vixa in a hushed voice.

"Why? They can come in through the pool anytime they want," said Gundabyr.

"Yes, and if there was any kind of digging to be done, you

can bet they'd have us doing it," Vanthanoris commented.

Armantaro circled the large chamber. "It's loudest here. What direction is that?" Harmanutis, Vanthanoris, and the dwarves had a brisk disagreement about this. Their voices rose.

"Quiet!" Vixa commanded. "That's the direction of the Mortas Trench!"

The revelation hit them like a lightning bolt. No Dargonesti would dare stray into the trench. It was thoroughly infested by . . .

"The chilkit," whispered Harmanutis.

"They're digging through to flank Coryphene's wall!" Vanthanoris exclaimed. In his shock, he backed away from the sound of digging and bumped into Gundabyr. The dwarf sat down hard in a deep puddle of water.

Vanthanoris apologized. Gundabyr started to complain loudly, but his remarks halted abruptly as he leaned down to sniff the puddle. Then he stuck a finger in the water.

"This isn't dew," he reported. "It's seawater."

The group ran back to the inhabited end of the grotto. Armantaro climbed up on an outcropping of rock and shouted for everyone's attention.

"We've found signs that the chilkit are boring into this tunnel!" he reported. The prisoners erupted into terrified exclamations. Armantaro held up his hands for silence, but had to shout over the tumult. "Listen to me!" he cried. "We must throw up a barricade!"

"If they can dig through solid rock, how can we stop them with ships' timbers and dunnage?" yelled a human.

"We need to buy time," Vixa countered. "We'll need air-shells to get out of here. Someone will have to go out and tell the Dargonesti."

"That's suicide!"

"Better to drown than face the chilkit alone," put in another slave.

"Who's the best swimmer here?" Armantaro shouted. No one came forward. Finally, Vanthanoris stepped out of the crowd.

The old colonel regarded the youngest of the Qualinesti

somberly. "You, Van?"

The elf shrugged. "Who else is there?"

"If the chilkit breach the mountain, this cave will probably flood," Gundabyr warned.

Groans and lamentations filled the air.

Armantaro jumped down from his perch and led the prisoners in piling up all the wreckage they had—bolstered with rocks, gravel, even their meager bedrolls.

Gundabyr and Garnath ferried their newly made store of gnomefire behind the barrier. Vixa stood atop the growing barricade, staring into the depths of the cave.

"Keep some of those pots handy," she said quietly to the dwarves. "We may need them to discourage the chilkit."

While she spoke, a thin stream of water came rolling down the cave floor. Some of the captives saw this and let out screams of fright.

"Vanthanoris, stand ready," Armantaro called. The young elf was poised by the edge of the pool.

There was a loud crash, and a cloud of dust spurted down the passage. A knee-deep surge of water followed, splashing against the foot of the hastily built barricade. Parts of the makeshift wall were swiftly washed away. Prisoners quickly armed themselves with stones or rude clubs made from ship timbers. Vixa stood atop a heap of flattened crates, heart pounding.

The mining noises ceased. The level of water slowly rose, seeping through the barrier. Then another, more sinister sound reached those on the barricade: the clicking of chilkit feet on stone. Vague shadowy forms appeared in the dark recesses of the cave.

"Astra, be with us," Armantaro whispered. Then he yelled, "Go, Van!"

Vanthanoris dove into the pool.

The prisoners stood behind the debris barricade, straining every nerve to see the enemy. The clicking grew louder.

"Ah! There!"

All eyes went to where Vixa pointed. Clinging to the roof of the grotto was a chilkit. The sight sent panic through the slaves. Armantaro shouted for them to stand fast. The old colonel's voice, long used to command, froze most of the fearful in their tracks.

Tentatively, the chilkit entered the illumination cast by the weak Dargonesti light globes. Its long antennae swept the air. It seemed confused and hesitant.

A second chilkit appeared, near the left wall. A third came slowly out of the darkness at floor level.

"Have at them!" Armantaro cried.

A barrage of stones hit the monster clinging to the ceiling, forcing it to back away. It waved one claw to ward off missiles, batted some aside. The chilkit on the wall rushed forward with startling speed and crashed into the pile of wreckage. Timber balks and broken yardarms fell apart, trapping several men underneath. The crates Vixa stood on slid sideways, throwing her off. She splashed down into six inches of water and rolled to a stop against something hard.

A chilkit's legs. She'd landed on the wrong side of the barricade, at the feet of the monster who'd advanced across the floor. For an endless second the creature regarded her with inky eyes. An antenna flicked lightly across her face. Vixa had a fleeting notion that the creature might not be hostile—until it raised a claw over her. The sharp inner edges were hard and white, in contrast to the bright red of the rest of the claw.

She wriggled between the monster's legs until she was directly under it. The claw raked the stone floor just behind her feet. Vixa kept crawling, using her elbows and knees. The dripping wet belly of the chilkit was inches above her. Oh, for Armantaro's dagger right now!

The chilkit did a fast turn, stepping over and uncovering Vixa. One of its spiny-fingered hands closed around her ankle. She yelled and kicked at it.

A red-bearded man darted in and hammered the chilkit with a club. After the third blow, his waterlogged weapon snapped. The monster thrust forward a closed claw, spearing the human in the chest. The chilkit easily lifted its victim off his feet and threw him back across the barricade.

By this time the grotto was a perfect riot of noise: shouts, screams, the smash and splinter of wood, the clatter of stone on flesh and stone. Vixa was still flailing in the shallow water, trying to free herself from the chilkit's grip when the burly Garnath approached. With a rock weighing as much as Vixa herself, the dwarf smashed the monster's arm, right on the joint. The crimson shell splintered and pink flesh tore. Vixa pulled away, the chilkit's four-fingered hand still locked around her leg.

Brave Garnath did not long survive that mighty blow. Stuttering in pain, the chilkit swung a massive claw sideways at the dwarf. It connected with a solid thud. Amazingly, Garnath kept his feet, though blood flowed from his lips. Vixa grabbed the first thing she could find: the stump of an oar. She whacked at the chilkit, but to no effect. The monster opened its claw around Garnath's neck. The dwarf threw up his arms to hold the deadly pincers apart, but the scissor claw closed with a hideous crunch. The gallant dwarf's head was severed from his body.

Vixa shouted a torrent of obscenity, yanking the chilkit hand from her leg. She climbed over the barricade, snatching up one of Gundabyr's pots of gnomefire paste. Her aim was true. The pot hit the chilkit that had slain Garnath, splattering sticky liquid over its armored chest.

The steady hail of rocks and missiles dislodged the chilkit clinging to the ceiling. It fell with a crash and lay squirming on its back. The other monster climbing along the left-hand wall was pushing through the tumbledown barrier, slaying anyone within claw-reach.

Blinking back tears of rage and sadness, Vixa climbed atop the remnants of the barricade. The now one-handed chilkit she'd hit with gnomefire paste was busy trying to drag Garnath's body back into the shadows. The yellow paste ran in slow streams down its front pair of legs. Several yards back into the darkness, the level of the steadily rising water reached the paste and ignited it.

The monster released Garnath's body and whirled frantically, trying to scrape off the flaming mess. This only spread the flames to the rest of its body. Then the chilkit lowered itself into the water, trying to wash the gnomefire away. This fanned the blaze farther. The burning monster made strange bubbling sounds. The other two chilkit stopped their attacks and went to their comrade's aid.

"Hit them with the gnomefire!" Vixa cried. "Seawater ignites it! Throw the pots!"

Armantaro and Harmanutis led the charge. All of Gundabyr's supply of gnomefire was on their side of the barrier, so they had ample ammunition. Harmanutis proved to have a strong arm and good aim. He hit the nearest chilkit twice in succession. Flames roared in the tight passage, the heat driving the prisoners back. The chilkit collapsed, his body blazing. The one-handed monster, grievously burned, staggered backward. When it was nearly out of range, a pot smashed into the wall above it, and paste rained down on its head. The chilkit turned and fled, and the gnomefire burst into flame. The last chilkit beat a fast retreat, leaving its two fellows blazing.

The grotto resounded with cheers. Some of the men waded out from behind the barricade and battered the dead monsters with their clubs.

"Come back! Come back!" Armantaro called. "The water is still rising! We must get to higher ground!"

The immediate danger from the chilkit was over, but the more insidious peril of drowning was growing stronger. Despite Armantaro's urging, there wasn't really any higher ground in the grotto—the entire cave sloped downward to the pool entrance. All the prisoners collected by the pool. Water was streaming from the rear of the cave. Pots and jars of gnomefire floated everywhere. Gundabyr, his face bloody, reminded them of the danger. If the gnomefire got wet . . .

"Where are the Quoowahb?" someone shouted.

"Will they leave us to drown?" cried another.

"Vanthanoris may not have gotten through," Harmanutis said grimly. He was cradling his left arm against his chest. A chilkit had gashed him badly.

The gnomefires at the rear still burned. By this light, and the feeble illumination of the Dargonesti globes, three hundred prisoners stared at each other helplessly, clinging to floating debris, the rough walls, or each other.

"E'li save us! They're back!"

Four more chilkit had appeared near the original barricade. They stayed where they were out of respect for the firepots, but busily demolished the wreckage that was damming the water coming in from their excavation.

"Now would be a good time for an idea," Vixa said, bumping into Gundabyr.

"Don't ask this dwarf. I'm stumped." Gundabyr wiped blood and soot from his face. He looked around at the floating prisoners. "Where's Garnath got to? Garnath! Hey, Brother!"

Vixa clamped a hand on his arm and shook her head. Her anguished expression told him more than he wanted to know.

The sight of the chilkit had spurred some of the prisoners into taking a desperate gamble. They drew in great breaths of air and then went under, heading for the open sea outside. They could only hope that the Dargonesti would find them before they drowned. Vixa remained where she was, treading water valiantly. She couldn't wager her life on so slim a hope. Not yet, anyway.

The four chilkit, reinforced by three newcomers, were advancing cautiously down the tunnel toward them. More and more men vanished below the water, fleeing the grotto. A chittering cry echoed through the cave. One of the chilkit had bumped a pot of gnomefire. It tilted, dumping its cargo into the water. Flames enveloped the creature, and its six cohorts promptly fled.

Rising water and burning gnomefire were using up the precious air. "It's getting harder to breathe," Vixa gasped.

"My lady," Armantaro wheezed, "it has been a privilege serving—"

"Save your breath, Colonel!"

The chilkit regrouped, this time advancing with timbers clutched in their claws. They gently pushed aside all floating containers. Their comrade had succumbed to the fire. Its charred body spiraled slowly down to the pool, trailing noxious smoke. The stench was overpowering.

Vixa was nearly blind. Smoke was making her eyes

stream. "I think drowning is preferable to this!" she said, gagging.

Gundabyr, miserable over the loss of his twin, said nothing. Armantaro agreed with her. "We'll have to risk it," he said. "On three—one, two, three!"

Taking a deep breath of the fetid air, Vixa ducked under the dark water. Kicking and sweeping out with her hands, she soon cleared the grotto's mouth, the last drylander out. The sea was full of people—swimming, fighting, drowning. What looked like the whole Dargonesti army was massed on the plain in front of Urione. Vixa looked toward the wall across the Mortas Trench. What she saw stunned her.

The entire center section of the wall had fallen, and the area was filled with red-shelled chilkit. Hundreds and hundreds of them.

She bumped into something. Turning in the water, she saw the lifeless form of one of her fellow prisoners. The man's long dark hair drifted across his face like a shroud, waving in the ocean currents.

Pressure built in Vixa's chest. She had no breath left. She searched frantically for Armantaro, Harmanutis, or Gundabyr, but couldn't make out any individuals in the dimness of the depths. Her limbs burned. Movement became harder and harder. Vixa began to sink.

Soft mud cradled her fall, covering her like a blanket. It was warm, so very warm and comfortable. She opened her mouth and let cold seawater fill her lungs.

Chapter 11

Transformation

"How could this have happened?" Coryphene raged. His watch captain, Telletinor, stood rigidly at attention. The warrior had several minor wounds, but he held his stance proudly, eyes fixed ahead.

"Well?" demanded Coryphene. "How did the enemy bring down my wall?"

"They mined under the foundation, Excellence. The first we knew of it was when the center span collapsed."

"How many were lost?"

"Most of the Silverside regiment. The Sea Horse regiment and the Queen's Killer Whales were far enough from the wall that they weren't affected."

"And no one saw them coming—because I sent Naxos and the sea brothers to some far-off coastline!" Coryphene grabbed his heavy helmet and pulled it on. "Muster all troops! I will lead the guard out myself. I—"

A lightly clad Dargonesti youth, green blood streaming from a gash on his forehead, stumbled up to Coryphene and his assembled officers.

"Excellence . . . the enemy . . . at Four Squids Quay!" he panted.

"Zura take them! They're in the city!" fumed the Protector. He turned to another of his officers. "Kantren, muster the army in the kelp gardens. You are in command. I will take the guard and repel the enemy at Four Squids Quay." The officer saluted and raced away.

Urione rang with conch shell alarms and the tramp of many feet. Coryphene assembled his iron-armed troops in the fish market square. Ordinary folk had vanished from sight, blocking their windows and doors. Just as five hundred of Coryphene's personal guard gathered in place, a scream tore the air.

Coryphene spun around and saw a melee spilling into the square. A column of six chilkit were trying to force their way up the street. Blocking their path were a dozen Dargonesti warriors, some of them weaponless. An equal number of fisherfolk, armed with nets and gaffs, had taken up the defense of their homes. From windows facing the street, other Dargonesti bombarded the invaders with stones, pots, and endless torrents of oyster shells. The chilkit, ignoring the onslaught of rubbish, attacked.

"Forward!" Coryphene shouted. Out came five hundred scavenged iron and steel swords.

"Close up there!" he barked. "Bring your shields together! First rank, follow me! The rest, hold here!"

He led fifty warriors at a dead run across the square. The beleaguered defenders were fragmenting. The undisciplined civilians were suffering badly as the chilkit ran them down one at a time. Then Coryphene's shock troop hit the scene.

The Protector of Urione did not shirk his place in the fore. He fended off a backhand blow by a chilkit claw and slashed at the monster with Vixa's Qualinesti blade. His first strike cracked the chilkit's armor shell. The creature gave ground, lashing at Coryphene's face with its antennae, trying to scratch his eyes. With a quick overhand swipe, he managed to cut off the antennae. The chilkit staggered and collided with the creature on its right. It tried to wrest Coryphene's shield away. Coryphene relinquished the shield and thrust straight at the monster's upright torso. A crunch, and the shell gave. Roaring a war cry, Coryphene rammed the blade home and out the chilkit's back. He put a foot to its chest and recovered his blade. The lifeless creature fell back, twitching in its death throes.

Looking over the scene, Coryphene realized that these six were the only foes in sight. A raiding party, he decided, to draw off his troops from the main attack. He had to get outside.

No sooner was his attention diverted than the chilkit mustered their resolve and resumed their furious attack. Two of them forced their way past the line of Dargonesti swords. The remaining three kept up the pressure on the front. Coryphene ordered his line to fall back.

"Excellence! Shall I summon the rest of the guard?" panted one of his lieutenants.

"For what reason? There are only five of them," was the acid retort.

The chilkit attacked singly, first from one side, then the other. One Dargonesti was dragged out of place and harried. The other warriors, infuriated, charged on their own initiative. Two chilkit were trapped between the Dargonesti and the houses of the fisherfolk. It took three or four elves to handle one chilkit, but they separated the two monsters and hacked away at them. Coryphene cleaved one creature's blunt head in two with his sword. Any warm-blooded foe would have dropped instantly, but the chilkit fought on, its actions violent and undirected. Two warriors were knocked down by its flailing limbs. Coryphene's shield caught a blow that was so strong it bent the tortoiseshell double. Down went the Protector of Urione.

Across the square, Captain Telletinor saw his commander fall. "Close ranks!" he cried shrilly. "At the double, charge!"

A tide of blue-skinned fury blasted across the market to crush the remaining chilkit. Afterward, sorting through the carnage, Telletinor and his brother officers found Coryphene, bruised but undefeated. The chilkit's last act before expiring had been to fall on top of him, and he had been pinned there, the monster's corpse too heavy for him to lift.

Tired and dehydrated warriors were lining up at the water spouts to douse their gills. Coryphene walked among them, shouting, "Back in ranks! Back, I say! You'll be wet soon enough!"

He led the guards to the quay and marched them out into the sea.

Behind him, the fisherfolk emerged from their houses to survey the scene of battle. A dozen Dargonesti lay dead in the square. They were tenderly taken up so the proper rites could be performed. Seawater was poured on the pavements to wash away the blood.

Axes appeared, and the fisherfolk set to lopping the limbs off the dead chilkit. The creatures were crustaceans, after all, just like crabs or lobsters. The sea elves always ate dead chilkit, just as the chilkit would have done to them.

* * * * *

A small spark lit the darkness that shrouded Vixa Ambrodel.

Tiny points of light, like the stars she gazed at from her window in the Speaker's house, twinkled above her. She floated under a canopy of cold stars. A red disk appeared on the horizon, a great staring eye—no, it was the red moon, Lunitari.

She tried to move. Pain lanced through her chest. Vixa inhaled sharply, found cool air, and coughed seawater. She was on the surface of the ocean! How had she gotten here? The last thing she remembered was escaping from the flooded Nissia Grotto—and drowning! She had drowned!

"Be still. Breathe."

Stiffly, Vixa turned her head. The face of Naxos hovered close by. His arms held her up, keeping her head above the sea swell.

"Naxos." Her voice was a raspy croak.

"Be still," he repeated softly. "You were nearly dead when I found you."

She swallowed painfully. "Ar-Armantaro," she hissed. "Where are my companions?"

He shook his head. "I do not know. You were the first one I saw. I used the magic of my necklace to bring you to the surface safely."

It was strange to feel wind on her face again. The pain in her chest and head gradually faded, but she was so weary she let Naxos continue to support her. He was treading water effortlessly, his long legs scissoring in slow, powerful strokes.

"How goes the battle?" she asked.

"The battle is over, for now. The chilkit have breached the wall. Many hundreds of them occupy the plain around the city. Coryphene was able to keep them out of Urione proper, but he lacks the power to defeat them."

"A siege."

"Yes. You and I have our own problems, however."

You and I. "What problems?"

"Coryphene sent the sea brothers to the coast of Silvanesti to search for a route for Uriona's invasion. I was called back and arrived in time to see the chilkit on the plain, and all the land-dwellers fleeing the grotto. No wonder, with the chilkit on the loose and a volcano erupting."

"Volcano? What volcano?"

"In the grotto. There was fire coming from the mouth of the grotto."

Vixa blinked at him, uncomprehending. Then she remembered. "The gnomefire! Of course, it burns underwater! I'll wager you've never seen fire like that before."

"You would be right. By its light, I saw you lying on the bottom. Your soul had nearly left your body, so the only thing to do was take you to the surface."

He was looking at her with an expression Vixa couldn't read in the dim red moonlight. It disconcerted her. "You said we had problems."

"Urione is too far away for you to reach without an airshell, and my necklace's magic is depleted."

"Couldn't you change into a dolphin and tow me to land?"

"It's two hundred leagues at least, but even if I could, would you leave your friends behind?"

He knew her that well at least. She couldn't leave Armantaro and the rest. She had to know if they were all right.

"Then what can I do?" she asked, anguished.

The unreadable expression returned to his face. "There is a way you can return to Urione," he said. The usual brash tone was gone from his voice. "It will require you to make a difficult choice, a choice you cannot go back on."

Cool wind raised goosebumps on Vixa's exposed skin. "What choice?" she finally asked.

"With my help, you could become a brother of the sea." His insolent grin flashed for an instant. "Or I should say, a sister."

"You mean, become a shapeshifter—with gills?"

"A shapeshifter, yes. But you would remain Qualinesti otherwise."

Strange as the idea was, Vixa also found it surprisingly inviting. She pondered silently as they bobbed in the waves.

"The ability is permanent?" she asked.

"Once I make the spell, it will be with you always."

"How do I control the transformation?"

"To assume dolphin shape you must be in the sea. Simply form in your mind the image of the dolphin. By concentrating on that image, you will change."

"And how do I regain my elven body?"

"Call up a vision of yourself on two legs. Whether you are dry or wet, the change will reverse."

It sounded simple enough, and what choice had she? Unable to return to Urione, unable to leave her friends. What else was there to do?

"I'll do it."

Naxos's golden eyes bored into her brown ones. "Be certain! This is not like the choosing of a gown. This will change you forever."

She bristled. "I'm a soldier and no stranger to hard decisions. I've made up my mind."

"As you wish."

From a pouch tied around his waist, Naxos took a small

object. By the red moonlight, Vixa saw that it was the tiny image of a dolphin, carved from some lustrous white stone. Naxos told her to lie on her back in the water. She stretched out her legs as he supported her with his left hand under her back. Whispering words in the sea tongue, Naxos touched Vixa's nose with the beak of the tiny carving. Reaching across her, he touched the side flipper to her right hand, and the other fin to her left. A shiver ran through her.

She stared up at the stars, pushing her fear aside. The tiny points of fire seemed to brighten. Water lapping in her ears carried sounds new and peculiar to her—grunts and wheezes she'd never heard before. Naxos's voice dropped to a murmur as he continued to touch the ritual carving to Vixa's body.

Her trembling ceased. Heat flowed through her blood, radiating outward from her heart. Vixa closed her eyes. Her muscles tensed. Her arms were pulled tight to her sides. She felt a moment of panic as she realized she couldn't move them any longer, but Naxos continued to drone on and on. She grew dizzy, feeling as though she were falling, or perhaps sinking.

Vixa wanted to tell Naxos to steady her, to pull her upright, but instead of words, all that came out of her mouth was a raucous squeak.

Holy Astra! Vixa's eyes flew open. The world had changed. The stars and moonlight were so bright—it was like daylight! Naxos was no longer treading water beside her. She rolled over, burying her face in the sea. A lean gray shape lolled in the ocean at her side. Naxos.

"Welcome to the sea," he said. His mouth didn't move at all, for he spoke in the clicks and whistles of the water-tongue. She understood him as though he were speaking Elvish.

"Naxos? Am I—am I changed?" Intuitively, she also spoke the strange language.

"Of course, silly dryfoot."

Vixa couldn't take it in. The change was too enormous. "You're as powerful a mage as Uriona!" she exclaimed.

She could have sworn that Naxos's dolphin face frowned

at her. "No," he said harshly. "It is a gift given to me as leader of the sea brothers. It has nothing to do with Uriona or her evil spellcasting." He rolled sideways and commanded, "Take a deep breath and hold it. Now, follow me!"

Naxos dove. He aimed his long snout almost straight down and drove himself with long sweeps of his flukes. Vixa imitated his posture, awkwardly at first, but quickly discovered that her new body was far more graceful and powerful than her old. She sped into the depths. With her eyes rolled back, she could see her own tail flexing. Her back was black, her flanks and belly snow white.

Another dolphin joined them. "Kios!" Naxos called, "are the brothers back from Silvanesti?"

"We heard of the great battle and came home. Who is this?" asked the other dolphin.

"Vixa, of the land-dwelling elves. She is one of us now."

Kios ducked under Naxos, coming up on Vixa's other side. Though they were speeding through the water, Kios maneuvered with ease.

"A land-dweller, become a brother of the sea? Such has not happened in ten lifetimes!" he exclaimed.

"Where are the other brothers?" Naxos asked.

"In the sargasso fields, east of the city. The chilkit have surrounded the city. None of the city-dwellers have ventured out since yestereve."

"Go there and bid them join me. Now may be the time to compel Coryphene to make concessions to us. The sea brothers are his best hope for defeating the enemy."

Kios departed. Vixa heard him long after his shape was lost in the dark waters. The sea was a constant symphony of sounds.

Vixa concentrated on keeping up with the larger and faster Naxos. What a sensation it was to be a dolphin! She felt the depth of the water, cleaved it like an arrow. The one giant breath she'd taken at the surface still sustained her. The awful pressure, the burning need for air hadn't come back. Could natural dolphins hold their breath this long? She would have to remember to ask Naxos.

Before she could, the glow of Urione appeared below them. Naxos slowed. Exuberant with her newfound mobility, Vixa circled the larger dolphin excitedly.

"What are you waiting for?" she chattered.

"I am thinking," he replied. After a minute, while Vixa continued to swim around him, Naxos said firmly, "Coryphene must not know of your transformation. We might have need of this secret. You should enter the city unseen, in your true form. I will come later and face the Protector."

"What do you plan to do?"

"If the chilkit are defeated—*when* the chilkit are defeated—I will lead the sea brothers against Coryphene and Uriona."

They parted. Vixa swam slowly above the iridescent city shell, looking down on the horde of chilkit spread out around Urione. In the distance, the mouth of Nissia Grotto still belched flame. With all the gnomefire Gundabyr had made, the prison might burn for days.

The sight of the grotto brought back thoughts of her friends. Her excitement over her transformation gave way to fear that Armantaro and the others might not have survived. Immediately, she dove to the lowest level of the city and barreled through an open doorway. As her dolphin head broke the surface, she saw Dargonesti soldiers standing watch. No good. She tried another entrance. The pool there was even more crowded.

On her fifth try she found an empty quay. With two sweeps of her tail, Vixa leapt out of the water and onto the stone ramp. In an instant she felt the difference. The sea no longer buoyed her, no longer cooled her massive body. On land, her elegant dolphin form weighed her down, quickly became uncomfortably hot. Breathing was difficult. Red mist filled her vision. She struggled to follow Naxos's instructions. Vixa imagined herself standing in front of a full-length mirror. She recreated in her mind an exact reflection of herself—a strong warrior's body, short blond hair, and honey-brown eyes.

The heat was becoming unbearable. She gasped, forcing all thoughts from her mind except one. You are an *elf*, she admonished herself. You are Vixa Ambrodel, princess and warrior of the Qualinesti.

A sudden chill shook her, set her teeth to chattering. She stayed her aching jaw with one hand. Hand? She looked down at her arm. The dark shade of her dolphin skin faded as her normal coloring returned. She was elven again!

Vixa sat up. Before, the heat had been intensely painful, now all of a sudden she was freezing. She hugged her knees to her chest, shaking violently.

"You! Drylander! What are you doing?"

She looked up to see a Dargonesti soldier standing in an open archway leading into the city. He challenged her again.

"I c-came here from N-Nissia Gr-Grotto," she said, forcing the words through rattling teeth.

"You can't run loose in Urione, drylander. Come with me."

"I-I'm fr-fr-freezing!" The sea elf gestured for her to get up, but she remained obstinately where she was.

The sea elf shook his head in disgust. He unclasped his cloak and dropped it unceremoniously over her head. Vixa wrapped it around herself, then got to her feet and followed him into the city.

She found herself in the fish market square, on the side opposite to where she and Armantaro had first entered. The square was carpeted with wounded Dargonesti. Sea elves in pale blue robes moved through the mass of injured, tending their hurts. She guessed them to be acolytes of Quen, the goddess of healing.

The warrior led her down a long line of wounded Dargonesti. There were not enough healers to tend them all. Dozens of warriors writhed in pain from claw wounds or lost limbs. She followed the guard until they came to a pavilion set up in the center of the square. Under this awning sat Coryphene, surrounded by warriors and priests. The crowd parted for her. When Vixa reached him, she saw that his cuirass was scarred by blows from chilkit claws. The Protector was being treated for a wound in his left forearm.

"The redshell cut right through my best shield," he said, seeing the direction of her gaze. The wound went deep into both sides of his forearm. Another inch or so, Vixa overheard the attending priest say, and Coryphene's arm would have been severed.

"Yes, yes," was the Protector's irritable response. To Vixa, he said, "I am surprised you are alive, lady."

"So am I, Excellence. Is there news of my companions?"

Coryphene's lips thinned in pain. The healer was dabbing at his wound with a bit of sponge. Steeling himself, he replied, "Few of them survived."

Vixa's face whitened. Fear twisted in her stomach. "Who lives?" she whispered.

"The two younger warriors are dead. The dark-haired one drowned. The other died fighting the enemy."

Harmanutis and Vanthanoris, both gone. "What else?"

Coryphene winced as the healer applied a roll of damp brown seaweed to his arm. "Careful, wretch!" he hissed. The priest drew back in alarm. Coryphene mastered his anger, told the healer to proceed.

"The younger, white-haired warrior, what was his name?"

"Van—" She cleared her throat. "Vanthanoris."

"He warned my left flank column that the chilkit were in the grotto. He was given an airshell, but would not return to the city. He took a spear from the battlefield and died fighting a chilkit. His warning allowed my army to withdraw to a safer position and prevented a rout. Your Vanthanoris died well. Is he typical of the warriors found in Qualinesti?"

Sunk in misery, she nodded.

"I see." There was a pause; then Coryphene beckoned to one of his many aides. The Protector said a quick word in the elf's ear, and the young Dargonesti departed on some errand.

The nervous healer now tried to tie the free ends of the seaweed bandage around Coryphene's arm. Coryphene made a fist and stared at the healer's hands while the knot was made fast.

"Enough. Begone!" The priest bowed and fled.

"Excellence," Vixa said, her heart heavy. "Have you any word of my other companion, Armantaro?"

"He survived. He is in the House of Arms with the other drylanders." A ray of happiness eased Vixa's sorrow. Coryphene held out a goblet. One of the soldiers stepped up to fill it with a greenish fluid. Coryphene drank deeply. His face was flushed when he lowered the cup.

"What about you?" he asked suddenly. "How did you survive the chilkit and the sea for so long?"

"Someone helped me," she said stiffly. "A Dargonesti gave me air. I had to hide in the open ocean until the battle ended."

Coryphene picked at the ends of his bandage while she talked. When she paused, he asked, still staring at his arm, "Was it Naxos?"

She stiffened in surprise, but feigned ignorance, saying, "Naxos? Your herald? No, Excellence. It was not a dolphin."

He nodded slowly, apparently satisfied. At that instant the young elf Coryphene had sent away returned. He bore in his arms several items of clothing. Coryphene made a quick gesture, and the elf handed the clothes to Vixa.

"What happened in the grotto?" the Protector asked. "That fire came from no volcano. Was it a chilkit weapon?"

Vixa couldn't think of any reason to lie, and she was too weary to make an effort. "It was gnomefire, Excellence. A dwarven smith among the prisoners made it from minerals he found in the caverns. We slaves were using it to try to keep warm. Gnomefire burns when it meets water. We were able to kill several chilkit with it."

"Can he make more, this dwarf?"

"I suppose so—if he's still alive," she finished sadly.

"Go to the House of Arms then. Find this dwarf for me. If he can make more of this fire, perhaps we can defeat our ancient enemy. Bear in mind, lady, if we defeat the chilkit, then we'll have no more need for troublesome dryland labor."

His words pierced her gloom. "No more need—you mean you'll set us free?"

"Let us see what your dwarf friend can contrive, shall we?" He turned away and called to one of his soldiers. "Egriun."

A sea elf with blue-streaked emerald hair stepped out of the pack of warriors. "Take her to the House of Arms," Coryphene said. "Find the dwarf smith, and see that he gets what he needs to make this . . . this . . ."

"Gnomefire," Vixa supplied.

Egriun gestured for Vixa to precede him. She walked out of the pavilion, and the two of them crossed the square to the central spiral ramp.

"What do you think, soldier?" she asked. "Can you defeat the chilkit?"

"One Dargonesti is worth ten redshells," Egriun replied. He looked around at the wounded elves covering the square. "But there are fewer Dargonesti left to bear arms."

"You should arm the citizenry."

"That rabble? They have no stomach for battle!"

"If they were trained—"

"Might as well train a halibut before putting it on the table. The chilkit would devour them where they stood."

Chapter 12
The Promise

Vixa made use of an empty alley to change into the green vest and short kilt Coryphene had given her. Eight levels up from the fish market, Egriun led her off the ramp. They wound up at a squat, square building whose towers merged into the roof of this level. A gate of polished stone, cut in the shape of a disk ten feet wide, rolled closed behind Vixa and her escort. She knew a fortress when she saw one—a fortress, and a prison.

Egriun took her down a long straight passage, darker even than Nissia Grotto. The walls and floor were made of dark blue slate that absorbed whatever light fell on it. Somewhere not far away Vixa heard the ring of hammer on metal. It was very warm in this place. She started to sweat.

The passage ended at a circular room with other tunnels radiating out from it. The stone floor was covered with an inlay of rainbow-hued scales, the hide of some enormous sea beast. Leather banners studded with gems and shells hung from the walls. Suits of armor wrought from tortoiseshell, sharkskin, and bronze plates stood on frames around the room's perimeter. Seated on the floor in this warriors' chamber were the survivors from Nissia Grotto. There weren't more than thirty.

Vixa immediately spotted Armantaro and broke from Egriun to greet him. "Hail, Colonel!" she cried.

"Highness!"

The princess threw her arms around the elder elf.

"I thought you were dead!" he exclaimed when they parted. "But you look well enough."

"You look as if you've been wrestling a dragon." It was true. The colonel's clothes were scorched, and he had scores of shallow cuts and scrapes on his face and arms.

"I'm too old for this nonsense," he said ruefully, his breath wheezing in his chest. "Two hundred years ago I could have knocked Coryphene from here to the Mortas Trench."

Vixa's smile was fleeting. Sobering, she said softly, "I heard about Harm and Van."

"A lot of good folk died yesterday. These sea elves claim they had other worries and couldn't take the time to check on their captives." Armantaro's voice was low and bitter.

Vixa tightened her grip on his arm. She had no comfort to give the colonel. And none for herself, either.

Slowly, afraid his answer might be more bad news, she asked, "Did Gundabyr survive?"

"Yes!" Armantaro turned to survey the room. "There he is," said the colonel. Gundabyr lay by the far wall, his back to the room. "Poor fellow, he's taken his twin's death hard. Very hard."

Vixa and Egriun went to the dwarf. She laid a gentle hand on his shoulder. "Wake up there. They need you at the forge."

Gundabyr rolled his head back so he could see who spoke. "Hello, Princess," he rumbled.

"Hello yourself, Gundabyr."

The dwarf noticed Egriun looming behind her. He rubbed his face and sat up. "What's this long drink of water here for?"

"Coryphene wants to see you," Vixa explained. "He knows about the gnomefire. He wants you to make more, to use against the chilkit."

The dwarf turned his bearded face to the wall. "Tell him to go and . . . soak his head."

"Listen to me!" Vixa shook his shoulder hard. "You have a chance—*we* have a chance—to help ourselves as well as the Dargonesti. The chilkit have surrounded Urione. The siege must be broken. Gnomefire may be the only thing that can do it!"

"So what." His voice was flat and emotionless. "Let the redshells have the city. We'll never see the sun again, no matter who wins."

Vixa yanked his arm, turning him to face her. She whispered fiercely, "I saw what happened to Garnath! Do you want the same fate for us all? If the gnomefire helps defeat the chilkit, Coryphene has hinted he'll let us go. Our lives are in your hands, Gundabyr. Garnath saved my life. Can you save us all?" She stood and stared down at him. "Show the blueskins what a forgemaster of Thorbardin can do!"

Gundabyr stared at her for a long time. Suddenly, he exhaled sharply and hopped to his feet. He stalked past Vixa and the patient Egriun.

"Well," he said to the sea elf, "what are you waiting for? Take me to your Protector. If he wants gnomefire, I'll give him a crab boil he won't soon forget!"

The dwarf's proud words echoed through the chamber. When he and his escort had departed, Vixa allowed her trembling knees to bend at last. She sank to the ground. The terror and excitement of the past twenty-four hours had left her weak and wrung out. Her mind was filled with thoughts of Harmanutis and Vanthanoris, of Captain Esquelamar and all the others who'd been lost on this journey.

Her first command was supposed to have been a simple task: pick up the ambassador—what was his name? Quenavalen?—and take him safely home to Qualinost. She hadn't thought of Quenavalen or the Ergothian civil war in many days.

How many days had it been? The lack of day and night

made things extremely confusing. The weary princess occupied her mind for several moments trying to determine exactly how long she'd been in this city of sea elves. She guessed five days since they'd been brought here by the dolphin shapeshifters. It certainly seemed much longer.

She was so very tired. Vixa's eyelids began to droop. Armantaro came to sit beside her. She dozed, leaning against his shoulder, while he watched the comings and goings of their captors. Racks of arms were dragged out and rapidly distributed to those who'd lost their weapons in the previous battle. Helmets were repaired or replaced. A single warrior casually stood watch over the former slaves. Even this guardian seemed unnecessary. None of the exhausted, bedraggled slaves appeared capable of making an escape, and even then they would have to get past the chilkit surrounding the city.

Vixa had been sleeping only a short time when the sound of Armantaro's coughing roused her. "Are you ill?" she asked groggily.

"Not at all. I just swallowed more of the ocean than is prudent."

She had to smile. "Adversity never wears you down, does it, Colonel?"

"So," said Armantaro in a very low voice, "how did you survive in the sea, lady?"

"You wouldn't believe me if I told you."

He feigned amazement. "I? Doubt the word of my princess and commander?"

She sat up, stretching and yawning. "I thought I was dead," she finally replied. "But someone took me up and restored me to life." The colonel's only reply was an upraised eyebrow. "Naxos, the dolphin herald," she whispered.

"By Astra!"

"That's not the half of it. There was no way for me to return to Urione, since I had no airshell, so Naxos offered me a solution." She hesitated, now that the time had come to speak of it. Armantaro begged her to continue. "Naxos said I could become like him," she finished.

The old colonel paled. "Like him? You mean, become a dolphin?"

Vixa nodded, watching the Dargonesti moving around them. "It was the only choice I could make."

"But you're an excellent swimmer, lady! You could have reached land!"

"Two hundred leagues? Besides, do you think I would leave you and the others behind? Is that what a Qualinesti officer does in time of danger?"

"No, lady. Forgive me. No child of Verhanna Kanan would abandon her troops."

Armantaro's mention of her mother brought that lady strongly to Vixa's mind. The princess pondered what might be happening in Qualinost now. Did they even know she was missing? Somehow the bright, leafy beauty of her home didn't seem real now. The only reality was Urione, the chilkit, and the life-and-death struggle being waged.

"Did I ever tell you about my son, Vintarellin?" Armantaro asked.

"No," she replied, surprised. "I didn't know you had a son."

"My only child—he's perhaps twenty years older than you. I was thinking of him just now. When he was very young, he came to me and asked permission to enter the priesthood of Astra. He had no interest in becoming a soldier, but wanted to learn the ways of leaf and vine."

"An admirable ambition."

Armantaro sighed heavily. "I didn't think so at the time. The family of Ramantalus have always been fighters in their prime, and stewards of the Speaker in their old age. I told Vintarellin he would have to learn the duty of combat first."

This harsh attitude seemed unlike the Armantaro Vixa knew. She asked, "And did he?"

"Oh, yes. I sent him off to a frontier post in northern Qualinesti. He became a remarkable archer and hunter. It was said my son could pierce the eye of a hawk on the wing. Unfortunately, blood and sport took control of him. He came to love the hunt, not as a necessary craft, but for the killing itself."

Vixa didn't know what to say. "I'm sorry, Colonel," she finally murmured.

"It's a hard thing to say, but I despise my son. We haven't spoken in over thirty years. He lives in the high forest, feared and hated by all—an outcast. It's my fault, of course. I should have let him have his heart's desire when he asked for it."

"Maybe the blood lust was always in him. At least he expends it in the forest and not on his fellows."

Armantaro said softly, "Parents complain when their children are foolish. They blame it on youth. I think it's *we* who are foolish, because we're old. We forget what it's like to be young."

Vixa patted his battle-scarred hand. "Parents and children always have problems. Look at my mother and me. I'm one of Qualinesti's most acclaimed fighters, yet nothing I do is ever good enough for her," she said ruefully. "I lack fire in my soul, she says. I'm sure she wonders if I am truly her daughter."

It was the old colonel's turn to comfort his princess. He spoke up quickly. "I believe the lyremaster set her straight on that score. As I recall, he told your mother in no uncertain terms that you were far too, ah, *fiery* for the arts."

The memory surprised a chuckle from Vixa. She squeezed his hand and grinned. "You heard about that? Oh, he was a sour pickle, was Master Picalum."

"No doubt he was, once you broke your lyre over his head. What had he done to anger you so?"

"He told me I had no rhythm in my fingers!" was the indignant response.

Armantaro laughed softly.

A troop of Dargonesti, their armor restored and refurbished, marched out of the House of Arms. New warriors straggled in, looking shocked and pale. From snatches of conversation that drifted their way, Vixa and Armantaro discerned that a sizable contingent of sea elves had been lured into a trap and slaughtered by the chilkit.

"This can't go on," Armantaro stated. "Coryphene will have to risk all in a final throw against them. If he sits tight, they'll strangle this city and cut his troops apart, like gardeners pruning grapevines."

Vixa agreed. Gundabyr had better hurry with the gnomefire.

* * * * *

A tense silence fell over the city of Urione. Within its graceful shell, a hundred thousand Dargonesti waited for the outcome of a strange race. Who would win, the dwarf or the chilkit?

No one was more uncertain than Vixa. She and Armantaro had remained in the House of Arms for a full day, not knowing what might be happening. Then a soldier had come, and they were taken to the Square of Artisans, where the dwarf toiled. Ostensibly they were there to help in the work, but the old colonel was of the opinion that their presence was more intended to keep the irascible dwarf calm and on the job.

In the Square of Artisans, where all the city's workshops were concentrated, Gundabyr had the finest crafters beneath the sea at his disposal. They worked feverishly mixing the minerals the dwarf needed. Fortunately, the Dargonesti had supplies of each ingredient stockpiled in the city. They used the components for different purposes—for example, raw bitumen as the cement in their mosaic floors—so everything was on hand.

Making gnomefire itself was the simplest of Gundabyr's tasks. How to deliver it, though? This question occupied the dwarf's every waking moment. How could the Dargonesti spread the fire paste on the chilkit without spilling it on themselves?

"On land, I'd just tell 'em to toss the jars," Gundabyr grumbled.

"Underwater the jars wouldn't hit hard enough to shatter," Armantaro pointed out.

"Yes, I know," said the dwarf sourly.

Vixa made a suggestion. "How about some type of catapult?"

Gundabyr scratched a few calculations on the white tabletop. A cadre of Dargonesti crafters craned their necks to follow Gundabyr's odd markings. They shook their long blue faces, exchanged worried looks. The drylander was mad, utterly mad.

"Thunderation!" Gundabyr bellowed, smearing the numbers with the heel of his hand. "A catapult won't work underwater either! No skein could keep tension when wet, and anyway, we've got no wood for the frame! Blast and thunderation!"

Vixa folded her arms. "The main difficulty is that water is much thicker than air, yes?"

"Yes, yes," Gundabyr replied testily.

"Yet fish move freely in it." She thought of her own recent experience. "And the dolphins practically fly through it. Why? Because they have fins and flukes, and muscles to power them."

"Hmm. Perhaps we could strap firepots to the dolphins," the dwarf mused.

Numerous blue faces registered shock as the Dargonesti protested this idea loudly. Vixa held up her hands for peace. "No," she agreed. "That's a terrible idea."

Gundabyr scowled.

Armantaro had been sipping from a shell of fresh water. "We're making this too complex," he said. "Simple answers are usually the best. How would we fight the chilkit on land? We'd charge them with cavalry armed with lances!"

The old colonel grabbed the shard of coal from Gundabyr and began to sketch on the table. "If we were to use long shafts, thicker and stronger than the Dargonesti spears, attaching a pot of gnomefire to the ends—"

"We could ram the chilkit from a safe distance!" Gundabyr finished. He jotted down some figures. "The lance will be heavy, so we'll put two soldiers on each one. Congratulations, Colonel, you've invented the firelance!"

The Dargonesti artisans quickly grasped the idea, and a basic model was made. Normally, the sea elves used a species of seaweed for their spearshafts. Dried and treated with certain minerals, the strands of seaweed became rigid and stayed that way, even in water. However, the strands weren't thick enough for Armantaro's firelance. This problem was easily solved by braiding a great many strands together before the hardening process.

"How much time do we have?" asked the colonel.

"It's been two and a half days since the last chilkit attack," Vixa said. "They're still massing outside the city. There's no time to lose."

Virtually every artisan in Urione was drafted. Painters and house builders joined the shapers and toolmakers in turning out strong, thick shafts by the score.

Everyone worked that day, through the night, and all the next day as well. Armantaro caught snatches of sleep in the potters' den. Here pots were fired over a volcanic vent. It was the warmest, driest place in the city. Gundabyr spent most of his time supervising the making of more gnomefire than had ever been concocted at one time. Vixa helped inspect the final products before they were assembled and the gnomefire added to the pots.

The pots themselves were cylindrical, with a socket on one end, a lid on the other. The shaft of the lance went into the socket, and a pair of bronze pins was inserted to hold everything together. The gnomefire paste was poured in, and the lid anchored with a sticky, waterproof jelly made from mashed kelp. The resulting firelance was twenty feet long, weighing almost one hundred pounds.

On the second night of work, Vixa was alone in the warehouse, counting pots and shafts. Coryphene arrived with only a single warrior as escort. The Protector of Urione watched the Qualinesti princess from the doorway until she turned and saw him. Vixa dipped her head in a brief salute.

"Excellence."

"How many are there?" he asked.

"Four hundred twenty-seven. By daybreak, there will be five hundred."

"That will have to do. The sea brothers report that the chilkit are plundering and murdering in our outlying domain. We have no more time. I must save my people!"

This last was said with such fierce conviction that Vixa gave him a quick, startled glance. During these last few days as the Dargonesti and the drylanders worked together, it had been all too easy to forget that she and her friends were prisoners, captives of Coryphene and his divine queen. Vixa thought she understood him a bit better now, understood his single-minded quest for power. Above all, Coryphene was a patriot.

"Are you certain the firelances will work?" he demanded. She nodded. With hard eyes, he looked over the array of cylindrical pots and lance shafts.

"I pray so, lady," Coryphene said at last. "If we defeat the chilkit by this weapon of yours, you and all the drylanders shall be freed. I swear it."

He walked away without looking back.

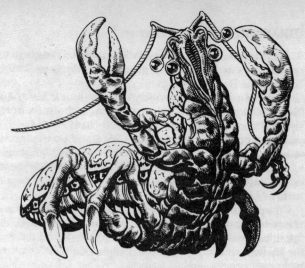

Chapter 13

Extermination

By morning, Coryphene had convened a council of war. His warrior chiefs and the priests of the great temples gathered to listen as the Protector and Queen Uriona laid out their plans.

The warriors filled the plaza in the center of the palace level. Their faces were hard and grim. There were gaps in their ranks. The priests and priestesses, on the other hand, prayed where they stood, calling on divine aid to save them from the chilkit. This annoyed the soldiers. Honor the gods, said the warriors, but listen to Coryphene Wallbuilder, Protector of Urione.

A dais ringed by curtains was set up for Queen Uriona. Her handmaids entered the plaza and flanked the dais. In unison they bowed their heads. The elves in the plaza did likewise as Uriona entered the enclosure. Coryphene, clad in his finest armor, appeared next.

The warrior chiefs raised both hands in salute and roared, "Coryphene! *Quoowahb kadai!*" which meant "The Dargonesti are with you!"

"Let there be silence," Coryphene intoned. "We are in the presence of our divine ruler, the goddess among us, Uriona Firstborn!"

A pall of silence fell instantly over the hundreds assembled in the plaza. Uriona's voice reached out from the veiled dais. Her words carried perfectly to every ear.

"My people," she proclaimed, "we stand on the threshold of our destiny. Today, the hated enemy will fall to us. I have asked the gods to bring us a weapon by which the foe can be destroyed. As always, my brother gods have seen fit to do as I asked."

Coryphene tipped a pot of gnomefire into a basin of seawater set up on the floor before the dais. It sputtered and burst into hissing flame. The priests recoiled, and many of the soldiers shifted uneasily away from a sight sea creatures had never beheld—naked flames.

"With this weapon, we cannot be defeated," Uriona went on. "I have seen our victory, and it will be glorious."

"Uriona!" Coryphene shouted. "*Quoowahb kadai!*"

The crowd took up and echoed his call over and over, until Coryphene raised a hand, signaling for silence. "The army will assemble on the plain of the kelp gardens," ordered the Protector. "All the firelances will be distributed to the left and right wings. When the battle commences, the wing commanders will attack, forcing the chilkit back. The wings will advance until the enemy breaks, then they will join to enclose the center. None shall escape us. None shall be spared!"

Once more Coryphene had to silence their cheers before he could speak. "Keep clear of the lance heads," he told them. "The yellow mixture inside burns when touched by water. If a pot bursts prematurely, the only way to put out the fire is to smother it with sand. Is that understood?" A clatter of weapons against shields signified the warriors' approval. Coryphene raised his voice, the words ringing through the square. "You know your places, soldiers! To victory! To victory!"

"To victory!" they shouted in return. "Coryphene! *Quoowahb kadai!* Uriona! *Quoowahb kadai!*"

The chiefs marched out to join their units. The priests and priestesses waited until the fighters were gone, then bowed and filed out silently. Uriona called to her warlord.

"Coryphene."

He went swiftly to the curtained enclosure. She seldom spoke his name. Hearing it now, feeling himself poised on the brink of his greatest victory, an intoxicating thrill went through his body. He knelt just outside the thin curtain.

"Yes, Divine Majesty?"

"Guard yourself, Coryphene. You are my instrument of destiny. Be valiant, but be careful as well."

"With Your Divinity to watch over me, nothing can touch me."

"Victory is assured. I have foreseen it. But—" The soft silhouette of the queen shifted on her ornate chair. "But our individual lives cannot be vouchsafed. Do you understand?"

"Yes, Divine Majesty, with all my heart."

He rose. Before he could take his leave, Uriona spoke again. "After the battle, there is a task to do. Only you can be trusted to accomplish it, Coryphene."

"You have only to name it, my queen."

"The drylanders must die. All of them. If any survive, it will endanger our expedition to Silvanost."

Coryphene, despite his absolute devotion to her, was shaken. "*All* of them? Even the princess of the Qualinesti?"

"Especially her. And the old colonel and the dwarf. They are a great danger to me, Coryphene. There is one other who must die. One of our own people."

He had no trouble guessing. "Naxos," he stated.

"Yes. He has already betrayed us to the drylanders. He plots with them to destroy us. To destroy me."

"He will not survive the battle! I vow it, Majesty!"

"Be wary of him. My brother gods may try to protect him."

"I fear no power but that of my divine queen," Coryphene said fervently. To his amazement, Uriona extended her hand through the curtain and held it for him to kiss. He took the hand in his, gazing at it as though he would memorize every line. The skin was fine as musselbeard silk, the webbing between the long, elegant fingers a translucent turquoise. Slowly, with all possible deference, Coryphene touched his lips to the soft hand.

"I am Your Majesty's slave," he whispered.

The hand was withdrawn, and Uriona spoke no more. Coryphene rose and strode from the empty plaza. Purpose blazed in his heart. Today would be the day of reckoning. Today the Dargonesti would defeat their dread enemy.

*   *   *   *   *

Rank upon rank of Dargonesti soldiers marched through the market square on their way to battle. The common folk of Urione lined the way, waving and singing. Some tossed scented water on the passing troops, a sign of special favor. The warriors filed into the quays and marched into the pools.

Of all the dryland prisoners, only three were in the square watching the soldiers go to meet the chilkit invaders. Vixa, Armantaro, and Gundabyr stood together. The old colonel stood straight as a pikestaff while the Dargonesti marched by, as if he were reviewing the troops. Vixa leaned on one arm against a low wall and counted the ranks. In a quarter hour she noted five thousand Dargonesti warriors had passed her.

"And still they come," she marveled. "Where does Coryphene get them?"

"Perhaps they're marching out, reentering the city, and marching past again, in a loop," Gundabyr wryly suggested. His bearded, craggy face was deeply shadowed from lack of sleep. "You know, to fool the hometown folks."

"You're wrong," Armantaro said. "I've not seen a face repeat." His martial stance and hawk-faced profile had attracted the attention of some of the Dargonesti soldiers. They'd begun to turn toward the Qualinesti colonel as they passed, giving a perfect "eyes left."

"A lot of these lads are new to arms. Look at the fit of their equipment. They're untried soldiers," the colonel remarked.

Vixa looked more closely and had to agree with his assessment. The spears were not ported at a sharp angle, the way veterans would carry them. Helmets seemed either too big or too small. Some of the Dargonesti even had empty scabbards flapping at their sides, as there were not enough weapons to go around.

A contingent of firelancers marched by, the new weapons on their shoulders. These were the best of Coryphene's troops, hand-picked for size and strength. Many had come from the ranks of the Protector's own guard. Considering the ferocity and size of the enemy they were to meet, their numbers seemed terribly small.

The sight of the ill-prepared youngsters and the too-few veterans galvanized Vixa into action. "I'm going out, too," she declared.

"What? Lady, you mustn't!" Armantaro objected.

"Can I stand idly by while others fight for my life? No!"

"I can," Gundabyr said calmly. "They took me prisoner, made me a slave, caused me to lose my brother. I made their damned gnomefire. Now it's their fight, Highness. Let 'em fight it."

"If you fight, then I shall be at your side," said the colonel.

Vixa clasped his arms. "No, my friend. Even if you won't admit it, I must—you're ill. That cough of yours gets worse daily."

Even as she said this, Armantaro's body shook as he smothered a cough. "It's nothing," he insisted.

"Stay here, Colonel. They'd never give you an airshell anyway."

"What about you?" asked Gundabyr. "What'll *you* do for air?"

"I have my own resources." Vixa moved to fall in with the passing ranks of soldiers. Armantaro would have followed, but she put a hand on his chest to stop him. "I order you to remain, Colonel," she said firmly. "As your commander and your princess."

"But, Your Highness—"

"No, Colonel. It is my official order—and my private

wish—that you stay in the city. If anything should happen to me, tell my mother . . ." She frowned, her voice trailing off.

He saluted. "I'll tell her you died bravely, in battle."

"You'll do no such thing. Tell my family to visit the seaside every year on Midsummer's Day. Tell them—" She smiled and departed without finishing the thought, merging into the column of tall sea elves. Armantaro quickly lost sight of her.

"What did she mean—visit the seashore?" asked Gundabyr.

"A joke, my friend." But the colonel looked anything but amused. Suddenly, an attack of coughing seized him. He turned his back on the ranks of marching elves, leaning on the wall for support. Gundabyr saw blood flecking his lips as he gasped for air.

At the quayside, a Dargonesti officer was directing lines of warriors into the water. Vixa remained hidden among the slow-moving ranks until she drew near the officer.

"You! Drylander! What are you doing here?"

"Going out," Vixa replied tersely.

"Are you mad? There's going to be a battle!"

"I know."

The lines of soldiery were walking down the ramp into the water. The rest of the pool was empty. Vixa spun, leapt, and hit the water in an arcing dive.

"Stupid drylander!" the officer yelled. "Where do you think you can go? You there—soldiers! Get her!"

Vixa swam hard for the passage leading into open water. She kicked furiously toward the archway. However, she felt hands seize her ankles. Three sea elves had caught her. She had no hope of shaking them off. The princess emptied her mind of everything but the memory of her dolphin body. The sleek black-and-white form filled her thoughts.

Heat flooded her body. The chill of the water was replaced by an expanding warmth. Vixa wanted to kick at the Dargonesti hands that held her ankles, but her legs had grown rigid. Of their own volition, her arms drew in tight against her sides. She knew an instant's panic as she felt herself being hauled back by the Dargonesti. The world tilted crazily.

Her Dargonesti captors suddenly cried out and fell back in shock. The leg they had been holding had become a muscular dolphin's tail. Though they were accustomed to the shapeshifters among their own people, this sudden transformation of a drylander took them completely by surprise.

Vixa fanned the water with her tail and shot out through the yawning arch. She turned up, gaining height over the sea bottom. The voices of her sea brethren were all around her.

"Hurry, hurry!" cried a dolphin voice. "The battle is joined!"

Vixa swam hard toward the sound. She sped through the water like a bird on the wing, passing schools of small fish. More dolphins gathered in the gloomy water. She fell in with a charging school of Dargonesti shapeshifters.

The ocean was filled with the sounds of battle. From below, the Dargonesti were calling every dolphin to come to their aid. Glancing back, Vixa saw hundreds streaming toward the scene of the conflict.

The chilkit were formed into a huge crescent, the horns of which threatened to close around Urione. The sea elves had sortied at four points and formed troops. The two center divisions of Dargonesti were being forced back under heavy chilkit attack. So far no gnomefire could be seen. Vixa prayed the formula would work. Everything had been prepared in such haste.

A dolphin hailed the princess. She didn't recognize him until he told her his name. He was Kios, the shapeshifter she'd met before. Following him, Vixa angled down with a hundred other dolphins to join the fight. A square of Dargonesti, bristling with spears, had been backed into the coral gardens on this side of the city. The chilkit, fighting in close ranks, sometimes almost standing on top of each other, advanced on them. Sand churned up around the feet of a thousand fighters. Blood drifted in the water like smoky clouds.

Kios let out a high-pitched cry and rammed into the back

of a chilkit. A half-second later, Vixa hit the next creature in line. The shock went through her from nose to tail, but she felt the red shell crack under the blow. Flexing her flukes, Vixa climbed out of reach of the chilkit's claws, circled, and dove again. Another shapeshifter streaked by her and hit the same target. The chilkit met him head-on. The monster's claws caught him on both flanks. Blood obscured them both for a moment, then Vixa saw the lifeless body of the shapeshifter sinking to the sandy bottom.

Shocked by his death and her own narrow escape, Vixa pointed her snout toward the surface. She raced upward in blind panic until her black-and-white head broke into the air in a blast of spray. Her thoughts whirled. The sun dazzled her.

Vixa rotated her body, scanning the horizon for possible landmarks. There was nothing to be seen but endless rolling waves. No hint of land marred the perfect line between sea and sky.

She knew she was somewhere in the great southern ocean called Turbidus. If she swam directly north she would find land eventually. Her dolphin form could make the trip with ease, no matter how long it took. Should she go? Didn't she have a duty to escape, to warn the nations of Ansalon about the threat of the Dargonesti and—most especially—about Queen Uriona's mad plan to conquer the elven nations?

What about her friends? Coryphene had sworn to free them if the battle was won. That was her first duty. She couldn't simply leave them to their fates. Vixa took in a great breath and dove once more for the depths.

Descending toward the city, the princess circled the battle site. The underwater cries of the Dargonesti added to the cacophony. From her position, Vixa saw that the chilkit had fought through the coral garden to the base of Urione itself. The Dargonesti wings had held, so now the chilkit formation resembled a giant red horseshoe. What was Coryphene waiting for? It was time to use the gnomefire!

Throwing caution to the wind, she dove hard at the center of the Dargonesti position. Coryphene was easy to spot, in the front ranks surrounded by the remainder of his guard. His tall, decorated helmet stood up above the rest. Hurtling over his head, she shouted his name. The Protector was too busy battling a chilkit to reply. Vixa doubled back and rammed the chilkit he fought.

"You there! Sea brother!"

She cruised by him, regarding him with one bright eye. "Thank you for your aid," he called in the water-tongue. "Do I know you?"

"Why have you not used the firelances?" she demanded.

"By the Abyss! Who are you to give me counsel?" Beneath his heavy helm, Coryphene's brow knitted. Suddenly, the frown lifted, to be replaced by a look of astonishment. "I *do* know you! Vixa Ambrodel! What—what are you doing in this guise?"

She ignored the question. "You'll be backed into your own plaza soon! Why don't you bring up the firelances?"

Coryphene was hailed by several other sea brothers. They'd brought the same question from his flank commanders.

"You have so little faith in our queen's genius," he told them all darkly. "Very well," the Protector said at last. "Bring forth the firelances! To the fore, all firelances!"

Vixa sped off to the left flank. She shouted Coryphene's order in her dolphin voice. Her words carried far. By the time she reached the left flank, the long lances tipped with the pottery cylinders were hoisted and ready. The chilkit were obviously not impressed by the unusual weapons. They closed ranks and came on.

"Now!"

The first line of firelancers dashed their weapons into the foe. Seawater mixed with the paste as the pots shattered, and a hundred chilkit were immediately engulfed in flames. The front lines of both armies pulled back, leaving the burning creatures in a zone of fire.

Underwater, gnomefire burned fiercely, but there was no smoke. Instead, huge bubbles of combustive gases boiled out of the flaming paste. The bubbles hit like forge hammers, hot and hard, as the chilkit and dolphins found out. One struck Vixa a glancing blow in her belly, driving the wind from her body. She raced for the city shell and surfaced in one of the lower-level quays. After a moment to catch her breath, she returned once more to the fray.

On both flanks the chilkit line gave way. The firelancers pressed forward, backed by armed Dargonesti.

In the center, Coryphene called for his reserve corps. A thousand fresh sea elves sprang up from hollows in the sandy bottom. The chilkit line fragmented. Individual chilkit were easily mown down by the more numerous, faster-moving Dargonesti spear fighters. Wherever the chilkit managed to re-form to stand off the Dargonesti, firelancers were brought up. Hundreds of chilkit were consumed by fresh infernos.

Vixa swooped in and out of the fight, hammering chilkit, saving Dargonesti who were menaced or who had fallen to the enemy. Over the din of battle, she heard her name being called. She stiffened to alertness.

"Sea brothers, to me!" cried the voice. Vixa found herself turning to obey.

A larger dolphin blocked her path. "Kios?" A raucous dolphin chuckle told her she was wrong. "Naxos!" she exclaimed.

The chief of the shapeshifters bobbed his head in the affirmative. "How do you like battle, little dryfoot? Isn't this better than sucking air from an old whelk shell?"

"Naxos—don't you hear the call?"

"It's only Coryphene. Ignore him."

"I can't," she complained. "I am compelled!" It was true. The call acted like a powerful magnet drawing her toward its source.

Naxos circled her slowly. "It's a sorcery he uses on the weak-minded. Resist it! You are freeborn."

"Sea brothers! To me! I command you!" The pressure became stronger, pulling her away from Naxos.

"I must go!" she cried. Resistance seemed impossible. He followed, keeping pace with her.

A thick cloud of dolphins had formed over the center of the battlefield. Amid columns of coiling, bubbling water, Vixa maneuvered to reach Coryphene. The Protector and his personal guard were mounting the dolphins as though they were horses. Coryphene climbed onto a sea brother that Vixa recognized as Kios.

"They have broken!" Coryphene exulted in the water-tongue. "Now is the time to drive the chilkit back into the dark depths forever!"

The triumph in his voice and the victorious cries of the other Dargonesti—dolphin and elven alike—filled Vixa's brain and set her blood tingling. She joined some of the riderless dolphins who were swooping and swirling around their Protector.

"I am with you!" Vixa chirped.

Coryphene threw down his shield. A warrior handed him three spears. Coryphene raised them in a bundle over his head. "Death to the enemies of Urione! No quarter! No quarter!" he roared.

Less than a thousand Dargonesti, mounted on dolphins, rose up from the battlefield and swept down on the retreating chilkit. Vixa and the other riderless dolphins surged ahead, harrying the fragmented enemy. The chilkit armor was thinner on top and vulnerable to spear thrusts. Coryphene killed six chilkit with his first spear before it broke. He grabbed a second weapon.

"Go on! Go on!" he commanded. "Let none survive!"

Vixa ploughed onward, turning this way and that, helping the sea brothers chase down any chilkit they saw moving. The ocean became so thick with chilkit blood, she no longer tasted the sea's salt, only a sickening sweetness.

The broken wall at the mouth of the Mortas Trench appeared. Vixa rose and shot through the gap. Below, red-shelled creatures were pouring back down the dark slope, seeking escape from the vengeful sea elves.

Coryphene had no intention of letting them go. He rallied his scattered dolphin riders and ordered the last battalion of firelancers to follow them. Tired but exuberant Dargonesti cheered him and followed in his wake.

Vixa swam mechanically now. Exhaustion was sapping her will. The dolphins, with and without riders, sped deeper and deeper into the black water. A running fight

ensued as individual chilkit turned to make their stand in
the murky shadows. Their bravery surprised Vixa, who had
grown used to thinking of them as cruel and mindless monsters. They were not. They helped their own wounded comrades, defending them from fresh attacks. But they were too
scattered to offer an effective defense. Whenever four or
five chilkit banded together, firelancers were called to put
them to the torch. Soon the trench floor was lit by a dozen
burning gnomefires.

Vixa left only once, taking in fresh air. Angling back down
to the seafloor, she rounded a bend in the trench and saw a
red glow that wasn't gnomefire. Ripples of unpleasantly hot
water washed by her. The floor of the trench had split open,
and lava was oozing out of the seabed. The red snake of
molten rock filled the rift for miles.

Suddenly, Naxos appeared at her side. "Coryphene
means to slaughter them all!" he exclaimed.

"Why? The battle is won."

"He is drunk with destruction. The chilkit are completely
broken, yet still he wages war. Sea brothers are put in danger for no reason!"

"I'll talk to him," she said as she shot away from Naxos.
She had no idea what she might say, but she had to try.

In the hot, weird waters of the trench, Vixa swam slowly
along a line of Dargonesti foot soldiers. At their head she
found the dolphin riders, led by Coryphene.

"The day is ours, Princess!" he exulted.

"You have defeated them utterly, Excellence. The battle is
over."

He shook his head. "None must survive. They will only
threaten our children someday."

"Talk to them then. Make peace with them. There's no
need for more Dargonesti lives to be lost."

"Talk to monsters? You've seen them in battle—do they
know anything of mercy?" She had no answer.

Vixa swam away. The last chilkit had their backs to the
lava flow. Faced with gnomefire on the one hand and lava
on the other, they charged the Dargonesti. Many sea elves
died in that last charge, perishing in a battle they'd already

won. Coryphene pressed the enemy with firelances. The remaining chilkit withdrew to a low mound. Lava flowed around the base and climbed its sides. Coryphene called his warriors back at last.

The chilkit stood fast, holding steady in the midst of the lava stream. Gradually, the lava reached them, and covered them. When the last chilkit was engulfed, Coryphene ordered a quick retreat, for the ocean was near to boiling.

The plain between the Mortas Trench and Urione presented a grisly scene. Thousands of Dargonesti were pouring out of the city now that the chilkit were defeated. They covered the plain, dispatching wounded chilkit with clubs, gaffs, even rocks. Chilkit claws were hacked off as edible trophies, and the bodies thrown on the still-burning gnomefires. Patrolling dolphins kept the sharks at bay while the carnage went on.

Coryphene was spotted as he returned from the trench. Ten thousand arms raised in salute. Ten thousand Dargonesti voices keened in triumph. The Protector accepted the adulation with a wave of his last spear.

The moment of victory was spoiled, however, as a single dolphin hurtled into view. Naxos brushed Coryphene with his powerful flukes, knocking the Protector from Kios's back.

"Traitor!" Coryphene hissed. "Blasphemer!"

"Whom have I betrayed? You?"

"You have betrayed your lawful sovereign by consorting with the drylanders. You have blasphemed our divine queen, and shared our sacred mysteries with a land-dweller. There she is!"

He pointed to Vixa with his spear. Frightened and embarrassed, she glared at them both.

Coryphene's loyal troops drew close around him. Naxos taunted, "Leave your guards, Excellence. Face the sea brothers on your own!"

Hundreds of Dargonesti warriors shouted insults and threats at the lone shapeshifter. To her consternation, Vixa realized that none of the sea brothers were coming to their chief's defense. Not even Kios, his second-in-command, had a word to say for Naxos.

"Face the sea brothers, you say?" Coryphene jeered. "I see only a single traitor who has no brothers."

Naxos had been swimming with studied nonchalance several fathoms above Coryphene. In a flash of gray, he dove at the Protector. Coryphene stood ready, spear lying in the crook of his right arm. A dolphin Naxos's size could shatter the armor of a chilkit. If he rammed Coryphene, there was no way the Protector could survive.

Vixa had been so riveted by this interplay, she'd sacrificed vigilance. Several warriors seized her. She struggled, but was too exhausted and too outnumbered to escape.

Coryphene dropped his spear butt to the top of his right foot and, with one powerful kick, launched the weapon at Naxos. The shapeshifter twisted to avoid the flashing spear, but it caught him on the back, just behind his dorsal fin. Coryphene looked on impassively as Naxos thrashed and rolled, trying to dislodge the spear. Vixa heard the shaft snap. The head remained embedded. In a welter of sand and blood, Naxos sped away, inches off the ocean floor.

"Let him go," Coryphene told his guard. "The sharks shall be his healers."

The Protector glanced around. Kios and the other sea brothers had scattered. They were gone in the blink of an eye, their chance to support their chief likewise vanished. Coryphene Wallbuilder stood amid the scene of his greatest victory, uncontested master of Urione.

Chapter 14

Treachery

Four Dargonesti warriors towed Vixa back into the city. They heaved her out of the water and onto a quay. No sooner had her flukes left the water than she felt great heat wash over her. Concentrate, she told herself wearily. Visualize yourself as elven.

Without the water to cool her, the heat of her dolphin form continued to build. She shuddered and closed her eyes, trying to clear her mind of everything except the desire to be elven once more. She felt the strange stretching of her limbs as first arms, then legs returned. Instantly, cold flooded her elven body. Goosebumps rose on flesh that was still fading from dolphin-black to Qualinesti-pale. The quay upon which she lay felt like an ice floe.

Coryphene emerged from the pool. For the first time Vixa saw the many injuries he'd sustained in battle. Slashes, scratches, and violet bruises covered his bare torso and limbs. He beckoned to a waiting elf who held a long cloak of woven seaweed for the Protector. She was surprised when Coryphene had the cloak draped around her instead of himself. Then he helped her to stand.

Vixa's teeth chattered uncontrollably. Her knees buckled, but Coryphene supported her with one arm.

"I'm ill," she muttered through blue lips.

"Your body is not meant to take the shape of a sea brother," Coryphene said.

She shrugged free of his arm. "What punishment do you have planned for me?"

Wiping his wet hair back from his face with one hand, he exhaled gustily. "I am tired, lady. I must bear tidings of our victory to Her Divine Majesty now." Coryphene stepped away from her. Giving her a brief, unreadable look, he turned away. "I will consider your disposition later."

"Will you keep your word, Protector of Urione?" she called to his back. "Will you free the dryland captives?"

He gave no sign that he heard, but went to where his guard had formed up, in the archway leading into the city. The narrow street beyond was jammed with hysterical Dargonesti, intoxicated by the defeat of their enemy. Coryphene visibly steeled himself, squaring his shoulders and taking a deep breath, before plunging into the crowd.

He marched away with his warriors. Thousands cheered him as he passed.

The Qualinesti princess pulled the cloak more tightly around her shivering body and made her weary way toward the House of Arms.

* * * * *

The victory over the chilkit transformed the status of Gundabyr and the Qualinesti. No longer were they despised, for the population of Urione knew how the drylanders had contributed to the defeat of the enemy. Hostility turned to generosity. Armantaro and the dwarf could not show themselves in the street without being inundated with gifts and praise.

"If I eat any more, I'll burst!" Gundabyr said. His vest buttons were straining to contain his protruding belly.

Edible gifts filled the House of Arms—dried, seasoned fish, exotic sauces and jellies made from seaweed, live shrimp in tanks of water, Dargonesti nectar—on and on the list went. Armantaro divided the spoils among the remaining dryland captives. It was the best eating any of them had done in a long, long time.

Armantaro was staring into space, preoccupied with his own thoughts, so Gundabyr repeated his complaint.

"Then stop eating so much," the colonel snapped. He'd eaten very little himself. The fiery sensation in his chest had killed his appetite. He spent his time worrying about his absent princess.

"What in the name of the Abyss has happened to her?" Armantaro demanded. It had been two days since they'd last seen Vixa. She had returned to the House of Arms after the final battle, wan, worn, and barely able to stand. After sleeping all that night and half the next day, Vixa had departed, refusing to tell even Armantaro where she was bound.

Any news the colonel and the dwarf had of the great battle, they'd gleaned from passing soldiers. Vixa had told them nothing. They knew she'd fought as a dolphin. They also knew that Naxos, the chief of the sea brothers, had crossed Coryphene and had been killed for his disloyalty.

"Maybe she's with Coryphene," suggested Gundabyr.

Armantaro stood up suddenly. "If he harms her . . ." the colonel rasped darkly.

"Why should he? She helped win the war, too."

"If he trifles with her, he'll wish the chilkit had taken him!" The vehemence of this statement surprised Gundabyr. He hadn't realized the depth of fatherly feeling the old Qualinesti colonel had for his young commander.

"If she can fight off red-shelled monsters, she can probably handle one blueskin," Gundabyr said dryly "She did pretty well as a dolphin."

Armantaro frowned. That aspect of the situation did not please him either. The colonel felt Naxos had manipulated her into becoming a shapeshifter. The more he thought about it, the angrier it made him. He stalked away from the dwarf.

"Where are you going?" Gundabyr called.

"To find Princess Vixa."

Gundabyr, opening a fresh pot of caviar, sighed. "You know how the blueskins are these days. You'll be mobbed by adoring Quoowahb before you get five paces out the door."

This was only too true. Armantaro rummaged through the gifts of clothing piled in the center of the great room. Among these was a fine sharkskin cape covered in silver scales. He whipped this around his neck and pulled the hood up.

"I'll pass for one of them," he said confidently. "They'll leave me alone."

"Oh, yes, a short albino Quoowahb—that's you all right. You're a stubborn cuss, you know that? Here the Dargonesti are finally beginning to make up for their treatment of us, and you want to go and antagonize their leader, a fellow with a temper the size of the whole southern sea. Don't you remember Nissia, Colonel? Do you want to end up a prisoner again?"

"As far as I can tell, I still am a prisoner. Better fed and warmer, maybe, but a prisoner nonetheless."

Armantaro swept from the room. No Dargonesti stood guard, so no one challenged him.

The victory celebrations had finally died down, and the streets were nearly deserted. Armantaro kept the hood close around his face. The House of Arms was some twenty levels below the palace. Climbing the wide ramp upward took most of Armantaro's strength. More than once he had to sit down and gasp for breath. On the floor just below the palace, he left the central way. No sense barging right in—Coryphene's magical barrier would warn him if anyone entered the palace by that means.

This level housed the armory, the barracks of the Protector's guards, storehouses of food and drink for the royal residence, and the Dargonesti treasury. Armantaro avoided the well-guarded barracks and treasury, skulking instead beside the silent warehouses. There ought to be a back stair around here somewhere.

Sure enough, down an alley between a row of stone storage huts, Armantaro found steps leading up. From the wear on them, he guessed servants had been using them for many, many years. Cautiously, he climbed into the darkness.

He could smell cooking—most unusual, since the Dargonesti ate their food raw or dried.

The steps led up through a large slot cut in the thick granite floor. Armantaro had entered the palace larder. The only light came from an open doorway. A rattle of pottery and a few distant words came through the opening as well. He crept forward, peering through the doorway.

Two Dargonesti were dipping dirty plates in a kettle of water to clean them. Both were grimacing ferociously.

"What a stink!" said one of the sea elves. "What is the Protector doing out there?"

The other glared at the dishes, saying tartly, "Does His Excellence tell me his business? What an awful smell!"

Armantaro got to his hands and knees and crawled behind a long table laden with kitchen implements. The servants had their backs to him and never heard him pass. In the pantry beyond the kitchen, the colonel got shakily to his feet. Curtains wavered in the doorway. He peeked through, saw an empty corridor, and started down it.

When he drew near the far end, he saw to his right the audience hall used by Queen Uriona. Vixa had described in detail her meeting with the queen there, and he had no trouble recognizing the place. To his left was a smaller chamber, set up as a dining room. Coryphene stood by a waist-high brazier, atop which blazed a stone crucible filled with hissing gnomefire. Thin smoke rose from the fire. Coryphene laid a bit of white meat atop the crucible. A few paces from the brazier was a single small table, and seated at it was the queen herself.

Armantaro halted, momentarily taken aback. This was his first sight of Queen Uriona, and he had to admit the princess's quick description of her had not done her justice. Her complexion was dark blue, her eyes large and lustrous violet, like twin amethysts. She had silver hair of a metallic sheen he'd never seen before. It was pulled back from her face in gentle waves, leaving her upswept ears free. Seated as she was, the thick braid of her hair—twined through with strands of shells and pearls—brushed the floor. Her cheekbones were high and prominent, her nose narrow and tilted slightly upward at the end. She appeared to be somewhere in her second century and certainly looked the part of a goddess. Her words, which came to Armantaro's acute ears, were frighteningly at variance with her elegant beauty.

"—your cleansing of the chilkit vermin," she was saying. "We could not afford to let a single beast live. They would certainly have returned to harass us someday."

"It is possible that some still live on some far-off abyssal plain," Coryphene reminded her.

She waved a slender hand. "They will not bother us again. As I look into the future, I see no chilkit to impede us." Uriona lifted to her lips an exquisitely fashioned goblet of shell and silver inlay. "Put more on the fire, Coryphene," she commanded.

The Protector dropped another bit of white meat on the gnomefire. "It smells terrible, Divine Queen," he said, his face stony with disgust.

"If I am to rule on land, I must become accustomed to eating food burned by fire. Bring me more of the chilkit."

With Armantaro's own dagger, Coryphene speared a chunk of some slain chilkit—and transferred it to a scallop-shell plate. The meat was seared on the ends, but the middle was still pink. Though it smelled remarkably like crab, Armantaro felt his stomach twisting with nausea. A warrior did not eat his enemies—even if his enemy was a chilkit. It was nothing short of cannibalism.

Coryphene presented the dish to Uriona like a priest making an offering. She picked apart the meat with her long nails. Wordlessly, she ate a tiny tidbit.

"Divinity?"

"Yes?"

"Is it—is it necessary that the drylander girl be slain?"

The words speared Armantaro through the heart. He held his breath as Coryphene continued. "She has become one of the sea brothers. Now that Naxos is dead, Kios has given me his fealty. In time I believe Vixa Ambrodel will become your loyal servant, like the others."

Uriona smiled. She really was remarkably beautiful. Yet the light that shone behind her startling eyes was not the light of wisdom, courage, or love. Armantaro saw only madness there.

"You admire her, don't you?" she murmured. Coryphene's blue coloring deepened. "Do you want her for your own?"

"Your Majesty knows I love only you! There is no other for me!" he said loudly. He returned to the sputtering fire. After a moment, he said more calmly, "Naxos was an insolent, traitorous wretch. I felt no pity at his death. The old dryland elf can die as well, but I feel it is unjust to slay the Qualinesti princess and the dwarf. It is because of them that we have our victory."

Uriona's customarily serene expression dissolved into a flash of anger. She stood abruptly and swept the table clean of implements. "Fool!" she cried. "Your victory is due to *me*, the divine queen of the sea! How dare you share my honor with mortal drylanders!"

Instantly, Coryphene went down on one knee, begging forgiveness, but Uriona turned away and stalked to the far end of the room, keeping her back to Coryphene. Armantaro ached to have his dagger in hand.

The Protector rose and went around the table. He stopped only a few feet from the angry queen.

"No one has served you better than I," he said, his voice tight and low. "From the day I saw you in your father's court in Watermere, I have loved you. Because of this love I have performed many difficult tasks for you—some shameful, some a stain on my warrior's honor. You owe me a boon, Uriona." He closed in, taking her by the shoulders. "Give me these two lives!"

"Release me!" she hissed, shocked at this liberty. Yet, he did not obey. She lifted one hand, palm facing the warlord. A surge of power shot out. Even from his hiding place, Armantaro felt it. It was like standing too near the open door of a dwarven blast furnace. Naked heat seared his body. He trembled. The Qualinesti colonel was amazed that Coryphene could withstand the queen's magic at such close range.

"Strike me dead, if you choose," the Protector said flatly, "but I will not be dissuaded."

The need to cough finally became too much for Armantaro. Coughing exploded from his mouth. He reeled away, blundering against the wall. He'd gone only a few paces back toward the kitchen when strong hands seized him from behind.

"So! You dare spy on Her Divine Majesty?"

Coryphene dragged the weakened Armantaro into the room and hurled him to the floor. The Qualinesti couldn't control his coughing, and blood from his spittle stained the white marble. Once the spasm had ended, Armantaro pushed himself up on his hands and knees.

"You see, Coryphene!" Uriona said triumphantly. "The drylanders invade my sacred precinct! And these are the people you would spare. We will never be safe from such as he."

"Foolish drylander," snarled Coryphene. The warlord hauled the old colonel to his feet, gripping him by the neck of the sharkskin cape. His words were as icy as the deep ocean. "Had you stayed in your place, I might have saved your princess. By your treachery you have condemned her to death as well."

"Your designs cannot succeed," Armantaro said hoarsely.

Coryphene drew the dagger from his waist. "No mortal hand can stop us. My queen rules all destiny. You brought the instrument of your own death with you. I give it back to you now."

There was steel yet in the old colonel's limbs. He'd hung limp in Coryphene's grasp. Now he grabbed the dagger hilt in both hands, surprising the warlord and wrestling the weapon from him. The Protector's reaction was that of a seasoned fighter: he threw himself back, out of Armantaro's reach.

Without pause, the colonel thrust the knife at the unprotected queen. Uriona put out her hand—not to ward off his blow, but to deliver one of her own.

A blast of heat hit Armantaro in the chest. He was lifted off his feet and flung backward. The dagger hilt was still in his hand, but the blade was gone. Spatters of molten iron on the floor testified to the force of Uriona's power.

"Finish him," she said disdainfully. Coryphene took Armantaro by the throat and lifted him. His powerful webbed fingers closed around the Qualinesti's neck. Blood thundered in Armantaro's head, and a red haze closed in around him.

A servant ran in and prostrated himself on the floor, careful not to look upon the divine face of his queen. "Gracious goddess!" he cried. "Lord Kios of the sea brothers begs for an immediate audience with Lord Protector Coryphene!"

His fury distracted, Coryphene released his death grip on Armantaro. The colonel dropped to the floor, racked with gasping coughs. Coryphene took two deep breaths. His gills flared out and relaxed again behind his ears.

"It is not fitting for you to see death, Divine One," he said to Uriona. "I will take the drylander out and dispose of him."

He gestured to the servant, who dragged the helpless Armantaro into the audience hall. Coryphene strode out after them.

"I have not given you leave to go," Uriona said sharply.

He turned. "I did not ask it. I will hear Kios and dispose of the drylander. Then I shall return, Majesty."

He walked out, proud and fierce. Alone in the chamber, Uriona smiled. It had taken a long time, but she had finally provoked Coryphene into asserting himself. If he was to be her consort, as she fervently wished, he'd better learn to speak up and stop playing the toady.

* * * * *

Vixa swam slowly along the bottom, probing the gloom around her. The Mortas Trench was hardly an inviting place at the best of times. In the aftermath of the climactic battle, it was hellish. Moray eels, sharks, and other carnivores prowled the dark recesses, feeding on dead chilkit drifting in the current. Strange how they lost their vivid crimson color after death. The chilkit bodies had turned pure white.

For two days Vixa had searched for Naxos in the unfamiliar environs around Urione. She had been encouraged by not finding his body, but her hope was giving way to despair. There were no clues at all. The gardens of kelp and coral were empty. No trace of the sea brothers' former chief could be found near the shrimp pens, the quarry, or the shell heaps where the Dargonesti discarded all the shellfish debris from the city. That left only one other place to search: Mortas.

Vixa had learned that as a dolphin her hearing was her greatest strength. Swimming slowly along the floor of the trench, she heard a constant background of noises, but nothing that sounded like the wounded Naxos.

She called to him. There was no response. She called more loudly. The only answer was the susurration of water lapping against the excavations made by the chilkit.

She cruised over to a large opening in the mountainside. This must be the tunnel the chilkit had made to enter Nissia Grotto. Cautiously, she swam inside the black pit. Small creatures scurried away as she approached. The sea was already claiming the tunnel for its own.

Ripples above her indicated a surface to the water. Her beak broke into air. She found herself in a small air pocket, perhaps ten paces wide. It was very cold in here. Mist jetted from Vixa's open mouth. She swam quietly in a circle, surveying the walls of the cave. By the marks on the stone she could tell that this area had been carved out by the chilkit.

Suddenly, Vixa saw something protruding between the rocks. She moved closer. It was a foot. She reared up and nudged the foot with her beak. To her shock, it moved.

"Who's there?" asked a weak voice, speaking Elvish.

She squeaked in response. A pale face appeared among the dark rocks. Naxos!

"Vixa Ambrodel, how nice to see you," he said as casually as though they were meeting on the street.

She called up her human form. Though she'd transformed several times now, the sensation still astonished her.

Her limbs stretched and the world changed. The dense muscularity of the dolphin was replaced by the tall litheness of the elf maiden. Soon she was treading water, her teeth chattering with the chill. She levered herself onto the narrow shelf of rock.

"Forgive me if I don't rise," Naxos whispered, gesturing to his injury. Coryphene's spear had taken him in the hip. The wound was clean, but large.

"Praise Astra! You're alive!" she exclaimed. "I've been looking for you for days!"

"Looking for me?" His face twisted. "For Coryphene, I suppose."

Her eyes flashed. "You say such a thing! Coryphene thinks you're dead, you stupid blueskin!"

He smiled wanly. "I beg your pardon, Princess. Pain and hunger have taken away all my charm, I fear."

He lay in a depression in the rock, with nothing to soothe his wound or make his berth comfortable. Vixa couldn't believe he still lived after lying in this damp, cold place for three days. She knelt beside him.

"So Coryphene thinks me dead? Let us hope that mistake will prove fatal for him," Naxos said softly. He winced as he shifted position.

"Kios has pledged his loyalty and that of the sea brothers to Coryphene and Uriona."

"Ah, brotherhood," Naxos sighed, but his heart wasn't in the sarcasm.

Vixa said, more cheerfully, "Now that I've found you, we can all escape. You and I can carry Armantaro and Gundabyr to land."

He gestured to his hip. "I'm not going anywhere like this. The muscle's damaged, and if I start bleeding in the water, the sharks will finish what our Protector started."

They looked at each other silently, pondering their predicament. Water dripped from overhead. "I'll bring you food and find some medicine," Vixa said firmly. "We'll heal your wound, *then* we'll escape."

"No."

"What?"

"Coryphene will notice your comings and goings. If he suspects I still live, he and that witch-queen of his will smell me out with their magic."

Naxos sat up, aggravating his injury and causing him to give vent to a howl of pain and anger. His breath hissed between his teeth, and he went on more calmly, "Listen, Princess. Do you know the precinct of the temples, in the city?" She nodded. "In the temple of Zura you will find a cistern fed by fresh water pouring from the mouth of the god's image. You must go there, fill an amphora with the water, and bring it back here to me."

"Why? Will it heal you?"

"Yes. . . . Yes, it will." There was a slight hesitancy to his words.

"And what else?" she asked suspiciously.

"Nothing that matters. Bring me the water, but be certain to seal the amphora before you swim out here. Don't let the water of Zura mix with seawater."

Vixa slid back into the pool and resumed dolphin form. She caught some small fish and brought them back for Naxos. The ravenous Dargonesti ate them with gusto. At his instruction, she brought him several long strands of kelp. These he made into a thick pad, pressing it to his wound.

"Bring back the water of Zura, Princess, and we will escape the same day!" he adjured her.

She bobbed her dolphin head vigorously in reply and sank beneath the water.

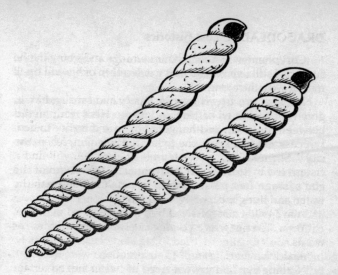

Chapter 15

Water of Zura

As the days went by, the thirty or so slaves who'd survived the flooding of Nissia Grotto began to drift out of the House of Arms. Singly and in pairs, as boredom overcame their fear of the Dargonesti, they wandered out of the citadel and into the city.

What Gundabyr found strange was that he never saw any of them on his jaunts through the streets, and none of the former slaves ever returned to the House of Arms. Six days after the battle, only a handful of men remained in the headquarters of the Urionan army. These were drylanders too sick or too injured to be up and about.

Three days earlier Armantaro had stormed off to locate Vixa, and he'd not returned either. A messenger had come from the palace bringing word to Gundabyr that the colonel was remaining there, to be with his princess and because his cough needed treatment. Still, the dwarf felt a bit like the kender cavalry commander in the famous story. "Charge the foe!" cried the kender commander, and five hundred kender on ponies charged—back the way they'd come. The commander, oblivious to this fact, rode on to meet the enemy alone.

Gundabyr resolved to seek out Armantaro and Vixa. Anything had to be better than sitting on his rump in this citadel day after day with nothing to do and no one to do it with. He needed something to occupy his mind, other than sad thoughts of Garnath.

There was no disguising his squat dwarven frame in a city of seven-foot-tall people, so he didn't try. The majority of the sea elves had finally moved on to other diversions, and the crowds that followed him now consisted mainly of children. Ten or twelve young sea elves, some of them as tall as adult Qualinesti, tried to tag along behind him as he mounted the central ramp. Their attentions were innocent, but Gundabyr had grown tired of being stared at. He whirled around and shouted, "Go home!" The startled children fled. Gundabyr stumped onward.

When he reached the top of the ramp, he was surprised to discover the magic barrier that usually concealed its entrance was no more. Beyond the ramp, he could see the green of the palace glimmering. There were no guards in sight. He entered the palace plaza and received another surprise.

The great courtyard was clogged with equipment: stands of spears by the thousands, sacks of provisions, armor, helmets, and most astonishing of all, enormous piles of cylindrical clay pots, just like the ones he'd designed to hold the gnomefire for the firelances. The Dargonesti were obviously stockpiling fresh supplies, but why? The chilkit menace was gone.

He could hear Dargonesti moving about in other parts of the plaza, but the heaps of goods screened his view. The dwarf made his way along an aisle that snaked through the military equipment. He soon came to a clearing in which stood a table. Kelp paper was strewn on the tabletop. He scanned the first document that came to hand. It was a map. Gundabyr couldn't read the angular Dargonesti printing, but by the shape of the river delta and coastline, he guessed this was a chart of southern Silvanesti.

"You there! Drylander! Do not move!"

Gundabyr hadn't been addressed in that tone for quite some time. A quartet of Dargonesti soldiers approached rapidly. Their leader snatched the map from the dwarf's hand and shoved him backward.

"Remove this drylander from the royal residence," said the officer in a nasty tone.

When the three Dargonesti soldiers advanced, Gundabyr clenched a fist the size of a nail keg and punched the Dargonesti officer in the stomach. The lightly built sea elf went over backward, air whooshing out of his mouth. He collided with his squad. All four went down like ninepins.

The sprawling Dargonesti made a most diverting sight, but the sound of marching feet told Gundabyr that reinforcements were coming. This was no place for a lone forgemaster! He grabbed the map of the Silvanesti coast, shoved it under his vest, then ran. The fact that they hadn't wanted him to see the map told him it must be important.

The masses of arms and supplies had turned the formerly open plaza into a maze. Gundabyr went down one winding aisle after another, but he kept running into Dargonesti. He decided to make his own path. Kicking over a stand of spears, he bulled through the rows of equipment. Shouts echoed through the plaza. Someone cast a spear at him. It missed, clattering harmlessly against the hard floor. Gundabyr put his head down and stormed through a wall of shields. His stumpy legs got caught, and he tripped. The shields toppled over, covering him.

He lay still. The Dargonesti were searching nearby. When he heard their footfalls recede, he crawled slowly out from under the shields. He got about five yards before the way was blocked by a large bundle lying on the floor. The dwarf shoved, but the bundle was heavy. As he pushed against it, his hands felt its contents. It felt almost like—

Casting quick glances left and right, Gundabyr worked at the lacing on the brown seaweed covering. Sure enough, a knobby human hand poked out of the hole he made. Why was a dead human lying in the palace plaza?

He realized there were a number of bundles here, pretty

much identical. Cold anger seized his heart. No wonder the slaves had never returned to the House of Arms. Coryphene had had them murdered!

A heavy stone had been placed in each makeshift shroud. The dwarf raged silently against Coryphene. After the drylanders had been instrumental in the defeat of the chilkit, the Protector couldn't simply execute the prisoners. That might disrupt the victory atmosphere. No, he had let the slaves think they were going to be freed, then secretly had them killed! Reorx take his eyes, he had given his word!

One bundle was noticeably longer than the rest. Swallowing hard, Gundabyr inched toward its head and pulled the seaweed cloth apart.

Armantaro.

Now he was truly afraid. He hadn't seen Princess Vixa in days. Perhaps she was dead as well. Aside from the few sick and injured humans in the House of Arms, Gundabyr might be the only drylander left in Urione.

"Things don't look good for our young dwarf," he murmured.

Reverently, he covered Armantaro's face. The Qualinesti colonel had been a good fellow, a brave fighter, and a wise elf. Gundabyr said a little prayer to Reorx, asking him to put in a good word with Astra, highest god of the Qualinesti. When he was done, he said a second prayer for himself. He would need plenty of divine aid if he was going to get out of this predicament alive.

He crawled on, using his powerful arms to drag himself forward. He reached the line of columns that encircled the plaza. The clutter of goods did not extend into the colonnade, so Gundabyr stood. He could hear the clash and clatter as the soldiers combed the stockpile behind him. Now was the time to make his move.

Skulking along the shadowed wall, Gundabyr went as quietly as his bulky physique allowed. There were numerous doorways to cross, and he never knew, when he dashed from one side to the other, if someone in the passage would see him and raise the alarm. After six such heart-pounding crossings, he paused, flattening himself against the palace wall. There were voices ahead.

Coryphene and two soldiers had emerged from a corridor and were standing under the portico. "Join the search," Coryphene told the soldiers. "Find the dwarf, immediately."

"And the other prisoner?" asked one of the Quoowahb.

The Protector glanced back the way they'd come. "She is secure. Go."

She! That could only be Vixa Ambrodel. She must still be alive! Gundabyr waited until Coryphene walked away before slipping into the corridor. There were several arched openings off this passage, and Gundabyr, with bated breath, crossed them all.

At the rear of the corridor he found a door whose surface was marred by a simple locking mechanism. The bolt had not been thrown home, but it was the first lock the dwarf had seen in Urione, and it made him curious. He put his ear against the cold granite. No sound came from within. He would have to chance it. He eased open the door.

Vixa was sitting in a heavy chair, her back to the door. She wore a green Dargonesti robe, but her short golden hair was unmistakable. Gundabyr slipped into the room.

"Release me, Coryphene!" Vixa cried, hearing the door close. "Is this how you repay those who help you?"

"Shh, lady, it's me. Gundabyr Ironbender."

"Gundabyr! Get me out of this!"

He came around the front of the chair and saw a bizarre sight. Vixa was not shackled or bound in any way. She was sitting bolt upright in the chair, facing the wall. Poised in midair, its barbed tip a hairbreadth from her chest, was a Dargonesti spear. Midway down the horizontal shaft, a gold ring glittered.

"What's this?"

"Coryphene's little joke, long since grown stale! He used that ring of his to set up this spell. If I move, the spear will impale me."

"What if I remove the spear?"

"No! Don't touch it! The only thing you can do is take off the ring. Slide it down the shaft to the butt, but don't let it touch the spear. Once the ring's off, the spell will be broken."

Gundabyr grimaced. "Move the ring without letting it touch the spear? That's a tall order, Princess. No wonder Coryphene felt no need to lock the door."

"You can do it, Gundabyr. Your hands are skillful, and your nerve is like the iron you forge."

"It's not my skill or nerve I'm worried about. It's these thick fingers of mine."

"Do it, Gundabyr! You must! I've got us a way out of here, a way to get home!"

The dwarf nodded, rubbing his hands along the tops of his trousers. He held out his right hand, flexing his stubby fingers as they neared the floating ring. An inch away, he stopped, pulling his hand back.

"I can't, lady! I'm too clumsy, I tell you! You'll die if I try it."

"We'll both die if you don't."

Gundabyr sat back on his haunches to think. There had to be a way to move the ring without letting it touch the spear shaft. If only he had a feather, he could slip it between the floating ring and the spear. But he had no feather, no tools, nothing. He sighed.

His gust of breath made the floating ring quiver. Was that it?

He explained his idea to Vixa. Sweating profusely, the princess agreed he should try it. Gundabyr moved around behind her. Leaning forward over her shoulder, he blew against the ring. It quivered, but didn't move. He blew harder. Coryphene's ring skittered two inches toward the spear butt.

"Hurrah!" Vixa rejoiced. "You can do it!"

"It's going to take a lot of wind."

During Gundabyr's many pauses for breath, Vixa told him about her explorations as a dolphin, the chilkit tunnel she'd found, and the discovery she'd made there. By which time, Gundabyr had moved the ring only half the distance necessary.

"So he's alive." The dwarf panted with exertion, his

cheeks red. "Glad to hear it. Anything that thwarts Cory-phene makes me happy."

A few more minutes of huffing and puffing and the ring was only scant inches from the end of the spear shaft. Gundabyr took a short break and outlined what had been happening in the city since the battle. When he got to the part about finding their fellow prisoners dead and pre-pared for disposal at sea, Vixa blanched.

"And Armantaro?" she whispered. The dwarf nodded curtly, his eyes fixed on the ring. He started blowing again, faster and harder, looking down to avoid the tears glisten-ing in Vixa's eyes. "He was ill. Did he die of his cough or was it murder?"

"The others weren't sick, lady, and they're dead."

"Coryphene gave his word! He promised he would free us!"

"He obviously changed his mind."

Hatred welled up inside Vixa. Armantaro was dead. Like Harmanutis, Vanthanoris, Captain Esquelamar, and for all she knew, everyone she'd left on *Evenstar*. All gone. Mur-dered by Coryphene and his insane queen.

"Hold still, lady!" Gundabyr hissed. Vixa forced herself to relax, pushing away her grief. It would serve no purpose now. Almost inaudibly, she said, "I will kill them both."

The icy coldness of her tone made Gundabyr stare at her. Her face, considered "humanlike" back in Qualinost because of her quarter-human ancestry, had worn thin under the hardships she'd endured. Poor food and privation had sharpened her features and bled most of the color from her skin. The dwarf could see the rage burning in her eyes.

"Princess, I'm about done," he said. "Are you ready?"

"I am."

He filled his cheeks, blew smartly. The ring flew off, rico-cheting against the wall. No sooner had it left the shaft than the spear dropped harmlessly to the floor. Vixa was up in an instant, the weapon in her hands.

"Thank you, my friend! Let's go."

He restrained her with one hand. "Escape, Princess, yes? Revenge can't be enjoyed when you're dead."

Before she could reply, they heard voices outside. Vixa sat back in the chair. Gundabyr scurried to the far corner and hid behind a stone column.

Coryphene entered, leaving a pair of guards in the corridor. "Hello, Princess," he called out. "Still here, I see." From his position he couldn't tell that Vixa, rather than his spell, was holding the spear in place.

"When are you going to keep your word and release me?"

There was the slightest of pauses. "Soon," he replied evenly. "Right now my warriors are looking for the dwarf Gundabyr. I thought he might have found his way in here."

"No such fortune. Is Armantaro nearby? I'd like to speak to him."

"That's impossible. Her Divine Majesty has forbidden it."

Vixa resisted a powerful urge to hurl the spear at him. She must remember that Gundabyr, too, would be endangered if the guards were to rush in.

"Where's your honor, Coryphene? Don't the Quoowahb believe in keeping their word?"

"You would be well advised not to provoke me. You're alive now only—" He stopped abruptly.

"Yes? Go on, Coryphene. What truth were you about to let slip?"

He made a fist. "You're alive because I have defied my divine queen! She has ordered your death, Vixa Ambrodel, but I have secreted you here instead!"

"How kind of you, but why?"

"Because the Protector of Urione *does* possess honor."

Vixa's arm, holding the spear by its head, was beginning to ache. "So, what's to become of me?"

"After we take Silvanost and Uriona is crowned queen of all the elven nations, I will set you free. Perhaps you would make a good viceroy, to rule in Qualinost in Her Divine Majesty's name."

Astonishment momentarily left the princess bereft of speech. Coryphene must be as crazy as his queen, if he thought she would become the tool of a conqueror. How little he knew her!

"I believe that, in time, you will come to accept Her Divinity's power," the Protector went on. "My queen will reward me in the future for not killing you now."

Vixa heard Coryphene's footfalls as he moved from the doorway, coming farther into the room. If he drew too near, he would see his spell had been thwarted. Sweat trickled down her forehead.

"My lord!" A soldier had appeared in the doorway. "The watch reports a disturbance at the House of Arms."

"What kind of disturbance?"

"A dispute—a riot between the surviving drylanders and the sea brothers."

Smothering an oath, Coryphene hurried from the room. Gundabyr emerged from his hiding place, and Vixa, with a relieved gasp, let the spear drop.

"Damn him!" she fumed, rubbing her aching wrist. "Did you hear that? I would make a good viceroy to rule in Qualinost, he said. What kind of weak-minded simpleton does he take me for?"

"Lady, we must go," insisted the dwarf.

Once outside under the colonnade, Vixa whispered, "We must hurry to the temple of Zura. Naxos needs water from the fountain there to heal his wound."

They had to take the central ramp, at least part of the way. Vixa dropped down on her stomach and started crawling into the plaza. The war supplies hid them both from the remaining guards until they reached the entrance to the spiral ramp. Gundabyr rolled into the opening. Vixa ducked after him. The ramp was clear.

Noises drifted up to them from the lower levels. Creeping down the ramp, Vixa and Gundabyr speculated on what might be happening below.

"A riot? That doesn't make sense," Gundabyr mused. "The only drylanders left in the House of Arms are too sick and weak even to walk, much less riot."

"Well, in any event, the timing was perfect." Perhaps a little too perfect, Vixa added silently.

The thick scent of incense told them they were nearing

the temple level. Farther on, and they could see robed priests and priestesses coming and going. It seemed impossible for Vixa and the dwarf to slip by unseen. Gundabyr, a practical soul, reached out from their hidden vantage point and grabbed an unsuspecting Dargonesti acolyte. A good solid blow to the back of his head, and the acolyte was in dreamland. Now they had a robe to wear.

"You're too short to pass for a Dargonesti," Vixa reminded him.

"Well, so are you, lady."

Vixa chewed her lip for a moment, then a smile broke out on her face. She leaned over and whispered in Gundabyr's ear. Soon he was grinning, too.

Moments later, a tall acolyte draped in a hooded gray robe joined the lines of worshipers in the courtyard outside Urione's temple complex. The new acolyte surreptitiously studied the inscriptions at the entrance to the various sanctuaries.

"Can you read them?" said a low, strained voice from the vicinity of the acolyte's waist.

"Shh, legs can't talk. I'll let you know."

Sitting astride Gundabyr's shoulders, Vixa tapped him with her left heel to steer him down a narrow lane. The usual Dargonesti script eluded Vixa's understanding, but here in the temple precinct the priests still used Old Elvish, just as was written in Silvanost more than a millennium ago. It was awkward and archaic, but Vixa, always an avid reader, had at least a general comprehension. She puzzled her way past structures sacred to gods named El-ai, the Fisher, and Ke-en. She decided these were the Dargonesti equivalents of E'li, the Blue Phoenix, and Quen. Then they entered a smaller, circular courtyard, faced by three lesser temples. The names on these were Matheri, Estarin, and Zura.

"What's the matter?" hissed Gundabyr in response to her soft exclamation.

"These Dargonesti are strange elves," she replied. "I just figured out that these three temples are sacred to Mantis of the Rose, Astra, and Zeboim." This last name amazed the dwarf. In Thorbardin this goddess was called Bhezomiax, but there were no shrines dedicated to her. What use had a mountain race for a sea goddess? Daughter of Takhisis, the queen of evil, Zeboim was known to be impetuous, temperamental, and very, very dangerous.

"You mean they worship evil gods alongside the good?" Gundabyr asked.

"So it seems. Now I understand Naxos's nervousness about using the water of Zura."

Gundabyr smothered a groan. "Lady, you're no lightweight, you know. Do we go on?"

Vixa nodded curtly. "We have to. I don't know what else to do."

They walked up to the entrance of the temple of Zura. The building was a truncated pyramid made of alternating bands of jade and blood coral. Striking but gaudy, was Vixa's opinion. Monstrous carvings decorated the outer walls, depicting all the destructive forces of the sea: waterspouts, tidal waves, and the like.

A pair of priests came into view. Each wore on a thong around his neck a jade medallion decorated with Zeboim's——or rather Zura's—sign, a sea turtle. Vixa flinched when they drew near enough for her to see their faces. Unlike the usual blue tone of the Dargonesti elves, the priests of Zura had deathly gray complexions. Their eyes were strangely dull and colorless—much like the flat, gray shade of the ocean on a cloudy day. They walked with small, shuffling steps, their arms hanging straight and unmoving by their sides. No notice was taken of the tall, unknown acolyte who fell in behind them.

The temple's interior was damp and fetid. Smears of phosphorescent slime on the walls provided what little light there was. Ahead, the two priests ducked their heads periodically. At first Vixa thought they were observing some sort of ritual, then she felt a cold, fleeting contact on her forehead. Looking up, she noticed faint tendrils of smoke floating in the air, writhing like the tentacles of some phantom octopus. Vixa felt no pain at the contact, but a horrid smell of decay permeated her nostrils.

The priests disappeared down a side passage. Vixa and Gundabyr forged ahead. She watched for other tendrils and dodged them when they appeared. At last they reached the center of the pyramid. The main chamber mimicked the form of the outer structure, being a flat-topped pyramid itself. In the center, instead of an altar, there was a fountain. Water dribbled from the mouth of a statue of Zura, which was carved from a massive block of white onyx. Depicted in Quoowahb form, Zura wore an expression of pure malevolence. Her eyes were set with blue-green jade.

"I need a jar," Vixa said. "Turn around, Gundabyr." The dwarf swung her in a full circle. "Whoa! Not so fast! Again, more slowly."

Deep niches were cut into the walls. Piled in the hollows were white clay amphorae. Vixa pulled one out. It was empty. Smaller than a Qualinesti wine jug, it would hold perhaps a quart of liquid. She hoped that was sufficient for Naxos's purpose. A fitted stone stopper was set in the mouth with the same kind of sticky kelp paste they'd used to seal the gnomefire pots. It had a long, braided seaweed loop for a handle.

Gundabyr took her back to the fountain. Since no one was around, he hiked up the hem of the long robe and took a breath of air, as well as a look around. When he saw the statue, his mouth dropped in amazement. "I hope we don't meet her while we're here," he said, aghast at the dreadful image.

"Shh! Bend over so I can fill the jug."

He leaned forward, resting his hands on the rim of the pool. As Vixa held the amphora in the water, Gundabyr was able to see what was lying in the bottom of the pool. Skulls. A great many of them.

"Uh, Princess, I'm not sure this is a good idea. Look down here."

Vixa glanced down, almost dropping the jug. "By Astra! Where did those come from?"

"Sacrifices, maybe? Or all that's left of people who drank the water?"

She shuddered. "We've got to trust Naxos," she said, finishing her task. "He said to bring him the water, and that's what we're going to do."

She plugged the amphora, smeared the brown jelly around the stopper, then handed the jug to Gundabyr. He put its braided loop over his neck, and they rearranged the robe over him and his burden.

They garnered a few sidelong glances as they crossed the square and left the temple precinct, but no one challenged them. By the ramp, they discarded the robe, and Vixa recovered her hidden spear. Gundabyr and Vixa descended a few levels, then got off at a residential floor evidently reserved for Urione's more affluent citizens. The houses were larger and fewer, and the level had the advantage of being nearly empty just now.

"There are side stairs and ramps all over," Vixa said, rushing ahead. "As long as we keep going down, we'll find our way to the sea."

Puffing a little, the slender amphora cradled in his arms, the dwarf commented, "Not to be argumentative, but the sea's everywhere outside, ain't it?"

Vixa pulled up short, her face reddening. "You're right. I would've dragged us through the whole city, just so we could leave the same way we came in!"

"We have another problem, lady."

"What?"

"I know you shapeshifted dolphins can hold your breath from here to midnight. Me, I'm running out of wind on these stairways."

She clapped a hand to her head. "We need an airshell!"

"Yup."

Dejected, the pair crouched in an alley between two fine houses. Through open windows occupants of the buildings could be seen moving about. Faint music came from inside.

"Let's consider this logically," Vixa whispered. "All an airshell is, is a container for air. We never knew how much air any one of them would have. Right?"

"Right. So?"

"A container for air," she repeated, her eyes distant with

thought. "Gundabyr," she said abruptly, "how many breaths do you take in a minute?"

"Hammer me if I know."

She urged him to find out. Breathing normally, the dwarf counted his exhalations while Vixa counted off the seconds in a minute.

"Stop," Vixa ordered.

Gundabyr reported he'd taken thirty-one breaths. "How does that help?" he asked.

"It will take me fourteen—no, better say fifteen—fifteen minutes to get from the city to Naxos's cave, swimming flat out. All we need is enough air to last you—" With one finger, she scribbled on the dusty floor. "Four hundred sixty-five breaths!"

Vixa stood and tiptoed to the back of the dead-end alley. She explained that what she was looking for was a barrel or sack that could hold enough air to last him until they reached the cave where Naxos was hidden. Gundabyr could take sips of air from the barrel or sack, just as they had taken air from the airshells. The dwarf rolled his eyes.

The rear of the alley was piled with Dargonesti household rubbish. Some sacks were woven seaweed, useless as it was not airtight. Others turned out to be made of catfish skin. Not bad. Vixa pawed through several such sacks until she found one of the size she wanted. She emptied it of rubbish.

"It'll do," she pronounced. Gundabyr looked more than a little doubtful.

They stole back into the street. A few residents were out at the other end of the lane but didn't notice the two drylanders skulking about. At the end of the street, they came to the pink granite wall that was the city's outer shell, unbroken by the arched openings found on the upper floors.

Vixa snarled at the bad luck. Time was running out. She'd been worrying constantly about Naxos ever since Coryphene's soldiers had captured her. What if he was already dead in that cold, wet cave?

"Over here, Princess!"

Just a few yards away, Gundabyr had found a staircase leading down to the next level. He descended; Vixa hurried after him. She could see the flicker of light reflecting off water at the bottom of the stairway.

When she reached bottom, a glad sight greeted her eyes. There were pools in the floor of this level every dozen feet or so. Vixa sat on the edge of one. Before she entered, she said, "You won't understand me when I'm a dolphin, but I will understand you. Once I change, fill up the bag with air and get on my back."

She slipped into the water, picturing her dolphin form. The black-and-white shape was becoming as familiar as her elven one. She no longer felt afraid as her body stiffened. The immobility would pass quickly. She sank beneath the surface. In seconds, she was two-legged no more, but when her dolphin head broke the surface she saw that the situation had changed dramatically. A squad of Dargonesti warriors was coming on the run toward the pool. They had their spears leveled.

Since escaping the grotto, Gundabyr had been quite happy to stay dry, having no fondness for the water. Now, however, he didn't hesitate, but leapt into the pool. In a heartbeat, he was seated on Vixa's muscular back, clinging tightly with his knees. He whirled the sack about his head, filling it with air.

"Go, go!" he shouted, thumping his heels against her flanks. She shook her head side to side, gesturing with her beak toward the amphora still sitting by the pool.

"Reorx save me," groaned the dwarf. He snagged the braided handle of the jug, slipping it over his neck. The Dargonesti were only twenty paces away. Clutching his inflated sack in one hand, Gundabyr grabbed her dorsal fin with the other.

"Now, *go!*" he cried. Vixa submerged, taking him with her.

Behind her, the princess could hear loud splashes as the Dargonesti dove into the pool. Her course was erratic, as the unfamiliar weight of the dwarf on her back made it difficult for her to swim straight.

They swam through an archway into the open sea. Vixa heard numerous cries as the Dargonesti shouted for her to stop and called for sea brothers to intercept her. She headed toward the ruined wall across the Mortas Trench and thanked all the gods that the spears would not travel far underwater.

Gray dolphins flashed by her. Sea brothers! Vixa stubbornly stuck to her course. The big shapeshifted dolphins zoomed before and behind her. What were they playing at? she wondered. With their speed and power, they could ram her into submission easily. But they didn't.

"What are you doing?" she demanded in the high-pitched water-tongue.

"No need to shout," said a friendly voice close by. Vixa cocked an eye astern and saw Kios keeping pace with her.

"Are you chasing me or not?"

Kios surged ahead of her. "If we wanted to catch you, Sister, we would."

"Then what's your game?"

"This is a show, for Coryphene's troopers. We'll tell them you evaded us. For now, take me to Naxos."

Her only response was to swim harder. Vixa didn't trust Kios, but what could she do? With Gundabyr on her back, she knew she had no chance to outrun or outmaneuver the sea brothers.

Six dolphins blasted through the breach in the wall made by the chilkit—Vixa, Kios, and four more sea brothers. Vixa headed directly for the tunnel leading to Naxos's hiding place, all the while praying she wasn't bringing him his death.

As soon as Gundabyr's head burst into the air, he gave a glad cry. Vixa carried him to the pool's edge, by Naxos's hiding place. The dwarf clambered out of the water. Vixa reverted to elven form and joined him. Kios also resumed his two-legged shape, though the other shapeshifters remained as they were.

Naxos appeared to be unconscious. Most of the color had drained from his skin, and he wasn't moving. Vixa knelt by him.

"What's in that jug?" asked Kios as Vixa unplugged the amphora.

"The water of Zura," she said bluntly. "He said it would cure him."

"Oh, it will cure his wound. But he will become undead, like the Shades of Zura."

Appalled, Vixa shoved the plug back in the amphora. She remembered the bloodless, empty faces of the priests she'd seen in Zura's temple. Naxos would become like them!

"What can we do?" she moaned.

Naxos stirred. "Vixa," he murmured, "and the Fire-bringer. Who's that with you?"

"It is I, Kios."

"Come to finish me off, Brother?"

"I could. Coryphene would shower me with riches if I brought him your head."

"Traitor." The voice was weak, but the anger very apparent.

"Ah, the things you say. Where is your famous wit, Naxos? I thought you would trade quips with Death himself when the time came."

"I'm too tired to trade anything. Kill me, or give me the water of Zura. I am weary of pain and cold."

Kios took the amphora from Vixa. Without hesitation, he dashed the jug against the stone wall. Into the stunned silence, he said, "It wouldn't do for the chief of the sea brothers to become undead."

"Chief?" Naxos whispered. "Am I still?"

"You've never been anything else." Kios went to the edge of the pool and gave orders to the remaining shapeshifters. The four dolphins submerged. When he returned, Kios brought back seawater in his cupped hands. He trickled this over Naxos's drying gills. Vixa and Gundabyr rushed to follow his example.

"Look here, my brother," Kios said, as the other two continued to minister to Naxos, "you confronted Coryphene in the middle of a battlefield, surrounded by thousands of his loyal soldiers. By the Fisher, Naxos, he'd just led them to victory over the chilkit! I had to profess loyalty to him on the spot. You should have done the same."

"Coryphene has no confidence in my sincerity," Naxos murmured.

"But he does in mine. If I had defied him, it would have meant civil war, then and there. The time was not right for us to resist, but it soon will be. Coryphene and the queen are leaving the city."

"Leaving?" Naxos was stunned. "To go where?"

"They are marching on Silvanost," Vixa supplied. "Uriona says she's received a prophecy that if she is crowned in the Tower of the Stars, she will rule all the elven nations."

"Hail, goddess Uriona," mocked Naxos.

Kios shook his head. "Don't be so certain of her madness. I have seen the preparations. They will take ten thousand warriors to the dry land and attack the city of our ancestors. Uriona has persuaded four thousand of the Shoal Dwellers to join the attack as well."

Naxos snorted. "Dimernesti nomads can't be trusted."

"No, but they have been promised booty."

"What sort of troops does Coryphene have?" asked Vixa.

"Six thousand spearcarriers, two thousand netcasters, a thousand firelancers, and a thousand picked troops armed with drylander swords. Those include Coryphene's personal guard."

"All infantry," she mused. "Have they no cavalry?"

"In the old country, the Waveriders fought mounted on hippocampi, but none of them followed Uriona into exile. The army is all afoot. Except for the sea brothers." Kios grinned. Weak as he was, Naxos returned the wicked smile.

"What do you find so amusing?" Vixa asked suspiciously.

"Coryphene relies on us to be his scouts," Naxos said.

"And once he's on the march, he'll find that all the sea brothers have vanished," concluded Kios. He rubbed his pale blue palms together. "We'll double back and seize the city!"

"No," said Naxos, shaking his head. "You can't hope to hold the city against Coryphene's army. Better to disperse, live wild in the sea."

Gundabyr, who'd remained in the background during this discussion, finally spoke up. "Hey, what about us? How are we supposed to get home?"

"I sent my brothers for bandages and healing ointments for Naxos," Kios told him. "They will bring an airshell for you, little fellow. Our sister can carry you to land."

They helped Naxos to stand, Vixa supporting him on one side, Kios the other. The wounded shapeshifter felt heavy as oak to the Qualinesti princess. They got him upright, leaning on a boulder by the pool's edge.

One of the sea brothers returned, carrying a whelk shell in a bag clutched in his mouth. Kios took Gundabyr aside to adjust the fit of the airshell's mouthpiece. Vixa had a moment alone with Naxos.

"Will you be all right?" she asked softly.

"With my brothers' help, I think so. You've saved more than my life, Vixa. You've saved the sea brothers from servitude to Coryphene and Uriona." That said, he leaned forward and kissed her gently on the cheek, barely brushing her face with his lips.

Surprised, Vixa raised a hand to her cheek. Color invaded her face. "I-I only wish Armantaro and the others could have lived to escape with me," she stammered.

"As do I, Princess."

At that moment, the pool erupted as four sea brothers arrived—three sent by Kios to fetch medicines, and the healer they'd brought with them. The four changed to Dargonesti form and came to help Naxos.

"This airshell should last you two full days underwater," Kios was saying to Gundabyr. "To be safe, our sister should carry you on the surface as much as possible."

"My thanks, Master Kios," Gundabyr said.

"For the Firebringer, it is nothing."

It was time for them to go. Vixa slipped into the water. Before she transformed, Naxos called out to her.

"I *shall* see you again, Lady Dryfoot!" His golden eyes stared into her brown ones.

"I don't know if I'll ever be able to return. My life is on land."

Naxos smiled knowingly. It was not his usual arrogant grin, but more personal. "I shall see you again, Vixa Ambrodel."

Vixa assumed dolphin form. With the airshell firmly clamped between his teeth, Gundabyr mounted her back and tapped her flanks to signal he was ready.

Naxos waved as the dolphin and the dwarf submerged.

Chapter 16

Sister of the Sea

No sooner had Vixa and her escort emerged from the dark Mortas Trench than they saw a cloud of mud stirred up on the plain. The seafloor between the ruined wall and the city was alive with columns of Dargonesti, marching in formation. Vixa veered away from the massed ranks, angling up toward the surface.

From above she could see the Dargonesti were marching away from the city, parallel to Coryphene's old wall. They were organized into companies of two hundred or so warriors, and there were many companies—a *great* many—strung out in a long line. Large numbers of dolphins cruised over their heads. Vixa and the sea brothers accompanying her blended in. A slower swimmer than the powerful shapeshifters, she was soon laboring along at the rear and falling behind.

A company of blueskins grounded their weapons and faced about. As Vixa looked back, other Dargonesti warriors sprang in unison from the seafloor and began swimming vigorously toward her. That was enough. She called ahead to her escorts.

"Brothers! I need you!"

There was no response. Vixa tore her frightened gaze from the advancing sea elves. Her escort had disappeared. No sea brothers were in sight.

Vixa swam upward as fast as she dared. The Dargonesti were surprisingly fast swimmers, considering they had only webbed hands and feet instead of flukes. This fact, added to the weight of Gundabyr that she carried on her back, meant that Vixa could maintain only a moderate lead. She had to stay ahead of her pursuers, but could not go so fast that Gundabyr would be in danger of exploding. Again, she called for the sea brothers.

All at once a storm of gray muscle and churning tails broke around her. Vixa heard the loud thumps as the shape-shifters rammed the swimming Dargonesti, knocking them out of the pursuit. The warriors were at a great disadvantage, having laid aside their spears in order to swim more rapidly. They were no match for the sea brothers, and dispersed toward the sea bottom. A knot of dolphins formed around Vixa as she raced for the surface. One dolphin broke from the screen and swam to Vixa's side. It was Kios.

"Coryphene will hear of this," she told him as they sped through the water. "He'll realize you have betrayed him."

"Do I care?" Kios replied.

She noticed Kios and the other dolphins were dipping and rising erratically. "What are you doing?" she called.

"Beware the netters!" Kios warned. "Beware the netters!"

Dargonesti soldiers were hovering in the water ahead. Between each pair was stretched a net. The sun's rays, slanting into the depths, picked out the hooks and weights on the edges of the nets.

Gundabyr kicked his heels against her flanks. "I know! I see them!" she squeaked and swam harder.

"Away! Away!" Kios cried. The shield of dolphins broke up. Vixa automatically followed Kios. The Dargonesti netters, accustomed to hunting powerful game fish like tuna and marlin, wielded their nets with great skill. The sea brothers, however, were just as skilled at avoiding the nets, and lured the netters away from Vixa and Gundabyr.

The water was growing lighter as Vixa neared the surface. The green depths gave way to paler shades, full of the sun's warmth. The bright orb drew her upward. She pounded the sea with her broad flukes, all thought of the netters gone.

Vixa broke the surface, leaping eight feet above the waves, with Gundabyr clinging to her for all he was worth. The sun was hot on her sleek wet hide. She uttered a high, shrill cry and crashed back into the tossing ocean.

The impact of landing jarred Gundabyr loose. He sailed into the waves, his airshell flying from his grip. Though he flailed the water frantically, he sank like a stone. He'd only dropped a few yards before a dark shape rose underneath him. He felt himself being lifted, and when Vixa vented, Gundabyr got a faceful of salty mist.

"Pah!" He mopped his face with his hand. He was sitting astride Vixa just behind her dorsal fin. "Watch where you do that!" he told her.

Vixa understood him just fine, but the only response he heard was a loud treble screech.

"Apology accepted," said the dwarf, though Vixa had actually told him to stop complaining.

She put her tail to the wind, which made the waves break over Gundabyr's back rather than his face. The drenched dwarf scanned the horizon, squinting into the sun.

"That way," he stated firmly. Vixa spoke, but the dwarf shook his head. "It's no good burping and squeaking at me. I don't understand. Go that way. It's north, so we're bound to hit land eventually."

She leapt forward. Gundabyr nearly toppled off. "Yow!" he yelled. He held on tight and squeezed with his knees. Vixa ducked under the surface, then burst into the air, arcing in and out of the water as though born to it. The poor dwarf simply clenched his eyes shut and held on.

The sun was high and hot, but it felt good to Vixa as she bounded from wave to wave. When her head was underwater, she heard a myriad of sounds: the swish of swimming fish, the click and clatter of crabs and shellfish, the distant booming songs of the great whales. She found she could taste differences in seawater, too. Down deep the water was cool and still. At the surface it was charged with light and life.

At one point a silver fingerling darted past her, and she dove after it. The fingerling swam desperately to evade her, but Vixa closed in as if pulled by an invisible line. With a sideways snap of her jaws, she swallowed the fish whole.

Heels thumped her sides. By Astra! She was three fathoms down, and she'd completely forgotten she had a passenger! She arrowed back to the surface.

"Will you please not do that!" the dwarf exploded as he gasped for breath.

This time the noises she made were apologetic.

For the rest of the day Vixa kept to the surface, her nose pointed north. When she tired and slowed, Gundabyr climbed off her back and held himself up by clutching her dorsal fin. This gave her some respite from his weight, but they couldn't make much progress that way, so they kept such breaks to a minimum.

Late in the day they spied a ship, toiling under tack against the breeze. Vixa altered her course toward the wallowing two-master.

"Ahoy!" sang out Gundabyr.

A human sailor put his head over the high rail. "Ahoy! Who calls?"

"Down here!"

Vixa swam alongside the ship's port side. The sailor gawked when he spotted the dwarf riding a big black-and-white dolphin.

"Blow me to Balifor!" he yelped. "What in Rann's name are you doin' down there, mate?"

"Riding a dolphin, of course. Slow down, Vixa. I want a word with this fellow."

She complied, matching her speed to that of the creeping ship.

"Can you tell me where we are?" Gundabyr asked.

"We're eight days out of Balifor city," the sailor responded, his eyes starting from his head.

"Where'll we make landfall if we keep heading due north?"

"Uh, Silvanesti—but you don't want to go there, mate. They don't allow visitors."

"Did you hear that, Vixa? Silvanesti!"

She responded with a pleased affirmative.

"What did it say?" asked the sailor, awestruck.

"No idea," Gundabyr replied with a shrug.

Someone on deck called out. "Haynar, you laggard! Who're you talking to?"

The sailor turned away. "Captain! You won't believe it, sir! There's a dwarf in the water, ridin' a—"

By that time Vixa had rounded the bow of the slow-moving vessel and was cruising up the starboard side. No one else caught a glimpse of them. Vixa could imagine the poor sailor trying to explain what he'd seen. A dolphin chuckle shook her.

It was late evening their third day at sea when the wind changed to easterly and blue-black clouds piled up on the horizon. The smell of fresh rain wafted to Vixa from miles away. Soon they could see bolts of lightning snapping from cloud to sea.

"Looks as if we're in for it," Vixa chirped wearily.

"Hmm, looks as if we're in for it," Gundabyr said.

The ocean was getting rougher by the minute. Wind blew in gusts of hot and cold air, and cool rain pattered over the tossing waves. Gundabyr raised his salt-crusted face and let fresh water fill his mouth. He swallowed repeatedly.

"Rain," he sighed joyfully.

A thunderclap punctuated his sigh. The rain fell harder. Vixa found it more and more difficult to swim on the surface against the wind-driven waves. She bobbed her head and screeched to warn Gundabyr she was planning to submerge.

"What? What're you saying?" he demanded. As the water level reached his chin, he finally understood. He took a great gulp of air and pinched his nose shut.

Vixa dove no more than two fathoms, swam hard for twenty heartbeats, then surfaced so Gundabyr could breathe. This wasn't terribly successful. The wind was whipping the waves eight to ten feet high. Vixa struggled on, boring through the towering waves.

"Quite—a—storm!" Gundabyr shouted.

She agreed silently. She hadn't eaten since earlier that day when a few small fish blundered into her path. The constant hard work of swimming was draining her strength. Her body felt like a longbow held too long at full draw—ready to snap. Doggedly, she pressed on through the howling squall.

Lightning struck nearby. It left a bitter smell that was quickly washed away by the pouring rain.

It was black as night now. The only things visible were the waves, thrown out in bold relief by each flash of lightning. Vixa had no idea which direction she was traveling. The churning ocean could have spun her to any point of the compass. When the storm had first struck, the wind had been easterly, hitting her on the right flank. She decided to keep the wind on her right.

After a time, the water took on a new taste. Mud. Vixa rolled onto her side and peered through the dark water. She couldn't see the bottom, but there was a thick cloud of dirt in the water. Was it shallower here?

Each stroke of her flukes was like the blow of a lash. Vixa panted hard through her blowhole. Gundabyr was ominously quiet now. She could feel his heart beating, so she knew he was alive, and his hands were still clenched about her dorsal fin, but he hadn't spoken in a very long time.

On a downstroke of her tail, Vixa felt her flukes drag against something. She arched her back and ran her snout through sand. Land! They must have made land! Unless—she hated even to think it—unless Coryphene had managed to summon the kraken again.

She drove ahead until her belly dragged in the sand. Waves washed against her and the dwarf. Spray lashed her eyes, but Vixa heaved herself out of the water and flopped forward. Another roller caught her and shoved her higher on the beach. Gundabyr was knocked from her back and taken away by the surf. Vixa had no strength left even to cry out to him.

Another wave hit her. She rolled over in the wet sand, coming to a stop against a pile of driftwood. By a vivid bolt of lightning, she saw trees some distance away. No trees grew on the kraken's broad back. They had made it to land!

Vixa closed her eyes. She was so spent she could barely think, but had to will herself to transform. She filled her mind with her true form, envisioning legs, two arms, and her elven face. The change seemed to take an eternity. Exhaustion made concentration difficult. The heat of her dolphin blood was a growing agony. At last, she felt her skin crawl and her limbs stretching into place. Her dolphin squeal of triumph became the glad cry of an elf maiden. Now the cold knifed into her bones.

With her last ounce of strength, Vixa reached out her hand. Her fingers closed on a piece of slick driftwood lying nearby. Her eyelids fluttered down, and she lost consciousness.

The lightning flashed. The cool rain fell.

* * * * *

She awoke with the sun in her eyes and the squawk of wheeling sea gulls in her ears. Vixa turned her head and saw she was several yards from the hissing waves. She sat up slowly. The beach was wide and empty. The driftwood she had clung to was part of a shipwreck, sticking up from the sand.

Just as she'd begun to worry about Gundabyr, Vixa saw the dwarf's vest lying on the beach next to her. At least, it used to be his vest. Now it was in two pieces. The cotton lining had been torn away from the outer woolen material. She picked it up and studied it. A smile slowly appeared on her face. Without further ado, Vixa donned the two garments.

Vixa saw bare footprints leading into the woods. The dwarf had obviously regained consciousness first and gone exploring. She hoped he'd find them something to eat. And drink. Vixa's throat was parched. A long, cool drink of water would be paradise just now. That, and half a roasted ox.

185

As if on cue, Gundabyr appeared out of the trees, his thick arms laden with fruit. He nodded in response to her greeting, then dumped his load of plums, wild grapes, and thorn apples on the sand before her.

"If you're as hungry as I was, dig in," he said cheerfully. "I've had my fill already, so don't be shy."

Vixa took an apple in each hand and bit into them alternately. Juice ran down her chin. They were the finest apples she'd ever tasted.

"Yup, they're good," Gundabyr said, agreeing with her happy sigh.

She interrupted her chewing long enough to ask, "Do you know where we are?"

"The Silvanesti coast, I'd say. Or maybe Kharolis. I saw smoke over that way"—he pointed east—"so there may be a fisher's hut there."

Vixa ate all the apples, four plums, and most of the grapes before she ventured to stand. She still felt weak, but it was amazing how the fruit had restored her.

"Well, shall we introduce ourselves?" she said, gesturing eastward. They set off down the beach, and Vixa munched periodically on a handful of grapes.

It probably wasn't the safest thing to do—two strangers walking up to the first signs of life they'd found on a foreign beach. If this was indeed Silvanesti territory, there wouldn't be any brigands or slavers, but the Silvanesti themselves weren't very hospitable to outsiders, especially dwarves and Qualinesti. Still, they had invaluable information for the Speaker of the Stars. Coryphene's invasion force was probably only days behind them. Maybe only hours.

They'd spotted some dark objects on the beach ahead. As they drew nearer, Vixa recognized them as two small boats, keels up on the sand. The boats had the characteristic shape and decoration of elven craft. Between the upturned hulls a crude wooden rack had been set. Clean, gutted fish hung on the rack, drying in the hot sun. The smell of wood smoke, wafting from the trees nearby, was strong here.

"Hello?" Vixa called. "Anyone here?"

A tall figure emerged from the trees. Upswept ears marked him as elven, as did his long blond hair, drawn back in a queue. He shaded his eyes and saw Vixa and Gundabyr.

"Kenthrin!" he shouted over his shoulder. "Dannagel! Come here!"

Two more elves appeared out of the woods. They were definitely Silvanesti as well. All three had the fair skin, pale hair, and sharp features of eastern elves. They were dressed in white, knee-length robes.

"What in the name of the immortal gods is that?" exclaimed one of the newcomers.

"I believe it's a girl," said the other. "Or didn't you notice, Kenthrin?"

The first Silvanesti jogged down the gentle slope, his cloak flapping. "Were you shipwrecked?" he asked, skidding to a stop. "Are you all right?"

"Nope," said Gundabyr, just as Vixa replied, "Yes."

The elf looked puzzled, but Vixa said, "Do you have any water?"

The Silvanesti unslung a waterskin from his shoulder and handed it over. Vixa drank deeply, then passed the skin to the dwarf.

The other two elves joined them. The one with the impudent eyes—Dannagel—smilingly appraised Vixa's skimpy attire. Vixa's face, reddened by the time she'd spent lying unconscious on the beach, took on an even deeper hue. The first elf frowned at his companion and unhooked his own red-bordered cloak. He draped this around Vixa's shoulders.

"I am Samcadaris, son of Palindar," he said. "These are my friends, Kenthrin and Dannagel."

"Vixa Ambrodel."

"Gundabyr, forgemaster of the clan—"

Dannagel broke in, saying, "Ambrodel? Did you say Ambrodel?" Vixa, in the midst of another drink, nodded. "Of the line of Tamanier Ambrodel?"

She swallowed the cool water. "He was my grandfather."

"She's Qualinesti!" Dannagel declared, surprise in every syllable.

"Just call me Gundabyr. Everyone does," said the dwarf, irked at being ignored.

"It doesn't matter who or what they are," Samcadaris stated. "You're in trouble, aren't you?"

"That we are," Gundabyr said fervently.

"I am the daughter of Kemian Ambrodel and Verhanna Kanan," Vixa explained. "Master Gundabyr and I were on separate sea voyages when we were captured and held prisoner."

The three Silvanesti waited. "Captured by whom?" prompted Kenthrin.

"The Dargonesti."

The three elves exchanged bewildered looks. "The who?" said Samcadaris.

"The race of elves who live at the bottom of the ocean."

There was a moment of stunned silence, then Dannagel burst out laughing. "She's mad! Daughter of the commander of the Qualinesti army indeed! Elves living in the ocean? Throw her back, my friends. She's crazy."

Kenthrin's expression was more compassionate, but his words were not. "The Dargonesti are just an old legend. Tell us really, how came you here?"

"Listen to me," Vixa pleaded. "I *am* of the royal house of Qualinost. If you help me, I'll see that you are handsomely rewarded."

"Gold is not required," Samcadaris said firmly. "Contrary to appearances, we are not simple fishers. We are members of House Protector, and serve in the household guard of the Speaker of the Stars."

"Then you must take me to Silvanost! I have urgent news for the Speaker!"

"What could you possibly have to say that would interest His Majesty?" Kenthrin asked.

"News of an impending attack! The Dargonesti mean to make war on you!"

Her pronouncement fell flat. Dannagel and Kenthrin were openly skeptical. Samcadaris gave no opinion, but told her and Gundabyr to come to their campsite. There, in the woods above the beach, the Silvanesti were smoking some of their catch over a hardwood fire. Samcadaris offered them a breakfast of fish.

Gundabyr paled. "None for me! I've been living on fish forever! Anything but that!"

Seated on logs around the small, smoky fire, Vixa and Gundabyr recounted their story. The Qualinesti princess held nothing back. She described the war with the chilkit, the invention of gnomefire, and the murder of Colonel Armantaro after Coryphene had promised to release his captives.

"So you're saying you swam here in three days, in the form of a dolphin with the dwarf riding on your back?" Samcadaris tried not to sound incredulous.

"That's right."

"And ten thousand water-breathing elves equipped with firepots that burn under water are coming to conquer Silvanost?"

Vixa bit her lip. "Yes," she said weakly. Put that way, it sounded foolish to her, too. She stared miserably into the fire.

"I will take you to Thonbec," Samcadaris announced, surprising his companions as well as the Qualinesti princess. "The commander of the garrison there can decide whether the Speaker need be troubled with this fantastic tale." His two friends objected, but he added, "Let Axarandes judge the truth or falsity of their story. Can we afford to ignore any hint of invasion? Let General Axarandes decide, I say."

"They're mad," Dannagel insisted.

"Or Qualinesti spies," suggested Kenthrin.

"In either case, our safest course is to take them to the fortress of Thonbec. Foreigners can't be allowed to wander the countryside. If they're spies, they can be held at the general's pleasure. If they're telling the truth . . ." Samcadaris left it to his friends to judge the consequences of that.

Samcadaris went to his knapsack and pulled out a spare robe for Vixa. She took it gratefully. "We'll break camp immediately," he told her. "We boated down the shore from the Thon-Thalas, and that's how we'll return."

The Silvanesti packed their belongings and extinguished the fire. Vixa and Gundabyr sat on a log, watching them work. They passed Samcadaris's waterskin back and forth until it was empty.

"What do you think, Princess?" asked the dwarf.

"There's a chance," she murmured. "At least we're talking to warriors. Now all we have to do is convince this General Axarandes."

"Can we do it?"

She squeezed his arm. "We must."

Chapter 17

Thonbec

___

The three Silvanesti warriors loaded their gear into their boats and pushed them into the surf. Kenthrin, biggest of the trio, had a boat to himself. Vixa and Gundabyr rode with him.

The Silvanesti paddled out to smooth water just beyond the breakers. Dannagel and Samcadaris turned their boat's prow east, and Kenthrin followed. They paddled for a while, then both boats stepped light masts and got underway by wind power.

An hour later, the mouth of the Thon-Thalas appeared. It was a broad delta, with many separate channels emptying into the ocean. The main channel was wider than the rest, and the Silvanesti sailed into it. The islands of the delta were high and covered with scrubby pines and cedars. Gradually, the sandy islets gave way to more solid land— dark earth and clay soil forested with thick stands of oak and ash.

On the right bank, the east side of the river, loomed a large gray citadel. After rounding several loops in the river, the boats drew in under the frowning fortress. Banners of Silvanost whipped from the tower tops.

"Thonbec," Kenthrin announced.

"Is there no town nearby?" Vixa asked.

"The village of Brackenost lies on the other side of the fortress. The walls shield the fishers from sea squalls blowing up the river."

A pair of massive stone piers jutted out into the river. Vixa thought them large enough to accommodate sizable war galleys, but no such ships were present this day. Aside from a few fishing dories, no craft at all plied the river.

Thonbec was very old, as evidenced by its design. Built by the famous kender general Balif, its walls were constructed of huge blocks of granite, fitted together without mortar, as was the fashion in earlier times. In shape the fortress was an oval—two squat round towers joined by two sections of wall. The main gate was set in the center of the riverside wall.

A few warriors were idling on the pier when the two boats docked. The appearance of the Qualinesti girl and the dwarf caused quite a stir. Samcadaris ordered a runner to notify General Axarandes of their arrival. Before they had finished unloading their gear from the boats, a squad of Silvanesti, twelve strong and in full armor, came jogging down the hill to the dock.

"Our commander, Axarandes Magiteleran, requires that you come with us at once," said the sergeant leading the squad. Vixa gave Gundabyr a shrug.

"Lead on," she told the sergeant. Samcadaris and his friends fell in behind.

With her soldier's eye, Vixa could see the fortress had not been seriously tested in a long time. Shrubs had been allowed to grow close to the walls and would provide safe cover for an invading enemy. Arrow loops had been bricked up, no doubt to render tower rooms more snug in winter. The huge double gate of Thonbec had stood open so long moss had grown on the hinges. Only the soldiers themselves seemed ready and fit. Vixa took some comfort in that.

As they walked in the main gate, she noted with approval that the walls of the fortress were at least fifteen feet thick. The open bailey was dotted with wooden buildings, erected over the years as conveniences to the garrison. In the center of the grassy courtyard was a reviewing stand. A solitary Silvanesti was seated on it. His long hair had yellowed with age, but his blue eyes were piercing and alert.

The sergeant halted his squad. Gundabyr and Vixa kept going, mounting the steps to the platform. Vixa saluted, Qualinesti fashion, by placing her closed fist over her heart and bowing her head slightly. Gundabyr planted his hands on his hips and said, "Hello."

"Well," said General Axarandes. "It seems Samcadaris and his lads had quite a fishing trip. A rare catch indeed."

"Sir," Vixa began, "I am a princess of the royal house of Qualinost. My name is Vixa Ambrodel. I am the niece of the Speaker of the Sun."

"So you say," was the even reply. "Do you have any proof?"

She spread her hands. "Alas, no. I was held captive and all my belongings taken from me."

"Who held you prisoner?"

"Blueskins," Gundabyr said loudly. "Elves who live under the sea."

There was a ripple of laughter among the guards. Axarandes's arched eyebrows climbed a little higher. "Extraordinary!" he exclaimed. "Have you any proof of that?"

"We're here telling you, aren't we?" said Gundabyr belligerently.

"You might be here for any number of reasons, Master Dwarf. Silvanesti law does not permit outsiders within our borders. If you are who you say you are, lady, then you should know that."

Nettled, Vixa's voice rose. "Yes, I *do* know that! Look, General, we're not spies, and we're not lunatics. The Dargonesti elves are coming from a city called Urione, which lies two hundred leagues offshore, under the sea. Ten thousand soldiers, commanded by a warlord named Coryphene, are on their way right now to attack Silvanost!"

No one laughed now. Axarandes reacted decisively. "Very well," he said. "I have been a soldier too long to ignore such a warning. Patrols will be sent out to investigate your claim. Dannagel?" The young elf stepped forward. "Form a cavalry troop. Scout the west bank as far as Point Zara. Kenthrin, lead a company east along the shore for the same purpose. Go no farther than Sandpiper Beach."

Both elves saluted, and Samcadaris asked, "And I, sir?"

"You will muster the remaining garrison and drill them on the common in Brackenost. I want watchers on both towers night and day." Axarandes stood.

"Is that all?" Vixa asked. "Aren't you going to send a warning to Silvanost?"

"To what end, lady? We don't know if this is a real invasion or not. I will not risk a reputation for five hundred years of common sense by sending a false report to His Majesty."

Vixa traded a helpless look with Gundabyr. The dwarf scowled. "What about us?" he wanted to know.

"You will remain here, under guard."

"As prisoners?"

"Until the truth of your story can be checked, you are foreigners on Silvanesti soil and must be detained." In seconds the pair was surrounded by armed elves.

"That's the thanks we get," grumbled Gundabyr.

"I don't wish to be harsh," Axarandes replied decently. "But the law is the law."

Vixa and Gundabyr were marched away. They were taken to a large room high up in the south tower. The thick door clanked shut, the bolt slid home, and they were captives once more.

"The luck is still with us," Gundabyr said sourly, "and it's still all bad. We shoulda just gone home."

"No," Vixa answered with a sigh. "This was the right thing to do. Coryphene and Uriona must be stopped."

"Do you think this general fella can do it?"

"He's taking precautions—that's good. But he simply doesn't understand who and what he's dealing with." She sighed again.

Gundabyr dragged a chair over to the high slit window. He climbed up and peered outside. The afternoon sun illuminated a narrow view of the Thon-Thalas delta and, in the distance, a blue strip of sea.

"I wonder how long it'll be?" he mused. "How long before we see blueskins marching out of the water?"

Vixa shivered, though the day was quite hot. She drew the Silvanesti cloak closer about her and said nothing.

* * * * *

As prisons went, their room in Thonbec wasn't too bad. The Silvanesti fed them regularly—no fish after the first meal, when Gundabyr's anguished complaints rang through the stone fortress. The thick walls kept the room cool, despite the intense afternoon sun, and by night the stones had absorbed enough heat to maintain a pleasant temperature, though cool sea breezes whistled in the slit windows.

Two days after being shut in the tower, Vixa and Gundabyr had a visitor. It was Samcadaris, looking grim.

"Kenthrin and Dannagel have returned," he reported. "They found no sign of an invading army. When did these Dargonesti supposedly start moving?"

"Five, six days ago," Vixa estimated. "They're all on foot, though. It will take them a while to march—or swim—here."

"All infantry, you say? No cavalry?"

"Horses don't fare too well forty fathoms down." Samcadaris merely nodded at Gundabyr's sarcastic comment. The grim look on his face didn't alter.

"It may not mean much to you now," the Silvanesti said, "but I agree with you that Silvanost should be warned. I don't think we can afford not to believe you. However, the general has lost what little faith he had in you. I fear you may be consigned to the dungeon shortly."

"But I am of the House of Kith-Kanan!" Vixa exploded.

"If that were true, we would treat you accordingly. But there seems to be no way you can prove what you say."

Gundabyr smacked his forehead with the palm of his hand. "I know what'll show 'em, Princess!" he said. He tugged her elbow, drawing her down to him. The dwarf whispered in her ear. Vixa smiled.

"I agree," she said. "Captain Samcadaris, if you will conduct me down to the river, I will be able to demonstrate the truth of my tale."

"The river? Do you think I can be fooled into allowing you to escape?"

Gundabyr threw up his hands, but Vixa said patiently, "I give you my word, I won't attempt escape. Take me to the river, and I can prove myself. Gundabyr will remain with you as hostage. If I fail, you can always toss us back in here, and I won't ask for another chance."

Samcadaris hesitated a moment longer, but the calm of her demeanor decided him. He conducted them out of their tower room. It was several hours after the midday meal, and the fortress bailey was bustling with activity. The path down to the river was quiet. Through the trees, Vixa could see barges on the water, flying the banners of Silvanost. Troops rowed back and forth, searching for signs of an attack. Part of her almost wished the Dargonesti would hurry and get here, proving that she and Gundabyr weren't lying. Or spies. Or crazy.

They walked out on the stone pier. Vixa kicked off her borrowed boots and pulled her robe over her head.

"What are you doing?" asked Samcadaris, mystified.

"I have to be in the water," she said. "Just be patient."

Clad only in her cotton shift, Vixa stepped off the dock. The water was neck-deep here. She closed her eyes and began the now-familiar process of visualizing her dolphin shape. The sleek black-and-white body filled her mind. She ignored everything except that one idea.

Nothing happened. Gundabyr cleared his throat.

"Well," he said, "get to it."

She glared up at him. "I'm trying!" Vixa closed her eyes again. Once more she concentrated. She remembered the sensation of hurtling through the water. She thought of the ease and grace her muscular form gave her, of the loops and circles she'd swum around Naxos during her first transformation. She remembered the exhilaration of leaping from wave to wave.

"Captain Samcadaris, what is the meaning of this?"

General Axarandes was striding across the dock. Samcadaris snapped to rigid attention and saluted.

"Sir! Lady Vixa said she had a way of proving the truth of her report, if I would bring her to the river—"

"Lady," the general interrupted, "please come out of the water."

"No," she said, glaring up at him. "Not yet!"

"What's wrong?" Gundabyr asked her.

She shook her head, at a loss to explain her failure. "I don't know. I—wait a minute!" Vixa's expression brightened. "Naxos said I had to be in the sea! Captain, take me to the sea! I can prove—"

The general's voice was firm. "Lady, come out of the water. Now."

Still protesting, Vixa did as he ordered. When she demanded again to be taken to the sea, Axarandes held up a hand for quiet.

"We have learned one thing here at least," he said softly. Vixa's confusion at his words turned to outrage as she saw that every elf wore the same expression—pity! They thought she was a lunatic, and they felt sorry for her!

"I'm not mad!" she shouted. "If you'll just take me to the ocean—"

"There are learned elves in Silvanost who can help you, lady," Axarandes said kindly. "Magic can be a great boon to a wandering mind."

"My mind is not wandering! I tell you I can prove what I say!"

When the general signaled for two elves to take hold of her, Vixa's patience ended. Planting her feet, she delivered a hard blow to the chest of the nearer warrior, sending him stumbling back. The second she seized by his tunic and flung into the river.

Axarandes sighed. "Take them," he said wearily.

Gundabyr let out a yell of dwarven anger and lashed out with his fists. Two Silvanesti went sprawling, but the rest overcame him by sheer numbers and pinioned his arms

197

and legs. Vixa evaded a rush by two more elves and grabbed for the hilt of the elderly Axarandes's fine sword. Unfortunately, the old general was quicker and stronger than he looked. Her wrist was seized in an iron grip. He broke her hold on the hilt and reversed her arm. Gasping with pain, she spun involuntarily until he had her arm tight against her back.

"Do be calm, lady. I've no wish to hurt you," he said. Vixa struggled, but she couldn't escape his armlock.

"All right. This is getting us nowhere," she said, relaxing.

Vixa and Gundabyr were surrounded by a phalanx of chagrined Silvanesti soldiers, all rubbing their jaws or nursing bruised knuckles. "Take them to the dungeon," Axarandes ordered. "Separate them."

Samcadaris had stood quietly by during this altercation, his face torn. Now, however, pity had replaced confusion. The girl's mind was obviously unstable. Axarandes turned to him.

"Captain, call in the patrols. This farce has gone on long enough."

His words horrified Vixa. "General, you must believe me! The Dargonesti are coming! You must be prepared!"

They marched back to Thonbec in disgrace. Along the way, Gundabyr muttered, "Well, that went fine, didn't it? Now they're certain we're nuts—or at least you are. I'm just the idiot who believes you!"

"Oh, shut up," she said crossly.

The rest of the journey was completed in angry silence. The Silvanesti locked them in separate cells in the fortress dungeon. The rooms were clean and dry, though far smaller than their previous tower chamber. The clanging of the bolt shooting home sounded like a death knell to Vixa.

The Qualinesti princess slumped against the wall and let her head rest heavily on her hands.

* * * * *

When she awoke, Vixa had no idea how much time had passed. The only light in her cell came from the small wicket in the oak door. She put her face next to the strips of black iron that barred the wicket and peered down the passage. Torches sputtered in wall sconces, but the low-ceilinged passage was empty. She called Gundabyr's name several times. There was no response.

It was all so frustrating! She was certain she could transform if only these fools would take her to the ocean! That *must* be why she'd failed. She had to be in salt water.

But was that the problem? For all she knew, her ability was temporary. Naxos had said "forever"—but the shape-shifter could have lied. That thought stung almost as much as her failure.

Disgusted, Vixa let her head fall against the doorjamb. Immediately, she felt strange vibrations echoing through the cold stone. She pulled back in surprise, and the sensation went away. Vixa pressed an ear to the wall beside the cell door. The stones were vibrating. Was the entire garrison marching on the battlements? Perhaps a mighty storm lashed the fortress. In moments a sound broke the silence of the dungeon—the sound of running feet, growing louder.

Vixa pressed her face against the iron straps over the wicket. "Hello!" she called. "Who's there? Let me out!"

Samcadaris rounded the far corner and raced toward her cell. She saw that he was dirty and spattered with blood.

"What's happening?" she asked.

"We're under attack!" He threw back the bolt on her door. "An hour after sundown they came out of the river! Warriors, giants with blue skin, just as you said!"

"Has the fortress fallen?"

"No! Axarandes led a counterattack and saved the troops trapped outside the walls. They've taken Brackenost, though. The village is burning."

She emerged from her cell. "Where's Gundabyr? He must be freed."

Samcadaris took her down the passage and around the corner. When Gundabyr was awakened and the situation explained to him, he got to his feet with a sigh, saying, "First they call us loonies, then they want us to fight for 'em. I tell you, the luck's still with us, and it's—"

"All bad," finished Vixa impatiently. "Captain, we need weapons."

"You shall have them," said Samcadaris. He led them down the passage and up the stairs, grabbing a torch as he went.

As they ran, the dwarf muttered, "I don't s'pose there's a decent axe around here. I can't fight with these fancy elf weapons."

They emerged in the ground floor chamber of the north tower, the fort's armory. The torchlight was reflected by racks of pole weapons, swords, shields, and various other implements of battle. Shouts and the clangor of battle filtered through the thick stone walls.

"Help yourselves," said the Silvanesti, stabbing the torch into a handy wall sconce. "I must return to the wall!"

Vixa chose a burnished bronze breastplate and helmet. There was no time to bother with greaves, vambraces, or the like. She tugged the helmet on and wriggled into the heavy cuirass. Gundabyr turned up his nose at the bronze armor—it was much too large for him anyway—and went straight to a rack of polearms. He took out a six-foot halberd and cut several feet of its shaft away. Now he had a large but serviceable hand axe.

"Let's go!" Vixa shouted, hefting a borrowed sword.

"Right behind you, Princess."

They dashed into the courtyard. The bailey was littered with wounded and dying Silvanesti. Long torches planted into the ground gave the scene an eerie, shifting illumination.

The walls teemed with fighting elves. Fires blazed on the far side of the walls, casting the parapets into sharp relief. Mixed in with the Silvanesti defenders were disturbing numbers of tall, blue-skinned Dargonesti. Now and then an elf toppled from the wall, trailing screams in the smoky air.

"The gate's where the fight will be hardest," Vixa shouted over the din. "That's where I'm going!" She ran for the entrance, Gundabyr right behind. They had to weave through the piles of wounded and dead.

They reached the front gate just as the fight was turning in favor of the defenders. General Axarandes was there, directing his troops with cool efficiency. He had solidified the defense. Vixa and Gundabyr pitched in, helping to shove the massive oak doors shut. When Axarandes saw them, he simply nodded.

Locking bars, made from entire tree trunks, were slid into place to hold the portal secure. Axarandes called for water and bandages for the wounded. There were no healers in Thonbec. They were usually brought in from Brackenost to tend the garrison's simple needs. Unfortunately, Brackenost had been conquered. The burning village brightly illuminated the eastern wall.

Vixa, Gundabyr, and the general climbed to the battlements. Vixa was furious that her warning had gone unheeded. Many of these deaths might have been prevented if only the Silvanesti had listened.

"After dark, the first of the enemy emerged from the river and seized the docks." Axarandes said. "Half the garrison was outside the walls, patrolling or on relieved duty. Before the alarm could be raised, the enemy were in the streets of Brackenost. They have an incendiary liquid that is difficult to extinguish."

"Gnomefire," Gundabyr said ruefully. "I'm afraid I gave them that."

"Captain Dannagel was in the village and mustered what warriors he could to resist the enemy attack. They came out of the river all along the bank, hundreds of them. Dannagel died defending the open gate. I brought his troops in, and only barely managed to keep the invaders out, as you saw for yourselves."

The Qualinesti princess shook her head as she stared down at the burning village beyond the wall. Of course the Dargonesti had come from the river! She'd told the Silvanesti they were a water-breathing race. But she cast these resentments aside. The objective now had to be the defense of Thonbec and Silvanost.

"Have you sent word to the Speaker?" she asked. Axarandes shook his head, and she quickly added, "Silvanost is their objective, General, make no mistake. You must warn the Speaker of the Stars to prepare for the defense of the city."

To her disbelief, he said, "You are too rash, lady. The enemy has not taken this fortress. In truth, now that their surprise attack has failed, I don't see that we have much to fear. I regret my lack of faith in your warning, but we are prepared now. A force of ten thousand infantry cannot have a siege train of the size necessary to reduce Thonbec. They might as well return to the sea now and spare their own blood."

"That's an easy thing to say," Gundabyr remarked. "But you don't know these blueskins the way we do. Coryphene didn't come all this way just to give up. Rest assured, he has some plan in mind for your fortress."

Axarandes regarded them for a minute. His aquiline features glowed in the light from the burning city. "Very well," he acquiesced. "A courier will be sent to Silvanost. Would you two like the job?"

Vixa's response was prompt. "No, thank you, General. I doubt they'd believe us any more than you did."

He nodded, turned away. Vixa and Gundabyr remained, watching the fire consume the last of Brackenost.

Chapter 18
The Fortress Destroyed

The night was not yet over.

After the fire in the village had burned itself out, bringing the darkness of a summer night back to the gray walls of Thonbec, Dargonesti crept out of the river again and massed on the riverbanks. Keen-eyed Silvanesti sentinels spotted them and sounded the call to arms on their trumpets.

First to the walls were the archers. The garrison of Thonbec consisted of fifteen hundred warriors, three hundred of whom were some of Silvanesti's most skilled archers. Though night shrouded the lower slopes of the riverbank, the archers showered death on the attackers. Stung by the hail, a band of fifty Dargonesti tried to rush the gate. Only half made it to the top of the hill, and none made it to the gate. The survivors broke and fled back to the safety of the Thon-Thalas.

"Hurrah!" a young sentinel shouted from the parapet. "They can't bear up under our arrows!"

"Not surprising," Vixa said dryly. She was tired and cross, wanting to sleep but not daring to. "They've never faced arrows before."

The sentinel said excitedly, "We should sortie and strike them! With a hundred swords we could—"

"—reduce the garrison by a hundred," Samcadaris finished. "Back to your post, soldier."

"The Dargonesti are just feeling out your defenses. They've never fought a land foe before," Vixa explained.

Long after the moons set, mere hours before dawn, it became very quiet. Axarandes, fresh from a well-deserved rest, came to the battlements with the dispatch he'd prepared for the Speaker of the Stars. He asked Vixa to read it, to check for factual errors regarding the might of the Dargonesti. She approved it all, and he sealed it in a deerskin wallet. Axarandes called for a courier, the fastest runner in Thonbec. The importance of his mission was explained to him, and the courier was lowered by rope over the east wall. Silently, he raced away from the fort, vanishing in the trees.

"I hope he makes it," Vixa murmured.

"I'll send a second courier in a few hours," Axarandes assured her. "And another at midday. One of them will get through."

A lookout atop the south tower sang out, "Turn out! Turn out! Something is happening in the river!"

All hands rushed to the west wall. By the time Vixa and Gundabyr reached the parapet the place was so crowded the dwarf couldn't see anything but elven posteriors.

"What is it? What do you see, Princess?" he demanded.

Vixa wasn't sure what she was seeing. The dark waters of the Thon-Thalas were rising. The surge was coming from the delta, not upstream. Water rose over the two stone docks, inundated the banks, and crept slowly up the hill toward the fortress.

A cold sensation settled in Vixa's stomach. "General," she whispered, "you'd better clear the walls."

"Why? What sorcery is this?" he wanted to know.

"Just clear the walls!" she repeated.

The rising water writhed, and a gelatinous mass appeared on the surface. To the Silvanesti, it looked like a swarm of giant snakes emerging from the river. One of the snakes rose into the air, as high as the walls of Thonbec. The elves gaped. The snake—or rather the tentacle—was six feet thick and studded with bright yellow suckers. Though she had never seen this part of the monster, Vixa knew what it was.

"They've called up the kraken."

Her whispered statement fell like a lightning bolt upon Gundabyr. "That does it," he said flatly, then turned and ran.

More of the monster humped out of the water. The boneless kraken filled the river from bank to bank. Its terrible tentacles reached out of the river, grasping tree trunks for support. More and more of its whitish, translucent bulk spilled out of the water.

The archers, unbidden, peppered the kraken with arrows. They might as well have blown kisses. The wooden shafts made no impression on the slick, rubbery hide of the massive creature. A tentacle touched the foot of the fortress wall, coiled around it, retracted again. Another came, feeling the stonework with a delicacy strange for so massive a limb. A third arm grasped the rim of the high wall, bowling over a dozen Silvanesti warriors as an elf brushes ants from his sleeve.

Vixa couldn't move. The dreadful sight kept her rooted to the spot, staring in horrified fascination. In the center of the monstrous mass of tentacles and flesh a single eye appeared, black as the Abyss and twice as wide as the gate of Thonbec. It glistened in the starlight, then she saw the immense organ swivel in her direction.

Five tentacles leapt up and grasped the parapet. Silvanesti attacked with sword and halberd, to no effect. The kraken's limbs knotted, drawing the monster farther out of the water.

Axarandes was shouting orders. Oil was brought from the towers and dumped onto the monster's grasping tentacles. Torches were cast. Though weak flames hissed, the sodden flesh of the kraken was nearly impossible to ignite.

They could smell the beast now. The fetid odor brought to Vixa's mind her horrible first encounter with the kraken. She shuddered violently, and her terrified paralysis ended abruptly. Vixa grabbed the general.

"You can't fight it like this! It's too big, too powerful! Sound retreat, General! Save the garrison!" she shouted into his face.

Already, stones on the parapet were breaking off under the kraken's grip. A half-dozen Silvanesti were crushed in one swipe as a tentacle thrashed against the south tower. The monster was halfway up the hill now, more of its arms reaching out to the fortress. Vixa ducked; limbs eight feet thick and two hundred feet long swept over their heads. Huge blocks of granite tumbled as the kraken tugged on the wall.

Axarandes gave the command. Trumpets sounded "Reform and retreat." Silvanesti spilled off the wall and formed ranks on the far side.

Vixa searched for Gundabyr. The monster was raking the courtyard. Warriors tried to hold ranks, but the threat was too great. The disciplined Silvanesti soldiers broke and ran for their lives. Hundreds of elves raced for the landside wall, to squeeze through the smaller postern gate there.

Masonry fell around Vixa. She was nearly crushed by a four-ton wall block. The sky was growing brighter as dawn approached, and against this purple background she saw the south tower of Thonbec in the kraken's grip. Screeching came from the giant suckers as they gripped the smooth stones. Then the grinding thunder of collapse sounded. The south tower slid into ruin before her astonished eyes.

The air was filled with dust, the pounding of toppling granite, the shrieks of injured and frightened elves. Vixa, shielding her nose and mouth from the flying dirt, ran for the postern gate, midway along the eastern wall. A tentacle lay in her path. Steeling herself, she clambered over it. It was cold and soft, like a mound of damp leather. It didn't stir as she dropped down on the other side, but a gruesome sight met her eyes: arms and legs of crushed Silvanesti protruded from underneath. Vixa looked away and resumed running.

The postern was partially blocked by rubble. The Qualinesti princess wormed through a tangle of stones. An elf lay dead under a large fragment of the gate arch. Bending low to crawl by the obstruction, she recognized the dead Silvanesti. It was Kenthrin, one of the first three she and Gundabyr had met on the beach.

Vixa crawled through a small gap, tearing her clothes and scratching her face and hands on sharp edges. The postern gate was standing open. Staggering to her feet, she dashed through. Outside, all she could see were the backs of many Silvanesti, running for the woods. Gundabyr was nowhere to be found.

The kraken turned its attention to the north tower. As Vixa stumbled away, she saw the same merciless grip enfolding that stout structure, with the same terrible result. Balif's great fortress, built with skill and care a thousand years earlier, crumbled under the monster's assault.

Vixa reached the line of trees, paused for breath, and looked back. Dargonesti warriors, their heads and shoulders sheathed in damp, turbanlike cloths, were marching up the hill, giving the kraken a wide berth. When they caught up with fleeing Silvanesti, they struck them down without mercy. Grinding her teeth in anger, the Qualinesti princess shucked off her cuirass and helmet. Alone, she couldn't save those who were dying. All she could try to do was save herself. The heavy armor would only slow her now.

The forest east of Thonbec was an old one, of large, widely spaced oaks and yews. The way was clear for rapid movement. Vixa ran until her lungs were bursting. When she could run no farther, she leaned against a broad yew tree and gasped for breath. Shame rose hot in her breast, shame for her panicked retreat and for the ignominious defeat.

In the distance, the eastern sky brightened behind a tall cloud of gray dust, rising from the ruins of Thonbec.

* * * * *

Gundabyr's early flight from the wall had been prompted not only by fear, but by his practical nature as well. He knew the power of the kraken. He knew there was nothing for a fellow to do in the face of such power but be elsewhere. Vowing to live to fight another day, the dwarf had fled.

When he reached the postern gate, he looked back. The tentacles of the kraken were gripping the riverside wall. Gundabyr was torn for a moment, wanting to go back for Vixa yet wanting to put as much distance as possible between himself and that ocean-dwelling horror. He, like most dwarves, was a very poor swimmer because of his stocky body and heavy bones. The sight of the kraken had brought back all the old terror, when the monster had sunk his ship and he and Garnath had been captured.

The kraken's tentacles swept the first elves from the battlement, and Gundabyr hesitated no longer. He ran down the east slope to the woods. The area was deserted. The Dargonesti hadn't bothered to surround the landward side of Thonbec. They probably didn't want to risk being cut off from the river.

Axe in hand, the dwarf plunged into the woods. His flight took him down this slope and up the next hill. As the eastern sky lightened to gold, he was forced to stop and catch his breath. On the bald crest of a hill, he turned to survey Thonbec. Nothing remained of the ancient fortress but an enormous mound of gray stone. A column of dust rose like smoke straight up in the still air. Real smoke from the sacked village of Brackenost made a thin plume next to the vast dust cloud.

Gundabyr leaned on his axe handle, chest heaving. He realized he couldn't simply run away. He was too stubborn for that and, he had to admit it, he liked that young elf princess. She wasn't nearly as stuck-up as most elves. Besides, if the Dargonesti were allowed to take over Silvanesti, no country on Krynn would be safe. He would have to go back. He had to find Vixa.

When his breathing came under control, he shouldered his weapon and started back down the hill. The return trip, not conducted at a blind run, was much slower. By the time

Gundabyr reached the clearing where the east wall had stood, the morning sun was bathing the ruins of the fortress. There were no Dargonesti in sight. Many Silvanesti lay dead on the field, slain in flight by Dargonesti spears. He looked them over, thankful Vixa couldn't be found among them.

The kraken was gone, presumably back into the sea, but its nasty smell still fouled the air. Gundabyr picked his way up the hill through the litter of broken stones and dead elves. He reached the top and could see a long distance in all directions. Nothing was stirring. No elves—of any nation—no sea monsters, not even any animals broke the unnatural quiet.

As the dwarf clambered down the north side of the ruins, all the while his mind was working. Where had the Dargonesti gone? They had taken the fort, or the kraken had, yet they'd left the site of their great victory.

The low sun blinded Gundabyr as he continued to search the ruins for Vixa. When he shielded his eyes against the glare, a thought came to him. Perhaps that was why the Dargonesti had departed so hastily. They wanted to avoid the sunlight. Taking this line of reasoning further, Gundabyr decided they were not likely to attack again until dusk at the least. Living in the ocean depths as they did, they were most likely unable to bear the direct heat and light of the sun. That could be a boon for the Silvanesti, and right now they needed any advantage.

He was satisfied that Vixa had not been killed at the fortress. Now, he just had to find her. His knowledge of Silvanesti geography was meager, but he knew the city of Silvanost lay upriver, on an island in the midst of the Thon-Thalas. Shouldering his axe, he started north, keeping a discreet distance from the water's edge. No sense tempting the blueskins to try their luck during the day.

Near midday, when the sun was scorching his bare head, Gundabyr smelled smoke—a campfire, he thought. He slipped into the brush beside the river road and worked his way toward the source. Care was needed. He didn't think the Dargonesti had taken to frying their fish these days, but he was a foreigner in Silvanesti territory and he'd seen enough elven prisons to last him several lifetimes.

Voices filtered through the foliage. He tightened his grip on his axe. The weight of it was comforting. Gundabyr caught a glimpse of movement in a clearing ahead. The odor of cooking was much stronger. It smelled like apples baking. His mouth watered.

"These will be ready soon," said a familiar voice. Samcadaris?

"I hope so. The general is in a bad way. He needs food."

Vixa! Popping out of a tangle of ivy, Gundabyr called, "Save an apple for me, Princess!"

The dwarf's sudden appearance startled the group around the campfire. Vixa, Samcadaris, and four Silvanesti soldiers leapt to their feet. Gundabyr found arrows and swords aimed at his broad chest.

"Wait!" he cried, throwing up his arms. "It's me!"

"Hold!" Vixa commanded. The warriors lowered their weapons. The Qualinesti princess shook her head. "Gundabyr, it's good to see you, but it's dangerous sneaking up like that."

"My apologies!" He stepped out into the open. "I'm mighty glad to see you, too."

"What happened to you?"

He briefly sketched his morning activities, including his return to Thonbec.

"And there was no one left alive?" Samcadaris asked grimly.

The dwarf shook his head. "Are you all that's left?" he asked, gesturing around at the small group.

Vixa replied, "We scattered when the walls and towers came down around us. I found Samca here, and we picked up the others with General Axarandes."

She cast a worried look upon the still figure that lay on a crude stretcher made from a cloak and two green saplings. A terrible wound showed on the general's head. He'd been hit by falling masonry, Vixa explained.

"Will he live?" whispered Gundabyr.

"It's very serious, but if we can get him to a healer soon—"

Her voice trailed off, then she added, "Have you seen any Dargonesti?"

"Not this morning." He told them his theory that the sea elves couldn't bear direct sunlight. Vixa concurred.

"We've seen signs they've raided both sides of the river," Samcadaris said. "We've encountered no farmers or fishers at all."

They were camped on the outskirts of the extensive orchard country that surrounded Silvanost. Green apples, plucked from the trees, were all they could find to eat. The soldiers were cooking the fruit to make it more palatable. The little band crouched around the fire, digging browned apples from the ashes and eating the hot fruit gingerly.

Gundabyr watched Vixa for several minutes. She talked and even joked with the others, keeping their spirits up in the face of their crushing defeat. She herself looked surprisingly well, considering all that had happened. The dwarf commented on this.

"I'm on dry land," she said simply. "It's amazing what a difference that simple fact makes. Everything else can be dealt with."

Samcadaris frowned. "I wish I shared your confidence, lady," he said. "I'm not afraid of these blue-skinned warriors, but if they can command monsters of the deep, then all may be lost."

Vixa swallowed a bite of warm apple. She pointed through the widely spaced trees to the river, visible as a sparkling ribbon at the bottom of the hill. "How wide would you say the river is here, Samca?"

"How wide? Maybe two hundred yards, two-fifty at most."

"The kraken is more than a mile wide. I know. I walked on its back and mistook it for an island. I doubt it can drag itself this far from deep water. Even at Thonbec it was too large for the river channel and stayed in the much broader delta area. And once the sun came up, it went back to deep water with the sea elves. Silvanost is safe from it, I think."

Samcadaris looked at the distant Thon-Thalas. "Thank Astarin for that, at least."

211

"What we really need are horses," Vixa said, rising. "We need to take a warning to Silvanost with all possible speed."

The elf captain managed a smile. He stood and dusted his hands. "I can do something about that, lady."

He went to General Axarandes. Vixa and Gundabyr followed. They could see the general's thin chest rising and falling as he breathed. Samcadaris knelt by his commander, placed a gentle hand on his shoulder.

"Sir? My lord Axarandes?"

Under a bruised brow, the general's eyes slowly opened. "Samca," he rasped.

"Sir, we need horses. We must get to Silvanost as quickly as possible."

"Sent . . . couriers."

"Yes, sir, I know," Samcadaris said patiently. "But we don't know if they got through. And you, my lord, are in need of a healer. Your wound is very serious."

"I should be dead. My citadel pulled down like a wattle hut, elves of Silvanesti fleeing in panic . . . you should have left me in the rubble."

Vixa knelt on the general's other side. "Look here, General. You're alive and there's a lot of fighting to be done yet. Will you give up on your country when it needs you most?"

He regarded her with bloodshot eyes. "Are you really a princess of the House of Kith-Kanan?"

Her back stiffened. She looked down on him with proud eyes. "I am Vixa Ambrodel, granddaughter of Kith-Kanan, first Speaker of the Sun."

A tiny smile lifted Axarandes's lips. "I'm sorry I doubted you, lady. You have the spirit, the carriage of a princess. I should have known it."

"Don't let it trouble you, sir. If I'd been in your shoes, I wouldn't have believed me either."

Samcadaris cleared his throat. "Sir, the horses?"

"Ah, yes."

Axarandes raised a hand stiffly to his neck and groped in the folds of his tunic. He produced a small golden talisman, which hung around his neck on a thong. It was a horse rampant, beautifully worked. Closing his hand around the figurine, he began to speak, though no sound passed his lips.

Gundabyr leaned over Vixa's shoulder and whispered loudly, "What's up? Is he praying?"

"The general is summoning horses," Samcadaris explained quietly. "Some elders of House Protector have the ability to call horses to them in times of emergency."

It was a long spell Axarandes soundlessly chanted. When at last the talisman fell from his fingers, he lost consciousness from the exertion. Samcadaris and Vixa stood up.

"Is that it?" asked the dwarf, unimpressed.

"Wait," said Samcadaris. "You must be patient."

Gundabyr shrugged his broad shoulders and went back to the fire for another apple. He'd taken only a few bites when a distant thundering reached his ears. Soon, the sound was recognizable as the pounding of hooves. Gundabyr was happily surprised by the sight of ten horses cantering into the clearing. They were of all colors and sizes—from heavy farm animals still wearing leather collars around their necks to half-wild ponies with ragged coats and unshod hooves. As only eight mounts were needed, the elves sorted out the best of the lot and sent the remaining two on their way.

The soldiers made halters out of rawhide for each of the animals. General Axarandes's makeshift stretcher was lashed behind one of the muscular farm horses. The travois wasn't ideal, but he was in no condition to ride. Gundabyr was provided with a wicked-looking pony. It bared yellow teeth at him and pranced nervously when he approached. The dwarf put his face up close to the pony's and bared his own yellow teeth. The fractious horse settled down after that. Gundabyr led it to convenient stump, and was soon mounted.

"Remarkable," said Samcadaris. "I doubt that animal's ever been ridden. How did you tame him so quickly?"

"Nothing to it. I just let him know that if he bites me, I'll bite back!"

For the first time since arriving in Silvanesti, Vixa Ambrodel laughed.

Chapter 19

City of the Stars

The trip to Silvanost passed quickly. It was nearly sunset when they came in sight of the fabled capital of the eastern elven realm. Tired though she was, Vixa sat up straight as the first silver towers gleamed over the distant trees. No one she knew, not even Colonel Armantaro, had seen this ancient city. He had often spoken of his desire to see the city of their ancestors. Vixa's excitement was tempered with sadness at the thought that he would never get his wish.

Unlike the buildings of Qualinost, which were formed from naturally occurring rose quartz, the spires of Silvanost were constructed of white marble. They soared to remark-able heights and were so slender and sharply peaked as to resemble giant inverted icicles or spikes of the purest white glass.

At least one of General Axarandes's couriers must have gotten to Silvanost ahead of them. Samcadaris pointed out that the river was devoid of the usual collection of small water craft. Large, heavy barges, their sides lined with bronze shields, were anchored in midstream to bar the way to enemy ships. The warning had not been ignored completely.

Banners flew from every masthead and tower peak. The setting sun warmed the white walls of Silvanost, and against that majestic backdrop, Vixa saw troops moving along the lengthy battlements.

They left behind the orchards and neatly tended gardens and entered a grassy plain that rolled down to the river. At once they were surrounded and challenged by handsomely outfitted cavalry on snow-white horses.

"Stand!" called a rider in herald's plumage. "Name yourselves!"

"Samcadaris, of House Protector. I have General Axarandes of Thonbec with me, gravely wounded. These are his warriors."

"Who are the outlanders?"

Samcadaris nodded to Vixa and Gundabyr, indicating they should speak for themselves. Vixa drew herself up and said in a loud, clear voice, "Vixa Ambrodel, daughter of Verhanna Kanan and Kemian Ambrodel, niece of Silveran, Speaker of the Sun!"

The dwarf merely waved a hand and said tiredly, "Gundabyr. Forgemaster. Thorbardin."

"You will come with me." The herald reined his prancing horse and sent it galloping off toward the shore. Vixa, Samcadaris, and the rest thumped heels against their ragged mounts and followed.

At the water's edge, a broad stone ramp slanted at a gentle angle into the river. The herald halted and put a golden horn to his lips. Two crystalline notes echoed across the Thon-Thalas. He sounded them once more.

"Now what?" rumbled Gundabyr. Vixa shrugged in reply.

In moments, they saw a stately barge of considerable size coming across the river toward them. At first she and Gundabyr couldn't figure out how it was powered. It had no sails, oars, or sweeps. A pair of thick chains ran taut from the bow out into the water ahead of the vessel. Gundabyr asked about their purpose, but before anyone could reply, the answer rose to the surface. A vast green dome emerged from the river in front of the barge. It loomed higher and higher. Unconsciously, both newcomers edged their horses away from the shore.

The dome was jointed, made up of dozens of smaller plates. Vixa was astonished to realize that it was a creature of some sort. Its head, the size of a fishing dory, rose dripping from the water, and huge brown eyes stared impassively at her.

"It's a turtle!" yelped Gundabyr. "The father of all turtles!"

"They are bred as tow beasts for the cross-river ferry." Samcadaris was grinning.

"Fantastic," Vixa breathed. "How do you control such a monster?"

"They are gentle as lambs, lady. Priests of the Blue Phoenix train them to work. I do not know what spells they use."

It didn't take long for the giant turtle to cross the Thon-Thalas. Soon it was hauling itself out of the water onto the stone ramp, laboriously turning the barge for the return trip. The vessel bumped along until the barge master whistled for the beast to halt. A gangplank was lowered, and two soldiers from Thonbec carried Axarandes aboard. Vixa, Gundabyr, and Samcadaris followed.

The barge was crammed with Silvanesti—by the look of them, river sailors hastily pressed into service as soldiers. Unlike the splendidly dressed cavalry, the barge marines were decked out in an assortment of ill-fitting cuirasses and helms. Like all the Silvanesti, they were tall and slender, with light eyes and hair. Vixa was used to the mixture of races found in Qualinost. Elves—many descended from the darker, stockier Kagonesti line—humans, some dwarves, and a few kender all called Qualinost home. The peaceful coexistence of the races was what her grandfather, Kith-Kanan, had envisioned for the city he founded. No such mixing of the races occurred in Silvanost.

Hundreds of years earlier, when Silvanesti was home to all elves, Speaker of the Stars Sithel had been slain by a party of humans hunting the fringes of Silvanesti territory.

Though the humans insisted the death had been accidental, the outraged elves had set about ridding their land of all nonelves, especially humans, many of whom had intermarried with the ancient race. The humans resisted, and so was begun the Kinslayer War.

When the fighting was over, the elves withdrew into their country, disdaining any contact with those not of the—to their way of thinking—superior race. Their natural arrogance had blossomed into outright bigotry.

However, some elves chafed under the rigid traditions and rules that governed their land. They were championed by Kith-Kanan, son of former Speaker Sithel and twin brother of Speaker of the Stars Sithas. This rift widened until it brought about the sundering of the elven nation. Kith-Kanan led his followers west, to found a new country called Qualinesti, where all races would be welcome.

Only Silvanesti feet had trodden the streets of Silvanost these last four hundred years. Now the eastern elves were faced with not only a dwarven intruder, but a Qualinesti one as well. They had a deep mistrust of their western cousins, as some Qualinesti had sided with the humans during the Kinslayer War. The Silvanesti also believed that if elves had never married humans, bringing the humans into Silvanesti, the entire bloody conflict would never have happened. There were even those who worried that the exiles—as the eastern elves called the Qualinesti—would one day try to return to Silvanesti to take back their ancestral home by force.

Vixa had always stood out among the inhabitants of her own country, with her height, light coloring, and bright blond hair. Here, she blended into the crowd.

It was obvious the Silvanesti didn't see it that way, however. Once Vixa and Gundabyr were on the barge, conversation among the crew quickly died. The dwarf and the Qualinesti girl were greeted with stares, some curious, but none welcoming.

"What's the matter with them?" muttered Gundabyr.

"Nothing," she replied just as softly. "They just don't get many—*any*—strangers here."

From his tower at the ferry's prow, the barge master gave a whistle. The turtle lurched into motion again, heading down the muddy ramp into the water. The barge did a swift right turn, sending the landlubbers skittering to the port bulwark. When the ride smoothed out, Samcadaris cornered the herald.

"Has the enemy been seen near the city?" he asked.

"No. I'm not even sure who the enemy is," the young herald replied. He eyed Vixa. "Are the Qualinesti attacking us?"

Vixa opened her mouth to protest, but Samcadaris intervened. "Indeed not," the captain said. "These brave foreigners brought us warning of the coming invasion."

The herald's gaze lost some of its hostility, but he still looked skeptical. "How was General Axarandes wounded? In battle?"

"His fortress fell on him," Gundabyr said bluntly. "When the kraken knocked it down."

"The what?"

Samcadaris explained grimly. "Thonbec is no more. The enemy command a great sea monster, which tore the fortress apart as though it were made of parchment. Its tentacles—"

"Hadn't you better save the report for the Speaker?" Vixa interrupted, noting the terrified looks Samcadaris's words were generating among the others on the ferry.

One of the crew, fear draining the color from his face, blurted, "Sea monster, Captain?"

Another put in, "What sort of fearsome beast could destroy an entire fortress?"

"Don't worry," Gundabyr said in a loud, genial voice. "The kraken can swallow three-masters for breakfast and swamp cities with a single belch, but it won't come to Silvanost."

The elves stared at him, openmouthed. "Why not?" asked one.

"Your river's too small. The kraken's a mile across, after all."

The Silvanesti did not look reassured.

They docked at an elegant white marble gatehouse, with raised drawbridge and arrow loops bristling with wary elven archers. The herald went ashore as soon as the bridge was lowered. The four soldiers from Thonbec bore their wounded general off the barge and took him away to be tended. Silvanesti from all over the quayside gathered to see the strange outlanders. As Vixa and Gundabyr awaited their turn to come ashore, quite a crowd collected.

"Make way! Make way! I am on the Speaker's business!" cried the herald, clearing a path for them through the curious throng.

The Silvanesti parted for him, but did not disperse. They began to murmur and point as the two outsiders came down the gangplank. Vixa felt the heat of attention. After weeks of living underwater, then fighting and escaping from Thonbec, she hardly resembled the regal daughter of a neighboring kingdom. She would have preferred to visit fabled Silvanost under different circumstances. It was obvious Gundabyr was feeling much the same way, despite his studied nonchalance. He hardly earned much respect for Thorbardin by his scruffy appearance. Still, Vixa held her head high and strode purposefully behind the herald. She might not be dressed as a princess, but she could certainly act like one.

"Hey, is this . . . a race?" Gundabyr panted, jogging to keep up with her.

Vixa didn't respond. The hostility of the Silvanesti was reminding her of her first sight of the common folk of Urione, when she and Armantaro had been taken through the streets to the palace. She was growing weary of such arrogant treatment. The fact she had come here only to save these ill-mannered elves made her angrier still.

After a few minutes the crowds thinned. Here the streets were wider as well, paved in white granite and spotlessly clean. Elaborate gardens peeped over the walls and roofs of private homes. White roses and lilac twined around doorways, giving off a heady scent. The air felt oddly charged, as though a thunderstorm had just passed, though there wasn't a cloud in the sky.

Gundabyr remarked upon it as well.

Samcadaris said, "We are used to it. Some sages say it is the presence of godly favor, bestowed upon us as the first race in the world. Others say it's the collective auras of so many Silvanesti living in one place. Still another opinion is that the presence of the Speaker of the Stars causes it."

"What do you believe?" Vixa asked.

He shrugged. "I am just a soldier, lady. I leave such mysteries for others to ponder."

Vixa liked his answer. Instead of trying to impress her with mysticism, he told the simple truth.

From a quiet residential street the procession entered a marvelous thoroughfare, paved in marble and gold. Here they had a clear view of the mightiest spire in the city, the Tower of the Stars. Vixa caught her breath at its beauty. This was Uriona's goal, the seat of power for the monarch of the first elven kingdom. Six hundred feet tall, made of the purest white marble, in the dimness of the twilit evening the Tower of the Stars glowed with its own light, shining like a beacon.

"I wouldn't mind seeing that up close," Gundabyr confided to Vixa.

The herald, overhearing, remarked, "No outsider has set foot inside the Tower since the beginning of the Kinslayer War."

The very matter-of-factness of his tone caused Gundabyr to bristle. To forestall any argument, Vixa asked, "Who is Speaker now? Is it still Sithas, son of Sithel? News from Silvanost is hard to come by."

"Great Sithas died two decades ago. His fourth son, Elendar, now holds the Throne of the Stars."

A beautiful carriage of red maple inlaid with carnelian and drawn by a team of three black horses rolled past them. The herald hailed this vision. To Vixa's delight, it proved to be for hire.

"Take us to Tower Protector," the herald ordered. When everyone was aboard, the driver clucked his tongue, and the trio of horses trotted away.

Nestled in butter-soft leather cushions, Vixa and Gundabyr found themselves playing tourist. They pointed to striking buildings and quizzed Samcadaris and the herald (whose name, they learned, was Tiahmoro) to identify them. The Qualinesti princess was especially delighted to see the Temple of Astra—or Astarin, as the Bard King was known in Silvanesti. This was the great founding temple, more ancient than any other in the world. They saw the dwellings of the nobility, richly faced with gold and silver, surrounded by trees that had been magically formed into fantastic shapes.

The boulevard led them to a circular plaza. In its center stood a square building of yellow stone with a distinctly military flavor. Just behind it was a thick tower of white marble. The tower rose some seventy feet into the darkening sky. Next to it were several smaller towers, each only fifty feet tall. The carriage stopped. All four of them dismounted.

This, Vixa surmised, was the headquarters of the Speaker's household guard, House Protector. They entered the square building through monumental front doors. Armed guards snapped to attention as they passed.

From her childhood lessons, Vixa knew that Silvanesti society was highly stratified, arranged in a rigid caste system. Every elf belonged to a certain house. There were many of these, from House Royal (the rulers descended from the first Speaker, Silvanos) through House Cleric, House Mason, and down to House Servitor. House Protector was the official army of Silvanost.

They wound through several corridors, ending at last in a central rotunda. This room, located in the main tower itself, rose seven stories to a massive dome. Diminished by these titanic proportions, Vixa and Gundabyr unconsciously inched closer together.

Samcadaris, unmoved by his familiar surroundings, strode through the echoing rotunda. He led them to a raised platform in the center of the great hall. An elderly elf in military garb sat at a high desk there.

"Ah, Samcadaris, son of Palindar, is it not? What have we

here?" the old fellow said, his pale blue eyes fastening on Vixa.

"Sir, I wish to report the destruction of the citadel of Thonbec," Samcadaris said calmly.

"What?" the ancient elf's shocked exclamation caused heads to turn throughout the rotunda.

Samcadaris recited the story once more: how he and his friends had found the two outsiders on the beach, how they had warned General Axarandes of the Dargonesti invasion, how the invasion had come, and how the undersea kraken had destroyed the fortress. As he spoke, idle warriors gathered around, listening intently.

"Where is Axarandes?" asked the desk officer.

"In the arms of Quenesti Pah," replied Samcadaris. "The goddess willing, he will live."

The old officer took out a sheet of parchment and a stylus. He wrote for several seconds, then said, "Herald, you will go to the court. Here is your pass. Ask that the Speaker see these people as soon as possible."

Many of the warriors in the rotunda protested his hasty decision. The old officer glowered and hammered on his desktop with the pommel of his dagger. The warriors fell silent. He finished writing, dusted the parchment with sand, and rolled it up. Tying it with a silken cord, he handed the scroll to Tiahmoro.

"You may wait here until the Speaker grants an audience, lady," said the desk officer. "I will send word to those on watch."

For the first time in many days, Vixa relaxed, at least a little. A flush of satisfaction warmed her tired body. She saluted smartly, saying, "Thank you, sir!"

The warriors dispersed, still arguing among themselves about the strange story. Tiahmoro departed, and Vixa lingered at the desk.

"Sir, may I make a request?" she asked softly.

"What is it?"

"If I am to meet the Speaker of the Stars, I would like to make myself more presentable. A bath and clean clothes would be most welcome."

"Me, too," grunted the dwarf.

The old elf eyed her torn and stained attire. "We have no female garments here, lady."

"Soldier's attire would suit me well, sir."

He looked at her for a long, considering moment, seeing for the first time the warrior's bearing beneath the privation and grime. He made up his mind. "Samcadaris," he called. "See to their needs."

The soldier led Vixa and Gundabyr away. The dwarf was taken to the soldiers' common bathing room. Samcadaris escorted the Qualinesti princess to his own room. He called for a bath to be drawn, then departed. Servants brought fresh linen underclothes and an officer's knee-length robe. Vixa washed the salt and dirt of many days from her sunburned skin. When she got out of the bath, she found the new clothes were an excellent fit. Sometimes her height was an advantage.

Half an hour after she'd left, Vixa was back in the rotunda, refreshed and ready to meet the Speaker of the Stars. Gundabyr was there as well, dressed in clean clothing. The elves had scrounged up leggings and a tunic for the dwarf. The hem dangled below his knees.

"Word has come back," said the desk officer. "The Speaker of the Stars will see you this night. His Privy Councillors will be in attendance. Your audience will be in the Quinari Palace."

Gundabyr grumbled at this. He'd hoped to see inside the Tower of the Stars.

The old Silvanesti went on, "Captain Samcadaris will accompany you. Herald Tiahmoro will conduct you."

A short time later, Samcadaris and the herald reappeared. They had changed attire as well and were now clad in their finest dress uniforms: polished steel breastplates, greaves, and vambraces etched in gold with the monogram of the Speaker, and short red capes. Samcadaris's helmet bore a plume from the rare golden peacock, the sacred bird of House Protector, indicating that he had distinguished himself greatly in battle.

An honor guard of forty warriors was drawn up in the

street outside. Vixa and Gundabyr took their places in the center of the column. With Herald Tiahmoro in the lead, they marched away to the Quinari Palace. Idlers and couples strolling in the mild evening air stepped back and watched the glittering procession go by. They looked at Vixa and Gundabyr with surprise and unconcealed suspicion.

The cavalcade approached the gleaming facade of the palace down a long, ceremonial avenue lined with statues of former Speakers. Silvanos, in the guise of warrior, lawgiver, and father, was here. Next came Sithel, in similar poses, and then Sithas, the tragic Speaker who'd reigned through the Kinslayer War and the sundering of the elven nation.

The Quinari Palace was far larger than the residence of the Speaker of the Sun in Qualinost, and far more elaborate. Three three-story wings radiated out from a central tower. Three hundred feet tall, the tower was made of rose-veined marble. The wings were faced with colonnades of green marble, and each column had been formed by powerful magic into a graceful spiral, in imitation of a unicorn's horn.

The honor guard halted and opened ranks. Samcadaris waved Vixa and Gundabyr forward. They mounted a long set of wide steps between double rows of fantastically clad warriors. At the top of the steps, two Silvanesti awaited them, one in armor, helmet, and the swinging gold cape of a marshal of the realm, the other richly robed in midnight blue and wearing a heavy necklace of star sapphires.

Samcadaris bowed to these two worthies. "My lord Druzenalis! My lord Agavenes! I and my charges beg leave to enter the palace of the Speaker of the Stars."

The marshal, Druzenalis, held up his baton of command. "Enter, all. His Majesty awaits within," he intoned. The civilian called Agavenes said nothing, but Gundabyr and Vixa felt his hard gaze raking over them as they passed.

The interior of the palace was cool and dimly lit. It gave off an essence of great age, and to the nervous Vixa, felt cold and forbidding. She still remembered running and playing with her cousins and siblings in the corridors of Speaker

Silveran's residence. She couldn't imagine anyone rough-housing or talking above a whisper in this place. It was as solemn as a temple.

Courtiers gathered in side passages to stare at them. The Silvanesti ladies were all fabulously beautiful and fabulously dressed. Vixa tugged uncomfortably at the neck of her borrowed attire. One nervous hand combed her damp hair, which had a tendency to dry into unruly ringlets.

Stop it, she commanded herself. You're behaving like a fool. How many of these delicate, ethereal beauties, in their robes of silver silk or tissue of ruby, have ever fought chilkit on the bottom of the ocean? These fine damsels in their gauzy trains wouldn't know one end of a sword from the other. It was certain that none of them had raced through the ocean waves in the guise of a black-and-white dolphin. Vixa's back straightened. The Silvanesti ladies were surprised to see a smile appear on the sun-reddened face of the tall Qualinesti girl.

Bronze doors two stories tall swung apart for them. The black polished floor beyond was like a mirror. A scarlet carpet led from the doorway deep into the throne room. Columns soared to the dark ceiling. Druzenalis and Agavenes entered first, bowed to the distant throne, stepped aside. Glancing right and left, Vixa saw that Tiahmoro and Samcadaris were as nervous as she. Their faces were frozen; their hands clenched the hilts of their ornamental swords. Only Gundabyr appeared relaxed in the face of this magnificence. Vixa envied him his composure.

They passed beneath living arches of ivy and vines laden with grapes. Off to one side, a band of musicians played a delicate tune on instruments made entirely of glass. Vixa could see a dais ahead, with the throne upon it. Like the Speaker of the Sun in Qualinost, the Speaker of the Stars used a chamber in his palace for the day-to-day running of his kingdom. The audience hall in the great Tower of the Stars was saved for more auspicious gatherings.

Vixa found herself squinting at the throne. It was occupied, but she couldn't make out any details. It was as if fog veiled the throne dais. Gundabyr, too, rubbed his eyes.

The air around them shimmered. For a moment it seemed a magical illusion, but then they felt a light touch on their heads and faces. It was like a cobweb, no more substantial than that. Gundabyr put out his hand and snagged a wisp of something. The dwarf peered closely at the gossamer threads. Gold! Spun as fine as any spider's web. *Now* he was impressed.

Three more wispy veils, and they could see the throne more clearly. The larger, taller seat was occupied, but the consort's chair next to it was empty. Nobles of the realm stood in two lines on either side of the dais. About five paces from its base, the crimson runner ended. Vixa stopped there, and held Gundabyr back so he wouldn't violate protocol by approaching too close.

The absolute ruler of the Silvanesti sat in an oddly casual posture—slouched down in his marble throne, one leg straight out in front of him, the other bent. A scroll lay across his lap. Its length spilled down his stretched leg and lay loosely coiled on the floor. The Speaker of the Stars appeared to be engrossed in his scroll. He didn't even look up at his visitors' approach.

Vixa cleared her throat. The Silvanesti lords glared at her. The Speaker looked up from his reading.

He was moderately young, less than two hundred years old, Vixa guessed. He had the hazel eyes and white-blond hair of the line of Silvanos, but Speaker Elendar's face was surprisingly free of the haughty expression that seemed the norm for his courtiers. While Vixa and Gundabyr studied him, he studied them as well, peering through a gold wire frame in which was set a polished glass disk.

"A dwarf. I've never seen a dwarf before," the Speaker said, his voice deep and resonant.

Quite devoid of self-consciousness, Gundabyr stumped forward and held out his hand. "Pleased to meet you, Your Majesty." The air was filled with elven gasps. Gundabyr compounded his indiscretion by asking, "What is that thing you're holding?"

"My crystal? Oh, I have a weakness in my eyes that keeps me from seeing clearly things that are more than an arm's length away," was the calm reply. The courtiers seethed with indignation at the dwarf's informality, but the Speaker of the Stars seemed unconcerned. "It enlarges things. See?"

Gundabyr took the proffered object and held the two-inch-wide glass disk to his eye. "By Reorx!" Turning to Vixa, he exclaimed, "I want one of these things! All those late nights I spent at the forge, trying to read recipes from the *Forgemaster's Journal* . . ."

Speaker Elendar regarded the dwarf with unconcealed amusement. "I shall have one made for you, Master Gundabyr. And you," he said to Vixa, "are said to be my cousin. Is this true?"

She bowed as she would to her uncle, Speaker Silveran. "I am Vixa Ambrodel, Sire. Your father and my grandfather were brothers."

"Yes, but not very good brothers." There was no malice in his tone. He smiled at her and added, "And now you've had quite an adventure, haven't you? Oh, yes, I've heard it all, Cousin. You lead an active life, like all those of the line of Kith-Kanan." The Speaker sighed.

Vixa could have sworn that there was a wistful quality to his words, as though the Speaker of the Stars, for all his power and prestige, envied her.

Agavenes and Druzenalis had come up behind the others. The Speaker asked the marshal about the current military situation.

"Great Speaker, since the destruction of Thonbec, there has been little sign of the invaders. We have reports from farmers and fisherfolk of the enemy on both sides of the river, but none have been seen more than a league north of the fortress," reported Druzenalis.

"And what do you make of that, Marshal?"

Druzenalis did not even glance at Vixa and Gundabyr. "I say it is a diversion, Majesty. It smells of Qualinesti duplicity," he replied coldly.

Vixa was outraged. "What? How dare—"

"What sort of invasion is it that fails to follow up on a significant victory?" the marshal went on. "Thonbec has fallen—so where are the enemy? Had they struck within a day of the citadel's fall, the element of surprise would have been on their side. I believe, if anything, this is a diversion from the true attack, which will come from the west."

More shocking than the marshal's accusation were the nods of agreement from the assembled Silvanesti nobility. Vixa exploded, "That's ridiculous! The Speaker of the Sun is devoted to peace! Everyone knows that!"

"I have stated my opinion." Druzenalis put a hand on the hilt of his short ceremonial sword. "Great Speaker, I think this girl is a spy and a deceiver. I say she should be thrown into prison. Let her ponder the unwisdom of trying to make fools of the Silvanesti."

The Speaker leaned forward, his blond eyebrows rising. "It *is* strange the enemy has not invaded Silvanost yet. Have you an answer for that, Cousin?"

Vixa took a deep breath. Angry ranting would do her no good. She must make her case calmly, sensibly. "Majesty, the Dargonesti are used to living in the depths of the sea. I can think of many reasons why they have delayed—the sunlight blinds them, the fresh water of the river could be distasteful to them, their kraken may be unmanageable—"

"The outlander is delaying," Druzenalis cut in. "Send her to prison, Sire. And the dwarf as well."

Until now, Samcadaris had remained silent, intimidated by his surroundings. At last he found his tongue. "Great Speaker," he said cautiously, "may one who witnessed the fall of Thonbec speak his mind?"

The Speaker nodded. "By our leave."

"Everything Lady Vixa and Master Gundabyr told us at Thonbec proved to be true. The Dargonesti are real. I have seen them, fought them. Twice the warriors from the sea attacked the fort, but always by night. If I were their commander—" He glanced around nervously as if to gauge how far he could go. "If I were the Dargonesti commander, I would not have attacked yet either."

"And why not?" sneered the marshal.

"Silvanost is an island. The surest way for a water-dwelling foe to lay siege to a city as large as ours is to envelop the island."

"With ten thousand troops? It cannot be done," Druzenalis snapped. "A hundred thousand, or more, would be required to encircle Fallan!"

"In conventional terms, yes, sir. But the Dargonesti have an advantage. They can attack us on land, but we can't touch them under the water."

Vixa saw what the captain was driving at. "Yes," she said, nodding. "The Dargonesti don't need to defend their lines against attack, therefore they don't need thousands of troops. By strategically placing their forces around the island, they can attack at will. And they can always retreat to the safety of the river."

The Speaker's relaxed posture vanished in an instant. He turned an intense gaze upon Druzenalis. "Could this be true, Marshal?"

Druzenalis was looking disconcerted, but he tried to wave off his junior's ideas. "Assuming these enemies even exist, then *perhaps*—"

"I saw them!" Samcadaris said with heat.

"Me too," Gundabyr put in. "And an Ironbender doesn't lie!"

Gundabyr and Vixa were glaring at the marshal. Druzenalis kept his eyes fixed on the Speaker. The growing tension was diffused by calm words from Speaker Elendar.

"It seems you have brought a timely warning, Cousin," he said, smiling at Vixa. "You and Master Gundabyr will remain here in the palace as my guests. Captain Samcadaris, you have served your country bravely. You are dismissed as well, with our thanks."

At a gesture from the Speaker, two servants stepped forward. Vixa and Gundabyr bowed to the throne, and the servants escorted them from the room. She sent Samcadaris a questioning look, but the Silvanesti captain only shrugged. Vixa sighed. They had delivered the warning. Now it was up to the Silvanesti.

As they were ushered out of the audience hall, the Qualinesti princess heard Druzenalis begin a haughty denunciation of her and her story. Lord Agavenes joined in, agreeing with the marshal. Vixa was surprised to find herself feeling a bit sorry for the Speaker. He seemed to have inherited retainers from his father's reign. Like most old retainers, each thought he knew better than anyone else—better, even, than the Speaker of the Stars.

Chapter 20

The Sword of Balif

Under the wind-tossed waves near the mouth of the Thon-Thalas, the Dargonesti were gathering. Queen Uriona's servants erected a seaweed canopy to protect their queen from the sun's rays in the relatively shallow water. Uriona's throne, laboriously borne here from the distant city, was set under the canopy. The throne itself was a low, four-legged, back-less chair carved of blood coral and inlaid with precious stones. Its wide seat curved up slightly on each side into arms shaped to resemble leaping dolphins.

Coryphene escorted Uriona to the place prepared for her. The queen, her face covered by a soft silver mask, seated herself.

"When will you be ready to attack?" she asked in the shrill, clicking tones of the water-tongue.

"Soon, Divine One," Coryphene replied. "The army even now moves to encircle Silvanost. Once I join them, we shall begin the assault."

She nodded. Her lavender eyes—all that was visible

beneath her mask—stared absently at the pearls stitched down the sleeve of her robe. After a moment, Uriona murmured, "I should be with you at the ancient capital. I should be ready to enter my city once the land-dwellers are defeated."

"Majesty, we have discussed this. You must not be placed in danger unnecessarily. Wait, just a little while, until the enemy is conquered."

"Are you so certain they will be overcome? Your army is few. The drylanders are many."

"They cannot stand against us!"

"Perhaps," she replied. "But it is well I have brought the Shades of Zura with me. If the fight proves too much for you, their magic can be brought to bear on the Silvanesti."

"I have no need of them," he said angrily. "I shall conquer by spear and lance, not by veils of clouds."

All at once her abstracted expression vanished, and she turned a penetrating look upon him. "Victory is within our grasp, Coryphene," she said softly. "I see the city in our hands. I hear Quoowahb cheers ringing through the Tower of the Stars as I am crowned queen of the ancient race. Go, Lord Protector. Liberate my city."

"Silvanost will soon be yours, Divine One. I swear it on my life!"

Coryphene sprang up, his powerful legs sending him racing through the water. Once he was lost from sight, Uriona waved a hand, dismissing her hovering attendants. The mask moved slightly as the queen smiled.

"Soon, my brother gods, soon Uriona Firstborn will sit upon the most ancient throne of the elves," she whispered. "Once I am crowned in the Tower of the Stars, my destiny will be complete. No power on Krynn will be able to oppose me. No power on Krynn!"

* * * * *

None of the Dargonesti had ever been in fresh water before, nor so close to land. A few were made ill, but the nausea and light-headedness passed quickly. The great majority found it exhilarating, like swimming through water churned up by a great storm. Coryphene was among the latter. The Protector of Urione, with a small escort, moved swiftly through the river. Once he had joined his troops, the battle for Silvanost would begin.

The sun was low in the western sky when Coryphene and his escort came within sight of the city. He was amazed by its beauty. Its very strangeness, glimmering in the dry air, caused him to beam with anticipation. Soon, he and his queen would walk its streets, explore its mysteries, and fulfill their destiny. She would be its ruler, and he its defender. It would be the first of many victories.

The Dargonesti of Urione had too long been isolated in their city. It was time for them to make their presence known. Coryphene, under the guidance of the divine Uriona, intended to remind the world that the sea was the true power on Krynn.

He swam to the eastern side of the city, which was already in deep shadow. He and his troops watched as night closed over Silvanost and sparkling points of light appeared in its windows. Once more he marveled at the soaring towers and the strange growths called trees.

The sight of the gracefully shaped trees brought to his mind the drylander girl, Vixa Ambrodel, who'd first explained them to Uriona. She'd been spotted among the defenders of Thonbec, and it was assumed she'd perished with them. The Protector found himself genuinely regretting her death. Brave and resourceful, she would've made a fine ally.

As he stared at the drylander city, Coryphene felt excitement building in him. Soon, very soon, the land-dwellers would know that the legends were true. They would see that the Dargonesti were very real. The power of the sea would again be respected—and feared.

*　*　*　*　*

Vixa and Gundabyr had been invited to dine this evening with the Speaker of the Stars. Unlike the usual state occasions, when as many as fifty might sit down with the ruler of the Silvanesti, only the three of them were present for this meal. In one of the palace's smaller rooms a table, laden with food and drink, was set up. Three places were laid with gold plates and silken napkins.

The Qualinesti princess felt she had spent a very unfruitful day. She had slept until nearly noon and had absolutely no duties to occupy her time. Her requests for information on the progress of the city's defenses were met with ignorance (from the servants) or unhelpful politeness (from everyone else). Lord Agavenes had sent a barely civil request that the Qualinesti girl and her dwarven companion remain within the palace, so as not to disrupt the citizens of Silvanost by wandering about the streets. Vixa had been furious, but Gundabyr—feeling he'd earned a respite—bluntly told her to stop her grumbling. He said they should take what rest they could, since once the Dargonesti got here there'd be no sleep for any of them.

The Speaker's summons had been most welcome to Vixa. She assumed he would answer her many questions about the plans for Silvanost's defense. She was wrong.

Speaker Elendar seated himself at the table and bade his guests do likewise. He was a charming host, and with his own hand filled three slender goblets with nectar. Once these were distributed, he dismissed his attendants so he and his guests could speak in private.

When Gundabyr tasted the nectar, his bushy black eyebrows rose. An excellent vintage. He'd never tasted better. He downed the entire contents of the goblet in one gulp, then held it out for more. Speaker Elendar smilingly refilled it. Once this amount was reduced by half, Gundabyr partook of some of the delicacies set before him. The food was a little light for his tastes, but certainly more than palatable. The dwarf gave the Speaker a puzzled look.

"Majesty, don't get me wrong, but I thought you Silvanesti were all like Agavenes and Druzenalis, and didn't care for outsiders."

Elendar sipped his own nectar. He held the goblet in both hands, staring at the pattern of stars engraved on its slender bowl.

"I am my father's fourth son," he said by way of explanation. "The previous Speaker was the last of my brothers. When he died, most unexpectedly, none of his sons was old enough to rule, so I came to the throne." Vixa and the dwarf regarded him blankly. He sipped his nectar and went on. "My point is, it was never expected that I would become Speaker, so I wasn't trained for the role. As I had a bent for scholarship, I spent most of my early life with tutors. I know a great deal about Qualinesti and Thorbardin, but it has all come from books. Meeting you has been the most interesting thing to happen to me in ages."

"Lately, my life's been nothing but interesting," Vixa said dryly.

"The end is in sight, lady," was his serene rejoinder.

Gundabyr set his delicate goblet down so hard it rang against the tabletop. "You're not thinking of surrendering?" he blurted.

"Of course not."

"Sire, what plans have you made for the defense of the city?" Vixa asked.

"Last night an edict went out to every corner of the realm, summoning all freeborn males to our service. In a week, two hundred thousand Silvanesti will arrive to defend their capital. Of course, an enemy that breathes water is a formidable foe. I don't know that the levies will be of much use against the Dargonesti."

Vixa was silent, but her expression spoke eloquently of her inability to understand his calmness in the face of such a threat.

"Don't trouble yourself, Cousin," the Speaker added soothingly. "Coryphene cannot succeed. In a week, he will either be dead or captured and Silvanost will be saved.

This simple pronouncement was too much for the Qualinesti princess. She demanded, "How is this so, Majesty? You cannot do battle underwater!"

The Speaker broke a round loaf of bread into three portions, handing one to each of them. He took a bite of the sweet bread, chewed, and swallowed, then said, "Once we were warned of the sea elves' advance, any chance they had to overwhelm us disappeared. Did this Coryphene and his queen imagine they could defeat a nation of one million Silvanesti with an army of ten thousand? Coryphene is bold, I'll grant, and we have been burdened by old fools like Druzenalis and Agavenes for too long, but Silvanost is home to some of the greatest thaumaturges on Krynn." He nodded slowly. "The fact that the Dargonesti will most likely surround the city works to our advantage—they will be spread thin. When the blow falls, Coryphene won't be able to rally them."

"What blow?" asked Gundabyr, mystified.

"My friends, you must be patient. I am not yet ready to reveal all." The Speaker would say no more. Instead, he filled his plate from the bounty before them. Vixa and Gundabyr exchanged helpless looks, but had to content themselves with talking of other things. They answered the Speaker's questions about their homelands and the other places they'd seen. A peaceful hour sped by.

At the conclusion of the meal, the Speaker of the Stars rose and offered his arm to Vixa—a great honor. "Would you like to see the Tower of the Stars?" he asked. "It's always beautiful, but at night it is particularly so."

They accepted with enthusiasm. Not even Vixa's worry over the coming invasion could keep her from taking advantage of such a generous invitation. She might very well be the only living Qualinesti to enjoy such an opportunity.

The sun had set a short while before. As they crossed the plaza that separated the palace from the Tower of the Stars, Gundabyr kept up a steady stream of questions and comments. The dwarf fell silent once they entered the main hall in the Tower. The aura of power and majesty in the great structure made any noise at all seem sacrilegious.

The Tower of the Stars was basically a hollow shaft six hundred feet high. Three levels of small chambers ringed its base. Lines of window openings and precious jewels spiraled up the interior walls. This evening the jewels reflected the light of the red moon, Lunitari, and the white, Solinari, filling the interior with flashing rainbows. The Tower's domed ceiling was dark and unadorned, pierced by a single opening that allowed a shaft of pearly moonlight to reach the floor far below.

Vixa and Gundabyr stared, their heads thrown back to take it all in. No columns supported the interior, and the vast open breadth of this central chamber was awe-inspiring. Vixa had thought the golden beauty of the Tower of the Sun in Qualinost could never be equaled, but this white and shining monument left her gasping.

Ahead of them, at the rear of the audience hall, seven steps led up to a raised platform. Three additional, wider steps led from this platform to the throne dais. The emerald Throne of the Stars sat in silent splendor on the dais.

The beauty of the Tower still moved the Speaker. When he spoke, it was in a whisper. "Behind the throne is a small door. It leads to a tightly spiraling stair that reaches to the battlements near the Tower's apex."

"Can we go up?" asked Gundabyr eagerly.

Before the Speaker could reply, an interruption occurred. "Sire, may I enter?" a voice called from the doorway.

They turned and saw an elf standing in the Tower's main entrance. The Speaker told the newcomer to enter. When he stepped into the moonlight illuminating the hall, they saw he wore the green tabard of a herald. His clothing was muddied, and he obviously had been running hard. His breathing was labored.

"I beg to report attacks, Sire, the first attacks on the city!" he panted.

As these dreadful words rang out, a group of elves appeared in the entrance behind the courier. They crowded into the audience hall. In the group were Druzenalis, Agavenes, and several priests and warriors, Samcadaris among the latter.

Druzenalis boomed, "Majesty, I have received reports that the city is under attack!"

"I have just heard the same news," the Speaker said dryly. "Herald, where is the enemy?"

"They have attacked from the east, Great Speaker, at the Gate of Astarin." This was the point at which Vixa and Gundabyr had entered the city. "They have slain the sacred turtle that drew the eastern ferry, and stormed the gate-house itself," the herald replied.

The Speaker thrust a finger at Samcadaris. "You," he said, "take half the royal guard and go to the Astarin Gate. Drive the enemy from our city."

The young captain saluted crisply. "It shall be done, Great Speaker, or I will not return alive!"

"Sire? Cousin?" Vixa said quickly. "May I join the fight?"

Speaker Elendar smiled faintly. "By all means. I hear your parents are most formidable warriors—especially Lady Verhanna. I welcome her daughter to our ranks. But you cannot meet the enemy unarmed. Druzenalis, give her your sword."

"Majesty!" The marshal was obviously taken aback. When Vixa had asked to join the battle, he hadn't bothered to hide his displeasure. His Speaker's command, however, caused Druzenalis's pale face to flush. "You cannot mean it. Give up my sword to this . . . this *outsider?*"

The loathing in those words stung her. Vixa held out her hand. The marshal did not move.

One of the Speaker's silver-white brows rose question-ingly. In a calm voice, he said, "Loan my cousin your sword, Marshal. Oblige me."

Druzenalis yanked the brilliant blade from its scabbard. It was only two feet long—obviously ceremonial. For a moment, Vixa thought she was going to receive it point-first. But he reversed his grip and handed the hilt to her.

"I promise to do it honor, my lord," Vixa said gravely, though Druzenalis pointedly ignored her. She looked to Gundabyr, who was grinning. "How about you? Want to come?"

He winked. "I got nothin' better to do right now."

Vixa, Samcadaris, and the dwarf rushed from the Tower of the Stars, preceded by the mud-spattered herald. Vixa heard heated words flash between the Marshal of Silvanost and his Speaker.

Outdoors, an orange glow lit the night sky. A fire was burning, a big one, in the wooded park that covered much of the south end of the island. Silvanesti elves ran to and fro in the streets, clutching bundles and sometimes weapons. Nevertheless, it was remarkably orderly.

"If Thorbardin were under attack, every dwarf in the kingdom would be at his front door, yelling at the top of his lungs," Gundabyr said.

"Why?" asked Samcadaris.

"For the enemy to come and face them, of course."

The dwarf dashed into the palace to retrieve the axe he'd fashioned at Thonbec. A cadre of five hundred elves, the cream of the Silvanesti army, was drawn up and ready in the neighboring street. Samcadaris went to the center of the boulevard and called the subordinate commanders together. He apprised them of the situation, and told them what was expected. In minutes the royal guard was surging through the streets, heading for the embattled Astarin Gate. Gundabyr, axe in hand, ran by Vixa's side.

They saw a small blaze burning outside the wall when they reached the gate, no doubt started by Gundabyr's gift of gnomefire. Though it was full night, the glare of the fire made it easy for the oncoming warriors to see the swarm of figures crowded into the open gatehouse. The Dargonesti were easily distinguished by their greater height, and the firelight gave their blue skin an odd tint.

Vixa found herself elbowing past the Silvanesti warriors to get at the enemy first. She was finally going to meet her enslavers on dry land, with a sword in her hand.

Weapons of the fallen littered the street, and Vixa was able to add to her armament a shield. While she paused to take it up, Gundabyr rushed by her with a whoop, leaving the ordered ranks of elves behind.

From the gatehouse roof, a rain of arrows fell. Though the scene was a jumble of blue skin and white, the well-aimed arrows of the Silvanesti archers hit only enemy bodies. Their skill was marvelous to behold. The hail of missiles was all that kept the Dargonesti from breaking through the shelter of the gate and rampaging through the city streets.

Some of the sea elves formed a line of green shields across the open gate and held off the Silvanesti defenders as others started to climb the steps inside the gatehouse to get at the pesky archers on the roof. All the while, flames leapt up from the other side of the wall, bathing the scene in hellish, shifting light.

The royal guard charged, hacking at the opposing side with their swords. Vixa traded a few blows with a spear carrier. As she closed in, she realized that this sea elf looked different from those she'd encountered in Urione. Though still fully seven feet tall, his skin was a much lighter blue and his hair was silver, not green. It was bound in a thick braid that reached below his shoulder blades, the braid studded with dozens of tiny shells. A large pearl dangled from a tiny hole in his right earlobe. He and his compatriots must be the Dimernesti, or shoal elves, she'd heard were fighting alongside Coryphene's troops.

Screams rang out above. Some of the Silvanesti archers tumbled from the gatehouse roof, thrown down by Dimernesti who'd gained the heights. Vixa saw quickly that the real battle was up there. She backed out of range and shouted to Gundabyr, "Can you climb?"

He saw the danger, too. "You bet. After you, Princess!"

She ran around to the side of the white marble gatehouse. Here, in the quiet shadows, the wounded had crawled away to suffer or die. There was no time to help them. The Qualinesti princess and the dwarf hurried to the foot of the gatehouse wall. The marble was smooth as glass, offering no handholds.

"That line of windows, up there!" Gundabyr said, pointing. "It must be a stairwell."

Vixa made a stirrup of her hands. Shaking his head, the dwarf told her, "You may be a warrior-hero, Princess, but you couldn't lift me. Climb on!"

He slapped his broad shoulders. Vixa wasted no time arguing. She placed one foot on his bent knee and clambered up to his shoulders. Gundabyr swayed and grunted, but he held. The added height allowed Vixa to reach the sill of the lowest window. She hauled herself up. The dwarf's guess had been correct—she found herself in a dimly lit stairwell.

"Princess! Catch!" Vixa leaned out the window. Gundabyr extended a discarded spear. He climbed the shaft as she anchored it, throwing her weight against the pull of his. Weeks of slavery had thinned the stocky dwarf sufficiently that he was able, just barely, to squeeze into the narrow window opening.

Once they were both inside, the Qualinesti princess cried, "Let's go!" They charged up the steps. The thumping of Gundabyr's feet behind her was a reassuring sound. Above them, the noise of the fighting rose. As Vixa rounded the fourth bend in the stairwell, a body came tumbling down, nearly knocking her from her feet. The Silvanesti soldier slid to a lifeless stop against the curving wall.

There was a landing ahead, clogged with wounded and dead from both sides. From there, the steps passed through a narrow opening and wound in a tighter spiral to the roof. Vixa stepped carefully over the fallen fighters. Just as she did, a Dimernesti with a long silver braid of hair loomed out of the darkness. His eyes widened in surprise. He backed a step and brought up his barbed spear. Vixa batted it aside with the flat of her blade, pushing forward all the time. Gundabyr crouched nearby, waiting for an opening.

The shoal elf hefted his spear and hurled it at Vixa. She easily deflected it with her shield, but while she was busy doing so, the Dimernesti's hands flashed to his waist. They came away with a weighted throwing net studded with gleaming fishhooks.

"Vixa! Look out!" roared the dwarf. The Dimernesti swung the net once and let fly. Instinctively, Vixa put up her shield. The weighted net wrapped around it and her. The fishhooks took hold. She tried to back away from her advancing foe, but tripped on the fallen warriors.

As the Dimernesti brought out a short-handled trident, Gundabyr bellowed a war cry and swung his axe. The nimble shoal elf leapt over the low swing. The dwarf's intervention allowed Vixa to struggle to her knees. She tried to discard her encumbered shield, but the fishhooks had pierced her clothing and, quite painfully, her skin.

The Dimernesti closed in. He kicked at Vixa's netted shield, and the blows sent her reeling once more. Her side exposed, he lunged with the trident. Vixa, flat on her back, flung up Druzenalis's short sword. As she thrust it at her opponent, she felt a surge like lightning flow from the hilt and travel along the blade. A flash of light jumped from the blade tip. In the next instant, the astonished Dimernesti found himself impaled on the blade. The trident fell from his webbed fingers. He collapsed sideways, taking the sword with him.

Gundabyr was at her side. "Get this damn net off me!" she fumed. The dwarf wound the net around the trident, like noodles on a fork.

As he worked to untangle the barbed net, Gundabyr demanded, "What just happened? I'd swear that little sword of yours just reached out and—and *grabbed* him!"

"There is certainly some power in it," she agreed, wincing from the pain of the fishhooks. "Trust the marshal of Silvanost to carry a magical weapon!" Her arm was free at last, and she impatiently flung her shield aside.

They ran up the last few turns of the stairs and emerged onto the roof. As Gundabyr was fond of saying, the luck was with them—and it was all bad. They faced eight Dimernesti, and no Silvanesti archers remained to help them.

"Uh, suggestions?" Vixa asked as the seven-foot-tall enemy turned to face them.

"Trust the gods and have at 'em!" cried the dwarf, rushing forward.

Caught by surprise, she gathered herself and followed him. "Great plan!" she shouted as they raced across the rooftop.

The mercenaries were used to fighting elves of their own stature, and the axe-wielding dwarf was new to them. By the time they figured him out, Gundabyr had knocked two down with great sweeps of his axe. Vixa accounted for a third very quickly by rushing in and allowing her magical sword to do its stuff. In a flash, the opposition had shrunk from eight to five—a definite improvement.

The Dimernesti separated, trying to surround their

attackers. Vixa and Gundabyr closed together, standing back to back. As their opponents sized them up, Vixa said to the dwarf, "I like this sword. Maybe I'll keep it."

"The marshal doesn't strike me as the generous type," commented Gundabyr, trying to keep a wary eye on two Dimernesti simultaneously.

With keening yells, the five shoal elves rushed them. Vixa parried one spear, thrust through the belly of the Dimernesti wielding it, snatched back her weapon, and parried her other opponent's attack. Gundabyr, fighting three foes, shoved the axe head into one fellow's chest, knocking him down. As he fell, another elf speared the dwarf in the shoulder. Roaring from pain and anger, Gundabyr chopped the spear off, and his attacker's hands as well. The third elf swung his spear at the dwarf, catching him on the side of the head. The dwarf staggered forward, trying to ward off further attacks with wild swings of his axe.

"Vixa!" he cried, falling to his knees.

The Qualinesti princess was busy defending her own life. Her opponent jabbed his spear at her face and chest. Her sword tip flashed under his nose. He backed to the edge of the roof. Suddenly, he gave a cry and toppled. A Silvanesti arrow had sprouted from his back.

The last Dimernesti, realizing he was alone, ceased his attacks on Gundabyr and sprinted for the steps. Vixa let him go, rushing to where Gundabyr lay.

The tough dwarf was still breathing, but his shoulder was bleeding freely. Vixa tore a wide strip from the hem of her kilt and jammed it against Gundabyr's wound.

"Aaah!" he moaned. "You're killing me!"

"Shut up!" she said fiercely. She pressed the bleeding wound harder.

From below came scraping and vibration as the ponderous gates were swung shut. That told her that the Silvanesti had prevailed, and the gate was now secure. A few moments later, Samcadaris and a score of fresh archers spilled onto the roof of the gatehouse.

"Lady! Are you well?" he called. His lean face was blackened by soot and streaked with blood—green Dimernesti blood. His red cape was bloodied as well.

"I'm all right, but Gundabyr needs a healer," she told him.

Samcadaris surveyed the carnage on the rooftop. "The sisters of Quenesti Pah are in the street below. Here, you two, take Master Gundabyr to them. Take him with all care and honor!"

Two elves carried the grumbling dwarf away. Vixa picked up Druzenalis's magic sword and shoved it through her belt.

"That was magnificent," Samcadaris told her when they were alone. "I never saw a finer fight. Two against eight—and they larger than you!"

"It was stupid," she said flatly. "Barging up here, just me and Gundabyr. Suppose there had been twenty instead of eight? I'd've ended up on the pavement down there, like your brave archers. I might have anyway, if not for this sword." She patted the pommel of the marshal's weapon.

"Ah, yes, Balif's sword. Longreacher."

Vixa stared at him and then at the sword. "Balif? This weapon belonged to him?"

"Yes, indeed. Great Silvanos had it wrought specially for his friend. He wanted the kender general to have a weapon that would make up for his lack of height. The sword has always been carried by the first soldier of the realm, the marshal of Silvanost."

Vixa withdrew it reverently from her belt and held it out to him. "I feel privileged to have held it, much less borne it into battle. But it's not right. Druzenalis should have it."

Samcadaris put his hand on the hilt, gently pushing it away. "Druzenalis has served the nation long and honorably. Of late, he has quarreled openly with the Speaker. His Majesty took the sword from him for good reason. He loaned it to you as a sign of favor."

Before she could say anything, runners appeared in the street below, crying out a summons from the Speaker of the Stars. All warriors not engaged in active defense were commanded to gather back at the Quinari Palace immediately.

With weary steps, Samcadaris and Vixa left the rooftop. In the street, scores of Silvanesti were being treated by healers from the temple of Quenesti Pah. A small band of Dimernesti, looking sullen and dejected, were under guard by Samcadaris's troops. Their gills were shriveled, and most of them swayed weakly where they stood.

"Better give those fellows water," Vixa advised the captain. "They'll perish in the dry air."

Samcadaris ordered that water be brought for the captives, and he appointed half his contingent to remain at the gate for its defense. The rest, somewhat less than two hundred elves, would march back to the Quinari as ordered.

Vixa found Gundabyr sitting up on the pavement, his left arm in a sling. Though pale, he was lively enough to curse the pain as he struggled to his feet.

"Keep still," she said genially.

He insisted on walking back to the palace with her, and Vixa was glad for his company. The fire in the south had gone out, and clouds obscured the stars. By the time they reached the front steps of the Quinari, the street was alive with torchbearers and armed elves, standing in eerily silent ranks.

"What's going on?" muttered the dwarf.

Vixa replied out of the side of her mouth, "Nothing good, I'll wager."

Samcadaris and his warriors took their places in the ranks, leaving Vixa and Gundabyr at loose ends. Tired and aching, the dwarf lowered himself to sit on the fine stone steps.

"I must find Druzenalis and return his sword," Vixa said.

"Do that. I'll stay here and catch forty winks." He lay down, pillowing his head on his good arm, and sighed. Vixa mounted the steps. She approached several Silvanesti officers and asked for the marshal. None of them said a word, but one pointed to the palace door.

Vixa went inside. She wandered back toward the audience chamber, and as she drew near, the sound of weeping reached her ears. At the entrance to the throne room, she realized that the weeping came from within. Something had happened. Someone important must be dead. An icy hand closed on her heart. Surely it wasn't the Speaker of the Stars!

As Vixa hurried into the darkened audience hall, she could see shadowy figures standing around the room's perimeter. Her eyes were drawn to the throne dais. A bier was set up on it, and a corpse laid out, covered by a shroud of blazing red silk. A single figure stood at the bier, with his back to Vixa. She slowed her hurried approach.

"My lord?" she said, her voice weak and uncertain.

The figure turned. It was Agavenes, the chamberlain.

"So, the Qualinesti princess. You live. Not surprising."

"Who lies there?"

Without a word, Agavenes flicked back the shroud from the corpse's face.

"Druzenalis!" Vixa exclaimed.

"Yes, the Marshal of Silvanost is dead." Agavenes's voice was icy.

"How did it happen?"

"After his humiliation by the Speaker, Druzenalis left the palace and placed himself at the head of his troops. They marched out of Red Rose Gate to confront the enemy in the southern forest. A fire was burning there, and Druzenalis wanted to extinguish it, lest it threaten the city. But it was a trap. The enemy attacked on three sides with fire and sword. Very few Silvanesti escaped."

"Five thousand brave elves went out. Less than five hundred returned."

Vixa was horrified. It was a terrible defeat, and it far outweighed their small success at Astarin Gate. She whispered, "Where is the Speaker?"

"With the army at Red Rose Gate. He has taken personal command." Agavenes held out a skeletal hand. "The sword. Give it to me."

Vixa drew Longreacher, then hesitated. "No," she finally said. "I will return it to the Speaker."

"Impudent girl! Isn't it enough that you caused the marshal's death? Or is that your purpose, to weaken and disunite us so that we fall to these barbarians? Are these water-breathing creatures part of some Qualinesti plot to overthrow Silvanost?"

Vixa shoved Longreacher back into her belt. "I have shed blood for your country," she growled. "Do not trifle with me. I am a princess of the blood of Kith-Kanan. I did not ask for this sword, nor did I steal the marshal's wits and send him into an obvious trap. This sword belongs to the Speaker of the Stars, and I will not soil it by placing it in your hands!"

She spun on her heel and strode away. Agavenes called after her. "You may have the favor of His Majesty, but this land will not tolerate mongrels and outlanders, no matter how noble some of their ancestors may have been. I will see the end of you, lady!"

Without looking back or raising her voice, Vixa replied, "You may try, Lord Chamberlain."

* * * * *

Dawn broke, and the city settled into an uneasy rest as the sea elves withdrew into the Thon-Thalas.

Speaker Elendar held a council in the Tower of the Stars. Looking very tired, the Speaker sat, in full martial panoply, on his emerald throne. Clustered on the raised platform before him were clerics representing the great temples. The priests and priestesses wore golden headbands, white robes, and a sash in the color of their patron deity—silver for E'li, red for Matheri, sky-blue for Quenesti Pah, and so on. By ancient law they went unshod, so as to be closer to the sacred soil of Silvanesti. Gathered in the audience hall were high officers of the army, heads of the city guilds, servants, and courtiers. It was easy to see who'd been involved in the battle of the previous night. Gundabyr's was not the only bandage in evidence.

The Speaker began to talk in a low, even voice. He'd been up all night, conferring with his warlords and sages. There were plans to save Silvanost, he said, but he was not yet ready to reveal the details.

Vixa stepped out of the crowd and asked permission to

approach. The Speaker nodded. She drew Longreacher slowly.

"Great Speaker, I would like to return this sword. It is not mine to carry," she said.

"I am told you acquitted yourself with honor at Astarin Gate, lady. Why shouldn't you carry the sword of Balif?" he responded, weariness not lessening the deep tone of his voice.

Vixa shook her head firmly. Couldn't he see the disapproval on the faces of his own people? Agavenes was positively livid.

"This is the blade of the marshal of Silvanost," she insisted. "It should not be given to another."

"Today there is no marshal."

Agavenes spoke out. "Name one, Sire! Give us a new marshal!" Others around the circular chamber took up the cry. The various factions called out suggestions. As the noise increased, the Speaker leaned forward and spoke softly to Vixa.

"Why don't you keep it, lady? I think you are as much a warrior as any other present. And you are of royal blood."

"No, Sire!" she hissed fiercely. "Do you want a civil war? Choose a Silvanesti!"

"Who do you suggest?"

Vixa was furious with him for asking such an inappropriate question, for not acting as she thought a Speaker ought. Then she saw the twinkle in his eyes. He was teasing her! She went along with him, saying, "I know few of your officers, Great Speaker, but Captain Samcadaris seems both wise and brave."

He raised an eyebrow, surprised perhaps that she had actually ventured a choice. However, he considered the idea with a thoughtful expression. "So? Captain to marshal in one bound? Agavenes will expire." His hazel eyes danced.

The Speaker leaned back in his throne, held up a hand. The tumult in the Tower subsided. When all was quiet, Elendar declaimed, "Summon Captain Samcadaris to our presence!"

The captain entered, looking more than a little surprised. He'd been detailed to stand guard with the royal watch. The summons from the Speaker was most unexpected.

Elendar held out a hand to Vixa. Into it, she placed the hilt of Balif's sword. She stepped back, and the Speaker bade Samcadaris approach. The captain complied.

"Accept this sword, sir, with my love and trust," said the Speaker. "Bear it with honor and justice in my name."

Samcadaris stiffened visibly, realizing what was being asked of him. He took Longreacher in a hand that trembled, then raised the sword in a salute. "I accept the honor and the responsibility, Great Speaker. I shall not fail you or my country," he said, his voice breaking.

"Loyal subjects, I present to you the Marshal of Silvanost!"

Speaker Elendar had barely pronounced these words when Agavenes exploded into anger. Casting a look of pure hatred at Vixa, the chamberlain cried, "Do foreigners choose our leaders now? Is this girl to be our master? I would rather take my chances with the blue-skinned barbarians. At least they fight openly, elf to elf!"

"Shut up, Lord Chamberlain," the Speaker said pleasantly. "You seem to forget you are addressing my blood cousin. And me."

"I am of a house no less ancient and noble, Majesty. I will not be passed over, like an incompetent underling!"

"Lord Agavenes, none of your stratagems has worked. You convinced me Druzenalis could destroy the enemy— but he lost the better part of our army and his own life. You said the Dargonesti attack on Thonbec was a diversion, that the true threat would come from the west. You were wrong there as well. I cannot afford your mistakes, Agavenes. Go from my sight."

All this was said in a patient, even voice, but to proud Agavenes it was as though the Speaker had slapped him. The color drained from his face, leaving him a waxen ghost. Jaw clenched in fury, the chamberlain whirled and stalked out of the Tower, his rich blue robes flapping. Several of the nobles went with him.

"They're showing their true loyalties," Samcadaris said angrily.

The Speaker stated, "Let them go. When this is over, there will be time to reckon with them."

He stood to address the assembly. "An edict has been issued calling all freeborn Silvanesti males to the defense of the city. Until they arrive, we must maintain our vigilance. More precise orders will be issued later from Marshal Samcadaris."

The elves began to file out. Gundabyr and Vixa shook hands with the new marshal, who was still reeling from his sudden elevation. Behind them, the Speaker, seated once more on his elegant throne, watched impassively. At last he commanded, "Go, Marshal, and see to the defenses. Remember, too, a great rise is sometimes followed by a great fall."

Samcadaris exited with a low bow. The Qualinesti princess and the dwarf likewise bowed to the ruler of Silvanost and followed on the marshal's heels.

Chapter 21

Escalade!

Queen Uriona impatiently drummed her long blue fingers on the arm of her throne. The seaweed canopy that shielded her during the day had just been removed. The sun was sinking beneath the western horizon. Despite the attentiveness of her loyal servants, Uriona was angry.

"Where is Lord Protector Coryphene?" she demanded for the fifth time in thirty minutes. "Why hasn't he been summoned?"

"He has, Divine Majesty," said one of the servants, patiently. He kept his eyes downcast.

More time dragged by. At last, a swirl of mud and sand in the water presaged the arrival of newcomers from the river. Coryphene swept into his queen's presence. He bowed deeply.

"My eternal regret for keeping Your Divinity waiting," he said.

"I summoned you hours ago."

"Apologies, Majesty. The river is murky and strange to

us. It is difficult to move quickly through it."

The strain of the invasion showed on Coryphene's face and in his posture. He'd fought all the night before in the dry forest south of the city, fought and slain a dozen foes single-handed. He had intended to launch another strike on the city this night. The peremptory summons from the queen had delayed the attack.

"When do you expect the city to fall?" Uriona asked.

"Soon, Beloved Goddess. Thousands of drylanders were lost in the forest and at the city gate last night. There cannot be many left to defend the walls. We were to attack again this evening, but—" He paused. "Our people need time to recover. Tomorrow, at dusk, we will resume the assault, this time most heavily from the west. The drylanders will expect us to charge their gatehouses again, but we will not. With the timbers we took from Brackenost, we have made scaling ladders. We shall storm the wall between their towers. There will not be enough defenders to meet us, and the city will be ours."

"Be sure of it, Lord Protector! The tide of affairs is turning—I feel it. My fellow gods bestir themselves for our enemies' sake. My destiny is to be crowned in the Tower of the Stars. I will achieve my destiny! Do you hear?"

"Perfectly, Divine Queen. May I return to the army?"

Uriona tapped her fingers on her throne. "Yes, very well, go."

Before he turned away, he saw an expression of worry pass over her face. She raised one hand to her head.

"Are you well, Uriona?" he inquired.

His use of her name brought anger to her face. "Yes! Why do you tarry? Go back to your warriors, Lord Protector!"

He didn't move, but continued to regard her with genuine concern. "Do you tire of this shelter in the shallow water? Why not come back with me in the river?"

"You said it wasn't safe for me to enter the river!" she snapped.

"The enemy is less formidable than I supposed. They cannot reach us underwater and cannot defeat us when we fight on land." He held out a hand to her. "Come, Divine

Majesty. Come let me show you your future capital."

Slowly, the anger faded from her face. Her expression took on a quality of yearning. "My capital," she repeated softly. "My city."

She took his hand and rose from her throne. Swimming together, they left the sea behind and entered the fresh water of the Thon-Thalas.

* * * * *

The night passed without incident in Silvanost. Vixa was surprised that the Dargonesti did not attack, but the time was not wasted. Fortifications were strengthened, weapons repaired, and myriad other tasks attended to.

The Speaker of the Stars had dined once more with his foreign guests. After the midday meal was finished, they strolled the halls of the Quinari Palace, ending up in one of the high western towers. From there, they could see nearly the whole of Fallan Island. The Speaker leaned on the alabaster windowsill and nodded at the sublime vista. "What do you see?" he asked them.

Gundabyr winced as he hoisted his bandaged arm up. "The city, the city wall, and the river."

"What do you deduce from the river?"

Baffled, the Qualinesti princess stared hard. The Thon-Thalas seemed just the same as when she had arrived the day before yesterday. There were still no fishing craft on the water. The barges that had been deployed to impede enemy ships were gone as well. Vixa's information had shown the Speaker that such a tactic was unnecessary. All the river craft were tied up on the north end of the island, tied to docks that stood long-legged out of the water, like so many herons. The fishing dories closer to shore had their prows buried in the mud. Vixa stiffened. *Buried in the mud?*

"The water level has receded!" Vixa exclaimed, seeing it at last.

"By Reorx! A good four feet, at least!" added Gundabyr.

"Closer to five," corrected the Speaker. "It will go lower still."

"But how? Why?"

Elendar's voice took on a note of pride. "The clerics of Silvanost are second to none in the esteem of the gods. I commanded them to work a mighty conjuration—*all* of them. The entire college of priests and priestesses are at their altars, minds linked into one magnificent whole, performing a fantastic evocation."

Vixa was stunned. "To lower the river?"

He nodded with satisfaction. "In two more days the Thon-Thalas will be half its normal depth. In six, it will be a muddy gutter. If the Dargonesti remain, they will dry in the sun like so many beached fish."

Vixa felt light-headed. That such power was available to the Speaker of the Stars . . . she could only shake her head in wonder. It was incredible. That she was here to witness it was a blessing. The Qualinesti princess bowed her head. "Great Speaker, forgive me for doubting you," she murmured.

He grinned at her. "Nonsense, Cousin. Would not the Speaker of the Sun do as much for Qualinost? Master Gundabyr, to what end would your High King go to deliver Thorbardin from danger?"

"Fight to the last axe and shed his very last drop of blood," the dwarf said solemnly. He brightened. "But don't I feel like a dolt! Here the princess and me were breaking our, uh, backs to come to your aid, and you have ol' Coryphene in the palm of your hand!"

"Things are not quite that certain, my friend. This Coryphene is resourceful, and his army can still do great harm."

Vixa knew the truth of that. She thought of how remorselessly Coryphene had pursued the chilkit, obsessed with exterminating them root and branch.

"When he realizes the river is falling, he will rethink his strategy," she said. "I fear the worst may still be ahead of us."

The Speaker rubbed his smooth cheek. "Do you think so? I would have thought that when things looked hopeless, he would retreat to save his own skin."

"Any ordinary general would, but Coryphene has a heavy burden that prevents him from running away—that prevents rational thought," she finished. The other two quizzed her with wordless looks.

"Uriona," she said. "He is bound up in her visions, bound up in his love for her. He will never give up."

* * * * *

The night watch roamed the quiet streets of Silvanost, as they had for more than a thousand years. This night, they were reinforced by bands of royal guards. Marshal Samcadaris knew he didn't have enough warriors to guard the entire perimeter of the great city. Until the levies arrived, he was forced to rely on two methods of defense: all the towers and gatehouses were strongly fortified and garrisoned with archers, and the remaining foot soldiers and dismounted cavalry were formed into flying corps, which would rush to the scene of any attack. In the Speaker's words, they would "plug holes in the Ship of State from the inside."

The sky had just turned from indigo to deep purple when the sentries atop Red Rose Gate heard a commotion in the southern forest beyond the wall. The previous fire and subsequent battle had done great damage to the ornamental gardens located by the edge of the forest. More than enough trees remained, however, to screen Dargonesti movements from the sharp-eyed sentries.

A herald was dispatched to Marshal Samcadaris, who was standing at the head of a thousand warriors in a street next to the Quinari Palace. Word of the enemy activity filtered through the ranks. The Silvanesti stirred nervously.

Speaker Elendar, Vixa, and Gundabyr were with Samcadaris. The Speaker said, "What do you think, Marshal?"

"A few soldiers can make a lot of noise," the young warrior replied. "I counsel that we wait."

A few minutes later, a second courier came running from Red Rose Gate. "Sir! Enemy in sight!" he cried. The warriors in the neat ranks began to murmur softly.

"Wait. We must wait," Samcadaris repeated, shaking his head slowly.

Back at the southern gate, the nervous Silvanesti defenders

watched as a double line of Dargonesti elves, fresh from the river, marched forward in closed ranks. On their shoulders, they bore long poles, which the archers took to be scaling ladders. The cry of "Escalade!" went up among the Silvanesti. The archers lofted a few arrows at them, but the Dargonesti halted just out of range.

The air was alive with the sound of snapping wood. The Silvanesti looked on in confusion as a giant ball of tree limbs and brush appeared out of the trees. The ball was fully twenty feet across and was being pushed forward—straight to the gate—by gangs of captured Silvanesti.

At the palace, Vixa heard the report of this and said immediately, "Coryphene means to burn down the gate." She explained that the long poles the archers had taken for ladders were probably firelances.

"You say water won't put out this gnomefire?" Samcadaris said. Gundabyr nodded regretfully. "Well, what will extinguish it?"

"Only smothering will douse a gnomefire. Dirt, sand, that sort of thing," said the dwarf.

Samcadaris gave orders that certain items be collected and taken to the gate. A few hundred warriors scattered to obey.

The archers atop the wall held their fire as the brush ball rolled slowly toward them. The Dargonesti were careful to keep behind it, beating their captives with sticks to ensure that the ball continued its forward momentum. Pairs of firelancers left the line and followed in the wake of the brush ball. Careless Quoowahb paid with their lives as the archers picked off any who strayed too far from the rolling shield.

Samcadaris's troops, a hundred fifty strong, arrived at the threatened gate. The special items they'd brought were passed up to the defenders on the wall. Tense, the Silvanesti waited.

The ground sloped upward to the gate, so the last few yards were slow going for the captives pushing the brush ball. When the ball drew near enough that the Silvanesti archers at last had a shot at those behind it, they realized the only targets available were their own countrymen. The Dargonesti slashing at the captives with seaweed whips were protected by a wooden mantelet. This shield had been fashioned from house timbers, doors, and any other bits of wood scavenged from Brackenost and the surrounding forests.

The Silvanesti archers ground their teeth in anger at this sight. Samcadaris had sent word they were to hold their fire. The marshal had a plan, and killing the unfortunate captives was not part of it.

Amid much cursing and shouting from the Dargonesti, the huge mass of tinder was shoved up next to the oaken gate. Then the mantelet retreated, but only to provide cover to the advancing firelancers, who readied, then cast their heavy projectiles into the brush.

For land fighting, Coryphene's armorers had modified Gundabyr's original design. The pot containing the paste was divided in half, one side containing gnomefire paste, the other filled with water. When the pot shattered, the two mixed, the paste exploding into flame.

Smoke boiled out of the brush pile. Two, three, four firelances were hurled against it. Liquid flames ran down the green saplings in the ball and pooled on the ground.

From the gate roof, many Silvanesti voices shouted, "Now!"

Down came grappling hooks on ropes. This was the special equipment ordered by Samcadaris. The hooks easily snagged the tangled brush. The elves heaved on the long lines, raising the burning heap off the ground. Flames shot up over the battlements, forcing the archers back. Once the ball had sufficient height, the ropes were cut. The momentum of the falling brush ball caused it to roll down the slope away from the gate, directly toward the Dargonesti line. With the jeers of the defenders ringing in their ears, the sea elves scattered before the hurtling blaze.

Back at the palace, everyone enjoyed a good laugh when descriptions of the Battle of the Bush arrived. No one, however, believed the night's fighting was over.

More wooden mantelets appeared from the woods.

Behind these makeshift shields, gangs of Dargonesti crept toward the wall. Arrows immediately began dropping down on them, but the attackers pushed on. Nearly twenty mantelets, covering several hundred Quoowahb, reached the foot of the wall and Red Rose Gate. The tall, powerfully muscled sea elves cast spears up at the defenders as other Dargonesti, equipped with captured tools, attacked the gate. Chips flew, but the oak barrier was ten inches thick. Behind it stood another gate, this one of rock crystal, magically cast in the days of Silvanos. The defenders let the Dargonesti waste their time and energy chipping at the wooden gate, secure in the knowledge that the crystal barrier could not be breached. All the while, arrows, large stones, and hot oil were poured on the attackers.

"This is stupid," Gundabyr remarked, when the latest report was brought back to the Quinari. "I thought the blue-skins were smarter than this!"

"I don't suppose they've ever attacked a walled city before," Samcadaris mused.

"They're getting a hard education," the Speaker said grimly.

The attack continued for over an hour, during which the attention of every elf in Silvanost was fixed on Red Rose Gate, in the south.

Unbeknownst to them, Dargonesti warriors were stealing silently out of the muddy Thon-Thalas and gathering among the piers and docks on the city's west side. Scaling ladders, knocked together from scavenged wood, were carried out of the water and readied at the base of the city wall. The army waited, poised for the signal. Coryphene's point of attack was exactly halfway between two towers.

Coryphene himself surfaced, holding the hand of Queen Uriona. The sorceress monarch had never been above the water in her life, and she was fiercely excited by the experience. The air here was very different than what she breathed in her city every day. A myriad of strange smells filled her nostrils. She gripped Coryphene's hand hard as she gazed up at the walls and towers of Silvanost.

"My city," she whispered. "My capital!"

"Not yet, Divine One. Let me shed a little blood for you, then it shall be yours in truth," he said.

She relinquished his hand. "Go! I will call on my powers to aid you!"

He slogged ashore. One thousand warriors, including his own sword-armed personal guard, were below the wall.

"Up ladders," he said quietly. Brawny blue arms lifted the wooden structures. The movement of so many ladders could not escape notice. Sentries on the two flanking towers shouted alarms. Torches blazed from the battlement, exposing Coryphene's troops.

"Up! Up!" he roared, waving his sword over his head. He still wielded Vixa Ambrodel's Qualinesti blade. The topaz in its hilt flashed in the torchlight. "Now is the time! For Urione! For Uriona!"

"Urione! Uriona!" the Dargonesti shouted.

In moments, the alarm reached the Speaker and the others at the Quinari Palace. Samcadaris threw down his marshal's baton.

"A feint! All that nonsense in the south is a feint!" He shouted quick commands, and the waiting warriors fell into three columns. Vixa and Gundabyr found places in the fore, the dwarf vowing to make Coryphene pay for the death of Garnath, his twin.

Speaker Elendar performed the ritual blessings, as the columns began to move off. Once the warriors were gone, the Speaker dismissed the priests and servants hovering nearby. The square between the Quinari and the Tower of the Stars was empty save for himself. He removed a plain helmet from beneath his cloak and pulled it on.

"I'll not sit by while others fight for my city," he murmured.

After a glance at the pearlescent beauty of the Tower of the Stars, a sight which never failed to strengthen his soul, Elendar, Speaker of the Stars, great-grandson of Silvanos, stepped into the night, tightening the chin strap of his helmet.

Chapter 22

Vixa Falls

The ladders thumped against the parapet. Fewer than two hundred Silvanesti guarded this stretch of the wall. They sprang to arms and rushed to knock the ladders over. With sword and spear, the defenders pried one heavy ladder loose and shoved it backward. They cheered as Dargonesti went flying.

At that instant tiny globes of light appeared above each remaining ladder. These swelled rapidly until they were larger than an elf. When the Silvanesti tried to approach the ladders, an invisible force hurled them back. The light globes crackled and hissed. Other warriors shot arrows and cast spears into the fiery globes. These, too, were flung back at their owners, sometimes with fatal results.

When the first Dargonesti laid his hand atop the city wall, the globe protecting his ladder vanished with a thunderclap. He and his fellows poured onto the battlement and rushed the dazed defenders. In minutes all the globes were gone, clearing the way for the sea elves to gain the wall. Only one ladder had been upset. The other nine had done their jobs well, and the Dargonesti entered the city.

Uriona, standing on the shoulders of two of her servants, watched from midriver. She trembled violently beneath her mask, from emotion and the effort she had exerted to create the force spheres. Victory was hers—she could feel it!

Samcadaris's columns were filing up the steps. Now and then bodies—blue-skinned and white—came hurtling back down. Vixa also pounded up the steps, Gundabyr on her heels. At the top of the long staircase, the wall was thick with fighting elves. The Silvanesti who'd been on the wall when Coryphene had first attacked had withdrawn to the two towers. The doors were shut and bolted. The Dargonesti had seized the wall; now could they hold it?

Vixa saw no Dimernesti this time. She faced only her old captors, and from the swords in their webbed hands, she knew they were part of Coryphene's elite guard. Shoulder to shoulder with a dozen of Samcadaris's fighters and the redoubtable Gundabyr, she would have taken on any foe. Like the dwarf, she had a debt to settle with the Lord Protector of Urione. He had taken too many lives—by this own hand and by his command.

There was no room for fancy swordplay. This was hack-and-slash fighting at its most brutal. Strength and stamina were what counted. Vixa traded cuts with a Dargonesti until his blade became entangled with that of the elf on her left. When he left himself open, Vixa ran him through. His place was taken by another warrior in green tortoiseshell armor. This one wielded a heavy Ergothian sword as easily as if it were a feather.

The Qualinesti princess gave ground. Gundabyr squeezed in and deflected the blue-skinned giant's blows. The dwarf was not at his best. His wound made him stiff and clumsy. Vixa grabbed him by the collar, dragging him back.

"Thick-headed fool!" she yelled at him. "Your arm's not sound! Get clear!"

"Don't give me orders, your ladyship!" he shouted back. Their exchange was interrupted by the sea elf, making a renewed assault on Vixa. Gundabyr dropped his heavy axe and dove at the Dargonesti's knees. Vixa leapt over the dwarf and whipped a roundhouse at the enemy. The sea elf, struggling with the dwarf, was unable to parry. He dropped down dead, his throat slashed by Vixa's sword.

The Qualinesti girl felt herself fall as well. The parapet was slick with blood, and her foot slid out from under her. A forest of legs churned around her. Someone stomped on her hand, and she lost her grasp on her weapon. More blows, accidental and otherwise, rained on her ribs. She curled up to protect herself, spied Gundabyr's axe, and snatched it up.

A stunning impact on her back rolled her over. Blearily, she saw a Dargonesti looming over her, sword upraised. She flung the axe at him. The flat of the blade took him in the face, and down he went. Vixa stood shakily. The Dargonesti, his face streaming green blood, was getting to his feet as well. Empty-handed, she ran at him and shoved. With a screech, he slid off the parapet, disappearing below.

Vixa had lost track of Gundabyr. A Dargonesti rushed her. She ducked under his sword arm, turned, and kicked his legs out from under him. Because of their height and unfamiliarity with dry land, the sea elves were somewhat clumsy. Their reflexes and balance were both affected.

She picked up the fallen sea elf's sword. It was a sailor's cutlass, streaked with rust. Just the thing for a mad melee like this! Yelling her war cry of family names, Vixa tore into the Dargonesti who were just getting off their scaling ladder. She slew one before he had time to defend himself, then felt a slash across her back. Her steel cuirass saved her life, but the end of the blade caught her shoulder. Stinging blood poured from her wound as she turned, seeing that the Dargonesti who'd struck her was still standing with his sword upraised. Before she could counter, he crumpled, an arrow sticking out of his back.

No order existed anywhere along the embattled wall. Unable to call upon their powerful mages, the Silvanesti were forced to deal with their foe in a primitive manner: they had set up siege engines on the flanking towers. These raked the scaling ladders with lead missiles and fist-sized stones. The flow of Dargonesti was nearly choked off.

Vixa got her bloodied back against the rear of the parapet so no one else could strike her from behind. The fight had lessened in intensity as the number of able warriors on both sides diminished. Panting for air, the Qualinesti princess scanned the scene. Something white caught her eye. She wiped sweat from her eyes, bringing the image into focus. It was a helmet decorated with shells and gemstones.

Coryphene.

"Hai! Ambrodel! Kanan!" Her war cries were lost in the general uproar. Vixa dashed back into the press, slashing right and left to clear a path. She bored through the disorganized battle until she was only a few paces from the helmeted figure.

"Coryphene!" she screamed.

He turned. "Princess! You did not die at Thonbec?"

"Stupid question!" She sprang forward, aiming a cut at his face. He parried it deftly. "You've lost, Coryphene! Everything!"

"The whine of the defeated!" Quick as lightning, he counterattacked. He moved with astonishing speed, though he didn't reach her. Vixa edged toward the parapet on the city side of the wall and presented a formal fighting stance. Under his elaborately decorated helmet, Coryphene smiled.

"You are a brave fighter. I'm glad you escaped," he said, saluting with his blade. *Her* blade, she fumed silently.

Vixa hissed, "My friends and the other slaves were not so fortunate!" The cutlass she held had a sharply curved blade, no good at all for thrusting. He held her off without even shifting his feet. "You murdered them," she said through clenched teeth.

"Only the weak," he replied coolly. He disengaged his blade from hers in a nimble riposte. His sword whispered close enough to her throat to leave a hairline cut. He laughed.

Fate, in the form of a Silvanesti catapult, played a hand in their duel. Catapulters on the more southern tower had aimed their engine and flung two hundred pounds of lead weights at the Dargonesti ladders still standing. The sea elves were trying to carry firelances to the battlement. The catapult missiles smashed the ladders and set the firelances crashing to the ground. Fire exploded among the ruined ladders and wounded Dargonesti.

A great gout of flame soared up behind Coryphene. The heat singed him, and he leapt to one side to avoid being burnt. Taking the advantage, Vixa took her cutlass in both hands and swung. The rude iron blade bit through his shell armor and into the flesh of his left arm.

With a howl, Coryphene dropped his sword and flung his right hand out. There was a flash, bright as the noonday sun, and Vixa found herself falling over the wall. One thought filled her astonished brain: I didn't know he could do that!

Expecting to die on the paving stones of the street, Vixa felt herself hit, not hard marble, but a sloping roof. Breath whooshed from her lungs, and she rolled wildly down the incline. Then she was falling once more. Cold water slapped her back, and she was sinking. She fought her way to the surface, gasping for air. Hands seized her. She would've fought them as well, but had no strength left for the struggle. The hands dragged her out of the water.

She had landed in a fountain. The hands that held her belonged to two wide-eyed Silvanesti soldiers who'd been bathing their wounds in the fountain's pool. They hoisted her to the side of the pool and stood by, regarding her with awe.

"That was—that was amazing!" one of them breathed. "You fell forty feet to that rooftop, rolled down, and dropped another twenty feet straight into the fountain!"

The Qualinesti princess tried to stand. Her legs buckled, and she fell, knocking her head against the rim of the fountain. The warriors, still with awestruck expressions, obligingly hauled her up again. The Qualinesti princess sat on the cold green stone of the pool rim, holding her throbbing head and groaning at the pain of her cut shoulder.

The blaze started by the gnomefire spread rapidly among the docks. The Dargonesti reeled away from the searing heat. The Silvanesti closed in on those remaining atop the wall.

Coryphene rallied his fighters, with Dargonesti fighting on two fronts, toward each of the guard towers. The Protector shouted encouragement, but even as the more powerful Dargonesti were pressing the Silvanesti back, the elves in the towers readjusted their siege machines to bear along the wall.

Whomp! A boulder flew in a high arc over the Silvanesti fighters and crashed down among the Dargonesti. For the first time since gaining the wall, they wavered. Coryphene commanded them to capture the catapult, but the mass of Silvanesti between them and the machine was a powerful dissuasion. The catapult hurled a second stone, which bounced along the parapet, wreaking fearful havoc among the closely packed ranks of Dargonesti.

At this juncture, a lone figure appeared on the roof of the southern tower, climbing onto the stout timber frame of the catapult. Cupping his hands to his mouth, the Speaker of the Stars yelled, "What are you waiting for? Take them, my brave Silvanesti!" His gold-bordered white cape whipped back from his shoulders, and the Crown of Stars on his head flashed in the torchlight.

A screaming cheer rose from the throats of the Silvanesti elves. They drove forward on two sides. The enemy from the sea fought stubbornly, but couldn't hold out against deadly boulders, masses of patriotic warriors, and the runaway fire that threatened them from below.

The surviving sea elves, including Coryphene, fled down the remaining ladders. Even that did not save all of them, for when the defenders regained control of the wall, they pushed the heavily laden ladders over, sending scores of Dargonesti into the flames below.

By the first hour after midnight, the battle was over. The western waterfront was a smoking ruin. Hundreds of elves on both sides were dead or wounded. Vixa worked her way through the clogged streets to the southern tower; she'd been told the Speaker was there. She climbed the steps to the roof to see the catapult that had turned the tide of battle. Its crew was gathered in a tight group, and she called out praise to them. The elves said nothing, but stood aside, revealing a terrible sight.

The Speaker of the Stars lay by the catapult, a spear in his side. The dark gray slate around him was stained red with his blood.

"Great Speaker!" Vixa exclaimed, rushing to him.

"Cousin," he said weakly. "What luck, eh? The battle won, and I stop a javelin."

The spear stuck out below the ribs on his left side. A healer was working feverishly over him, but the Speaker's pale face was waxen from loss of blood.

"You must live, Majesty," Vixa said, pressing his cold hand. "Victory will be yours in a few days!"

"I'll see what I can do," he whispered. His eyes closed; his head lolled.

The young priestess pushed sweat-dampened hair from her face. "He will live," she said tiredly. "He only sleeps from the potion I gave him, to spare him pain."

Speaker Elendar was carried away on a litter to the temple of Quenesti Pah, goddess of healing. As the senior priestesses were still engaged in the great invocation to lower the Thon-Thalas, the younger healers would have to attend to him as best they could.

Vixa questioned the catapulters. "What happened? How did the Speaker of the Stars get wounded?"

The elves were in shock. One of them shook his head in bewilderment and tried to explain. "He climbed atop our machine to rally the warriors. As the last of the enemy was going down the wall, some of them cast spears at him. One struck."

Vixa clapped the brave elf on the shoulder, then wearily made her way back to the palace.

Just a few more days, she told herself fiercely. Soon, Coryphene will have to know the river is falling. Already it was more than six feet below normal. The middle channel, the deepest part of the Thon-Thalas, now carried but four-teen feet of water.

* * * * *

Coryphene trudged into the river, heading away from the city. Most of his fighters had thrown themselves face first into the muddy water along the riverbank, so badly were their gills beset by smoke and heat. The Protector of Urione had too much dignity for that. He waded out some yards from shore and with great deliberation raised a handful of water to his face.

The battle was over, lost, but he did not despair. Somewhere on the miles-long perimeter of Silvanost there had to be a weak spot, a place not easily accessible to reinforcements or those infernal rock-throwing monsters. He would find that weak spot. He would find it for his queen.

He walked farther into the river and submerged himself. As the life-giving water flowed through his gills, Coryphene looked around at Silvanost. For the first time he noticed the condition of the city's piers. Some of the shorter ones were surrounded by mud. The Protector of Urione frowned, bringing his head above water.

Queen Uriona had come forward from the deep channel, watching the survivors drift back, burned, dazed, gasping for water. Their suffering meant nothing to her. Only their failure was important. And where was Coryphene? She saw him now, standing there, staring as though dumbstruck.

"You live!" Uriona cried. Her relief was only momentary. Anger quickly displaced it. "You failed, Lord Protector! You are defeated!"

"Only in this battle, Divine One. The campaign is not over. Your Majesty must depart, however. There is great danger for you here."

His words fueled her anger. "What danger? The drylanders cannot reach me here in the river. You said so yourself."

"The river is shrinking," he stated bluntly.

"What? How?"

"I don't know. I know only that there is less water in the river than there was when we entered it. The level has declined during the battle and continues to dwindle even now."

Uriona, standing hip-deep in the Thon-Thalas, stared at

him. "Is this by natural means, or unnatural?"

"You would know better than I. Why don't you ask your brother gods?" he said irritably. "I must see to my soldiers. There will be no more fighting this night."

As he turned to leave, Uriona's voice stopped him. "We cannot remain in the river if it dries up," she said. "It is well I brought the Shades of Zura."

The Protector turned back, his face drawing down into a frown. "The undead priests are not needed," he insisted. "Once the army has rested for some hours, I intend to renew the attack by day."

She looked at him as if he were demented. "But the sunlight! Our eyes cannot bear it!"

"My warriors can bear anything but defeat. The enemy thinks themselves safe during daylight. We will teach them otherwise. After dawn, I intend to throw the whole army against the western gate. It will be our final onslaught. We must carry the day or perish. In either case, Your Divinity must return to the sea. We cannot allow—*I* cannot allow— you to be trapped here, at any cost."

Her expression softened. "What kind of goddess would I be if I abandoned my Protector at the hour of his glory? I shall remain."

"Uriona—"

"Silence. My pavilion has been erected at the deepest point in the channel. I will be safe there. And with great Zura to aid our endeavors, I shall enter the city in triumph before the next sunset."

To forestall further discussion, she left him and walked back to the depths of the river. Coryphene watched her go, the frown back on his face. Though an accomplished spellcaster, the Protector considered himself first a warrior, a soldier who preferred to win his battles by strength and cunning. However, he was also completely devoted to his queen. No matter his misgivings, he must bend himself to her divine will.

He called up his lieutenants and sent word to every company in his army to collect in the channel west of the city. The gathering of the Dargonesti was complete by sunrise, but since it took place underwater, no one in Silvanost had any inkling of it.

* * * * *

That morning, word of the Speaker's grievous injury spread, casting a pall over the city. Despite their victory at the west wall, the Silvanesti had lost fully a third of their trained warriors. Barely two thousand fighters remained, though the ranks were being augmented by volunteers. These recruits were brave, but they were ill-matched against Coryphene's veterans.

While Vixa slept, Gundabyr met with Marshal Samcadaris and other high-ranking Silvanesti officers. The marshal's greatest fear was that the Dargonesti would launch serious attacks simultaneously at more than one point. He no longer had enough troops to cover multiple fronts.

"What about the levies?" asked the dwarf. "Shouldn't they be close by now?"

"Some should. They were to gather at Ilist Glade," said Samcadaris. "The levies from the nearer provinces should already be there."

"Then let's send word!"

"The city is surrounded," objected a Silvanesti colonel named Eriscodera. "How can we get to the far shore without being attacked?"

"The blueskins don't move during the day, remember? I say we send a small band across at high noon to find the waiting levies and bring them back, quicker than quicksilver."

Samcadaris rubbed his pointed chin. "There is something in what Master Gundabyr proposes, only I would be even bolder than he. Go now, I say, and don't wait for noon."

He chose Colonel Eriscodera to lead the party. "Take twelve cavalry with you. Ride as though the Dragonqueen herself is after you, and bring back the levies that are already assembled." He smote his thigh with his fist. "Make all the noise you want on your return. Let the Dargonesti think a mighty army is coming to terminate the siege of Silvanost!"

"May I go, too?" asked Gundabyr. "With this hurt wing of mine, I'm not much good in a fight, but I want to do whatever I can to stop the blueskins."

"What do you say, Colonel?"

"An outlander riding with the cavalry of Silvanost?" said Eriscodera, eyeing the dwarf uncertainly. "I suppose it may serve to drive home how desperate things are."

"Kind of you to say so," Gundabyr remarked sourly.

"Master Gundabyr is brave and resourceful," Samcadaris said. "And he knows the enemy better than any of us. I do you an honor, Colonel, by sending him with you."

Eriscodera saluted smartly and departed with the dwarf. They went directly to the cavalry headquarters, Gundabyr not even taking time to have breakfast.

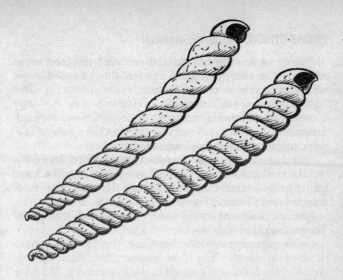

Chapter 23
By Sword and Spell

Ragged and bloodied, Vixa rested in a small chamber in the Quinari Palace. Once her shoulder had been bandaged, she simply found the nearest couch and dropped down on it. The Silvanesti quickly tired of whispering about her in the corridor. She slept, deeply and dreamlessly.

She awoke suddenly, sitting bolt upright on her couch. She had no idea how long she'd been asleep, but the sun was up, its rays slanting in the large windows on the palace's east facade. All was silent. The usual sounds—servants' soft voices, footsteps whispering on carpet—were absent. Yet, Vixa had the distinct impression she'd been awakened by a loud noise.

Slowly, her bandaged shoulder aching and stiff, Vixa got to her feet. Mud and blood had dried on her boots, flaking off with every step. She buckled on her borrowed sword and encountered no one as she walked through the sun-bright palace rooms. The audience hall was empty as well.

Where was everyone? she wondered. The streets outside

the palace were vacant as well—not so much as a cat showed itself. The air fairly pulsed with power, the harnessed magic of the entire priesthood of Silvanost. It overlaid the city like a wooly blanket. And there was something more. A steady hum, like the sound of an enormous beehive, filled the air. It came from nowhere and everywhere. Vixa felt a pang of fear. She had to know what was happening.

She jogged away from the palace, toward Pine Tree Gate, which guarded the western entrance to the city. The humming grew louder, funneled through the high canyons of houses and towers. Disoriented, she made several wrong turns into dead-end streets, but the noise steadily increased as she made her way west.

In the square above Pine Tree Gate, Vixa ran smack into a mob of Silvanesti. They were ordinary folk, standing side by side and holding the hands of their neighbors. The elven chain looped back and forth through the square and disappeared down the many side streets. All the elves had their eyes closed, their lips parted slightly. They were humming.

"What is it?" Vixa demanded. "What's happened?"

The elves did not answer, but held their places and hummed. Vixa grabbed the last one in line. As her hand closed around his arm, she felt a shock go through her. An image flashed across her mind's eye: the Thon-Thalas, wrapped from shore to shore in dense, white cloud. The cloud billowed and roiled, and gray shapes stirred inside. Though vague, they were somehow threatening—

She yanked her hand free and staggered backward. Vixa knew immediately what she'd seen. Through the eyes of thousands of Silvanesti, the image of the cloud was vivid and terrifying. Coryphene, or Uriona, had summoned up the strange white fog that had first carried *Evenstar* away from land. But why? What would it do now? And why were the people of Silvanost behaving so oddly?

The Qualinesti princess shouldered through the lines, ducking under linked hands until she reached the base of the city wall near Pine Tree Gate. The sound of humming grated on her nerves and caused an ache in her head. Atop the wall she saw Silvanesti warriors moving about and hurried to join them. Two score young elves, newly pressed into the depleted ranks of the Speaker's host, stood behind the crenelations that protected the parapet.

"Who commands here?" Vixa asked.

The elves were staring out toward the river. Without turning, a spear-armed youth replied, "Marshal Samcadaris, lady. He passed here an hour ago."

Frowning, Vixa followed the direction of his rapt gaze. Her frown became an expression of shock. The shrinking Thon-Thalas was completely obscured by a sea of white cloud. The cloud stretched upstream and down as far as Vixa could see and overlapped the banks by several yards. The top of the cloud was level with the wall upon which she stood, and it looked as solid.

"When did this fog come up?" she demanded.

The spear-carrier replied, "At sunrise. It has been thickening steadily ever since."

"Why do the people stand together humming?"

"It is the will of the Speaker, lady. The clerics of the high gods began to grow weak and fell as the mist closed in. The Speaker summoned the people to reinforce the magic."

Vixa shook her head as she looked back toward the city, at the rows and rows of humming Silvanesti. Of course, they weren't actually humming. The sound was in fact the rapid chanting of thousands upon thousands of Silvanesti voices. She shivered, and gooseflesh rose on her arms. The focused power of these eastern elves sent tingles racing along her spine.

Thunder rumbled overhead. Directly above the sea of snow-white cloud, a long serpent of blue-black thunderheads coalesced rapidly in the still air. Lightning flashed inside the dark mass.

"Looks as though we'll get wet today," Vixa noted. The recruits divided their anxious gazes between the white fog bank and the gathering storm.

"Lady, what shall we do?" asked the spear-carrier, fear tingeing his words.

"Are you afraid?" He nodded, and the others echoed his gesture. Vixa said firmly, "Good. Fear will put iron in your arm and fire in your belly. Then we shall win."

She walked on, past tired veterans and green recruits pressed into service to fill out their ranks. As she went by them, the Qualinesti princess offered low-voiced advice and encouragement in equal portions. Though not a Silvanesti, she still had two thousand years of royal blood in her veins. Her calm, expert manner garnered respect from the veterans and brought a measure of comfort to the frightened newcomers.

Vixa felt a fat raindrop strike her cheek. It ran down to the corner of her mouth, and she tasted salt. She stopped and looked up. The thunderclouds had expanded, filling the sky overhead. Several more drops landed on her face. They were salty as well.

The raindrops were made of seawater!

Hitching up her sword belt, she jogged to the tower ahead of her. On the open summit she found Samcadaris with most of his corps of dismounted cavalry.

"Marshal! It's Vixa Ambrodel!"

He waved to his troopers to let her through. Rain was falling more regularly now. A boom of thunder rolled over the high tower. Samcadaris was standing on a wooden platform that allowed him to see over the crenelation. Vixa climbed up beside him.

"Where have you been?" he inquired.

"Asleep in the palace. I nearly missed everything!"

Thunder crashed once more, and the heavens opened up. A torrent of salty rain fell on Silvanost. "You may wish you had missed this!" Samcadaris shouted over the deluge and thunder.

"Coryphene summoned this rain to sustain his army!"

The marshal nodded. "I have only a few thousand regulars left. The rest are mere children, artisans, and idlers scraped up and given arms. I pray Eriscodera and your dwarven friend get back in time."

"Gundabyr? Where's he gone?"

"They sneaked across the river before dawn to round up what militia had already gathered. If reinforcements don't arrive soon, I doubt we can hold the city."

Weird bleating erupted from various points along the length of the white cloud obscuring the river. The Dargonesti were blowing on conch shells. The sound lifted the hairs at the nape of Vixa's neck, but she realized the noise was probably meant to be practical rather than theatrical. It was likely that Coryphene's warriors couldn't see through the fog either. The noises were probably signals from the different commands.

A Silvanesti shouted from the wall. "They're coming!"

"Stand to arms," said Samcadaris sharply. Weapons rattled as the order was relayed along the city wall. "Archers, stand ready."

"Sir," said an officer at the marshal's elbow, "the archers have only one quiver left per elf."

"Then order them not to miss," was the grim reply.

Vixa wiped salt rain from her eyes and asked, "Where do you want me, Marshal?"

"Royalty may choose their own ground, lady." He smiled wanly. "And there are any number of weak areas on the wall. However, there"—he pointed at a spot farther along the battlement—"halfway between this watchtower and Pine Tree Gate, that's our nearest weakness."

She nodded briskly. "Give me twenty stout fighters, and I'll hold the wall against all comers!"

He agreed. Vixa and her picked squad ran down the steps from the watchtower to the place he'd indicated on the battlement. Halfway between Samcadaris's watchtower and Pine Tree Gate she halted her band. Salty rainwater pooled on the stone parapet, pouring off the wall through small openings in the crenelations. Vixa shucked her sodden cloak. The call of the Dargonesti conch shells abruptly ceased.

Despite the pounding rain, thick tentacles of white fog detached themselves from the main mass of cloud and crept up toward the battlements. Vixa found them uncomfortably similar to the massive limbs of the kraken, which had wrought such havoc on the fortress of Thonbec.

Under the astonished eyes of the Silvanesti, these foggy tentacles gripped the smooth stone walls just beneath the level of the parapet. They thickened and solidified. Now the rain splashed off their hardened surfaces and streamed down their inclined length. One elven warrior, smitten with curiosity, broke ranks and approached the odd growths. An instant later, he toppled from the wall, riddled with arrows.

Vixa cried out as more arrows flickered up from the fog bank. With shrill shouts, Dimernesti mercenaries, wielding captured Silvanesti bows, swarmed out of the mist. They ran up the solid tendril of fog to the top of the city wall.

"Lock shields!" Vixa commanded. Her band of hand-picked warriors obeyed just as a hail of arrows raked them. "Swords out! Attack!"

They rushed the lightly armed Dimernesti and in short order pushed them back over the crenelations. All along the wall, sea elves mounted to the parapet on pathways of solidified vapor.

"We must disrupt their assault," Vixa said quickly. "All of you! If you can shoulder a spear or swing a sword, follow me!"

The Qualinesti princess swallowed hard and leapt through a crenel toward the magical fog ramp. She wondered if it would support anyone, or only Coryphene's chosen. Her feet landed on a surface hard as marble. She looked back. Her twenty warriors were with her. The other Silvanesti stood watching.

"What are you waiting for? The enemy is gaining the wall! Come on!" She plunged down the ramp and into the fog below. The lack of visibility was disorienting, but Vixa found the going easier if she didn't worry about where her feet fell. She concentrated on listening for the enemy and on the sounds of the Silvanesti behind her.

Soon the brown mud of the riverbank appeared ahead. Vixa was vastly relieved when her feet splashed in the diminished Thon-Thalas.

The warriors arrived behind her. "Where now, lady?" one asked.

She turned. The city above was lost in the wall of white cloud, and none of them could see more than a few feet in front of their noses. Not even elven eyes could penetrate this magical fog bank. However, Vixa quickly discovered that the fog, though it veiled their eyes, did not affect their ears. She could hear the battle going on behind and above them. Ahead, Dargonesti were running to the fight, their wide, bare feet slapping loudly in the mud. The fog also seemed to act as a shield against the deluge of rain. Only a few raindrops splashed against Vixa's armor. She pointed with her sword to the right.

"That way," she said firmly. "The enemy seems to be coming from that direction."

They formed in a close column of twos. Some thirty volunteers had followed Vixa and her original band, making a total of fifty warriors under her command. Surrounded though they were by several thousand Dargonesti, Vixa was unafraid. The fog was a two-edged weapon. It would screen them from Coryphene's warriors just as well as it hid the sea elves from the Silvanesti.

Silently, Vixa and the Silvanesti made their way through the mist. Now and then, small groups of Dargonesti ran past, unaware. They also came upon sea elves who had crawled away from the city and died. Even as they tried to follow the edge of the river, it dwindled before them. Vixa called a halt when an odd odor reached her nostrils. At first sweet, then somehow sour and disagreeable, the odor was amazingly familiar. Where had she smelled it before?

Incense! It was the sour-sweet scent that had filled the temple level of Urione. The Dargonesti priests responsible for the strange fog and salty rain must be near.

She led her contingent of Silvanesti forward at a slower pace. To the left she spied a group of tall figures, standing close together. Whipping her sword in a circle overhead, Vixa signaled the attack.

They charged the enemy. Instead of evil priests, they found a band of Dargonesti warriors trying to slake their thirst in the rapidly shrinking river. The sight of the attacking Silvanesti sent the sea elves leaping for their spears, which they'd left driven into the mud nearby.

A melee ensued. Vixa was unsure how many of the foe

they'd flushed, but attack was their only option. The Silvanesti spread out, trying to envelope the sea elves. Unencumbered and unprotected by shield or helmet, Vixa eluded Dargonesti spear thrusts while striking home again and again with her sword. Panting from lack of water, the Dargonesti gave ground. In spite of the salt rain, the sea elves appeared to be in desperate straits.

Staggering with fatigue, one of the Dargonesti jabbed at Vixa. She dodged, spun, and drove her blade into his ribs. This exchange had taken her a short distance from the rest of her command, and when her opponent fell, she found herself looking at a circle of perhaps twenty gray-robed Dargonesti priests, facing inward, a seething cauldron in their midst. Sprigs of smoldering incense were woven into their long jade hair. The odor of incense was overwhelming, but above it rose the smell of death and decay. These were the undead priests of Zura.

"Silvanesti, to me!" Vixa shouted. "Slay the priests and break their spells!"

The fight was over in minutes. The mages were so engrossed in their incantation, they did not attempt to flee or fight back. Even when confronted by sword-wielding enemy, the faces of the Shades of Zura remained expressionless and devoid of life.

When the slaughter was done, Vixa stood with the remaining Silvanesti soldiers, panting with exertion.

"This is no work for warriors," muttered one of the Silvanesti. "Slaying unarmed clerics!"

"They were armed more mightily than any of us," Vixa retorted. She bent over, her hands resting on her knees, and panted. "By their spells Silvanost could be lost."

From her bent position, Vixa saw the green Dargonesti blood staining the muddy water at her feet. She also noticed something else—she could see her own shadow. Vixa stood erect and looked at the sky. The mist was thinning. A freshening wind and the heat of the sun were shredding the evil fog. With the priests of Zura dead, their conjurations were being dispersed by the living force of Silvanost's own clerics.

This was not altogether a positive occurrence from Vixa's point of view. As the mist lifted and the salt rain ceased, she and her command found themselves a lonely island in a sea of Dargonesti. Hastily they formed a circle, every elf facing outward, sword and shield ready. Vixa sheathed her blade and recovered a Dargonesti spear from the mud. Without a shield of her own, she needed the reach of the longer weapon.

Several hundred enemy warriors formed a short distance away. Vixa paced inside the small circle of her soldiers, giving orders in what she hoped was a steadying voice. Now and then she glanced up at the city. A furious fight still raged atop the wall. She uttered a brief, silent prayer for Samcadaris. Then there was time for nothing but survival.

The Dargonesti rushed them from all sides. They had rags tied around their heads to keep their gills damp, but the sun was out now and the air was warming rapidly. Vixa could see the powerful blue-skinned warriors gasping even as they tried to squeeze the small circle of Silvanesti into oblivion. At least, she thought, the city will be saved. Destroying the spell of the evil priests was worth all their lives.

The press of bodies was overpowering. Vixa raced around the inside of the circle of warriors, stabbing her spear at encroaching sea elves. The weapon was finally wrenched from her grasp. Two Silvanesti in front of her were knocked down by the sheer weight of Dargonesti pushing in. Vixa tried to back away, but she fetched up against the backs of the Silvanesti behind her. There was no place left to go.

She grabbed a sword from the lifeless hand of one of her soldiers and dueled with a pair of spear-armed Dargonesti. Something hard rapped Vixa sharply on the side of her head. Stunned, she went down. A wounded Silvanesti fell across her legs. The river mud gripped her. She felt herself sinking into it.

A horn blared above the clash of war. With the shouts and screams of combat around her, Vixa couldn't tell if it was a Dargonesti conch shell or Silvanesti brass. She struggled to rise. Her borrowed sword slipped away and was swallowed by the mud.

One of her soldiers cried out, "The silver moon banner of Eriscodera! It's the militia!"

Vixa grappled with fallen friends and foes and staggered upright. She nearly wept with relief at the sight that met her eyes. On the far shore were thousands of Silvanesti, those called to arms by the Speaker's edict. At their head was an auburn-haired elf on horseback. Silvanost was saved!

With a concerted shout, Eriscodera and his cavalry left the marching levies and charged down the dry, cracked riverbank onto the mud flats. The white-kilted infantry, armed with pikes and halberds, came after them to the music of elven pipes and drums. The music wafted across the narrow channel that was all that remained of the mighty Thon-Thalas. Vixa watched the cavalry flounder in the heavy mud, but they kept coming. They weren't making for the western gate of Silvanost though, but for a cluster of poles and banners in the center of the river.

"Silvanesti, rally!" she shouted hoarsely. "On your feet!"

Barely a dozen warriors remained to answer her call. The Dargonesti had fallen back when Eriscodera's trumpets had sounded. The sea elves seemed uncertain whether to finish off Vixa's little band or form and meet the oncoming cavalry.

Atop the city wall, Coryphene also heard the blaring of the horns, and he saw disaster looming for his army. Three-quarters of his depleted host was engaged in a wild fight along the walls. When the priests of Zura had died, the magical ramps of solidified fog had vanished. Coryphene's troops on the wall were trapped. The Protector was committed to this battle as the will of his queen, and he would not have ordered retreat even had the ramps still been in place. He was quite prepared to fight to the last elf. However, when he saw Eriscodera's cavalry divert from the city to Queen Uriona's pavilion in the river, his ambition failed him. His queen was alone and undefended but for her servants. The fact that she was still covered by seven feet of water didn't seem to register in his frantic mind. Coryphene saw drylanders bearing down upon his divine mistress, and he acted. He threw down his weapons and leapt from the wall in a graceful, arcing dive.

No land dweller could have survived so great a fall, but Coryphene's body, accustomed to the press of the ocean's depths, absorbed the shock of impact. He hit the sun-dried ground, rolled down to the line of mud, and got shakily to his feet. The blood streaming from his face and the cries of his officers, still atop the wall, were all ignored as he hurried toward Uriona's pavilion.

The remaining Dimernesti mercenaries had fled upon first sighting the levies. They were back in the Thon-Thalas heading for the sea even before Coryphene's prodigious leap. When the Dargonesti on the wall saw their leader leave the field of battle, the fight went out of them as well. Word quickly spread through their ranks that the Lord Protector had deserted them. They drew back from their exhausted enemies and grounded their arms. Amazed, Samcadaris sent an emissary forward to discover their intentions. The Silvanesti officer came back with word that the sea elves wished to surrender.

The dazed marshal accepted with alacrity. With his lieutenants at his side, Samcadaris came down from the watchtower to accept the surrender of the Dargonesti army.

*   *   *   *   *

"Uriona! Uriona!" Coryphene shouted. He shed breastplate and armor as he ran, limping, then dove into the brown river. Born as he was to the water, still he couldn't cover the distance in time to reach the queen before the Silvanesti cavalry did. They surrounded her pavilion and slew any servants who tried to do battle with them. Coryphene found himself hemmed in by lance-wielding soldiers long before he set eyes upon Uriona. He drew his dagger to die fighting. At that moment Eriscodera and Gundabyr arrived, the dwarf riding double with Eriscodera's standard-bearer.

"Take him alive," said the dwarf. "He's their leader."

Coryphene still struggled to reach his queen, flailing in

the chest-deep water until he was exhausted. The Silvanesti cavalry barred him from getting any closer. Uriona was out of the water now and on her way, under heavy guard, to the west bank. At last, Coryphene ceased his struggles. He bowed his head.

"I-I yield to you," he said, holding out his dagger hilt-first to Eriscodera.

The colonel took the proffered weapon. His troopers disarmed Coryphene and bound his hands with cord.

"Put Lord Coryphene on a horse," the colonel ordered. "We will present him and his royal mistress to the Speaker of the Stars."

Coryphene and his escort galloped to the city. Eriscodera and his herald, with Gundabyr riding pillion, returned to the west bank where Uriona was being held by the militia.

"Why does she wear that mask?" asked the colonel.

"No one is allowed to look on her face," Gundabyr explained. "Those that dare are killed."

"Shall we unmask her?" suggested a grinning soldier. Uriona stiffened visibly.

"Certainly not!" Eriscodera snapped. "You will show Her Majesty every courtesy! No one shall lay hands upon her until she is presented to the Speaker. Understood?" The soldier who'd spoken nodded quickly.

By the time Eriscodera's party reached the gate at Silvanost, a transformation had occurred within the city. Where scarcely an hour earlier only soldiers could be found in the streets, now the avenues were crowded with delighted Silvanesti. From every window in the city, flowers were thrown, filling the air with sweet-smelling petals. Vixa and her tiny band entered the city first and were showered with joyous greetings.

The cavalry, muddy but triumphant, entered the city next with the captive Coryphene. He did not look at Vixa as he passed by. Instead he scowled fiercely at the cheering Silvanesti who waved and flung flowers over their victorious troops. He shook the smothering blossoms from his own head with a violent gesture.

Three phalanxes of militia infantry, who'd never even

gotten to fight, swung jauntily into the city, smiling broadly at their reception. Then came Eriscodera, his herald, and a rough cart bearing the masked Uriona. The colonel had always been popular with the common folk of Silvanost, and they went wild as he came into view, breaking their orderly lines and mobbing his horse.

Vixa waved at Gundabyr, who slid down from the standard-bearer's saddle and pushed his way through the throng to his friend's side.

"Forgemaster," she said simply, gripping his hand in hers. "What a change in fortune! Can you believe it?"

"Believe it, lady." He showed her Coryphene's dagger. "The blueskins are finished!"

The levies finally cleared a path for Eriscodera's horse and Uriona's cart. After the militia came the warriors who had defended the city until Eriscodera's arrival. Marshal Samcadaris led his weary troops in a close column of fours, divided into two bands. Between the two came the captured Dargonesti soldiers, over three thousand of them. They were shackled or tied to each other, most of them staring at the street, ignoring the shameful downpour of flowers that rained upon their heads.

Vixa and Gundabyr joined Samcadaris in the impromptu victory parade. The marshal seemed disoriented. Vixa clapped him on the shoulder and asked him how he fared.

"I'm numb," he replied. "I-I had faith in our ultimate victory, but I never dreamed it would be so near a thing, or that it would happen so quickly!"

Vixa noticed the enthusiasm of the crowd was not so marked for Samcadaris and his brave warriors as it had been for Eriscodera and the militia. Fickle people, she thought to herself. They award the victory to those who'd made such a grand and timely arrival, not to the soldiers who'd labored so hard right before their very eyes.

The captured Dargonesti were diverted and taken to Tower Protector. There they were placed under guard and given water. Samcadaris detailed half his remaining troops to accompany them. He and the rest went on to the Quinari.

When they arrived, the streets were packed with spectators. Speaker Elendar, seated in a silk-draped litter atop the steps, with the robes of Silvanos around his shoulders, was receiving a report from Eriscodera about the conclusion of the battle. The huge crowd parted for Samcadaris, Vixa, and Gundabyr. They crossed the palace plaza. At the foot of the steps stood Coryphene, arms pinioned. Beside him, still masked, stood Uriona. The cart that had borne her was being wheeled away.

They mounted the steps of the palace. The crowd gradually quieted. Samcadaris gave a terse account of the battle. Vixa, covered in soot, dirt, and the blood of friend and foe alike, gave the Speaker a flashing smile.

"How fares Your Majesty?" she asked.

"I've been told I can expect to live no more than four or five hundred more years," he quipped. "What fine trophies my warriors have brought me. This is Coryphene, I presume, and the veiled lady his queen."

"Uriona," Vixa said. "The self-proclaimed goddess in mortal form."

"So it is sacrilegious to see her face? Well, Marshal, remove her mask. Let all of Silvanost behold it."

"Sire, I would not do that," Vixa said quickly. "Defeated she may be, but Uriona is a powerful sorceress. Also, humiliating her publicly might provoke the captured Dargonesti."

"Hmm, yes, I see what you mean. Very well. I shall retire to the Tower of the Stars. Bring them before me, one at a time."

He raised his hand, and four bearers hoisted his litter. The Speaker was borne across the plaza to the Tower of the Stars. Samcadaris and Eriscodera went to escort the prisoners.

"Now what happens?" asked Gundabyr.

"I'm in the dark same as you, my friend," Vixa replied. "Why doesn't the Speaker just throw them in the dungeon and forget about them?"

Once the leaders departed, the crowd of Silvanesti began to disperse. There was some discussion of the momentous events of the day, but for the most part the elves went quietly about their business. Gundabyr and Vixa watched them, both shaking their heads at the strangeness of it all. Just when she'd begun to think the Silvanesti were not so different from her own people, Vixa was reminded anew how different the two halves of the elven nation really were.

Chapter 24

Strange Justice

Speaker Elendar had taken his place on the emerald throne of Silvanesti. He was pale and drawn. White bandages were visible through the vents of his white and gold robe. An elven youth stood by with a silver ewer of nectar, ready to pour at the Speaker's nod.

Of Uriona, there was no sign. Coryphene stood proudly on the raised platform below the throne dais. Someone had provided him with water, which trickled from his jade hair and over his battered armor. Samcadaris and Eriscodera stood at his sides, their hands on their sword hilts. Vixa and the dwarf circled around them, coming to a halt beside the nectar bearer.

"Hey, lad, pour me a spot of that," Gundabyr whispered. The willowy youth turned a scandalized look upon his Speaker. Elendar nodded, his smile fleeting.

"So, Lord Coryphene, what have you to say for yourself?" the Speaker of the Stars asked.

"Nothing," was the reply. "You have won. I have lost.

There is nothing to say."

"Good. I hate long, pointless speeches. Tell me, Cousin, what should I do with this worthy?"

Vixa had been pondering just that question. Her expression as she looked at the captive Dargonesti had nothing of pity in it. "He's too dangerous to let go, Sire. I would have his head."

"I'm with her," said Gundabyr, wiping his lips with the back of his hand. He held out his cup for more nectar.

"What do you say, Marshal of Silvanost?"

The weary Samcadaris inhaled slowly, carefully considering the question. "From what I know, Great Speaker, this one is but an instrument of our true enemy. As such, he deserves some mercy. I would commend him to imprisonment for life."

"And you, Colonel? As his captor, your voice carries weight," said the Speaker of the Stars.

Eriscodera spoke without hesitation. "I, Great Speaker, would parole him." Vixa and Gundabyr started in surprise—the dwarf choking on his third cup of nectar.

"That's ridiculous!" Vixa exclaimed. "Parole him for what reason?"

The Silvanesti colonel ignored her, addressing himself directly to the Speaker. "Majesty, as lord of a defeated army, Coryphene has no power left. If we send him home in disgrace, his own people will likely disown him. We will not have the keeping of him, and he will not trouble us again."

There might have been something in what Eriscodera said, but Vixa couldn't countenance letting Coryphene go. She enumerated his many crimes, from the sinking of unsuspecting ships with the kraken, to his enslavement of free elves and men, and his murder of many of those same prisoners. To that she added the destruction of Thonbec, and the wrongful deaths of many Silvanesti subjects. During her long, impassioned plea, Coryphene stood straighter, as if proud of the record she recited.

"Enough," said the Speaker at last. "I am convinced of the villainy of Lord Coryphene. Hold him at our royal convenience until further notice." Four guards came forward to claim the Dargonesti. Before he was led away, his eyes met Vixa's. She flushed with fury at what she saw in them: an arrogance undiminished by his capture.

When Coryphene was gone, Speaker Elendar sagged back in his throne, his face growing paler. A healer came to him with a vial of yellowish fluid. The Speaker drank some of the nostrum. Coughing, he sat erect again and commanded, "Bring in Queen Uriona."

Samcadaris and Eriscodera went to one of the Tower's small side chambers and returned with the queen. Her silver gown had long since dried, the supple musselbeard cloth looking as fresh and unsullied as if Uriona had spent the day lounging on her throne. Her head was held high, the soft silver mask covering all but her violet eyes. She halted a few paces from the throne.

"So, lady, your plans are laid low," the Speaker began. "What are we to do with you now?"

"You dare not interfere with me," she intoned. "I am the divine queen of the sea."

"I believe we have already interfered with you, lady. As for your divinity, well, you need only exercise it and take yourself away from here." The Speaker paused, leaning forward. "Any time you wish."

Vixa saw the tendons in Uriona's throat tense and relax, but nothing happened. Titters of laughter circulated among the ladies of the court. Vixa—almost—felt sorry for Uriona.

"I see you have decided to stay with us," the Speaker said. "If that is the case, you are my guest. Guests do not hide their faces from their hosts, so I'll trouble you for your mask, lady."

Vixa held her breath. Nothing happened for a long minute. Just as the Speaker was about to order her unmasked, Uriona moved. One long-fingered blue hand came up in a slow, steady motion and took the covering from her face.

Her finely sculpted features were expressionless. Lavender eyes, surrounded by thick silver lashes, regarded the Speaker of the Stars steadily, unblinking. Without a word, she let the mask drop from her fingers and put up her hands to take the tortoiseshell combs from her hair. Released, it fell in a thick, shimmering mass down to her knees. Sunlight, refracted by the jewels encrusting the Tower walls, sent rainbows dancing in the silver tresses. Speaker Elendar didn't appear to notice that he had risen to his feet.

Uriona bowed her head, lifting a hand to her hair once more, as though ashamed of the display she was making. The webbing between her fingers appeared nearly transparent.

"Lady." The Speaker cleared his throat and tried again. "Your pardon, lady, for any rudeness," he murmured.

"As my conqueror, you have the right," she said.

Beside her, Vixa heard Gundabyr sigh. Even the tough dwarf appeared affected by the loveliness of Uriona. The Qualinesti princess was not. She found herself trying to decipher the expression on the queen's face. Was it contrition? Embarrassment? She doubted that Uriona was capable of either.

The Speaker sat down heavily, the pain of his injured side suddenly reminding him that rash movement was better avoided for now.

"The audience is at an end," he announced, wincing. "Depart, all of you."

Everyone bowed and began to file out. Samcadaris inquired, "Sire? What of the prisoner?"

"Take her—take her to Hermathya's Tower. See to her comfort and security. See to it personally, Marshal."

"It shall be done, Great Speaker."

* * * * *

The priests and priestesses of Silvanost released the river from its magical constraints. The process had to be done carefully. All that night and through the next day, the Thon-Thalas rose slowly, gradually. By evening, the river was well on its way to filling its banks once more.

Vixa sat in her palace room by an open window, watching the river's return. Bathed, fed, and dressed in clean clothing, she'd stayed by the window for hours. When the day ended, she didn't rise to light any lamps, but let the growing darkness fill the room.

The first stars were beginning to glimmer in the purple sky when a soft knock came on her door.

"Enter." She did not turn to see who came.

"Cousin?"

Vixa recognized the Speaker's voice. "Your Majesty," she said, rising quickly.

"Why, Cousin, I would not know you," Elendar said, gently mocking. Vixa had forsaken her warrior's garb for the admittedly more comfortable flowing gown of a high-born Silvanesti lady. The golden yellow robe was a luxury she felt she'd earned.

The Speaker entered, leaning on a staff and limping slightly. Vixa brought a chair for him, and he gratefully took it. He regarded her, merriment dancing in his almond eyes.

"The resemblance is even more pronounced now," he murmured.

"What resemblance?"

"To your grandfather, Kith-Kanan. He and my father were twins, if you recall. You have the look of him."

Vixa was mildly embarrassed. "I confess I don't see it. My grandmother, Suzine, was human, and sometimes that's all people see, all I see as well." She offered him nectar, which he politely refused. She asked, "What brings you here, Great Speaker?"

Now it was his turn to be embarrassed. "I-I would like to know your mind about certain things."

"Such as Queen Uriona?"

"Hmm, yes," he said, clearing his throat. "What is your opinion of her?"

"She is mad, hungry for power, and should never be allowed her freedom again."

"Yes, yes, but what do you *think* of her?"

She frowned. "I don't know what you mean."

"Cousin, is she not beautiful?"

Vixa felt her jaw dropping in surprise. So that was the way the wind was blowing. No answer came to her. Of course the Dargonesti queen was lovely to look at, but what had that to do with anything?

"You are well traveled, Cousin," the Speaker went on. "You know the ways of the world. My counselors have been pressuring me to marry since I came to the throne. Marriage brings stability, they say. But I've never met any maid who interested me. The ladies of the court are all light laughter and mocking gossip. When you arrived, I considered asking you to be my wife—"

"Me!"

"Why not? You're of royal blood, you're brave and honest, and not bad to look at."

"My thanks to Your Majesty," Vixa said tartly.

He grinned, then turned serious once more. "It was only a fleeting thought. The nobles and priests would never accept a Qualinesti marriage for me. There's too much bitterness remaining from the war, and the rivalry of Kith-Kanan and my father. Queen Uriona, however . . ." His voice trailed off.

This time Vixa could not conceal her astonishment. "Queen Uriona? You mean you want to marry her?" the Qualinesti princess's voice was loud with shock.

"We cannot simply release her. What better way to keep watch on her? She'll have no allies to plot with, no faction to support any policies of her own. She's elven, she's of royal lineage, and"—he shifted in his chair—"she is *very* beautiful. Why shouldn't I think of marrying her?"

"Because she's evil!" exclaimed Vixa, jumping to her feet. "Because she's a powerful sorceress capable of any treachery!" The Speaker's face reflected mild reproof, and Vixa struggled to rein in her temper. One did not screech at the Speaker of the Stars—even if he was talking blasted nonsense! She sat down again.

Elendar said calmly, "What better place to keep such a formidable opponent than here? There'll be none to aid her, and the mages of Silvanost are more than a match for one Dargonesti queen."

Vixa tried another approach. "What about the succession? The Silvanesti won't want a half-Dargonesti as ruler after you, will they?"

"No offspring of mine will ever become Speaker—be they half Dargonesti or full Silvanesti. That was settled long ago. When my brother, the previous Speaker, died, I was asked to rule as regent for my eldest nephew, but I refused. Then the privy council offered me the throne as Speaker of the Stars, if I would designate my nephew as heir apparent, even above any children I might have later. I agreed."

The complexities of Silvanesti politics were giving Vixa a headache. She could muster no argument to change his mind. He had obviously given this matter a great deal of consideration. Shrugging her shoulders, the Qualinesti princess said, "Sire, you must do as you see fit. As for Uriona, she will never love you, only herself. She may even try to murder you, thinking to capture the throne for herself. If you can live with that, then—well, it's not my place to argue."

The Speaker levered himself out of the chair. "I value your honesty, Cousin. Never doubt that my eyes are open to all Uriona's faults. But I think I shall marry her. I will have the queen of my heart's desire, foil the reactionary nobles, and live a long life to boot. Good night, lady!"

* * * * *

The next morning, the palace was abuzz with rumors that the Speaker of the Stars had made a marriage proposal to the Dargonesti queen. There were shocked mutterings, and several of the older courtiers were heard to say that such a thing would never have been allowed in the days of Speaker Sithas. However, since the succession was in no danger, the majority of the nobles supported their Speaker once the initial shock had worn off. The wedding would take place in a month's time. Repairs had begun on the damaged portions of the city, and the entire capital, of stunning beauty already, would have to be made radiant for the coming nuptials. Everyone, citizen and noble alike, anticipated a grand celebration.

Gundabyr couldn't believe his ears. "It's time for me to

go home," he said morosely. "I've heard of some strange marriages in my time, but I never heard of a bride who gained her groom by besieging his city!"

Vixa agreed heartily. "I've no wish to remain and see Uriona achieve her dream. Maybe not queen of all the elves, but certainly queen of Silvanesti!"

They went to make their good-byes to the Speaker. He was downcast when he learned they intended to depart. "The wedding will be immense," he promised. "Ten days of feasting! Actors, jugglers, and singers are being summoned. The clerics are building a chapel of glass under the river just for the ceremony! You should remain for that at least."

Gundabyr was tempted. Ten days of food and drink was certainly something to consider. The presence of Uriona, however, was certain to turn the food to ashes and the nectar to vinegar. They both declined. The Speaker settled for showering his new friends with rich gifts of clothing and jewels, not forgetting the magnifying lens he had promised Gundabyr. He asked how they planned to get home.

"Walk?" said the dwarf.

"Ride," said Vixa firmly. "If Your Majesty would loan us horses."

"I shall do no such thing. You will have a griffon from the royal stable. You can fly home faster than the wind!"

He clasped hands with Gundabyr, and Vixa was surprised to find herself embraced. She returned the gesture warmly.

"May the gods favor you in all things, Cousin," Elendar said sincerely. "Master Gundabyr, you and Lady Vixa are welcome in my realm at any time."

They thanked him again and took their leave. Outside, the morning sun was promising a hot day. Vixa looked across the city to Tower Protector, a frown on her face.

"I have one more errand left," she told Gundabyr. "I'll meet you at the royal stable in an hour."

"Whatever you say, Princess."

Vixa walked to Tower Protector and entered without challenge. Though the nobles of Silvanost might disparage her for her heritage, the warriors respected her valor. She found Samcadaris and told him she desired a favor.

"Anything, lady," he said simply.

"I want to talk to Coryphene."

The marshal was surprised. "You'll not harm him—he is in my charge."

"I won't touch him," Vixa promised.

She climbed to the top floor of one of the smaller towers. There in the center of a round room a large glass box had been formed by magic, sealed tight but for some finger-sized holes along its top. The box was filled with water. It was Coryphene's prison cell.

He stirred when she entered. He still wore his warrior's clothing, though without armor. Vixa came close to the thin glass barrier.

"What do you want?" he asked, addressing her in Elvish. His voice was muffled by the water and the glass, but she could understand him.

"I've come to say good-bye. I'm going home."

At her words his head came up, and he stared at her. "To Urione?"

"Qualinost," she corrected. "Why would you think otherwise?"

"You are a sister of the sea now. The call will be irresistible."

She laughed. "At Thonbec, when my freedom and credibility were at stake, it wasn't so irresistible. I couldn't even change into a dolphin."

"Foolish drylander. Do dolphins live in rivers? Only seawater makes the change possible."

"In any event, that's not important. I came to pass along some news no one else may have bothered to share."

"What news?"

"Uriona is marrying the Speaker of the Stars in one month's time."

If she had hit Coryphene with a club, she couldn't have stunned him more. His arrested expression and sudden stillness were most gratifying.

"You lie," he said at last. "You say so only to wound me. Uriona is mine."

"In a month, you'll be able to hear the marriage pipes from here," Vixa said with a shrug. "Uriona never loved you. You were only a tool for her ambition. When greater power came her way, she grabbed it." The Qualinesti princess stepped closer and raised one finger to tap the glass barrier that separated them. "Ponder that, Lord Protector. Think of Uriona in the palace with the Speaker of the Stars, as you live the rest of your days in this glass bowl."

The angry flush had gone, leaving his face pallid and frozen. Vixa turned to leave, her mission accomplished. Nothing disturbed her enjoyment of the moment. She had only to remember Armantaro, Harmanutis, and Vanthanoris—none of them ever to return to Qualinesti soil—and all pangs of conscience vanished instantly. Let him sit alone in his crystal prison thinking of his love marrying another.

Vixa descended to say farewell to Samcadaris. Halfway down the long staircase, she heard a crash above, followed by the sound of rushing water. Rivulets flowed down the steps behind her. She stood immobile for an instant, then another sound filled the air. It was a scream, which stopped abruptly.

The Qualinesti princess's face was blank. On the ground floor hall of the tower, she found the warriors rushing outside. She followed them. At the door stood Samcadaris.

"It's Coryphene!" he exclaimed. "Somehow he erupted out of his cage and threw himself from the window!"

"Is he dead?" Samcadaris nodded, and she said flatly, "Good."

He stared at her. "What did you say to him?" the marshal demanded.

"I only told him of the Speaker's coming marriage."

Samcadaris looked shocked. "You told him—"

"Coryphene chose his own path from Watermere to this tower," she responded in a cold voice. "I will not grieve for him."

The Marshal of Silvanost regarded her in silence for several seconds, then he did an odd thing. He saluted. Vixa returned the gesture. Her coldness melted, and she said warmly, "You are a fine elf, Samca. Thank you for believing in me back on that beach."

They said their good-byes, and Vixa made her way to the royal stables. A fine, large griffon was saddled and ready. It had the magnificent head, neck, and wings of an eagle and the torso and hindquarters of a lion. A plumed lion's tail fanned the air behind it. Panniers hung down on each flank, loaded with fine gifts and provisions. Gundabyr stood off to one side, regarding the beast dubiously.

"Are we supposed to ride this thing?" he asked. Since the high-backed saddle was even now being cinched on the griffon's back, his question was obviously rhetorical.

Vixa smiled. "What's the matter, afraid of flying?"

"So long as we stay dry, I can handle anything." The dwarf climbed onto a tall mounting block and was assisted into the saddle. Vixa mounted in front of him. The great animal shifted under their weight, turning its fierce head to regard them silently. The handler gave Vixa the reins. There was no bit, of course. The reins were connected to a leather halter. The Qualinesti princess had never flown a griffon before, but she wasn't about to let the Silvanesti know it. She took the reins confidently.

"What's his name?" she asked the handler.

"*Her* name is Lionheart, lady," was the smooth reply.

Vixa nodded as the handler stepped back. Looking over her shoulder, she said, "Ready, Gundabyr?" He grunted an affirmative, and Vixa snapped the reins. "Away, Lionheart!" she cried.

The beast spread its great wings, took a few steps forward, and leapt into the air.

Chapter 25

Homecoming

Vixa and Gundabyr flew straight to Thorbardin, where Lionheart landed at Northgate. Vixa tied the beast's reins to a handy outcropping of rock, and she and Gundabyr descended into the underground city. At Gundabyr's clan home in Daewar City, all of his family—and there were a lot of them—turned out to welcome him back and meet the Qualinesti princess. There was sadness, however, when Gundabyr relayed the news of his twin's death.

The two friends parted on the best of terms, each promising to visit the other. Gundabyr's multitudinous family all began planning a trip to Qualinost, hounding the poor fellow to give Vixa a firm date for the visit. Their attention grew so vexing, he drew Vixa aside and murmured, "Maybe I'll just come visit you now—alone!"

Vixa laughed and bade them all farewell. She returned to the patient Lionheart. They ascended high over the mountains, flying northwest toward Qualinost. Their route took them directly over Pax Tharkas, the great fortress guarding the pass between Qualinesti and Thorbardin. It had been built jointly by the two countries to celebrate their peaceful coexistence. Vixa's grandfather, the famous Kith-Kanan, had overseen its construction, and his tomb was deep inside it.

By the next morning, Vixa and Lionheart were circling Qualinost. The city was built on a plateau bounded by two rivers that flowed through deep gorges. The rivers merged at the northern point of the triangular plateau. Four silver-inlaid marble towers marked the cardinal points around the city. The towers were connected by arched bridges that encircled the city. The city's buildings were built of rose quartz, which reflected the morning sun in a dazzling display. As Lionheart came to a gentle landing beside the golden Tower of the Sun, crowds of Qualinesti began to fill the city's quartz-lined streets.

The last word any in Qualinost had received of Vixa and her party had been brought by Ambassador Quenavalen, who'd finally made it home himself only a week before. The ambassador, after speaking to Ergothian refugees at the mouth of the Greenthorn River, carried home the news that *Evenstar* had been lost, with all hands aboard, in a strange fog. Vixa was saddened to know the ship had never returned. It must have gone down when the kraken submerged beneath it.

Vixa walked up the grand steps and into the Speaker's house, a huge, happy crowd trailing behind her. Kemian Ambrodel and Verhanna Kanan were waiting. Still in mourning for their youngest child and only daughter, they could barely credit her amazing arrival. The three had a joyous reunion. Speaker Silveran himself came out and greeted his niece, to the tumultuous cheers of the crowd.

Eventually the whole story was told. A banquet was given, and the celebrations lasted four days. Throngs of celebrants—highborn, lowborn, elven, human, dwarven—filled the feasting hall to hear Vixa relate her tale. Scribes took down every word, and copies were posted throughout the city for the benefit of those who didn't hear the story firsthand.

When she finished recounting her adventures, Vixa was embraced by her mother. Tears sparkled in Verhanna's dark brown eyes. "You were magnificent, Daughter! I'll give you command of your own regiment—no, two regiments!"

"Thank you, Mother, but no." Vixa sat down, holding out her goblet for more nectar. "I've seen enough war for a dozen lifetimes."

"But, Vixa, you've proven yourself fit for higher command. The army—"

"Do you know what I really need, Mother?" Verhanna shook her head. "I need to disappear into a quiet forest glade for at least a month!"

Most of those assembled at the banquet laughed when they heard that, even the Speaker of the Sun, who was usually very solemn. Verhanna, however, was not at all amused. She returned to her place between the Speaker and her husband. For the rest of the evening she maintained an ominous silence.

Some time later, Vixa found herself alone in her old room. She was wandering around, reacquainting herself with her familiar possessions, when a knock came at the door.

"Enter," she called.

The door opened to reveal her father. "Am I disturbing you?" he asked.

She smiled at him. "No, Father, please come in."

Kemian Ambrodel was a handsome elf of some four hundred years. From him Vixa had inherited her fair coloring and her introspective nature. Verhanna was more likely responsible for Vixa's temper and strong will.

Her father pulled up a chair and sat down. Without preamble, he stated, "I want you to make peace with your mother. She was nearly mad with grief when we thought you lost. She blamed herself for everything. When you came back, it was as though she lost a century off her age." Kemian brushed a hand through his daughter's fair hair. "She sees so much of herself in you, you know."

Vixa took his hand. "I always wanted to be more like you."

"After all you've been through, you can't deny that you have your mother's courage and passionate nature. She and I are very different, yet here we are, married all this time. No one thought it would work."

"She married you after you bested her in a duel!" Vixa said indignantly. Kemian's almond-shaped blue eyes twinkled, and she added, "Very well, Father. I'll take what command she offers—but I need some time to rest and reflect."

"That's fine. Verhanna won't object to that. It will be good to have you close to home for a while."

Vixa slept in her own bed that night. Her dreams were filled with a kaleidoscope of images: Armantaro's familiar face; the battle for Silvanost, fought side by side with Gundabyr; and most strongly of all, the endless sea. She dreamt she was racing through the waves in dolphin form. The sensation was so powerful that she awoke breathless. Coryphene's words came back to her: "You are a sister of the sea now. The call will be irresistible."

Rolling over to a more comfortable position, Vixa banished the ghostly echo from her mind. Sister of the sea? No longer. Not here in Qualinost.

* * * * *

Vixa spent the remainder of the summer in the city, home with her parents. Her sleep continued to be troubled by dreams of the sea. To divert herself, she composed a long letter to Samcadaris, which she sent by the simple expedient of tying it to Lionheart's saddle and sending the griffon home.

Summer heat gave way to the gold-and-red chill of autumn. Vixa assumed command of the Wildrunners, the rangers of Kagonesti ancestry who'd served Kith-Kanan so well during the Kinslayer War. Her duties kept her in the northern woods for many weeks at a time. After her adventurous summer, she thought all she wanted was the peace and quiet of a remote outpost, yet she never felt at ease in the forest, not as she once had. Her nights were more disturbed now, the dreams of the sea frequently leaving her agitated and unable to sleep.

Winter was gray and silent, as woodland winters usually are. Vixa spent nearly a month sick with fever, hot bricks in her bed to ward off the chills. She talked wildly in her delirium, raving about Urione, Nissia Grotto, Naxos, and other things that confounded the healers. Her fever would lessen for a short time, but hope was dashed as the illness took hold of her once more. At times they despaired for her life, but she was young and strong, and by the time the snows melted, she was on her feet again, unusually thin, with dark hollows beneath her eyes.

The arrival of spring brought a courier from Qualinost. Among the other papers he carried was a strange letter addressed to Vixa. It had come, so the courier told her, when a griffon appeared over the city. The beast dropped a small scroll, upon which was written Vixa's name. The letter had finally found its way to her, deep in the northern forest.

Vixa untied the silk cord that bound the scroll. Tiny, elegant Silvanesti script filled the page. The letter read:

To Her Royal Highness
Princess Vixa Ambrodel

Greetings:

I regret not being able to respond sooner to your letter, but my duties have kept me quite busy. I am no longer marshal of Silvanost. That honor has fallen to Eriscodera, whom you met as a colonel last summer. An unlikely alliance has grown up between Eriscodera, Lord Agavenes, and the Speaker's wife, Lady Uriona. They have opposed the Speaker's attempts to restore contact with Qualinost. I fear Silvanost grows ever more insular. The Speaker has told me he hopes to abdicate in favor of his nephew. Uriona will oppose that, of course.

I trust you are well, Princess. Though it saddens me to say it, I sometimes feel all our fighting was for naught, as

*we are ruled by Uriona anyway. At least the succession is
assured and the line of Silvanos will continue. I remain*

> *Your friend,*
> *Samca*

A shudder ran through the Qualinesti princess. Perhaps
Uriona's prophecy had been right all along—at least in part.
She had indeed been crowned in the Tower of the Stars, and
now occupied the most ancient elven throne in the world.

Vixa put a hand to her head, attempting to massage the
ache from her temples. The pain would not go away. It had
been with her, off and on, for a week.

She called her lieutenant. "I'm turning over command to
you," she told him, writing out her orders on a scrap of
parchment. "As of today, you lead the Wildrunners."

The Kagonesti was stunned. "By why, lady? Is your
health still poor?" he asked.

"No, but I can't stay here. If I do, I'll go mad."

She packed a single cloth bag with a few necessities, as
Kerridar stood by helplessly, at a loss to explain his com-
mander's sudden departure. "What shall I tell the Speaker?
What shall I tell your mother?" he asked weakly.

"I've left letters for them. They'll understand." She didn't
intend to bandy words with Kerridar all day. "I'll probably
return some day to visit, but I'll never command the Wildrunners again. You're a good soldier, Kerridar. I've been
proud to serve with you."

She gripped his hand, ignoring his bewilderment. Vixa
tied her bag to her saddle and mounted. The chestnut horse
fretted in a circle. "Good-bye, Kerridar," she called.

"Fare you well, Lady Vixa. Astra go with you!"

She rode for days, stopping only for the horse's sake. The
rest periods had to be brief, because whenever she stopped,
the ache in her head grew unbearable. Once she was moving again, the pain would subside. She avoided roads and
villages, not wanting to meet anyone. By the evening of her
third day of travel, she arrived at the ocean shore. There
was nothing before her now but sand and rolling waves.

She unsaddled the horse and took the bridle from its head. "You're free, too," she said, giving the animal's rump a slap. The chestnut cantered away, snorting and shaking its head at the unaccustomed lack of restraint.

Her headache had gone away, as she knew it would. In its place were unintelligible whispers. She couldn't understand the words, but she knew what they signified. The voices wanted her to come into the water. Vixa dropped her bag on the sand and, like a sleepwalker, headed for the surf. As she went, she shed her clothing.

Though summer was more than a month away, the water felt warm and indescribably good. She dove headfirst into the waves, swimming out beyond the line of breakers. A last glance back at the beach, and she sank beneath the surface. She kicked her feet until they were feet no more. Never had the transformation been so effortless and so welcome. Faster and faster she coursed through the depths. Now she could understand the voices. They said, "Come, Sister. Come home. Come home."

Before she'd gone half a dozen leagues, she was surrounded by dolphins. The sea brothers greeted her by name as they cavorted around her.

"Why did you call me?" she asked in the water-tongue.

"Our brother, our chief, commanded it," they replied.

Her heartbeat quickened. "Naxos?"

"Naxos, yes. Our brother, our chief," said one mottled gray dolphin. "He sent us to tell you that we have left the city. We have no home but the sea now. Come with us, Sister! Be consort to our brother, our chief!"

"What has become of the Quoowahb of Urione?"

"They have a new master, but we are free. Come with us, Vixa Dryfoot!"

The pain and fatigue of her journey dropped away like a soiled cloak. Happiness filled her heart. Naxos was calling her. She would be free to roam the oceans, to live in peace. She would not have to fight wars or serve any master but nature itself.

She turned her dolphin body away from the land. "Take me to Naxos," she said to her brothers.

DRAGONS
of
SUMMER
FLAME

**An Excerpt
From a Work in Progress
by
Margaret Weis and Tracy Hickman**

Chapter One

Be Warned . . .

It was hot that morning, damnably hot.

Far too hot for late spring on Ansalon. Almost as hot as midsummer. The two knights, seated in the boat's stern, were sweaty and miserable in their heavy steel armor; they looked with envy at the nearly naked men plying the boat's oars. When the boat neared shore, the knights were first out, jumping into the shallow water, laving the water onto their reddening faces and sunburned necks. But the water was not particularly refreshing.

"Like wading in hot soup," one of the knights grumbled, splashing ashore. Even as he spoke, he scrutinized the shoreline carefully, eyeing bush and tree and dune for signs of life.

"More like blood," said his comrade. "Think of it as wading in the blood of our enemies, the enemies of our Queen. Do you see anything?"

"No," the other replied. He waved his hand, then, without looking back, heard the sound of men leaping into the water, their harsh laughter and conversation in their uncouth, guttural language.

One of the knights turned around. "Bring that boat to shore," he said, unnecessarily, for the men had already picked up the heavy boat and were running with it through the shallow water. Grinning, they dumped the boat on the sand beach and looked to the knight for further orders.

He mopped his forehead, marveled at their strength, and—not for the first time—thanked Queen Takhisis that these barbarians were on their side. The brutes, they were known as. Not the true name of their race. The name, their name for themselves, was unpronounceable, and so the knights who led the barbarians had begun calling them by the shortened version: brute.

The name suited the barbarians well. They came from the east, from a continent that few people on Ansalon knew existed. Every one of the men stood well over six feet; some were as tall as seven. Their bodies were as bulky and muscular as humans, but their movements were as swift and graceful as elves. Their ears were pointed like those of the elves, but their faces were heavily bearded like humans or dwarves. They were as strong as dwarves and loved battle as well as dwarves did. They fought fiercely, were loyal to those who commanded them, and, outside of a few grotesque customs such as cutting off various parts of the body of a dead enemy to keep as trophies, the brutes were ideal foot soldiers.

"Let the captain know we've arrived safely and that we've encountered no resistance," said the knight to his comrade. "We'll leave a couple of men here with the boat and move inland."

The other knight nodded. Taking a red silk pennant from his belt, he unfurled it, held it above his head, and waved it slowly three times. An answering flutter of red came from the enormous black, dragon-prowed ship anchored some distance away. This was a scouting mission, not an invasion. Orders had been quite clear on that point.

The knights sent out their patrols, dispatching some to range up and down the beach, sending others farther inland. This done, the two knights moved thankfully to the meager shadow cast by a squat and misshapen tree. Two of the brutes stood guard. The knights remained wary and watchful, even as they rested. Seating themselves, they drank sparingly of the fresh water they'd brought with them. One of them grimaced.

"The damn stuff's hot."

"You left the waterskin sitting in the sun. Of course it's hot."

"Where the devil was I supposed to put it? There was no shade on that cursed boat. I don't think there's any shade left in the whole blasted world. I don't like this place at all. I get a queer feeling about this island, like it's magicked or something."

"I know what you mean," agreed his comrade somberly. He kept glancing about, back into the trees, up and down the beach. All that could be seen were the brutes, and they were certainly not bothered by any ominous feelings. But then, they were barbarians. "We were warned not to come here, you know."

"What?" The other knight looked astonished. "I didn't know. Who told you that?"

"Brightblade. He had it from Lord Ariakan himself."

"Brightblade should know. He's on Ariakan's staff. The lord's his sponsor." The knight appeared nervous and asked softly, "Such information's not secret, is it?"

The other knight appeared amused. "You don't know Steele Brightblade very well if you think he would break any oath or pass along any information he was told to keep to himself. He'd sooner let his tongue be ripped out by red-hot tongs. No, Lord Ariakan discussed this openly with all the regimental commanders before deciding to proceed."

The knight shrugged. Picking up a handful of small rocks, he began tossing them idly into the water. "The Gray Robes started it all. Some sort of augury revealed the location of this island and that it was inhabited by large numbers of people."

"So who warned us not to come?"

"The Gray Robes. The same augury that told them of this island also warned them not to come near it. They tried to persuade Ariakan to leave well enough alone. Said that this place could mean disaster."

The other knight frowned, then glanced around with growing unease. "Then why were we sent?"

"The upcoming invasion of Ansalon. Lord Ariakan felt this move was necessary to protect his flanks. The Gray Robes couldn't say exactly what sort of threat this island represented. Nor could they say specifically that the disaster would be caused by our landing on the island. As Lord Ariakan pointed out, perhaps disaster would come even if we didn't do anything. And so he decided to follow the old dwarven dictum, 'It is better to go looking for the dragon than have the dragon come looking for you.' "

"Good thinking," his companion agreed. "If there is an army of elves on this island, it's better that we deal with them now. Not that it seems likely."

He gestured at the wide stretches of sand beach, at the dunes covered with some sort of grayish-green grass, and, farther inland, a forest of the ugly, misshapen trees. "Elves wouldn't live in a place like this."

"Neither would dwarves. Minotaurs would have attacked us by now. Kender would have walked off with the boat *and* our armor. Gnomes would have met us with some sort of fiend-driven fish-catching machine. Humans like us are the only race foolish enough to live in such a wretched place," the knight concluded cheerfully. He picked up another handful of rocks.

"It could be a rogue band of draconians or hobgoblins. Ogres even. Escaped twenty-some years ago, after the War of the Lance. Fled north, across the sea, to avoid capture by the Solamnic Knights."

"Yes, but they'd be on our side," his companion answered. "And our wizards wouldn't have their robes in a knot over it. Ah, here come our scouts, back to report. Now we'll find out."

The knights rose to their feet. The brutes who had been sent into the island's interior hurried forward to meet their leaders. The barbarians were grinning hugely. Their nearly naked bodies glistened with sweat. The blue paint with which they covered themselves, and which was supposed to possess some sort of magical properties said to cause arrows to bounce right off them, ran down their muscular bodies in rivulets. Long scalp locks, decorated with colorful feathers, bounced on their backs as they loped easily over the sand dunes.

The two knights exchanged glances, relaxed.

"What did you find?" the knight asked the leader, a gigantic red-haired fellow who towered over both knights and could have probably picked up each of them and held them over his head. He regarded both knights with unbounded reverence and respect.

"Men," answered the brute. They were quick to learn and had adapted easily to Common, spoken by most of the various races of Krynn. Unfortunately, to the brutes, all people not of their race were known as "men."

The brute lowered his hand near the ground to indicate small men, which might mean dwarves but was more probably children. He moved it to waist height, which most likely indicated women. This the brute confirmed by cupping two hands over his own breast and wiggling his hips. His own men laughed and nudged each other.

"Men, women, and children," said the knight. "Many men? Lots of men? Big buildings? Walls? Cities?"

The brutes apparently thought this was hilarious, for they all burst into raucous laughter.

"What did you find?" said the knight sharply, scowling. "Stop the nonsense."

The brutes sobered rapidly.

"Many men," said the leader, "but no walls. Houses." He made a face, shrugged, shook his head, and added something in his own language.

"What does that mean?" asked the knight of his comrade.

"Something to do with dogs," said the other, who had led brutes before and had started picking up some of their language. "I think he means that these men live in houses only dogs would live in."

Several of the brutes now began walking about stoop-shouldered, swinging their arms around their knees and grunting. Then they all straightened up, looked at each other, and laughed again.

"What in the name of our Dark Majesty are they doing now?" the knight demanded.

"Beats me," said his comrade. "I think we should go have a look for ourselves." He drew his sword partway out of its black leather scabbard. "Danger?" he asked the brute. "We need steel?"

The brute laughed again. Taking his own short sword—the brutes fought with two, long and short, as well as bow and arrows—he thrust it into the tree and turned his back on it.

The knight, reassured, returned his sword to its scabbard. The two followed their guides deeper into the forest.

They did not go far before they came to the village. They entered a cleared area among the trees.

Despite the antics of the brutes, the knights were completely unprepared for what they saw.

"By Hiddukel," one said in a low voice to the other. " 'Men' is too strong a term. *Are* these men? Or are they beasts?"

"They're men," said the other, staring around slowly, amazed. "But such men as we're told walked Krynn during the Age of Twilight. Look! Their tools are made of wood. They carry wooden spears, and crude ones at that."

"Wooden-tipped, not stone," said the other. "Mud huts for houses. Clay cooking pots. Not a piece of steel or iron in sight. What a pitiable lot! I can't see how they could be much danger, unless it's from filth. By the smell, they haven't bathed since the Age of Twilight either."

"Ugly bunch. More like apes than men. Don't laugh. Look stern and threatening."

Several of the male humans—if human they were; it was difficult to tell beneath the animal hides they wore—crept up to the knights. The "man-beasts" walked bent over, their arms swinging at their sides, knuckles almost dragging on the ground. Their heads were covered with long, shaggy hair; unkempt beards almost completely hid their faces.

They bobbed and shuffled and gazed at the knights in openmouthed awe. One of the man-beasts actually drew near enough to reach out a grimy hand to touch the black, shining armor.

A brute moved to interpose his own massive body in front of the knight.

The knight waved the brute off and drew his sword. The steel flashed in the sunlight. Turning to one of the trees, which, with their twisted limbs and gnarled trunks, resembled the people who lived beneath them, the knight raised his sword and sliced off a limb with one swift stroke.

The man-beast dropped to his knees and groveled in the dirt, making piteous blubbering sounds.

"I think I'm going to vomit," said the knight to his comrade. "Gully dwarves wouldn't associate with this lot."

"You're right there." The knight looked around. "Between us, you and I could wipe out the entire tribe."

"We'd never be able to clean the stench off our swords," said the other.

"What should we do? Kill them?"

"Small honor in it. These wretches obviously aren't any threat to us. Our orders were to find out who or what was inhabiting the island, then return. For all we know, these people may be the favorites of some god, who might be angered if we harmed them. Perhaps that is what the Gray Robes meant by disaster."

"I don't know," said the other knight dubiously. "I can't imagine any god treating his favorites like this."

"Morgion, perhaps," said the other with a wry grin.

The knight grunted. "Well, we've certainly done no harm just by looking. The Gray Robes can't fault us for that. Send out the brutes to scout the rest of the island. According to the reports from the dragons, it's not very big. Let's go back to the shore. I need some fresh air."

* * * * *

The two knights sat in the shade of the tree, talking of the upcoming invasion of Ansalon, discussing the vast armada of black dragon-prowed ships, manned by minotaurs, that was speeding its way across the Courrain Ocean, bearing thousands and thousands more barbarian warriors. All was nearly ready for the invasion, which would take place on Summer's Eve.

The knights of Takhisis did not know precisely where they were attacking; such information was kept secret. But they had no doubt of victory. This time the Dark Queen would succeed. This time her armies would be victorious. This time she knew the secret to victory.

The brutes returned within a few hours and made their report. The isle was not large. The brutes found no other people. The tribe of man-beasts had all slunk off fearfully and were hiding, cowering, in their mud huts until the strange beings left.

The knights returned to their shore boat. The brutes pushed it off the sand, leaped in, and grabbed the oars. The boat skimmed across the surface of the water, heading for the black ship that flew the multicolored flag of the five-headed dragon.

They left behind an empty, deserted beach. Or so it appeared.

But their leaving was noted, as their coming had been.